Dear readers,

It's Anna here, and I just wanted to thank you so much for picking up this book. Whether you've read it before and are celebrating the upcoming movie release, or you're a first-time reader, your support means so much to me.

If you've been a part of the *After* family, I just wanted to write something special here to celebrate how far we've come since that first chapter on Wattpad. You guys have taken this little story of ours and made it into a bestselling book series and now A FREAKING MOVIEEEE!! I know you'll love seeing the story come alive on the screen, and for the parts you miss, they can always be found here within these pages. I love you all more than I can ever explain, and I hope you'll love the movie that we created together. <3 Talk to you soon ;)

Anna Todd

AFTER

ANNA TODD

G

GALLERY BOOKS

New York   London   Toronto   Sydney   New Delhi

G

Gallery Books
An Imprint of Simon & Schuster, Inc.
1230 Avenue of the Americas
New York, NY 10020

The author is represented by Wattpad.

This Gallery Books trade paperback edition March 2019

GALLERY BOOKS and colophon are registered trademarks of Simon & Schuster, Inc.

For information about special discounts for bulk purchases, please contact Simon & Schuster Special Sales at 1-866-506-1949 or business@simonandschuster.com.

The Simon & Schuster Speakers Bureau can bring authors to your live event. For more information or to book an event, contact the Simon & Schuster Speakers Bureau at 1-866-248-3049 or visit our website at www.simonspeakers.com.

Interior design by Davina Mock

Manufactured in the United States of America

10 9 8 7 6 5 4 3 2

Library of Congress Cataloging-in-Publication Data is available.

ISBN 978-1-9821-1100-7
ISBN 978-1-4767-9254-5 (ebook)

To my readers from the start,
with so, so much love and gratitude.
You mean the entire world to me.

AFTER

prologue

College had always seemed so crucial, such an essential part of what measures a person's worth and determines their future. We live in a time where people ask which school you went to before asking your last name. From an early age I was taught, trained really, to prepare for my education. It had become this necessity that required an overwhelming amount of preparation and border-line obsession. Every class I chose, every assignment I completed since my first day of high school revolved around getting into college. And not just any college—my mother had it set in her mind that I attend Washington Central University, the same school that she attended, but never completed.

I had no idea that there would be so much more to college than academics. I had no idea that choosing which electives to take during my first semester would seem, just a few months later, like trivial affairs. I was naïve then, and in some ways I still am. But I couldn't have possibly known what lay ahead of me. Meeting my dorm-mate was intense and awkward from the start, and meeting her wild group of friends even more so. They were so different from anyone I had ever known and I was intimidated by their appearance, confused by their pure inattention to structure. I quickly became a part of their madness, indulging in it . . .

And that's when *he* crept into my heart.

From our first encounter, Hardin changed my life in ways that no amount of college prep courses or youth group lectures could have. Those movies I watched as a teen quickly became my life, and those ridiculous plotlines became my reality. Would I have done anything differently if I had known what was to come? I'm not sure. I would love to give a straight answer to that, but I can't. At times I am grateful, so utterly lost in the moment of passion that my judgment is clouded and all I can see is him. Other times, I think of the pain he caused me, the deep sting of loss for who I had been, the chaos of those moments when I felt as if my world had been turned upside down, and the answer isn't as clear as it once was.

All that I'm certain of is that my life and my heart will never be the same, not after Hardin crashed into them.

chapter one

My alarm is set to go off any minute. I've been awake for half the night, shifting back and forth, counting the lines between the ceiling tiles and repeating the course schedule in my head. Others may count sheep; I plan. My mind doesn't allow a break from planning, and today, the most important day in my entire eighteen years of life, is no exception.

"Tessa!" I hear my mother's voice call from downstairs. Groaning to myself, I roll out of my tiny bed. I take my time tucking the corners of my bedsheet against the headboard, because this is the last morning that this will be a part of my regular routine. After today, this bedroom is no longer my home.

"Tessa!" she calls again.

"I'm up!" I yell back. The noise of the cabinets opening and slamming closed downstairs makes it known that she is feeling just as panicked as I am. My stomach is tied in a tight knot, and as I start my shower I pray that the anxiety I feel will lessen as the day goes on. All of my life has been a series of tasks in preparation for this day, my first day of college.

I spent the last few years nervously anticipating this. I spent my weekends studying and preparing for this as my peers were hanging out, drinking, and doing whatever else it is teenagers do to get themselves in trouble. That wasn't me. I was the girl who spent her nights studying cross-legged on the living room floor with my mother while she gossiped and watched hours of QVC to find new ways to improve her appearance.

The day my acceptance letter to Washington Central University came I couldn't have been more thrilled—and my mother cried for what felt like hours. I can't deny that I was proud that all my hard work had finally paid off. I got into the only college I applied for and, because of our low income, I have enough grants to keep my student loans to a minimum. I had once, for just a moment, considered leaving Washington for college. But seeing all the color drain from my mother's face at the suggestion, and the way she paced around the living room for nearly an hour, I told her I really hadn't been serious about that.

The moment I step into the spray of shower water some of the tension leaves my strained muscles. I'm standing here, under the hot water, trying to calm my mind, but really doing the opposite, and I get so distracted that by the time I finally wash my hair and body, I barely have enough hot water to run a razor over my legs from the knees down.

As I wrap the towel around my wet body, my mother calls my name yet again. Knowing that it's her nerves getting the best of her, I give her some leeway but take the time to blow-dry my hair. I know that she's anxious for my arrival day at college, but I have had this day planned down to the hour for months. Only one of us can be a nervous wreck, and I need to do what I can to make sure it's not me by following my plan.

My hands shake as I fumble with the zipper on my dress. I don't care for the thing, but my mother insisted that I wear it. I finally win the battle with the zipper, and pull my favorite sweater from the back of my closet door. As soon as I'm dressed, I feel slightly less nervous, until I notice a small tear on the sleeve of my sweater. I toss it back onto my bed and slip my shoes onto my feet, knowing that my mother is growing more impatient with every second that passes.

My boyfriend, Noah, will be here soon to ride up with us.

He's a year younger than me but will turn eighteen soon. He's brilliant and has straight A's just like I did, and—I'm so excited—he's planning on joining me at WCU next year. I really wish he was coming now, especially considering that I won't know a single person at college, but I'm thankful that he's promised to visit as often as possible. I just need a decent roommate; that's the only thing I'm asking for and the only thing I can't control with my planning.

"Ther-e-saaaa!"

"Mother, I am coming down now. *Please* do not scream my name again!" I yell as I walk down the stairs. Noah is sitting at the table across from my mother, staring down at the watch on his wrist. The blue of his polo shirt matches the light blue of his eyes, and his blond hair is combed and lightly gelled to perfection.

"Hey, college girl." He smiles a bright, perfectly lined smile as he stands. He pulls me into a tight hug and I close my mouth when I catch his excessive cologne. Yeah, sometimes he overdoes it a bit with that.

"Hey." I give him an equally bright smile, trying to hide my nerves, and pull my dirty blond hair into a ponytail.

"Honey, we can wait a couple minutes while you fix your hair," my mother says quietly.

I make my way to the mirror and nod; she's right. My hair needs to be presentable for today, and of course she didn't hesitate to remind me. I should have curled it the way she likes anyhow, as a little goodbye gift.

"I'll put your bags in the car," Noah offers, opening his palm for my mother to drop the keys into. With a quick kiss on my cheek he disappears from the room, bags in hand, and my mother follows him.

Round two of styling my hair ends with a better result than the first, and I brush a lint roller over my gray dress one last time.

As I go outside and walk to the car packed up with my things, the butterflies in my stomach dance around, making me slightly relieved that I have a two-hour drive to make them disappear.

I have no idea what college will be like, and, unexpectedly, the question that keeps dominating my thoughts is: *Will I make any friends?*

chapter two

I wish I could say that the familiar scenery of my home state calmed me as we drove, or that a sense of adventure took hold of me with each sign that indicated we were getting closer and closer to Washington Central. But really I was mostly in a daze of planning and obsessing. I'm not even sure what Noah was really talking about, but I know he was trying to be reassuring and excited for me.

"Here we are!" my mother squeals when we drive through a stone gate and onto campus. It looks just as great in person as it did in the brochures and online, and I'm immediately impressed by the elegant stone buildings. Hundreds of people, parents hugging and kissing their children goodbye, clusters of freshmen dressed head to toe in WCU gear, and a few stragglers, lost and confused, fill the area. The size of the campus is intimidating, but hopefully after a few weeks I will feel at home.

My mother insists that she and Noah accompany me to freshman orientation. My mother manages to hold a smile on her face the entire three hours and Noah listens intently, the same way that I do.

"I would like to see your dorm room before we head out. I need to make sure everything's up to par," my mother says once orientation is over. Her eyes scan the old building, full of disapproval. She has a way of finding the worst in things. Noah smiles, lightening the mood, and my mother perks up.

"I just can't believe you're in college! My only daughter, a college student, living on her own. I just can't believe it," she whines, dabbing under her eyes, though careful not to mess up her makeup. Noah follows behind us, carrying my bags as we navigate through the corridors.

"It's B22 . . . we are in C hall," I tell them. Luckily, I see a large B painted on the wall. "Down here," I instruct when my mother begins to turn the opposite way. I'm thankful that I only brought a few clothes, a blanket, and some of my favorite books along so Noah doesn't have too much to carry and I won't have too much to unpack.

"B22," my mother huffs. Her heels are outrageously high for the amount of walking we endure. At the end of a long hallway, I slide the key into the old wooden door, and when it creaks open my mother lets out a loud gasp. The room is small, with two single beds and two desks. After a moment, my eyes travel to the reason behind my mother's surprise: one side of the room is covered in music posters of bands that I've never heard of, the faces on them covered in piercings and their bodies with tattoos. And then there's the girl lying across one bed, and her bright red hair, eyes lined with what looks like inches of black liner, and arms covered in colorful tattoos.

"Hey," she says, offering a smile, a smile that I find quite intriguing, much to my surprise. "I'm Steph." She sits up on her elbows, causing her cleavage to push tight against her laced-up top, and I gently kick at Noah's shoe when his eyes focus on her chest.

"H-hey. I'm Tessa," I choke, all of my manners flying out the door.

"Hey, Tessa, nice to meet you. Welcome to WCU, where the dorms are tiny and the parties are huge." The crimson-haired girl grins wider. Her head falls back into a fit of laughter as she takes in the three horrified expressions in front of her. My mother's jaw is wide open, practically on the carpet, and Noah shifts uncomfortably. Steph walks over, closing the gap between us, and wraps her thin arms around my body. I'm frozen for a moment, surprised by her affection, but I return her kind gesture. A knock sounds at the door just as Noah drops my bags onto the floor, and I can't help but hope that this is all some sort of joke.

"Come in!" my new roommate yells. The door opens and two boys walk inside before she finishes her greeting.

Boys inside the female dorms on the first day? Maybe Washington Central was a bad decision. Or perhaps I could have found a way to screen my roommate first? I assume by the pained expression covering my mother's face that her thoughts have taken the same course. The poor woman looks like she might pass out any moment.

"Hey, you Steph's roomie?" one of the boys asks. His blond hair is styled straight up and there are sections of brown peeking through. His arms are scattered with tattoos and the earrings in his ear are the size of a nickel.

"Um . . . yes. My name is Tessa," I manage to say.

"I'm Nate. Don't look so nervous," he says with a smile, reaching out to touch my shoulder. "You'll love it here." His expression is warm and inviting despite his harsh appearance.

"I'm ready, guys," Steph says, grabbing a heavy black bag from her bed. My eyes shift to the tall brown-haired boy leaning against the wall. His hair is a mop of thick waves on his head, pushed back off his forehead, and he has metal in his eyebrow and lip. My focus moves down his black T-shirt to his arms, which are *also* covered in tattoos; not an inch of untouched skin is seen. Unlike Steph's and Nate's, his appear to be all black, gray, and white. He's tall, lean, and I know that I'm staring at him in the most impolite way, but I can't seem to look away.

I expect him to introduce himself the way that his friend did, but he stays quiet, rolling his eyes in annoyance and pulling a cell phone from the pocket of his tight black jeans. He definitely isn't as friendly as Steph or Nate. He's more appealing, though; something about him makes it hard to tear my eyes from his face. I'm vaguely aware of Noah's eyes on me as I finally look away and pretend I was staring out of shock.

Because that's what it is, right?

"See you around, Tessa," Nate says and the three of them exit the room. I let out a long breath. Calling the last few minutes uncomfortable would be an understatement.

"You're getting a new dorm!" my mother roars as soon as the door clicks shut.

"No, I can't." I sigh. "It's fine, Mother." I do my best to hide my nerves. I don't know how well this will work out, either, but the last thing I want is my overbearing mother causing a scene on my *first day* of college. "I'm sure she won't be around much at all anyway," I try to convince her, along with myself.

"Absolutely not. We are going to switch now." Her clean appearance clashes with the anger in her face; her long blond hair is flipped to one shoulder, yet every curl is still perfectly intact. "You will not room with someone who allows men in like that—those punks, at that!"

I look into her gray eyes, then to Noah. "Mother, please, let's just see how it goes. Please," I beg. I can't begin to imagine the mess it would create trying to get a last-minute dorm change. And how humiliating it would feel.

My mother looks around to the room again, taking in the décor covering Steph's side, and huffs dramatically at the dark theme.

"Fine," she spits out, much to my surprise. "But we're going to have a little talk before I go."

chapter three

An hour later, after listening to my mother warn me against the dangers of parties and college men—and using some language that's rather uncomfortable for Noah and me to hear from her—she finally makes her move to leave. In her usual style, a quick hug and kiss, she exits the dorm room, informing Noah that she will wait for him in the car.

"I'll miss having you around every day," he says softly and pulls me into his arms. I inhale his cologne, the one I bought him two Christmases in a row, and sigh. Some of the overpowering scent has worn off, and I realize that I'll miss this smell and the comfort and familiarity that go along with it, no matter how many times I complained about it in the past.

"I'll miss you, too, but we can talk every day," I promise and tighten my arms around his torso and nuzzle into his neck. "I wish you were here this year." Noah is only a few inches taller than me, but I like that he doesn't tower over me. My mother used to tease me growing up, claiming that a man grows an inch for every lie he tells. My father was a tall man, so I won't argue with her logic there.

Noah brushes his lips across mine . . . and just then I hear a horn honking in the parking lot.

Noah laughs and breaks away from me. "Your mom. She's persistent." He kisses me on the cheek and hurries out the door, yelling, "Call you tonight!" as he goes.

Left alone, I think about his hasty exit for just a moment and then begin to unpack my bags. Shortly, half my clothes are neatly folded and stored in one of the small dressers; the remainder are hung neatly in my closet. I cringe at the sheer amount of leather and animal print filling the other closet. Still, my curiosity does get the best of me and I find myself running my finger along a dress made of some sort of metal, and another that's so thin it's barely there at all.

Feeling the beginnings of exhaustion from the day, I lie across the bed. An unfamiliar loneliness is creeping its way into me already, and it doesn't help that my roommate is gone, no matter how uncomfortable her friends make me. I have a feeling she will be gone a lot, or, worse, she may have company over too often. Why couldn't I get a roommate who loved to read and study? I suppose it could be a good thing, because I will have the small room to myself, but I don't have a good feeling about any of this. So far college is neither what I had dreamed of nor expected.

I remind myself that it's only been a few hours. Tomorrow will be better. It has to be.

I gather my planner and textbooks, taking the time to write down my classes for the semester and my potential meetings for the literary club I plan on joining; I'm still undecided on that, but I read a few student testimonials and want to check it out. I want to try to find a group of like-minded people I can talk to. I don't expect to make a lot of friends, just enough that I can have someone to maybe eat a meal with every once in a while. I plan for a trip off campus tomorrow to get some more things for my dorm room. I don't want to crowd my side of the room the way that Steph has, but I would like to add a few things of my own to make me feel more at home in the unfamiliar space. The fact that I don't have a car yet will make it a little difficult. The sooner I get one, the better. I have enough money from graduation gifts and savings from my summer job at a bookstore, but I'm not sure if I want the stress of owning a car right now. The fact that I live on campus gives me full access to public transport, and I've already researched the bus lines. With thoughts of schedules, red-haired girls, and unfriendly men covered in tattoos, I drift to sleep with my planner still in hand.

THE NEXT MORNING Steph is not in her bed. I would like to get to know her, but that might be difficult if she's never around. Maybe one of the two boys that she was with was her boyfriend? For her sake, I hope it was the blond one.

Grabbing my toiletry bag, I make my way to the shower room. I can already tell that one of my least favorite things about dorm life is going to be the shower situation—I wish each of the rooms had their own bathrooms. It's awkward, but at least they won't be coed.

Or . . . I had assumed they wouldn't be—wouldn't everyone assume that? But when I reach the door, sure enough, there are two stick figures printed on the sign, one male and one female. *Ugh.* I can't believe they let this kind of thing happen. I can't believe I didn't uncover it while I was researching WCU.

Spotting an open shower stall, I skirt through the half-naked boys and girls quickly, pull the curtain closed tight, and undress, then hang my clothes on the rack outside by blindly poking one hand out of the curtain. The shower takes too long to get warm and the entire time I'm in there I'm paranoid that someone will pull back the thin curtain separating my naked body from the rest of the guys and girls out there. Everyone seems to be comfortable with half-naked bodies of both genders walking around; college life is strange so far, and it's only the second day.

The shower stall is tiny, lined with a small rack to hang my clothes on while I shower and barely enough room to stretch my arms in front of me. I find my mind drifting to Noah and my life back home. Distracted, I turn around and my elbow knocks into the rack, knocking my clothes to the wet floor. The shower *pours* onto them, completely soaking them.

"You've got to be kidding me!" I groan to myself, hastily cutting the water off and wrapping my towel around myself. I grab my pile of heavy, soaked clothes and rush down the hall, desperately hoping no one sees me. I reach my room and shove the key in, instantly relaxing when I push the door closed behind me.

Until I turn around to see the rude, tattooed, brown-haired boy sprawled across Steph's bed.

chapter four

U m . . . Where is Steph?" I try to sound authoritative, but my voice comes out as more of a squeak. My hands are clenched around the soft fabric of my towel and my eyes keep darting down to make sure it's actually covering my naked body.

The boy looks at me, the corners of his mouth lifting slightly, but doesn't say a word.

"Did you hear me? I asked you where Steph is," I repeat, trying to be slightly more polite this time.

The expression on his face magnifies and he finally mumbles, "I don't know," and turns on the small flat screen on Steph's dresser. *What is he even doing in here? Doesn't he have his own room?* I bite my tongue, trying to keep my rude comments to myself.

"Okay? Well, could you like . . . leave or something so I can get dressed?" He hasn't even noticed I'm in a towel. Or maybe he has but it doesn't impress him.

"Don't flatter yourself, it's not like I'm going to look at you," he scoffs and rolls over, his hands covering his face. He has a thick English accent that I didn't notice at first. Probably because he was too rude to actually speak to me yesterday.

Unsure how I should respond to his rude remark, I huff and walk to my dresser. Maybe he isn't straight, maybe that's what he meant by "it's not like I'm going to look." Either that or he finds me unattractive. I hastily put on a bra and panties, followed by a plain white shirt and khaki shorts.

"Are you done yet?" he asks, snapping the last bit of patience I held.

"Could you be any more disrespectful? I did nothing to you. *What is your problem?!*" I shout, much louder than I had wanted to, but by the surprised look on his face, my words had the intended effect.

He silently stares at me for a moment. And while I await for his apology . . . he bursts into laughter. His laugh is deep and would be an almost lovely sound if he didn't come off so unpleasant. Dimples indent both of his cheeks as he continues on, and I feel like a complete idiot, unsure what to do or say. I don't usually like conflict and this boy seems like the last person I should start a fight with.

The door opens and Steph bursts in.

"Sorry I'm late. I have a hell of a hangover," she says dramatically, and her eyes dart back and forth between the two of us. "Sorry, Tess, I forgot to tell you Hardin would be coming by." She shrugs apologetically.

I would like to think me and Steph could make our living arrangement work, maybe even build some sort of a friendship, but with her choice of friends and late nights, I'm just not sure anymore.

"Your boyfriend is rude." The words tumble out before I can stop them.

Steph looks over at the boy. And then they *both* burst into laughter. *What is it with people laughing at me?* It's getting really annoying.

"Hardin Scott is *not* my boyfriend!" she spits out, nearly choking. Calming down, she turns and scowls at this *Hardin*. "What did you say to her?" Then, looking back at me: "Hardin has a . . . a unique way of conversing."

Lovely, so basically what she is saying is that Hardin is,

simply, at his core, a rude person. The English boy shrugs and changes the channel with the remote in his hand.

"There is a party tonight; you should come with us, Tessa," she says.

So now it's my turn to laugh.

"Parties aren't really my thing. Plus I have to go to get some things for my desk and walls." I look at Hardin, who, of course, is acting as if neither of us is in the room with him.

"C'mon . . . it's just one party! You're in college now, just one party won't hurt," she begs. "Wait, how are you getting to the store? I thought you didn't have a car?"

"I was going to take the bus. And besides, I can't go to a party—I don't even know anyone," I say, and Hardin laughs again—a subtle acknowledgment that he'll pay just enough attention to mock me. "I was going to read and Skype with Noah."

"You don't want to take the bus on a Saturday! They're way too packed. Hardin can drop you on the way to his place . . . right, Hardin? And you'll know *me* at the party. Just come . . . please?" She presses her hands together in a dramatic plea.

I've only known her for a day; should I trust her? My mother's warning about parties goes through my head. Steph seems quite sweet, from the small interaction that I've had with her. But a party?

"I don't know . . . and, no, I don't want Hardin to drive me to the store," I say.

Hardin rolls over across Steph's bed with an amused expression. "Oh no! I was really looking forward to hanging out with you," he dryly replies, his voice so full of sarcasm that I want to throw a book at his curly head. "Come on, Steph, you know this girl isn't going to show at the party," he says, laughing; his accent is so thick. The curious side of me, which I admit is quite large, is desperate to ask him where he is from. The competitive side of me wants to prove that smug face of his wrong.

"Actually, yeah, I'll come," I say with as sweet a smile as I can manage. "It sounds like it might be fun."

Hardin shakes his head in disbelief and Steph squeals before wrapping her arms around me in a tight hug.

"Yay! We'll have so much fun!" she shrieks. And a big part of me is practically praying that she'll be right.

chapter five

I'm thankful when Hardin finally leaves so Steph and I can discuss the party. I need more details to ease my nerves, and having him around is no help at all.

"Where is the party? Is it within walking distance?" I ask her, trying to sound calm as I align my books neatly on the shelf.

"Technically, it's a frat party, at one of the biggest frat houses here." Her mouth is wide open as she layers more mascara onto her lashes. "It's off campus, so we won't be walking but Nate will pick us up."

I'm grateful it won't be Hardin, even though I know he will be there. Somehow riding with him seems unbearable. Why is he so rude? If anything, he should be grateful that I'm not judging *him* for the way he has destroyed his body with holes and tattoos. Okay, maybe I am judging him a little, but not to his face. I'm at least polite about our differences. In my home, tattoos and piercings are not a normal thing. I always had to have my hair combed, my eyebrows plucked, and my clothes clean and ironed. It's just the way it is.

"Did you hear me?" Steph says and interrupts my thoughts.

"I'm sorry . . . what?" I hadn't realized my mind had wandered to the rude boy.

"I said let's get ready—you can help me pick my outfit," she says. The dresses she picks out are so inappropriate that I keep looking around for a hidden camera and someone to jump out and tell me this is all a joke. I cringe at each one and she laughs, obviously finding my distaste humorous.

The dress—no, piece of scrap material—she chooses is a black fishnet, which lets her red bra show through. The only thing keeping her from showing her entire body is a solid black slip. The dress barely reaches the tops of her thighs and she keeps tugging the material up to reveal more leg, then back down to reveal more cleavage. The heels of her shoes are at least four inches tall. Her flaming red hair is pulled into a wild bun with curls escaping down to her shoulders and her eyes are lined with blue and black liner, somehow even more eyeliner than she had on before.

"Did your tattoos hurt?" I ask her as I pull out my favorite maroon dress.

"The first one sort of did, but not as bad as you would think. It's almost like a bee stinging you over and over," she says with a shrug.

"That sounds terrible," I tell her and she laughs. It occurs to me that she probably finds me as strange as I find her. That we're both unfamiliar with each other is oddly comforting.

She gapes at my dress. "You're not really wearing that, are you?"

My hand slides over the fabric. This is my nicest dress, my favorite dress, and it's not like I really have all that many. "What is wrong with my dress?" I ask, trying to hide how offended I am. The maroon material is soft but sturdy, the same material business suits are made of. The collar goes up to my neck and the sleeves are three-quarter length, hitting just under my elbows.

"Nothing . . . it's just so . . . long?" she says.

"It's barely below my knee." I can't tell if she can see I'm offended or not, but for some reason I don't want her to know this about me.

"It's pretty. I just think it's a little too formal for a party. You could borrow something of mine?" she says in all sincerity. I cringe at the idea of trying to squeeze into one of her tiny dresses.

"Thanks, Steph. I'm fine wearing this, though," I say and plug in my curling iron.

chapter six

Later, when my hair is perfectly curled and lying down my back, I push two bobby pins in, one on each side to keep it out of my face.

"Do you want to use some of my makeup?" Steph asks, and I look in the mirror again.

My eyes always look a little too large for my face, but I prefer to wear minimal makeup and usually just put on a little mascara and lip balm.

"Maybe a little eyeliner?" I say, still unsure.

With a smile, she hands me three pencils: one purple, one black, and one brown. I roll them around in my fingers, deciding between the black and brown.

"The purple will look great with your eyes," she says, and I smile but shake my head. "Your eyes are so unique—want to trade?" she jokes.

But Steph has beautiful green eyes; why would she even joke about trading with me? I take the black pencil and draw the thinnest possible line around both eyes, earning a proud smile from Steph.

Her phone buzzes and she grabs her purse. "Nate's here," she says. I grab my purse, smooth my dress, and slip on my flat, white Toms, which she eyes but doesn't comment on.

Nate is waiting out front of the building, heavy rock music blaring out of his car's rolled-down windows. I can't help but glance around to see everyone staring. I keep my head down and just as I look up, I see Hardin lean up in the front seat. He must have been bending down. *Ugh.*

"Ladies," Nate greets us.

Hardin glares at me as I climb in behind Steph and end up getting stuck sitting directly behind him. "You do know that we are going to a party, not a church, right, Theresa?" he says, and I glance at the side mirror and find a smirk across his face.

"Please don't call me Theresa. I prefer Tessa," I warn him. How does he even know that's my name? Theresa reminds me of my father, and I would rather not hear it.

"Sure thing, Theresa."

I lean back against my seat and roll my eyes. I choose not to banter back and forth with him; it's not worth my time.

I stare out the window, trying to drown out the loud music as we drive. Finally, Nate parks on the side of a busy street lined with large, seemingly identical houses. Painted in black letters is the name of the fraternity, but I can't make out the words because of the overgrown vines sneaking up the side of the massive house in front of us. Messy strings of toilet paper sprawl up the white house, and the noise coming from inside adds to the stereotypical frat house theme.

"It's so big; how many people will be here?" I gulp. The lawn is full of people holding red cups, some of them dancing, right there on the lawn. I'm way out of my league here.

"A full house, hurry up," Hardin responds and gets out of the car, slamming the car door behind him. From the backseat, I watch as multiple people high-five and shake Nate's hand, ignoring Hardin. What surprises me is that no one else that I see is covered in tattoos like he, Nate, and Steph are. Maybe I can make some friends here tonight after all.

"Coming?" Steph says with a smile and pops open her door and hops out.

I nod, mostly to myself, as I climb out of the car, making sure to smooth my dress again.

chapter seven

Hardin has already disappeared into the house, which is great because maybe I won't see him again for the rest of the night. Considering the number of people crammed into this place, I probably won't. I follow Steph and Nate into the crowded living room and am handed a red cup. I turn to decline with a polite "No, thank you," but it's too late and I don't have a clue who gave it to me. I put the cup on the counter and continue to walk through the house with them. We stop walking when we reach a group of people crowded on and around a couch. I assume they are friends with Steph, given their appearance. They are all tattooed like her, and sitting in a row on the couch. Unfortunately, Hardin is on the right arm of the couch, but I avoid looking at him as Steph introduces me to the group.

"This is Tessa, my roommate. She just got here yesterday so I figured I would show her a good time for her first weekend at WCU," she explains.

One by one they nod or smile at me. All of them seem so friendly, except Hardin, of course. A very attractive boy with olive-toned skin reaches out his hand and shakes mine. His hands are slightly cold from the drink he was holding, but his smile is warm. The light reflects off his mouth, and I think I spot a piece of metal on his tongue, but he closes his mouth too quickly for me to be sure.

"I'm Zed. What's your major?" he asks me. I notice his eyes

travel down my bulky dress and he smiles a little but doesn't say anything.

"I'm an English major," I say proudly, smiling. Hardin snorts but I ignore him.

"Awesome," he says. "I'm into flowers." Zed laughs and I return one.

Flowers? What does that even mean?

"Want a drink?" he asks before I can inquire further about flowers.

"Oh, no. I don't drink," I tell him and he tries to hide his smile.

"Leave it to Steph to bring Little Miss Priss to a party," a tiny girl with pink hair says under her breath.

I pretend not to hear her so I can avoid any kind of confrontation. Miss Priss? I'm in no way "prissy," but I have worked and studied hard to get where I am, and since my father left us my mother has worked her entire life to make sure I have a good future.

"I'm going to get some air," I say and turn to walk away. I need to avoid party drama at all costs. I don't need to make any enemies when I don't have any friends to begin with.

"Do you want me to come with you?" Steph calls after me.

I shake my head and make my way to the door. I knew I shouldn't have come. I should be in my pajamas curled up with a novel right now. I could be Skyping with Noah, whom I miss terribly. Even sleeping would be better than sitting outside this dreadful party with a bunch of drunken strangers. I decide to text Noah. I walk to the edge of the yard, since it seems to be the least crowded space.

I miss you. College isn't very fun so far. I hit send and sit on the stone wall waiting for his reply. A group of drunk girls walk by giggling and stumbling over their own feet.

He responds quickly: Why not? I miss you too, Tessa. I wish I was there with you and I smile at his words.

"Shit, sorry!" a male voice says and a second later I feel cold liquid soak the front of my dress. The guy stumbles and pulls himself up to lean against the low wall. "My bad, really," he mumbles and sits down.

This party could not get any worse. First that girl called me prissy, and now my dress is soaked with God knows what type of alcohol—and it really smells. Sighing, I pick up my phone and walk inside to find a bathroom. I push my way through the crowded hall and try to open every door on the way, none of them budging. I try not to think about what people are doing in the rooms.

I make my way upstairs and continue my hunt for a bathroom. Finally, one of the doors does open. Unfortunately, it's not a bathroom. It's a bedroom, and, even more unfortunate for me, it's one in which Hardin is lying across the bed while the pink-haired girl straddles his lap, her mouth covering his.

chapter eight

The girl turns around and looks at me as I try to move my feet, but they just won't budge. "Can I help you?" she snarks.

Hardin sits up with her still on his torso. His face is flat—not amused or embarrassed at all. He must do this type of thing all the time. He must be used to being caught in frat houses practically having sex with strange girls.

"Oh . . . no. Sorry, I . . . I'm looking for a bathroom, someone spilled a drink on me," I quickly explain. This is so uncomfortable. The girl presses her mouth against Hardin's neck and I look away. These two seem to be a good match. Both tattooed, and both rude.

"Okay? So go find a bathroom." She rolls her eyes and I nod, leaving the room. After the door closes I lean my back against it. So far college isn't fun at all. I just can't wrap my head around how a party like this could be considered fun. Instead of trying to find a bathroom, I decide to find the kitchen and clean myself off there. The last thing I want to do is open another door and find drunken hormonal college students on top of one another. Again.

The kitchen isn't too hard to find, but it's crowded since most of the alcohol supply is in ice buckets on the counter and stacks of pizza boxes fill the countertops. I have to reach around a brunette puking in the sink to grab a paper towel and wet it. As I wipe it over my dress, small white flakes of the cheap paper towel cover the wet spot, making it worse. Frustrated, I groan and lean against the counter.

"Having fun?" Nate asks as he approaches me. I'm relieved to see a familiar face. He smiles sweetly and takes a sip of his drink.

"Not exactly . . . how long do these parties usually last?"

"All night . . . and half the day tomorrow." He laughs and my mouth drops. When would Steph want to leave? Hopefully soon.

"Wait." I begin to panic. "Who's going to drive us back to the dorm?" I ask him, well aware of his bloodshot eyes.

"I don't know . . . you can drive my car if you want," he says.

"That's really nice, but I can't drive your car. If I wreck or get pulled over with underage drinkers in the car I would get in so much trouble." I can just imagine my mother's face as she bails me out of jail.

"No, no, it's not a far drive—you should just take my car. You haven't even been drinking. If not, you'll have to stay here, or I could ask around to see if someone—"

"No, it's fine. I'll figure it out," I manage before the music gets turned way up and most everything is drowned out by bass and lyrics that are practically screamed.

My decision to come to this party is proving to be worse and worse as the night goes on.

chapter nine

Finally, after pointing around and yelling "Steph!" like ten times at Nate, the music drops into a quieter song and he nods and starts to laugh. His hand moves up into the air and he points into the next room. He is really a sweet guy—why does he hang out with Hardin?

As I turn to where he indicated, all I hear is my own gasp as I spot her. She, along with two other girls, are dancing on a table in the living room. A drunk guy climbs up and joins them, his hands gripping her hips. I expect her to swat his hands off but she just smiles and pushes her bottom against him. *Okay.*

"They're just dancing, Tessa," Nate says and gives a quick chuckle at my uneasy expression.

But they aren't *just dancing*; they're groping and grinding against each other.

"Yeah . . . I know." I shrug, even though it isn't as casual to me. I've never danced that way, not even with Noah, and we have been dating two years. Noah! I reach into my purse and check my messages from him.

You there Tess?
Hello? You okay?
Tessa? Should I call your mom? I'm getting worried.

I dial him as fast as my fingers will allow, praying that he hasn't called my mother yet. He doesn't pick up, but I text him assuring him that I'm okay and there is no need for him to call my mother. She will lose it if she thinks something happened to me on my first weekend of college.

"Heyyyy . . . Tessa!" Steph slurs and leans her head on my shoulder. "You having fun yet, roomie?" She giggles, obviously heavily intoxicated. "I think . . . I need . . . the room is starting to spend, Tess . . . I mean spin," she says, laughing, and her body lurches forward.

"She is going to get sick," I tell Nate. He nods and lifts her into his arms, draping her body over his shoulder.

"Follow me," he instructs and heads upstairs. He opens a door halfway down the hall, finding a bathroom quickly, of course. Right as he places her on the floor by the toilet, she begins to vomit. I look away but grab her red hair and gently hold it back away from her face.

Finally, after more vomit than I can handle seeing, she stops and Nate hands me a towel. "Let's get her to the room across the hall and lay her on the bed. She is going to need to sleep it off," he says. I nod, but what I'm really thinking is that I can't leave her here alone, passed out. "You can stay in there, too," he says, seeming to read my mind.

Together we get her up off the floor and help her walk across the hall and into a dark bedroom. We gently lay a groaning Steph onto the bed and Nate quickly takes off, telling me he'll check in on us later. I sit down on the bed next to Steph and make sure her head is comfortable.

Sober, with a drunk girl beside me and a party raging all around, I feel like I've hit a new low. I turn on a lamp and look around the room, my eyes immediately going to the bookshelves that cover one of the walls. Since this perks my mood up, I go over to it and scan through the titles. Whoever owns this collection is impressive; there are many classics, a whole range of different types of books, including all of my favorites. Spying *Wuthering Heights*, I pull it off the shelf. It's in bad shape, the binding giving away how many times it's been opened.

I'm so lost in Emily Brontë's words that I don't even notice the change in light when the door opens, or the presence of a third person in the space.

"Why the hell are you in my room?" an angry voice booms from behind me.

I know that accent by now.

Hardin.

"I asked you what the hell you're doing in my room," he repeats, just as harshly as the first time. I turn to see his long legs pulling him toward me and he snatches the book from my hand and tosses it back onto the shelf.

My mind is whirling. I thought the party couldn't get any worse, but here I am, caught in Hardin's personal place. He rudely clears his throat and waves his hand in front of my face.

"Nate told me to bring Steph in here . . ." My voice is soft, barely audible. He takes a step closer and lets out a deep breath. I gesture to his bed, causing his eyes to follow my hand. "She drank too much and Nate said—"

"I heard you the first time." He runs his hand through his messy hair, clearly upset. Why does he care so much if we are in his room? Wait . . .

"You are a part of this fraternity?" I ask him. It's impossible to hide the shock in my voice. Hardin is far from what I imagined a frat boy to be like.

"Yeah, so?" he answers and takes yet another step closer. The space between us is less than two feet, and when I try to inch away from him my back hits the bookcase. "Does that surprise you, Theresa?"

"Stop calling me Theresa." *He has me cornered.*

"That's your name, isn't it?" He smirks, his mood slightly lightening.

I sigh and turn away from him, basically facing into the wall of books. I have no idea where I'm going, but I need to get away from Hardin before I slap him. Or cry. It has been a long day, so I will most likely cry before slapping him. And what a sight that would be.

I turn and push past him.

"She can't stay in here," he says as I pass. When I turn around he has the small ring in his lip between his teeth. What made him decide to put a hole in his lip and eyebrow? That had to be painful . . . though the one piece does accent just how full and round his lips are.

"Why not? I thought you guys were friends?"

"We are," he says, "but no one stays in my room." His arms cross over his chest, and for the first time since I met him, I can make out the shape of one of his tattoos. It's a flower, printed in the middle of his covered forearm. Hardin, with a flower tattoo? The black and gray design resembles a rose from this distance, but there is something surrounding the flower that takes the beauty from it, adding darkness to the delicate form.

Feeling brave and annoyed, I let out a laugh. "Oh . . . I see. So only girls who make out with you can come into your room?" As the words leave my mouth his smile grows.

"That wasn't my room. But if you're trying to say you want to make out with me, sorry, you're not my type," he says. I'm not sure why but his words hurt my feelings. Hardin is far from my type, but I would never actually say that to him.

"You are . . . you are . . ." I can't find the words to express my annoyance toward him. The music through the wall is like an itching sensation. I'm embarrassed, annoyed, and exhausted from the party. Arguing with him isn't worth it. "Well . . . then *you* take her to another room, and I'll find a way back to the dorms," I say and head for the door.

As I go through it and slam it shut behind me, even through the noise of the party, I hear Hardin's mocking "Good night, *Theresa.*"

chapter ten

I can't help the tears that fall down my cheeks as I reach the top of the stairs. I hate college so far—and my classes haven't even started. Why couldn't I just get a roommate who was more like me? I should be asleep now, preparing for Monday. I don't belong at parties like this, and I certainly don't belong hanging out with these type of people. I do like Steph, but I just don't have it in me to deal with a scene like this and people like Hardin. He's such a mystery to me; why must he always be such a jerk? But then the next thing I think of is that wall of books of his—why does he have all of them? There is no way a rude, disrespectful, tattooed jerk like Hardin could possibly enjoy those amazing works. The only thing I can picture him reading is the back of a beer bottle.

Dabbing at my wet cheeks, I realize I have no idea where this house is located, or how to get back to the dorms. The more I think about my decisions tonight, the more frustrated and stressed I become.

I really should have thought this through; this is exactly why I plan everything, so things like this don't happen. The house is still packed and the music is too loud. Nate is nowhere to be found; neither is Zed. Maybe I should just find a random bedroom upstairs and sleep on the floor? There are at least fifteen rooms up there, and maybe I will get lucky and find an empty one? Despite my efforts to conceal my emotions, I can't, and I don't want to go down and have everyone see me like this. I turn back, find the bathroom I was in with Steph, and sit on the floor with my head between my knees.

I call Noah again, and this time he answers on the second ring.

"Tess? It's late, are you okay?" he says, his voice groggy.

"Yes. No. I went to a stupid party with my roommate and now I am stuck at a frat house with nowhere to sleep and no way to get back to my room," I sob through the line. I know my problem isn't life or death, but I'm beyond frustrated at myself for getting into this overwhelming situation.

"A party? With that redhead girl?" He sounds surprised.

"Yeah, with Steph. But she's passed out upstairs."

"Whoa, why are you even hanging out with her? She's so . . . just not someone you would ever hang around with," he says, and the scorn in his voice irritates me. I wanted him to tell me it will be okay, that tomorrow is a new day, something positive and encouraging. Something not so judgmental and harsh.

"That isn't the point, Noah . . ." I said with a sigh, but right then the door handle jingles and I sit up. "Just a minute!" I call to the person outside and wipe at my eyes with some toilet paper, but that only smears the eyeliner even more. This is exactly why I don't wear this stuff.

"I will call you back; someone needs the bathroom," I say to Noah and hang up before he can protest.

Whoever's on the other side of the door begins *pounding* on it and I groan as I hurry to open it, wiping my eyes again. "I said just a min—"

But I stop as glaring green eyes pour into mine.

chapter eleven

As I look into those amazing green eyes, I suddenly realize that I hadn't previously noticed their color before. And *then* I realize that it's because Hardin hasn't really made eye contact with me until just now. Amazing, deep, *surprised* green eyes. Hardin looks away quickly when I push past him. He grabs my arm and pulls me back.

"Don't touch me!" I yell, jerking my arm away.

"Have you been crying?" he asks, his tone curious. If this wasn't Hardin, I might actually think he was concerned for me.

"Just leave me alone, Hardin."

He moves in front of me, his tall frame blocking my movements. I can't take more of his games, not tonight.

"Hardin, please. I am begging you, if you have one decent bone in your body you will leave me be. Just save whatever mean comment you are going to say for tomorrow. Please." I don't care if he hears the embarrassment and desperation in my voice. I just *need* to be left alone by him.

A flash of confusion shows in his eyes before he opens his mouth. He watches me for a moment before any words come out. "There's a room down the hall you can sleep in. It's where I put Steph," he flatly states. I wait a second for him to say something else, but he doesn't. He just stares at me.

"Okay," I quietly say and he moves out of my way.

"It's the third door on the left," he instructs and heads down the hall and disappears into his bedroom.

What the hell was that? Hardin without any rude comments? I know I'm in for it if I see him tomorrow. He's probably got a planner for all his snide comments like I do for my classwork, and I'm sure I'll be on his agenda tomorrow.

The third room on the left is a plain room, much smaller than Hardin's and with two twin beds. It looks more like a dorm room than the larger space that Hardin has. Maybe he's the leader or something? The more likely explanation is that everyone is afraid of him and he bullied his way into the largest room. Steph is lying across the bed closest to the window, so I kick off my shoes and cover her with the blanket before locking the door and lying down on the other.

My thoughts are all over the place as I fall asleep, and images of clouded roses and angry green eyes flow through my dreams.

chapter twelve

When I wake, it takes my mind a moment to remember the events of last night that led me to this strange bedroom. Steph is still asleep, snoring unattractively with her mouth wide open. I decide to wait until I know how we are getting back to the dorms before waking her. I quickly put my shoes on, grab my purse, and step out. Should I knock on Hardin's door or try to find Nate? Is Nate even part of the frat? I would have never guessed that Hardin would be a part of an organized social group, so maybe Nate is, too.

Stepping over sleeping bodies in the hallway, I make my way downstairs.

"Nate?" I call, hoping to hear a reply. There are at least twenty-five people sleeping in the living room alone. The floor is littered with red cups and trash, which makes it hard to navigate through the mess, but also makes me realize how clean the upstairs hallway actually was, despite the people there. When I reach the kitchen, I have to force myself not to start cleaning it up. This will take the whole house all day to clean up. I would love to see Hardin cleaning up all this trash, and as the thought goes through my head I giggle a little.

"What's so funny?"

I turn around and find Hardin entering the kitchen, a trash bag in his hand. He sweeps his arm over the countertop, making the cups fall into the trash bag.

"Nothing," I lie. "Does Nate live here, too?"

He ignores me and continues to clean.

"Does he?" I ask again, more impatient this time. "The sooner you tell me if Nate lives here, the sooner I can leave."

"Okay, now you have my attention. But, no, he doesn't live here. Does he seem like a frat boy to you?" He smirks.

"No, but neither do you," I snap and his jaw tenses.

He moves around me and opens the cabinet next to my hip, pulling out a roll of paper towels.

"Is there a bus that runs close to here?" I ask, not expecting an answer.

"Yep, about a block away."

I follow him around the kitchen. "Could you tell me where it is?"

"Sure. It's about a block away." The corners of his mouth lift, taunting me.

I roll my eyes and walk out of the kitchen. Hardin's momentary civility last night was obviously a onetime thing and today he'll be coming at me full force. After the night I had, I can't stand to be around him.

I go wake up Steph, who wakes up surprisingly easily and smiles at me. I'm grateful that she's just as ready to get out of this damned fraternity house.

"Hardin said there is a bus stop around the block," I tell her as we walk downstairs together.

"We aren't taking the damn bus. One of these assholes will take us back to our room. He was probably just giving you a hard time," she says, her hand resting on my shoulder. As we enter the kitchen and find Hardin pulling some beer cans out of the oven, she's all authority. "Hardin, you ready to take us back now? My head is pounding."

"Yeah, sure, just give me a minute," he says like he's been waiting for us all along.

* * *

DURING THE DRIVE BACK to the dorms Steph sings along to whatever metal song is playing through the speakers and Hardin rolls all the windows down, despite my polite requests to roll them up. Silent the whole way, he mindlessly drums his long fingers on the steering wheel. Not that I was paying attention.

"I'll come by later, Steph," he tells her as she climbs out of the passenger seat. She nods and waves as I open my door.

"Bye, Theresa," he says with a smirk. I roll my eyes and follow Steph into the dorm.

chapter thirteen

The rest of the weekend goes quickly and I manage to avoid seeing Hardin. When I head out early Sunday to go shopping, I leave before he can come to the room, and I return after he's apparently left.

The new clothes I get fill up my small dresser, but as I put them away Hardin's obnoxious voice plays in my head: *You know we are going to a party, not church.*

I suspect he'd say the same about these new outfits, but I've decided that I am no longer going to be going to parties with Steph, or anywhere that Hardin may be. He isn't good company and bickering with him is exhausting.

Finally it's Monday morning, my first day of college classes, and I couldn't be more prepared. I wake up extra early to make sure I can take a shower—without boys around—and not be rushed. My white button-up shirt and tan pleated skirt are perfectly ironed and ready to be put on. I get dressed, pin my hair, and put my bag over my shoulder. I'm about to leave—about fifteen minutes early, to ensure that I won't be late—when Steph's alarm goes off. She hits the snooze button, but I wonder if I should I wake her. Her classes may start later than mine, or maybe she isn't planning on going. The idea of missing the first day of classes stresses me out, but she is a sophomore, so maybe she has it under control.

With one last glance in the mirror, I head to my first class. Studying the campus map proves to have been a good idea, and I find my first building within twenty minutes. When I walk into my freshman history class the room is empty, save one person.

Since this person obviously cares about being on time, too, I sit next to him. He could be my first new friend. "Where is everyone?" I ask, and he smiles. His smile alone puts me at ease.

"Probably running across campus to barely make it here on time," he jokes, and I instantly like him. That's exactly what I was thinking.

"I'm Tessa Young," I say and give him a friendly smile.

"Landon Gibson," he says with an equally adorable smile as the first one. We spend the rest of the time before class talking. I find out that he's an English major, like me, and he has a girlfriend named Dakota. Landon doesn't mock me or miss a beat in our easy conversation when I tell him that Noah is a grade below me. I decide now that he is someone whom I would like to see more of. As the class begins to fill, Landon and I make a point to introduce ourselves to the professor.

Afterward, as the day continues, I begin to regret taking five classes instead of four. I rush to my British Literature elective—thanking God it's the last class of the day—and barely make it on time. I am relieved when I see Landon sitting in the front row, the seat next to him empty.

"Hey again," he says with a smile as I sit down.

The professor begins the class, handing out the syllabus for the semester and giving a brief introduction about himself, what led to him to become a professor, and his excitement for the topic. I love that college is different from high school and the professors don't make you stand in front of the class and introduce yourself or do any other embarrassing and unnecessary things.

In the middle of the professor explaining our reading lists, the door creaks open and I hear myself groan as Hardin stumbles into the classroom.

"Great," I say under my breath sarcastically.

"You know Hardin?" Landon asks. Hardin must have quite
the reputation around the campus if someone as sweet as Landon
knows of him.

"Sort of. My roommate is friends with him. He's not my favorite person," I whisper.

As I do so, Hardin's green eyes lock on mine, and I worry that
he's heard me. What would he do if he had? But, honestly, I don't
care if he did—it's not like he isn't aware that we don't care for
each other.

I find myself curious about what Landon knows about him,
though, so I can't help but ask, "Do you know him?"

"Yeah . . . he's . . ." He stops talking and turns slightly to look
behind us. I look up and see Hardin sliding into the desk next to
me. Landon stays quiet for the rest of the class, keeping his eyes
focused on the professor the entire time.

"THAT'S ALL FOR TODAY. I will see you all again on Wednesday,"
Professor Hill says and dismisses us.

"I think this will be my favorite class," I tell Landon as we
walk outside, and he agrees. But his face falls when we realize
Hardin is walking next to us.

"What do you want, Hardin?" I ask, giving him a taste of his
own medicine. It doesn't work, or I don't have the right tone for it,
because all he seems is amused.

"Nothing. Nothing. I'm just so glad we have a class together,"
he says mockingly and runs his hands through his hair, shaking it
and pushing it up on his forehead. I notice an oddly shaped infinity symbol tattooed just above his wrist, and he lowers his hand as
I try to study the surrounding ink.

"I'll see you later, Tessa," Landon says, excusing himself.

"You would find the lamest kid in class to befriend," Hardin
says as he watches him go.

"Don't say that about him; he's a sweet guy. Unlike you." I'm shocked at my harsh words. He really brings out the worst in me.

Hardin turns back to me. "You're becoming more feisty with each chat we have, Theresa."

"If you call me Theresa one more time . . ." I warn and he laughs. I try to picture what he would look like without his tattoos and piercings. Even with them, he's very attractive, but his sour personality ruins him.

We begin walking along back in the direction of my dorm and get about twenty steps when all of a sudden he shouts out, "Stop staring at me!" turns a corner, and disappears down a pathway before I can even think of a response.

chapter fourteen

After several exhausting—but exciting—days, it's finally Friday, and my first week of college is almost over. Feeling pleased with the way the week has gone overall, I plan on just watching some movies, since Steph will most likely be at a party and it'll be quiet. Having all my classes' syllabi really makes things easier for me, and I can do a lot of the work ahead of time. I grab my bag and leave early, stopping by the café to grab a coffee to get an extra shot of energy for the beginning of the weekend.

"Tessa, right?" a girl's voice says behind me as I wait in line. I turn around to find the pink-haired girl from the party. Molly, I think Steph called her.

"Yeah. That's me," I answer and turn to face the counter, attempting to avoid further conversation.

"Are you coming to the party tonight?" she asks. She has to be mocking me, so, sighing, I turn around again and am about to shake my head no when she says, "You should, it's going to be awesome." She runs her tiny fingers over a large fairy tattooed on her forearm.

I pause for a moment, but do shake my head and say, "Sorry, I have plans."

"Too bad. I know Zed wanted to see you." At that I can't help but laugh, but she only smiles. "What? He was talking about you just yesterday."

"I doubt that . . . but even if he was, I have a boyfriend," I tell her, causing her smile to grow.

"Too bad, we could have double-dated," she says ambiguously, and I inwardly thank God when the barista calls my order. In my haste, I grab the cup too roughly and a little bit of coffee laps over the edge and burns my hand. I curse, hoping that this isn't setting the tone for my weekend. Molly waves goodbye to me and I smile politely before I exit the shop. Her comments replay in my mind; *Double-date with who? Her and Hardin? Are they actually dating?* As nice and attractive as Zed may be, Noah is my boyfriend and I would never do anything to hurt him. I know that we haven't spoken much this week, but that's only because we have both been so busy. I make a mental note to call him tonight and catch up, see how he's been doing without me.

After my coffee burn and awkward encounter with Miss Pink Hair, my day improves. Landon and I had made plans to start meeting at the coffee shop before the classes we have together, so he's leaning against the brick wall, and as I walk up to him he greets me with a big smile.

"I'm leaving about thirty minutes into class today. I forgot to tell you that I'm flying back to my hometown for the weekend," he says. I'm happy for him to visit Dakota, but I hate the idea of sitting through British Literature without him, and *with* Hardin, if he shows. He was absent Wednesday, not that I was paying attention.

I turn to him. "So soon? The semester just started."

"It's her birthday and I promised her months back that I would be there." He shrugs.

IN CLASS, Hardin takes his seat next to me but doesn't say a word, not even when, as promised, Landon leaves thirty minutes into class, which suddenly makes me even more aware of Hardin's presence beside me.

"Monday we begin our weeklong discussion of Jane Austen's

Pride and Prejudice," Professor Hill announces as class ends. I don't hide my excitement, and I'm fairly sure that I just let out a squeal. I have read that novel at least ten times and it's one of my favorites.

Although he hadn't really said anything to me all during class, Hardin walks up close beside me. I swear I could almost predict what he's going to say with that deadpan look in his eyes.

"Let me guess, you are just madly in love with Mr. Darcy."

"Every woman who has read the novel is," I say without meeting his eyes. We reach the intersection and I look both ways before crossing the street.

"Of course you do," he laughs, continuing to follow me along the busy sidewalk.

"I'm sure you aren't able to comprehend Mr. Darcy's appeal." My mind goes to the massive collection of novels in Hardin's room. They couldn't possibly be his. *Could they?*

"A man who is rude and intolerable being made into a romantic hero? It's ridiculous. If Elizabeth had any sense, she would have told him to fuck off from the beginning."

I laugh at his choice of words but cover my mouth, stopping myself. I was actually enjoying our little banter, and his presence, but it would only be a matter of time—three minutes, if I'm so lucky—until he says something hurtful. Looking up, I meet his dimpled grin and can't help but admire his good looks. Piercings and all.

"So you do agree that Elizabeth is an idiot?" He raises his eyebrow.

"No, she is one of the strongest, most complex characters ever written," I say in her defense, using the words from one of my favorite movies.

He laughs again and I join him. But after a few seconds, catching himself having a decent laugh with me, he stops suddenly and his laughter fades. Something flashes in his eyes. "I'll see you around, Theresa," he says and turns on his heel and disappears back where we'd come from.

What is with him? Before I can begin to analyze his actions, my phone rings. Noah's name flashes across my screen and I feel oddly guilty as I answer.

"Hey, Tess, I was going to text you back, but I figured I might as well call." Noah's voice is clipped, a bit distant.

"What are you doing? You sound busy."

"No, just on my way to meet some friends at the grill," he explains.

"Okay, well, I won't keep you. I'm so glad it's Friday. I am ready for the weekend!"

"Are you going to another party? Your mom is still disappointed."

Wait—why did he mention it to my mother? I love that he has a close relationship with her, but sometimes dating him is like having an annoying little brother who tattles on me. I hate to compare him that way, but it's true.

Rather than getting into it with him, I just tell him, "No, I'm staying in this weekend. I miss you."

"I miss you too, Tess. So much. Call me later, okay?"

I agree and we exchange "I love you's" before hanging up.

WHEN I GET BACK TO MY ROOM, Steph is getting ready for another party, which I assume is the one Molly mentioned at the café. I log into Netflix and browse the movies.

"I really wish you would come. I swear we won't stay overnight this time. Just come for a little bit. Watching movies alone in this small room will be hell!" Steph whines, and I laugh. She continues to beg me while she teases her hair and changes into three different outfits before deciding on a green dress that leaves very little to the imagination. The crisp color looks really good with her bright red hair, I have to admit. I envy her confidence. I'm confident to a certain extent, but I'm aware that my hips and breasts are larger than most women my age. I tend to wear clothes that hide my large bust, while she tries to draw as much attention as possible to hers.

"I know . . ." I say, humoring her. But then my laptop screen turns black and I press the power button and wait . . . and wait. The black screen remains.

"See! It's a sign that you should come. My laptop's at Nate's apartment, so you can't use mine." She smirks and teases her hair again.

Looking at her, I realize I really don't want to sit in the dorm alone without anything to do or watch.

"Fine," I say, and she jumps up and down, clapping her hands. "But we're leaving before midnight."

chapter fifteen

I change out of my pajamas and put on a new pair of jeans that I haven't worn yet. They are a little tighter than my usual pants, but I'm in desperate need of a trip to the laundry room, so I don't have much of a choice. My shirt is a simple black button-up, sleeveless shirt with lace trim on the shoulders.

"Wow, I actually like your outfit a lot," Steph tells me. I smile and she tries to offer me eyeliner again.

"Not this time," I tell her, remembering how it smeared from my tears last time. *Why did I agree to go back to that frat house again?*

"Okay. Molly is picking us up instead of Nate; she just texted that she'll be here any minute."

"I don't think she likes me," I say as I check myself out in the mirror.

Steph cocks her head to one side. "What? She does. She's just bitchy and too honest sometimes. And I think she is intimidated by you."

"Intimidated? By *me*? Why on earth would she be intimidated by me?" I say and laugh. Steph clearly has this backward.

"I think just because you're so different from us," she says and smiles. I know I'm different from them, but to me they are the "different" ones. "Don't worry about her, though; she'll be occupied tonight."

"By Hardin?" I ask before I can stop myself. I continue to

look at the mirror, but I can't help but notice the way she is looking at me with one eyebrow raised.

"No, by Zed probably. She changes guys every week."

That's a harsh thing to say about a friend, but she just smiles
and adjusts her top.

"She isn't dating Hardin?" The image of them making out on
the bed comes to mind.

"No way. Hardin doesn't date. He fucks with a lot of girls, but
he doesn't date anyone. Ever."

"Oh," is all I manage to say.

THE PARTY TONIGHT is the same as last week. The lawn and house
are crowded with drunk people everywhere. Why didn't I just stay
in and stare at my ceiling?

Molly disappears as soon as we arrive, and I end up getting a
spot on the couch and am sitting there for at least an hour when
Hardin walks by.

"You look . . . different," he says after a short pause. His eyes
rake down my body and back up to rest on my face. He doesn't
even try to be subtle about the way he's assessing me. I stay silent until his eyes meet mine. "Your clothes actually fit you
tonight."

I roll my eyes and adjust my shirt, suddenly wishing I was
wearing my normal loose clothing.

"It's a surprise to see you here."

"I'm a bit surprised that I ended up here again," I say and
walk away from him. He doesn't follow, but for some reason I find
myself wishing he would have.

A few hours later, Steph is drunk again. Well, as much as
everyone else is.

"Let's play Truth or Dare," Zed slurs and their small group of friends gather around the couch. Molly passes a bottle of clear al-cohol to Nate and he takes a swig. Hardin's hand is so large that it covers his entire red cup as he takes a sip. Another punk-looking girl joins the game, making it Hardin, Zed, Nate, Nate's room-mate Tristan, Molly, Steph, and the new girl.

I'm just thinking that a drunken game of Truth or Dare can't possibly end well when Molly says with a wicked smile, "You should play, too, Tessa."

"No, I'd rather not," I tell her and focus my attention on a brown stain on the carpet.

"To actually play, she would have to stop being a prude for five minutes," Hardin tells them and they all laugh except Steph. His words anger me. I am not a prude. Yeah, I will admit I'm not by any means wild, but I'm not some cloistered nun. I glare at Hardin and sit down cross-legged in their little circle, between Nate and another girl. Hardin laughs and whispers something to Zed before they start.

The first few truths and dares include Zed being dared to chug an entire can of beer, Molly being dared to flash her bare chest to the group, which she does, and Steph revealing the truth that her nipples are pierced.

"Truth or dare, Theresa?" Hardin asks and I gulp.

"Truth?" I squeak.

He laughs and mutters, "Of course," but I ignore him as Nate rubs his hands together.

"Okay. Are you . . . a virgin?" Zed asks, and I choke. No one seems fazed by the intrusive question besides me. I feel the heat in my cheeks and the humor in everyone's faces.

"Well?" Hardin presses. Despite how much I want to run away and hide, I just nod. Of course I'm a virgin; the furthest Noah and I have gone is making out and some slight groping, over our clothes, of course.

Still, no one seems outright surprised by my answer, just intrigued.

"So you have been dating Noah for two years and you haven't had sex?" Steph asks, and I shift uncomfortably.

I just shake my head. "Hardin's turn," I say quickly, hoping to take the attention off myself.

chapter sixteen

D are," Hardin answers before I even ask him. His green eyes bore through me with an intensity that says I'm the one on the spot, that I'm the one dared to do something.

And I falter, not having really thought this out, or expecting to be met with such a reaction. What should I dare him to do? I know he will do whatever it is, just because he won't want to back down from me.

"I . . . hmm. I dare you to . . ."

"To what?" he says impatiently. I almost dare him to say something nice about each person in the group but I decide against it, however amusing it would have been.

"Take your shirt off and keep it off the entire game!" Molly yells out, and I'm glad. Not because Hardin will be taking his shirt off, of course, but because I couldn't think of anything and it eases the pressure of my having to give him orders.

"How juvenile," he complains, but he lifts his shirt over his head. Without meaning to, my eyes go directly to his long torso and the way the black tattoo ink stretches across his surprisingly tan skin. Under the birds on his chest, he has a large tree inked onto the skin of his stomach. The branches are bare and haunting. His upper arms have many more tattoos than I expected; small, seemingly random images and icons are scattered along his shoulders and hips. Steph nudges me, and I tear my eyes away from him, praying that no one saw me staring.

The game continues. Molly kisses Tristan and Zed both.

Steph tells us about her first time having sex. Nate kisses the other girl.

How did I find myself in the middle of this group of hormonal college rock-and-roll misfits?

"Tessa, truth or dare?" Tristan asks.

"Why even ask? We know she will say truth—" Hardin starts.

"Dare," I say, surprising them and myself.

"Hmm . . . Tessa, I dare you to . . . take a shot of vodka," Tristan says, smiling.

"I don't drink."

"That's the point of the dare."

"Look, if you don't want to do it . . ." Nate starts to say and I look over at Hardin and Molly sharing a laugh at my expense.

"Fine, one shot," I say. I think Hardin will probably have yet another contemptuous expression at this, but when his eyes meet mine, I find he's giving me a strange look instead.

Someone hands me the clear bottle of vodka. I mistakenly put my nose against the top, smelling the foul liquid, which burns my nostrils. I scrunch my nose, trying to ignore the chuckles behind me. I try not to think of all the mouths that have been on the bottle before me, and I just tilt it back and take a drink. The vodka feels hot and burns all the way down to my stomach, but I manage to swallow it. It tastes horrible. The group claps and laughs a little—everyone except Hardin. If I didn't know him any better, I would think he was mad or disappointed. He is so strange.

After a short time, I can feel the heat in my cheeks and then, later, the small amount of alcohol in my veins that grows with each round that I am dared to take another shot. I oblige, and I have to admit I feel pretty relaxed for once. I feel good. With this feeling, everything seems a little easier. The people around me all seem a little more fun than before.

"Same dare," Zed says with a laugh and takes a swig from the bottle before handing it to me for the fifth time. I don't even re-member the dares and truths that have been happening around me for the last few rounds. This time I take two big drinks of the vodka before it's ripped from my grasp.

"I think you've had enough," Hardin says and hands the bottle to Nate, who takes a drink.

Who the hell is Hardin Scott to tell me when I have had enough? Everyone else is still drinking, so I can, too. I grab the bottle back from Nate and take a drink again, making sure to give Hardin a smirk as the bottle touches my lips.

"I can't believe you have never been drunk before, Tessa. It's fun, right?" Zed asks and I giggle. Thoughts of my mother's lec-tures on irresponsibility flood my mind, but I push them back. It's only one night.

"Hardin, truth or dare?" Molly asks. He answers "dare," of course.

"I dare you to kiss Tessa," she says and gives him a fake smile.

Hardin's eyes go wide, and though the alcohol is making everything more exciting, I really just want to run away from him.

"No, I have a boyfriend," I say, making everyone laugh at me for the hundredth time tonight. *Why am I even hanging around these people who keep laughing at me?*

"So? It's just a dare. Just do it," Molly says, pressuring me.

"No, I'm not kissing anyone," I snap and stand up. Without looking at me, Hardin just takes a drink from his cup. I hope he's offended. Actually, I don't care if he is. I'm through interacting with him like this. He hates me and is just too rude.

As I get to my feet, the full effect of the alcohol hits me. I stumble but manage to pull myself together and walk away from the group. Somehow I find the front door through the crowd. As soon as I'm outside, the fall breeze hits me. I close my eyes and breathe in the fresh air before going to sit on the familiar stone wall. Before I realize what I am doing, my phone is in my hands, dialing Noah.

"Hello?" he says. The familiarity of his voice and the vodka in my system make me miss him more.

"Hey . . . babe," I say and bring my knees to my chest.

A beat of silence passes. "Tessa, are you *drunk*?" His voice is full of judgment. I shouldn't have called him.

"No . . . of course not," I lie and hang up the phone. I press my finger down on the power button. I don't want him to call back. He's ruining the good feeling from the vodka, worse than even Hardin did.

I stumble back inside, ignoring whistles and crude comments from drunk frat guys. I grab a bottle of brown liquor off the counter in the kitchen and take a drink, too big of a drink. It tastes worse than the vodka and my throat feels like it's on fire. My hands fumble for a cup of anything to get the taste out of my mouth. I end up opening the cabinet and using a real glass to pour some water from the sink. It helps the burn a little, but not much. Through a break in the crowd, I see that the group of my "friends" are still sitting in a circle playing their stupid game.

Are they my friends? I don't think they are. They only want me around so they can laugh at my inexperience. How dare Molly tell Hardin to kiss me—she knows that I have a boyfriend. Unlike her, I don't go around making out with everyone. I've kissed only two boys in my life, Noah and Johnny, a freckle-faced kid in third grade who kicked me in the shin afterward. Would Hardin have gone along with the dare? I doubt it. His lips are so pink and full, and my head plays an image of Hardin leaning over to kiss me and my pulse begins to race.

What the hell? Why am I thinking about him like that? I am never drinking again.

Minutes later, the room begins to spin and I feel dizzy. My

feet lead me upstairs to the bathroom and I sit in front of the toilet, expecting to throw up. Nothing happens. I groan and pull myself up. I am ready to go back to the dorms, but I know Steph won't be ready for hours. I shouldn't have come here. Again.

Before I can stop myself, my hand is turning the knob on the only room I'm somewhat familiar with in this oversize house. Hardin's bedroom door opens without a problem. He claims to always lock his door, but he's proving otherwise. It looks the same as before, only this time the room is moving around beneath my unsteady feet. *Wuthering Heights* is missing from where it was on the shelf, but I find it on the bedside table, next to *Pride and Prejudice*. Hardin's comments about the novel replay in my mind. He has obviously read it before—and understood it—which is rare for our age group, and for a boy especially. Maybe he had to read it for class before, that's why. But why is this copy of *Wuthering Heights* out? I grab it and sit on the bed, opening the book halfway through. My eyes scan the pages and the room stops spinning.

I'm so lost in the world of Catherine and Heathcliff that when the door opens, I don't hear it.

"What part of 'No One Comes Into My Room' did you not understand?" Hardin booms. His angry expression scares me, but somehow humors me at the same time.

"S-sorry. I . . ."

"Get out," he spits, and I glare at him. The vodka is still fresh in my system, too fresh to let Hardin yell at me.

"You don't have to be such a jerk!" My voice comes out much louder than I had intended.

"You're in my room, again, after I told you not to be. So get out!" he yells, stepping closer to me.

And with Hardin looming in front of me, mad, seething with scorn and making it seem like I'm the worst person on earth to him, something inside me snaps. Any composure I had snaps in half, and I ask the question that's been at the front of my brain without my wanting to acknowledge it.

"Why don't you like me?" I demand, staring up at him.

It's a fair question, but, to be honest, I don't really think my already wounded ego can take the answer.

chapter seventeen

Hardin glares at me. It's aggressive. But unsure. "Why are you asking me this?"

"I don't know . . . because I have been nothing but nice to you, and you've been nothing but rude to me." And then I add, "And here I actually thought at one point we could be friends," which sounds so stupid that I pinch the bridge of my nose with my fingers while I wait for his answer.

"Us? Friends?" He laughs and throws up his hands. "Isn't it obvious why we can't be friends?"

"Not to me."

"Well, for starters you're too uptight—you probably grew up in some perfect little model home that looks like every other house on the block. Your parents probably bought you everything you ever asked for, and you never had to want for anything. With your stupid pleated skirts, I mean, honestly, who dresses like that at eighteen?"

My mouth falls open. "You know nothing about me, you condescending jerk! My life is nothing like that! My alcoholic dad left us when I was ten, and my mother worked her ass off to make sure I could go to college. I got my own job as soon I turned sixteen to help with bills, and I happen to *like* my clothes—sorry if I don't dress like a slut like all the girls around you! For someone who tries too hard to stand out and be different, you sure are judgmental about people who are different from *you!*" I scream and feel the tears well up in my eyes.

I turn around so he won't get to remember me like this, and I notice that he's balling his fists. Like he gets to be angry about this.

"You know what, I don't want to be friends with you anyway, Hardin," I tell him and reach for the door handle. The vodka, which had made me brave, is also making me feel the sadness of this situation, of our yelling.

"Where are you going?" he asks. So unpredictable. So moody.

"To the bus stop so I can go back to my room and never, ever come back here again. I am *done* trying to be friends with any of you."

"It's too late to take the bus alone."

I spin around to face him. "You are not seriously trying to act like you care if something happened to me." I laugh. I can't keep up with his changes in tone.

"I'm not saying I do . . . I'm just warning you. It's a bad idea."

"Well, Hardin, I don't have any other options. Everyone is drunk—including myself."

And then the tears come. I am beyond humiliated that Hardin, of all people, is seeing me cry. Again.

"Do you always cry at parties?" he asks and ducks his head a little, but with a small smile.

"Apparently, whenever you're at them. And since these are the only ones I've ever been to . . ." I reach the door again and open it.

"*Theresa*," he says so soft that I almost don't hear him. His face is unreadable. The room starts to spin again and I grab on to the dresser next to his door. "You okay?" he asks. I nod even though I feel nauseous. "Why don't you just sit down for a few minutes, then you can go to the bus station."

"I thought no one was allowed in your room," I state, then sit on the floor.

I hiccup and he immediately warns, "If you throw up in my room . . ."

"I think I just need some water," I say and move to stand up.

"Here," he says, putting a hand on my shoulder to keep me down and handing me his red cup.

I roll my eyes and push it away. "I said water, not beer."

"It *is* water. I don't drink," he says.

A noise somewhere between a gasp and a laugh escapes me. There is *no way* Hardin doesn't drink. "Hilarious. You're not going to sit here and babysit, are you?" I really just want to be alone in my pathetic state, and my buzz is wearing off, so I'm starting to feel guilty for yelling at Hardin. "You bring out the worst in me," I murmur aloud, not quite meaning to.

"That's harsh," he says, his tone serious. "And yes, I am going to sit here and babysit you. You are drunk for the first time in your life, and you have a habit of touching my things when I'm not around." He goes and takes a seat on his bed, kicking his legs up. I get up and grab the cup of water. Taking a big drink, I can taste a hint of mint on the rim and can't help but think about how Hardin's mouth would taste. But then the water hits the alcohol in my stomach and I don't feel so hot.

God, I am never drinking again, I remind myself as I sit back down on the floor.

After a few minutes of silence Hardin finally speaks up. "Can I ask you a question?"

The look on his face tells me I should say no but the room's still not feeling entirely solid, and I think maybe talking will help me focus, so I say, "Sure."

"What do you want to do after college?"

I look up at him with new eyes. That is literally the last thing I thought he would ask. I assumed he would ask why I'm a virgin, or why I don't drink.

"Well, I want to be an author or a publisher, whichever comes first." I probably shouldn't be honest with him; he will just make fun of me. But when he doesn't say anything back, I start feeling brave and ask him the same question, earning an eye roll from him but no answer.

Finally I ask, "Are those your books?" even though it's probably futile.

"They are," he mumbles.

"Which is your favorite?"

"I don't play favorites."

I sigh and pick at a small fray on my jeans.

"Does Mr. Rogers know you're at a party again?"

"Mr. Rogers?" I look back up at him. I don't get it.

"Your boyfriend. He is the biggest tool I have ever seen."

"Don't talk about him like that, he is . . . he is . . . nice," I stutter. When Hardin laughs, I stand up. He doesn't know Noah at all. "You could only dream of being as nice as he is," I say sharply.

"*Nice?* That's the first word that comes to your mind when talking about your boyfriend? Nice is your 'nice' way of calling him boring."

"You don't know him."

"Well, I know that he's boring. I could tell by his cardigan and *loafers.*" Hardin's head rolls back in laughter and I can't ignore his dimples.

"He doesn't wear loafers," I say, but have to cover my mouth so I don't laugh with him at my boyfriend's expense. I grab the water and take another drink.

"Well, he has been dating you for two years and hasn't fucked you yet, so I would say he is a square."

I spit the water back into the cup. "What the hell did you just say?" Just when I think we can get along he says something like that.

"You heard me, Theresa." His smile is cruel.

"You're an asshole, Hardin," I growl and throw the half-empty cup at him. His reaction is exactly what I hoped for: complete shock. While he wipes water off his face, I stagger to my feet using the bookshelf for leverage. A couple of books fall to the ground, but I ignore all that and storm out of the room. I stumble downstairs and push my way through the crowd into the kitchen. The anger I feel has overcome my nausea, and all I want is to get Hardin's evil smirk out of my head. I spot Zed's black hair through the crowd in the other room and go to where he's sitting with a cute preppy boy.

"Hey, Tessa, this is my friend Logan," Zed says, introducing us.

Logan smiles at me and offers the bottle he's holding. "Want some?" he asks and passes it to me. The familiar burn feels good; it ignites my body again and I momentarily forget about Hardin.

"Have you seen Steph?" I ask, but Zed shakes his head. "I think she and Tristan may have left."

She left? What the hell? I should care more but the vodka skews my judgment and I find myself thinking she and Tristan would make a cute couple. A couple of drinks later, I feel amazing.

This must be why people drink all the time. I vaguely remember having sworn off alcohol at some point tonight, but it's not so bad.

FIFTEEN MINUTES LATER, Zed and Logan have me laughing so hard that my stomach hurts. They are much better company than Hardin. "You know Hardin is a real ass," I tell them, which elicits wide grins from them both.

"Yeah, he can be sometimes," Zed says and snakes his arm around me. I want to move it but I don't want to make it awkward because I know he doesn't mean anything by it. Soon the crowd starts to die down and I start to feel tired. It dawns on me that I have no way to get back to the dorms.

"Do the buses run all night?" I slur. Zed shrugs, and just then Hardin's mop of curls appears in front of me.

"You and Zed then?" His voice is thick with an emotion that I can't quite register.

I get up and push past him, but he grabs my arm. He has no boundaries. "Let go of me, Hardin." Looking for another cup to toss in his face, I say, "I'm just trying to find out about the bus."

"Chill out . . . it's three a.m. There is no bus. Your newfound alcoholic lifestyle has you stuck here again." The glee in his eyes when he says this is so mocking that it makes me want to smack him. "Unless you want to go home with Zed . . ."

When he lets go of my arm, I do go back to the couch with Zed and Logan, because I know it will irritate him. After standing there and nodding for a moment, he turns in a huff. Hoping that that same room from last weekend is empty, I tell Zed to take me upstairs so we can find it.

chapter eighteen

We find the room. Unfortunately one of the beds is occupied by a snoring, passed-out guy.

"At least that bed is empty!" Zed says and laughs. "I'm going to walk back to my place, if you want to come. I have a couch you could sleep on," he says.

Cutting through the haze to try to think clearly for a second, I conclude that Zed, like Hardin, hooks up with a lot of different girls. If I agree to this it could mean I am offering to kiss him . . . well. I have a feeling with those good looks it's easy for Zed to get girls to do more than kiss.

"I think I will just stay here in case Steph comes back," I say.

His face falls a little but he gives me an understanding smile. He tells me to be careful and gives me a hug goodbye. The door closes as he leaves and I can't help but lock it. Who knows who will come in? I look over at the comatose snorer and feel secure that he isn't waking up anytime soon. The tiredness I felt downstairs has somehow faded, my mind going back to Hardin and his comment about how Noah hasn't slept with me yet. It may seem strange to Hardin, who's with a different girl every weekend, but Noah is a gentleman. We don't need to have sex; we have fun together doing other things like . . . well . . . we go to the movies and go for walks.

With that in mind, I lie down, but quickly find myself staring at the ceiling, counting the tiles in an attempt to go to sleep.

Occasionally the drunk guy rustles around on the other bed, but eventually my eyes close and I begin to drift off.

"I haven't seen you . . . around here before," a deep voice suddenly slurs in my ear. I jump up and his head bumps my chin, causing me to bite my tongue. His hand is on the bed, inches away from my thighs. His breathing is ragged and smells like vomit and liquor. "What's your name, cutie?" he breathes, and I gag. I lift one thin arm up to push him away from me, but it doesn't work, and he just laughs.

"I'm not going to hurt you—we're just going to have some fun," he says and licks his lips, leaving a string of saliva down his chin.

My stomach turns and the only thing I can think to do is to knee him, hard. Hard and right *there*. He grabs his crotch and stumbles back, giving me my chance to bolt. Once my shaky fingers finally open the lock, I rush out into the hallway, where several people give me odd stares.

"Come on, come back here!" I hear the disgusting voice say, not too far behind me. Strangely, nobody seems fazed by a girl being chased down the hall. He is only a few feet away, but fortunately is so drunk he keeps stumbling into the wall. My feet act of their own accord, taking me down the hall to the only place I know in this damned fraternity house.

"Hardin! Hardin, please open the door!" I yell, one hand banging on the door and one trying to twist the locked doorknob.

"Hardin!" I scream again and the door flies open. I don't know what made me come to *his* room of all places, but I would take Hardin's judgmentalism over the drunk guy trying to have his way with me any day.

"Tess?" Hardin asks, seeming confused. He wipes his eyes with his hand. He is wearing only black boxer briefs, and his hair is jutting out all over his head. Weirdly, I am more surprised by how good he looks than by the fact he called me "Tess" for once instead of "Theresa."

"Hardin, please can I come in? This guy . . ." I say and look behind me. Hardin pushes past me and looks down the hall. His eyes meet my stalker, and the creep changes from scary to frightened. He looks at me one more time before turning around and walking back down the hall.

"Do you know him?" My voice is shaky and small.

"Yeah, get inside," he says and pulls me by my arm into his room. I can't help but note the way his muscles move under his inked skin as he walks to his bed. His back has no tattoos on it, which is a little strange since his chest, arms, and stomach are covered. He rubs his eyes again. "Are you okay?" His voice is raspier than ever from just being woken up.

"Yeah . . . yes. I'm sorry for coming here and waking you up. I just didn't know what—"

"Don't worry about it." Hardin's hand runs through his messy hair and he sighs. "Did he touch you?" he asks, without any trace of sarcasm or humor.

"No, he tried, though. I was stupid enough to lock myself in a room with a drunk stranger, so I suppose it's my fault." The idea of that creep touching me makes me want to cry, again.

"It's not your fault that he did that. You aren't used to this type of . . . situation." His voice is kind and totally the opposite of his usual tone. I walk across the room toward his bed, silently asking him for permission. He pats the bed, and I sit down with my hands in my lap.

"I have no plans on getting used to it. This really is the last time I'm coming here, or to any parties, for that matter. I don't know why I even tried. And that guy . . . he was just so . . ."

"Don't cry, Tess," Hardin whispers.

And the funny thing is, I hadn't realized I was. Hardin brings his hand up, and I almost flinch away, but not before the pad of his thumb captures the tear from my cheek. My lips part in surprise from his gentle touch. *Who is this guy and where is the snarky, rude Hardin?* I look up to meet his green eyes and his pupils dilate.

"I hadn't noticed how gray your eyes are," he says, so low that I lean closer to hear him. His hand is still on my face, and my mind is racing. Pulling half of his bottom lip in his mouth, he takes his lip ring between his teeth. Our eyes meet, and I look down, unsure of what's going on. But when he removes his hand, I look at his lips once more, and I can feel my conscience and my hormones battling.

But my conscience loses, and I crash my lips against his, catching him totally off guard.

chapter nineteen

I have no idea what I'm doing, but I can't stop. As my lips touch Hardin's I feel his sharp intake of breath. Hardin's mouth tastes just like I had imagined. I can taste the faint hint of mint on his tongue as he opens his mouth and kisses me. Really kisses me. His warm tongue runs along mine and I can feel the cold metal of his lip ring on the corner of my mouth. My entire body feels like it's been ignited; I have never felt like this before. He brings his hand to my face, cupping my flushed cheeks, before both of his hands go to my hips. He pulls back a little and plants a small kiss on my lips.

"Tess," he breathes out, then quickly brings his mouth back to mine, his tongue sliding in once more. My mind is no longer in charge; the sensation has taken over every inch of me. Hardin pulls me by my hips closer to him as he lies back on the bed, never breaking our kiss. Unsure of what to do with my hands, I put them against his chest, and then climb onto his torso. His skin is hot and his chest is moving up and down with his rapid breaths. He pulls his mouth away from mine and I whimper at the loss of contact, but before I can complain he's at my neck. I feel every swipe and lick his tongue makes. His breath moves across me. He grabs hold of my hair to keep my head just above his as he continues to kiss my neck. His teeth graze my collarbone and I moan, the feeling shooting down my whole body when he begins gently sucking on my skin. I would be embarrassed if

I wasn't so intoxicated, by Hardin and the alcohol. I have never kissed anyone like this, not even Noah.

Noah!

I say, "Hardin . . . stop," but I don't recognize my voice. It's low and husky, and my mouth is dehydrated.

He doesn't stop.

"Hardin!" I say again, my voice clear and sharp, and he lets go of my hair. When I look into his eyes, they are darker, yet softer, and his lips are a deeper pink and swollen from kissing me. "We can't," I say. Even though I really want to keep kissing him, I know I can't.

The softness in his eyes disappears and he pulls himself up, knocking me onto the other side of the bed. *What just happened?*

"I'm sorry, I'm sorry," I say, and they are the only words I can think of. My heart feels like it will explode any second.

"Sorry for what?" he says and walks over to his dresser. He pulls out a black T-shirt and pulls it over his head. My eyes go down to his boxers again and they are noticeably tighter in the front.

I flush and look away. "For kissing you . . ." I say, though something in me really doesn't want to apologize for that. "I don't know why I did it."

"It was just a kiss; people kiss all the time," I hear him say.

His words hurt my feelings for some reason. Not that I care if he didn't feel what I did . . . *What did I feel?* I know I don't actually like him. I am just drunk and he is attractive. It has been a long night and the alcohol made me kiss him. Somewhere in the back of my mind I fight down the thoughts of how much I wanted it to happen again. He was just being so nice, that's why.

"Can we not make a big deal of it, then?" I ask. I would be humiliated if he told anyone. This isn't me. I don't get drunk, and I don't cheat on my boyfriend at parties.

"Trust me, I don't want anyone to know about this, either. Now, stop talking about it," he snaps.

And there's his arrogance again. "So now you're back to your old self, I see?"

"I never was anyone else—don't think because you kissed me, basically against my will, we have some sort of bond now."

Ouch. *Against his will?* I can still feel the way his hand gripped my hair, the way he pulled me on top of him, and the way his lips mouthed "Tess" before kissing me again.

I shoot up off the bed. "You could have stopped me."

"Hardly," he scoffs and I feel like crying again. He makes me too emotional. It's too humiliating, too painful how he's basically saying I forced him to kiss me. I bury my head in my hands for a moment and head for the door.

"You can stay in here tonight since you have nowhere else to go," he says quietly, but I shake my head. I don't want to be anywhere near him. This is all part of his little game. He will offer to let me stay in his room so I'll think he is a decent person, then he will probably draw some vulgar design on my forehead.

"No, thanks," I say and walk out. When I reach the stairs, I think I hear him call my name but I keep going. Outside, the cool breeze feels wonderful against my skin, I sit on the familiar stone wall and turn my phone back on. It's almost 4 a.m. I should be waking up in an hour to get an early shower and start studying. Instead I'm sitting on this broken stone wall, alone and in the dark.

With a few stragglers milling about, and unsure what to do, I pull out my phone and scroll through the text messages from Noah and my mother. *Of course* he told her. It's what he would do . . .

But I can't even be upset with him. I just cheated on him. What would give me the right?

chapter twenty

A block away from the frat house, the streets are dark and quiet. The other frat houses aren't as big as Hardin's. After an hour and a half of walking and GPS-obsessing, I finally reach the campus. Fully sober and figuring that I might as well stay awake, I stop at the 7-Eleven and grab a cup.

As the caffeine hits me, I realize that there are so many things I don't understand about Hardin. Like: why is he in a fraternity with a bunch of preppy rich kids if he is punk, and why does he go from hot to cold so quickly? It's all academic musing, though, since I don't know why I even bother to waste my time thinking about him, and after tonight I am beyond done trying to be friendly with him. I can't believe I kissed him. That was the biggest possible mistake I could have made, and the second I let my guard down he attacked, worse than ever. I'm not stupid enough to trust that he won't tell anyone, but I hope his embarrassment over kissing "the virgin" will keep him quiet. I will deny it until the grave if anyone asks.

I need to come up with a good explanation for my mother and Noah for my behavior tonight. Not the kissing—they will never know about that—but that I was at a party. Again. But I also really need to have a talk with Noah about telling my mother things; if I'm an adult now, she doesn't need to know what I am doing all the time.

By the time I reach my dorm, my legs and feet hurt and I actually sigh in relief as I turn the knob.

But then I nearly have a heart attack at the sight of Hardin sitting on my bed.

"You've got to be kidding me!" I half scream when I finally regain my composure.

"Where were you?" he asks calmly. "I drove around trying to find you for almost two hours."

What? "What? Why?" As in, if he was going to do that, why didn't he just offer to take me home earlier? More importantly, why didn't I ask him to as soon as I found out he hadn't been drinking?

"I just don't think it's a good idea for you to be walking around at night, alone."

And because I can no longer read his expressions, and because Steph is who-knows-where and I'm alone here with *him,* the person who seems to be the real danger to me, all I can do is laugh. It's a wild laugh, ragged and not really me. And it's definitely not because I find this funny, but because I'm too drained to do anything else.

Hardin furrows his brows, frowning at me, which only makes me laugh harder.

"Get out, Hardin—just get out!"

Hardin looks at me and runs his hands through his hair. Which is at least something; in the little time that I have known this frustrating man that is Hardin Scott, I have learned that he does that when he is either stressed or uncomfortable. Right now I hope it's both.

"Theresa, I'm—" he begins, but his words are cut off by a terrible pounding on the door, and screaming: "Theresa! Theresa Young, you open this door!"

My mother. It's my *mother.* At 6 a.m., when a boy is in my room.

Immediately I spring into action, as I always do when faced with her anger. "Oh my God, Hardin, get in the closet," I whisper-hiss and grab his arm, yanking him up off the bed and surprising us both with my strength.

He looks down at me, amused. "I am *not* hiding in the closet. You're *eighteen*."

He says it—and I know he's right—but he doesn't know my mother. I groan in frustration and she pounds again. The defiance with which his arms are crossed over his chest tells me I'm not moving him, so I check the mirror, wiping at the bags under my eyes, and grab my toothpaste, smearing a little on my tongue to conceal the smell of vodka even beyond my coffee breath. Maybe all three scents will confuse her nose or something.

I'm all ready with a pleasant face and greeting on my lips when I open the door, but it's then that I see my mother hasn't come alone. Noah is standing at her side—of course he is. She looks furious. And he looks . . . concerned? Hurt?

"Hey. What are you guys doing here?" I say to them, but my mother pushes by me and goes straight for Hardin. Noah slips silently into the room, letting her take the lead.

"So this is why you haven't been answering your phone? Because you have this . . . this . . ." She waves her arms around in his direction. "Tattooed *troublemaker* in your room at six a.m.!"

My blood boils. I am usually timid and sort of afraid when it comes to her. She has never hit me or anything but she isn't shy when it comes to pointing out my mistakes:

You aren't wearing that, *are you, Tessa?*

You should have brushed your hair again, Tessa.

I think you could have done better than that on your tests, Tessa.

She always puts so much pressure on me to be perfect all the time, it's exhausting.

For his part, Noah just stands there glaring at Hardin, and I want to scream at both of them—actually at all three of them. My mother for treating me like a child. Noah for telling on me. And Hardin for just being Hardin.

"Is this what you do in college, young lady? You stay up all night and bring boys back to your room? Poor Noah was worried sick about you, and we drive all this way to find you running around with these strangers," she says, and Noah and I both gasp.

"Actually, I just got here. And she wasn't doing anything wrong," Hardin says, and I am *shocked*. He has no idea what he is up against. Still: he's an immovable object, she's an unstoppable force. Maybe this would be a good fight. My subconscious temps me to grab a bag of popcorn and sit down in the front row to watch.

My mother's face gets mean. "Excuse me? I certainly was not speaking to you. I don't even know what someone like you is doing hanging around my daughter anyway."

Hardin absorbs the blow mutely and just remains standing and staring at her.

"Mother," I say through my teeth.

I'm not sure why I'm defending Hardin, but I am. Maybe part of it is that she sounds a bit too much like how I treated Hardin when I first met him myself. Noah looks at me, then at Hardin and back to me again. Can he tell that I just kissed Hardin? The memory is fresh in my mind and makes my skin tingle just thinking about it.

"Tessa, you are out of control. I can smell the liquor on you from here, and I can only assume that this is the influence of your lovely roommate and *him*," she says, punctuating it with an accusing finger.

"I am eighteen, Mother. I have never drank before and I didn't do anything wrong. I am just doing what every other college student is doing. I'm sorry that my cell phone battery died, and that you drove all the way here, but I'm fine." Suddenly exhausted from the last few hours, I sit down at my desk chair after my speech and she sighs.

Seeing my resignation gives my mother a calmer demeanor somehow; she's not a monster, after all. Turning to Hardin, she says, "Young man, could you leave us for a minute?"

Hardin looks at me as if asking if I will be okay. I nod and he nods back and walks out of the room. Noah swiftly closes the door behind him, his eyes trailing Hardin all the while. It's a strange sensation, Hardin and I together against my mother and my boyfriend. Somehow I know he'll be waiting somewhere just outside the door until they leave.

For the next twenty minutes, my mother sits on my bed and explains that she is just worried about me ruining my chance at an amazing education and doesn't want me to drink again. She also tells me that she doesn't approve of my friendship with Steph, Hardin, or anyone else in their group. She makes me promise that I will stop hanging around with them, and I agree. After tonight, I don't want to be around Hardin anyway, and I won't be going to any more parties with Steph, so there's no way my mother will know if I am friendly with her or not.

Finally, she stands up and claps her hands together. "Since we are already here, let's go get some breakfast and maybe do some shopping."

I nod in agreement, and Noah smiles from where he's leaning on my door. It does sound like a good idea and I am starving. My thoughts are still a little stifled by alcohol and tiredness, but my walk home, the coffee, and my mother's lecture have sobered me. I head for the door, but stop when my mother coughs.

"You'll need to clean up a little and change, of course." She smiles her condescending smile. I go get some clean clothes out of my dresser and change in the closet. I touch up last night's makeup and am ready to go. Noah opens the door for us, and we all three look at where Hardin is sitting on the floor, leaning against the door across the hall. When he looks up, Noah grasps my hand, tightly, protectively.

Still, I find myself wanting to pull my hand away from him. *What is wrong with me?*

"We are going to go into town," I tell Hardin.

In response, Hardin nods several times, like he's answered some question deep within himself. And for the first time he looks vulnerable, and maybe a little hurt.

He humiliated you, my subconscious reminds me. Which is true, but I can't help feeling guilty as Noah pulls me along past Hardin and my mother gives Hardin a victory smile, causing him to look away.

"I really don't like that guy," Noah says, and I nod.

"Me, either," I whisper.

But I know I'm lying.

chapter twenty-one

Breakfast with Noah and my mother is agonizingly slow. My mother continues to bring up my "wild night" and finds every opportunity to ask me if I am tired or hungover. Granted, last night was very out of character for me, but I don't really need to hear about it over and over. Has she always been this way? I know she just wants the best for me, but she seems to be worse now that I'm in college; or maybe being away from her for a week has given me a newfound outlook on her.

"Where should we shop?" Noah asks between mouthfuls of pancake, and I shrug. I wish he had just come alone. I would love to spend time with him. I do need to have a talk with him about not telling my mother every detail of my life, especially the bad, and if we were just alone that would be easier, too.

"Maybe we should go to the mall around the block. I'm not really familiar with the area yet," I tell them, cutting the last few bites of my French toast into pieces.

"Have you thought about where you want to work yet?" Noah asks.

"I'm not sure yet. A bookstore maybe? I wish I could find an internship or something related to publishing or writing," I tell them, which elicits from my mother an award-winning proud smile.

"That would be great, somewhere you could work until you finish college and that could then hire you full-time," she says, smiling again.

I try to hide my sarcasm with "Yeah, that would be ideal," but Noah catches it and grabs my hand to give it a little conspiratorial squeeze under the table.

As I put my fork into my mouth, the metal reminds me of Hardin's lip ring. And I pause for a moment. Noah catches this, too, and looks at me with questioning eyes.

I need to stop thinking about Hardin. Now. I smile at Noah and pull his hand up to kiss it.

After breakfast my mother drives us to the Benton Mall, which is huge and crowded. "I am going to go into Nordstrom's, so I'll call you when I am ready," she tells us, to my relief. Noah takes my hand again and we browse through a bunch of stores. He tells me about his soccer game on Friday, and how he shot the winning goal. I listen intently and tell him how great it all sounds.

"You look nice today," I tell him and he smiles. His perfect white smile is adorable. He is wearing a maroon cardigan, khakis, and dress shoes. Yes, he really does wear loafers, but they are cute and somehow fit his personality.

"You do, too, Tessa," he says and I cringe. I know I look like hell, but he is too unfalteringly kind to tell me so. Unlike Hardin, who would tell me in a heartbeat. *Ugh, Hardin.* Desperately wanting to get my mind off Mr. Rude, I pull Noah into me by the neck of his cardigan. When I go to kiss him, he smiles but pulls away.

"What are you doing, Tessa? Everyone's staring at us." He gestures toward a group of adults trying on sunglasses at a kiosk.

I shrug playfully. "No, they aren't. And so what?" I really don't care; usually I would, but I need him to kiss me. "Just kiss me, please," I practically beg.

He must see the desperation in my eyes because he tilts my chin up and kisses me. It's gentle and slow, no urgency behind it. His tongue barely touches mine but it's nice. Familiar and warm. I wait for a fire to ignite within me, but it doesn't.

I can't compare Noah to Hardin. Noah is my boyfriend,

whom I love, and Hardin is a jerk who has a roster of girls he hooks up with.

"What's gotten into you?" Noah teases as I try to pull his body against mine.

I flush and shake my head. "Nothing, I just missed you, that's all," I tell him. *Oh . . . and I cheated on you last night,* my subconscious adds. Ignoring that, I say, "But, Noah, could you please stop telling my mother when I do things? It makes me really uncomfortable. I love that you are close to her but I feel like a child when you basically tell on me." It feels good to get that off my chest.

"Tessa, I am *so* sorry. I was just worried about you. I promise I won't do it again. Honestly." He wraps his arm around my shoulder and kisses my forehead, and I believe him.

The rest of the day is better than the morning, mostly because my mother takes me to a salon and I get my hair trimmed and some layers added into it. It still hangs down my back but with my new cut it has more volume and looks much better. Noah showers me with compliments the entire drive back to my dorm, and everything just feels right. I say goodbye to them at the front door, once again promising to stay away from anyone with a tattoo and within a hundred-mile radius. When I walk into my dorm room, I feel a tinge of disappointment to find it empty, but I'm not sure if I was hoping to see Steph or someone else.

I don't even bother taking my shoes off before I lie in my bed. I'm too exhausted and in need of sleep. I sleep the night away and don't wake up until noon. When I wake up, Steph's asleep in her bed. I go study for the rest of Sunday, and when I return she's gone. Monday morning she's still not back, and I start feeling a strong urge to catch up on what she was doing all weekend.

chapter twenty-two

Before heading to my first class, I stop to grab my usual at the coffeehouse, where Landon is waiting for me with a smile. After our hellos, we're interrupted by a girl asking for intricate directions, and so we don't get the chance to catch up until we're walking to our last class of the day. The class that all day I have been dreading, but anticipating.

"How was your weekend?" Landon asks and I groan.

"Terrible, actually. I went to another party with Steph," I tell him and he makes a sour face and laughs. "I'm sure yours was much better. How is Dakota?"

His smile grows at the mention of her name and I realize that I didn't mention seeing Noah on Saturday. Landon tells me about Dakota applying to a ballet company in New York and how happy he is for her. All the while, I wonder if Noah's eyes light up like that when he talks about me.

As we walk into class, he's telling me how his father and step-mother were thrilled to see him, but I find myself searching the room and not listening very closely to him; Hardin's seat is empty.

"Won't it be hard if Dakota is gone so far?" I manage to ask as we take our seats.

"Well, we are already far from each other now, but it works. I really just want the best for her, and if New York is it, that's where I want her to be."

The professor walks in, silencing us. *Where's Hardin? He wouldn't skip class just to avoid me, would he?*

We dive into *Pride and Prejudice*—a magical book that I wish everyone would read—and before I realize it the class is over.

"You've cut your hair, Theresa." I turn around to see Hardin smiling behind me. He and Landon exchange awkward stares and I try to think of what to say. He wouldn't mention the kiss in front of Landon, would he? Those dimples, deep as ever, tell me that yes, yes he would.

"Hey, Hardin," I say.

"How was your weekend?" His expression is so smug.

I pull Landon by the arm. "Good. Well, see you around!" I yell nervously and Hardin laughs.

When we're outside, Landon asks, "What was that about?" obviously catching on to my strange behavior.

"Nothing, I just don't like Hardin."

"At least you don't have to see him often."

But there is something behind his voice, and why would he say that? Does he know about the kiss?

"Um . . . yeah. Thank God," is all I can muster.

He pauses. "I wasn't going to say anything, because I don't want you to associate me with him, but"—he smiles nervously—"Hardin's dad is sort of dating my mom."

What? "What?"

"Hardin's dad—"

"Yes, yes, I got that, but Hardin's dad lives *here*? Why is Hardin here—I thought he was British? If his dad lives here, why doesn't he live with him?" I flood Landon with questions before I can stop myself. He looks confused, but less nervous than a moment ago.

"He's from London; his dad and my mom live close to the campus, but Hardin and his dad don't have a good relationship. So please don't mention any of this to him. We already don't like each other."

I nod. "Sure, okay." A thousand more questions come to my

mind, but I stay quiet as my friend goes back to talking about Dakota, his eyes brightening with each word about her.

WHEN I GET BACK TO MY ROOM, Steph isn't back yet since her classes run two hours past mine. I start to lay out my books and notes to get ready to study, but decide to call Noah instead. He doesn't pick up, and it really makes me wish he was here with me at college. It would make things so much easier and comfortable. We could be studying or watching a movie together right now.

Still, I know that I'm thinking about this because of my guilt about kissing Hardin is consuming me—Noah is so sweet and he doesn't deserve to be cheated on. I am so lucky to have him in my life. He's always there for me, and he knows me better than anyone. We have known each other basically our whole lives. When his parents moved in down the street, I was ecstatic to have someone my age to hang out with, and the feeling only grew as I got to know him and learned he was an old soul like me. We spent our time reading, watching movies, and bringing life into the greenhouse behind my mother's place. The greenhouse has always been my safe haven; when my dad drank I would hide in there and no one except Noah knew where to find me. The night my dad left was a terrible night for me, and my mother refuses to speak of it, ever. Doing so would shatter the perfect façade she has created for herself, but I still want to talk about it sometimes. Even though I hated him for drinking so much, and for pushing my mother around, I still felt the deep need to have *a father*. That night, stowed away in the greenhouse while my dad screamed and went wild, I kept hearing glasses shattering in the kitchen, and then, when it stopped, footsteps. I was terrified my father was coming for me, but it was Noah. And I had never been so relieved in all my life to see someone safe. From that day on we were inseparable. Over the years, our friendship turned into more, and neither of us has ever dated anyone else.

I text Noah that I love him and decide to take a catnap before I begin my studies. I pull out my planner and check my work one more time, I can surely fit in a twenty-minute nap.

Not even ten minutes into my nap, there's a knock at the door. Figuring Steph must have forgotten her key, I groggily pull the door open.

Of course it isn't her. It's Hardin.

"Steph isn't back yet," I say and walk back to my bed, leaving the door open for him. I'm a little surprised he even bothered to knock, since I know Steph gave him an extra key as backup for herself. I will have to talk to her about that.

"I can wait," he says and plops down on Steph's bed.

"Suit yourself." I groan, ignoring his chuckle as I pull the blanket over my body and close my eyes. Or rather, trying to ignore it. There is no way I am going to be able to sleep knowing that Hardin is in my room, but I would rather pretend-sleep than face the awkward, rude talk we are bound to have. I try to ignore the sound of him gently tapping the headboard of her bed until my alarm goes off.

"Going somewhere?" he asks and I roll my eyes even though he can't see me.

"No, I was taking a twenty-minute nap," I tell him and sit up.

"You set an alarm to make sure your nap is only twenty minutes?" he says, amused.

"Yeah, I do. So what's it to you, anyway?" I grab my books and lay them out neatly, in order of my class schedule, and stack the notes for each class on top of them.

"Are you OCD or something?"

"No, Hardin. Not everyone's crazy because they just like things a certain way. There's nothing wrong with being organized," I snap.

And he laughs, of course. I refuse to look at him, but out of the corner of my eye, I can see him pushing up off the bed.

Please don't come over here. Please don't come . . .

And then he's standing over me, looking down at where I sit on my bed. He grabs my Literature notes and turns them over a couple of times exaggeratedly like he's staring at a rare artifact. I reach up for them but—like the annoying jerk he is—he lifts them higher, so I stand and swipe at them. But he tosses them in the air and they fall to the ground in a scattered mess.

"Pick those up!" I demand.

He smirks and says, "Okay, okay," but just grabs my Sociology notes and does the same thing to them. I scramble to pick them up before he steps on them, but that's only funny to him.

"Hardin, stop!" I yell, just as he does the same with the next stack. Infuriated, I stand up and shove him away from my bed.

"You mean, someone doesn't like their stuff being messed with?" he asks, still laughing. *Why must he always laugh at me?*

"No! I don't!" I yell and go to shove him again. He steps toward me and grabs my wrists, pushing me back against the wall. His face is inches from mine, and suddenly I'm aware I'm breathing way too hard. I want to scream at him to get off me, to let me go, and demand that he put my work back. I want to slap him, to make him leave. But I can't. I'm frozen against the wall and mesmerized by his green eyes burning into mine. "Hardin, please," are the only words I finally find. But they are soft. And I'm not sure if I am begging him to let me go, or kiss me. My breathing still hasn't slowed; I can feel his increasing, the way his chest rises powerfully. Seconds feel like hours, and finally he removes one hand from my wrists, but the other is large enough to hold both.

For a second, I think he might slap me. But his hand moves up to my cheekbone and then he gently tucks my hair behind my ear. I swear I can hear his pulse as he brings his lips to mine—and the fire crackles under my skin.

This is what I have been longing for since Saturday night. If I could only feel one thing for the rest of my life, this would be it.

I don't let myself think about why I am kissing him again or what terrible thing he will say afterward. All I want to focus on is the way he presses his body against mine when he lets go of my wrists, pinning me to the wall, and the way his mouth tastes like mint again. The way my tongue somehow follows his, and the way my hands slide over his broad shoulders. His hands grip the backs of my thighs and he lifts me up, my legs instinctively wrapping around his waist, and I'm amazed at the way my body somehow knows how to respond to him. I bury my fingers in his hair, gently tugging at it while he walks back toward my bed, his lips still molded to mine.

The responsible voice inside my head finds her way in, reminding me that this is a terrible idea—but I push her back. I am *not* stopping this time. I pull Hardin's hair harder, earning a moan from him. The sound elicits one of my own, the two mixing in the most heavenly way. It is the hottest sound I have ever heard and I want to do anything I can to hear it again. He sits back on my bed, pulling me so I'm on his lap. His long fingers dig into my skin, but the pain is wonderful. My body begins gently rocking back and forth on his lap, and his grip tightens.

"Fuck," he breathes into my mouth, and I experience a sensation I have never felt before as I feel him harden against me.

How far will I let this go? I ask myself, but I don't have an answer.

His hands find the hem of my shirt, and he tugs at it, pulling it up. I can't believe I'm letting him, but I don't want to stop. He pulls away from our heated kiss to get the shirt over my head. His eyes meet mine, then go down to my chest as he takes his lip between his teeth.

"You're so sexy, Tess."

The idea of dirty talk never appealed to me, but somehow Hardin saying those words becomes the most sensual thing I have ever heard. I never buy any fancy underwear because no one, literally no one, ever sees them, but right now I wish I had something besides this plain black bra. *He's probably seen every type of bra there is,* the annoying voice in my head reminds me. To try to get such thoughts out of my head, I rock harder against his lap, and he wraps his arms around my back and pulls my body to his, our chests touching . . .

The door handle jingles. I push myself off Hardin's lap and throw my shirt on, the trance I was in immediately broken.

Steph steps through the door and stops short when she sees me and Hardin. As she takes in the scene before her, her mouth forms an O.

I know my cheeks are bright red not only from the embarrassment but from the way Hardin has made me feel.

"What the hell did I miss?" she gasps, staring at us both with a huge grin. I swear her eyes are practically clapping with glee.

"Nothing much," Hardin says and stands. He walks to the door and doesn't look back as he walks out of the room, where I'm left panting and Steph laughing.

"What the actual hell was that!?" she asks me and then covers her face in mock horror. But she's too excited by the gossip and pops back quickly. "You and Hardin . . . You and Hardin are like messing around?"

I turn and pretend to look through the stuff on my desk. "No! No way! We aren't messing around," I tell her. *Are we?* No, we just happened to kiss, twice. And he took my shirt off, and I was basically humping him—but we aren't messing around, like regularly. "I have a boyfriend, remember?"

She comes over to face me. "So . . . that doesn't mean you can't mess around with Hardin—I just can't believe it! I thought you guys hated each other. Well, Hardin hates everyone. But I thought he hated *you* even more than his normal hatred for people," she says, then laughs. "When did this even . . . how did this happen?"

I sit on her bed and run my fingers through my hair. "I don't know. Well, Saturday when you left the party I ended up in his room because this creep tried to hit on me, and then I kissed Hardin. We promised to never speak of it again—but then he came by today and he started messing with me, not in that way." I point at the bed, which only makes her smirk grow. "Like he was throwing my stuff around and I pushed him and then somehow we ended up on the bed."

It sounds so bad as I repeat it. I really am acting so out of character, just like my mother said. I put my hands over my face. How could I do this to Noah—again?

"Whoa, that sounds hot," Steph says, and I roll my eyes.

"It's not—it's terrible and wrong. I love Noah, and Hardin is a jerk. I don't want to be another conquest of his."

"You could learn a lot from Hardin . . . you know *sexually*."

My mouth falls open. *Is she serious? Is that something she would do . . . wait, has she? Her and Hardin?*

"No way, I don't want to learn anything from Hardin. Or anyone besides Noah," I tell her. I can't imagine Noah and I making out like that. My mind replays Hardin's words: *You're so sexy, Tess*. Noah would never say something like that—no one has ever called me sexy before. I feel my cheeks heat up as I think about it. "Have *you*?" I ask a little sheepishly.

"With Hardin? *No*." And something inside me feels better when she says that. But then she continues. "Well . . . I haven't had sex with him, but we had a little fling when we first met, as embarrassing as that is to admit. But nothing came from it; we were sort of friends with benefits for about a week." She says it like it's no big deal, but I can't help the jealousy that stirs inside me.

"Oh . . . benefits?" I ask. My mouth is completely dry and I find myself suddenly annoyed by Steph.

"Yeah, nothing too big. Just like a few heavy makeout sessions, a grope here and there. Nothing serious," she says and my chest hurts. I'm not surprised really, but I wish I wouldn't have asked.

"Does Hardin have a lot of friends with benefits?" I don't want to hear the answer, but I can't help asking.

She snorts and sits down on her bed across from me. "Yeah, he does. I mean, not like hundreds, but he's a pretty . . . active guy."

I can tell she's seen how I reacted and is trying to sugarcoat it for my sake. I make the mental decision for what feels like the hundredth time to stay away from him. I will not be anyone's friends with benefits. Ever.

"He doesn't do it to be mean or use girls; they pretty much throw themselves at him, and he lets them know from the start that he doesn't date," she says. I remember her telling me that before. But it's not like he said that to *me* when we . . .

"Why doesn't he date?" *Why can't I stop asking these questions?*

"I don't know, really . . . Listen," she says, her voice full of concern, "I think you could have a lot of fun with Hardin, but I also think this could be dangerous for you. Unless you know you will never develop any sort of feelings for him, I would stay away. I have seen a lot of girls fall for him and it's not pretty."

"Oh, trust me, I do not have feelings for him. I don't know what I was thinking." I laugh, and hope that it at least *sounds* genuine.

Steph nods. "Good. So, how much trouble did you get into with your mom and Noah?"

I tell her all about my mother's lecture, minus the part about me promising not to be friends with her anymore. We spend the rest of the night talking about classes, Tristan, and anything I can think of besides Hardin.

chapter twenty-three

The next day Landon and I meet at the coffeehouse before class to compare notes for Sociology. It took me an hour to get all my notes in order after Hardin's annoying stunt yesterday. I want to tell Landon about it but I don't want him to think badly of me, especially now that I know about his mom and Hardin's dad. Landon must know a ton about Hardin, and I have to keep reminding myself not to ask questions about him. Besides, I don't care what Hardin does.

The day flies by and finally it's time for Literature. Per usual, Hardin is in the seat next to mine, but today he doesn't seem inclined to look my way at all.

"Today will be our last day on *Pride and Prejudice*," the professor informs us. "I hope you all have enjoyed it, and since you've all read the ending, it feels fitting to base today's discussion on Austen's use of foreshadowing. Let me ask: as a reader, did you expect her and Darcy to become a couple in the end?"

Several people murmur or randomly flip through their books like it'll provide an immediate answer for them, but only Landon and I raise our hands, as always.

"Miss Young," the professor calls on me.

"Well, the first time I read the novel, I was on the edge of my seat about whether or not they would end up together. Even now—and I have read it at least ten times—I still feel anxious during the beginning of their relationship. Mr. Darcy is so cruel and says such hateful things about Elizabeth and her family that

I never know if she can forgive him, let alone love him." Landon nods at my answer, and I smile.

"That's a load," a voice cuts through the stillness. Hardin's voice.

"Mr. Scott? Would you like to add something?" the professor asks, clearly surprised at Hardin's participation.

"Sure. I said that's a load. Women want what they can't have. Mr. Darcy's rude attitude is what drew Elizabeth to him, so it was obvious they would end up together," Hardin says, then picks at his fingernails as if he isn't the slightest bit interested in the discussion.

"That isn't true, about women wanting what they can't have. Mr. Darcy was only mean to her because he was too proud to admit he loved her. Once he stopped his hateful act, she saw that he really loved her," I say, much louder than I intended.

Much louder. I look around the room and find everyone is staring at me and Hardin.

Hardin exhales. "I don't know what kind of guys you normally go for, but I think that if he loved her, he wouldn't have been mean to her. The only reason he even ended up asking for her hand in marriage was because she wouldn't stop throwing herself at him," he says with emphasis, and my heart drops. But finally we're getting at what he's really thinking.

"She did not *throw herself* at him! He manipulated her into thinking he was kind and took advantage of her weakness!" I scream, and then the room really, truly goes silent. Hardin's face is flushed with anger, and I can't imagine mine looks much different.

"He 'manipulated' her? Try again, she is . . . I mean, she was so bored with her boring life that she had to find excitement somewhere so she certainly was throwing herself at him!" he yells back, his hand gripping the desk.

"Well, maybe if he wasn't such a manwhore, he could have

stopped it after the first time instead of showing up in her room!" After the words leave my mouth, I know that we've been exposed, and snickers and gasps are heard throughout the room.

"Okay, lively discussion. I think that's probably enough on that topic for today . . ." the professor begins, but I grab my bag and run out of the room.

From somewhere behind me in the halls, I hear Hardin's angry voice yell, "You don't get to run this time, Theresa!"

I get outside and am crossing the green lawn, about to reach the corner of the block, when he grabs my arm and I jerk away.

"Why do you always touch me like that? *Grab my arm again and I will slap you!*" I scream. I surprise myself at my harsh words, but I've had enough of his crap.

He grabs my arm again, but I can't manage to follow through on my promise. "What do you want, Hardin? To tell me how desperate I am? To laugh at me for letting you get to me again? I am so sick of this game with you—I won't play it any longer. I have a boyfriend who loves me, and you are a terrible person. You really should see a doctor and get some medication for your mood swings! I can't keep up with you. One second you're nice, then you're hateful. I want nothing to do with you, so do yourself a favor and find another girl to play your games, because I'm done!"

"I really do bring out the worst in you, don't I?" he asks.

I turn away and attempt to shift my focus to the busy sidewalk next to us. A few confused students' eyes linger on Hardin and me for a beat too long. When I face him again, he's running his fingers across a small hole at the bottom of his worn black T-shirt.

I expect him to be smiling or laughing, but he's not. If I didn't know any better I would think he was . . . hurt? But I do know better and I know he couldn't care less. "I'm not trying to play games with you," he says and runs his hand over his head.

"Then what are you doing—because your mood swings give me a headache," I snap. A small crowd has gathered around us, and I want to curl into a ball and disappear. But I have to know what he will say next.

Why can't I stay away from him? I know he's dangerous and toxic. I have never been as mean to someone as I am to him. He deserves it, I know, but I don't really like being mean to anyone.

Hardin grabs my arm yet again and pulls me into a small alleyway between two buildings, away from the crowd. "Tess, I . . . I don't know what I am doing. You kissed me first, remember?" he reminds me.

"Yeah . . . I was drunk, remember? And you kissed me first yesterday."

"Yeah . . . You didn't stop me." He pauses. "It must be exhausting," he says.

What? "What must be exhausting?"

"Acting like you don't want me, when we both know you do," he says, and steps closer.

"*What?* I do *not* want you. I have a boyfriend." The words tumble out too fast and reveal their absurdity, making him smile.

"A boyfriend that you're bored with. Admit it, Tess. Not to me, but to yourself. You're bored with him." His voice lowers, and slows to a sensual pace. "Has he ever made you feel the way I do?"

"W-What? Of course he has," I lie.

"No . . . he hasn't. I can tell that you've never been touched . . . *really* touched."

His words send a now-familiar burn through my body. "That's none of your business," I say and back away, making him take three steps toward me.

"You have no idea how good I can make you feel," he says, and I gasp. How does he go from yelling at me to *this*? And why do I like it so much? I have no words. Hardin's tone and dirty words make me weak, vulnerable, and confused. I have become a rabbit in a fox's trap.

"Really, you don't have to admit it. I can tell," he says, his voice thick with arrogance.

But all I can do is shake my head. His smile grows and I instinctively back against the wall. He takes a step toward me, and I take a deep, hopeful breath. Not again.

"Your pulse has quickened, hasn't it? Your mouth is dry. You're thinking about me and have that feeling . . . down *there*. Don't you, Theresa?"

Everything he is saying is true and the more he talks to me like this, the more I want him. It's strange to crave and hate someone at the same time. The attraction I feel is purely physical, which is surprising considering how opposite he is from Noah. I don't remember ever being attracted to anyone except Noah.

I know that if I don't say something now, he will win. I don't want him to have this power over me and *win,* too.

"You're wrong," I mutter.

But he smiles. And even that sends electricity through me.

"I'm never wrong," he says. "Not about this."

I step to the side before he fully traps me against the wall. "Why do you keep saying I throw myself at you if you're the one cornering me now?" I ask, my anger pushing past my lust for this maddening tattooed boy.

"Because you made the first move on me. Don't get me wrong, I was as surprised as you were."

"I was drunk and had a long night—as you already know. I was confused because you were being nice to me; well, your version of being nice." I scoot past him and sit down on the curb so I can get out of his space. Talking to him is so exhausting.

"I'm not that mean to you," he says, looming over me, but it sounds more like a question than a statement.

"Yeah, you are. You go out of your way to be mean to me. Not just me, but everyone. But it still seems like you are extra hard on me." I can't believe I am being this honest with him. I know it's a matter of minutes before he turns on me.

"That's just not true. I'm no meaner to you than I am to the rest of the general population."

I shoot up. I knew I couldn't have a normal discussion with him. "I don't know why I keep wasting my time!" I yell. I start walking back toward the main pathway and lawn.

"Hey, I'm sorry. Just come back over here."

I groan, but my feet react before my brain can catch up, and I end up standing a few feet away from him.

He sits on the curb where I was previously sitting. "Sit," he demands.

And I do.

"You're sitting awfully far away," he says, and I roll my eyes. "You don't trust me?"

"No, of course I don't. Why would I?"

His face falls slightly as my words hit him, but he recovers quickly. *Why would he care if I trusted him?*

"Can we just agree to either stay away from each other, or be friends? I don't have it in me to keep fighting with you." I sigh, and he moves a little closer.

He takes a deep breath before he speaks. "I don't want to stay away from you."

What? My heart beats out of my chest.

"I mean . . . I don't think we can stay away from each other, with one of my best friends being your roommate and all. So I suppose we should try to be friends."

Disappointment bubbles up from nowhere, but this is what I want, right? I can't keep kissing Hardin and cheating on Noah.

"Okay, so friends?" I say, pushing down this feeling.

"Friends," he agrees and reaches out his hand for me to shake.

"*Not* friends with benefits," I remind him as I shake, only to feel the blood rush to my cheeks.

He chuckles and moves his hand to play with his eyebrow ring. "What makes you say that?"

"Like you don't know. Steph already told me."

"What, about me and her?"

"You and her, and you and every other girl." I try to fake a laugh but it comes out as a cough, so I cough a little more to try to cover.

He raises his eyebrow at me but I ignore him. "Well, me and Steph . . . that was fun." He smiles as if remembering something and I swallow the bile rising in the back of my throat.

"And yeah, I have girls that I fuck. But why would that concern you, friend?"

He's so nonchalant about the whole thing, but I'm in shock. Hearing him admit to sleeping with other girls shouldn't bother me but it does. He isn't mine: Noah is. Noah is. *Noah is,* I remind myself.

"It doesn't. I just don't want you to think that I will be one of those girls."

"Aww . . . are you jealous, Theresa?" he mocks me, and I shove him. There is no way in hell I will ever admit that.

"No, absolutely not. I feel sorry for the girls."

He raises his eyebrows playfully. "Oh, you shouldn't. They enjoy it, trust me."

"Okay, okay. I get it. Can we please just change the subject?" I sigh and lift my head back to look at the sky. I need to clear the image of Hardin and his harem out of my mind. "So, will you try to be nicer to me?"

"Sure. Will you try not to be so uptight and bitchy all the time?"

Looking at the clouds, I dreamily say, "I'm not bitchy; you're just obnoxious."

I look at him and start laughing; fortunately he joins in. It's a nice change from screaming at each other. I know we haven't really resolved the big issue here, which is the feelings that I may or may not have for him, but if I can just get him to stop kissing me, I can focus back on Noah and stop this terrible cycle before it gets worse.

"Look at us, two friends." His accent is so cute when he isn't being rude.

Hell, even then it is, but when his voice is soft his accent makes it so much softer, like velvet. The way words roll off his tongue and through his pink lips . . . I can't think about his lips. I tear my eyes away from his face and stand up, wiping my skirt off.

"That skirt really is dreadful, Tess. If we're going to be friends you need to not wear that anymore."

For a second I'm hurt, but when I look up at him, he's smiling. This must be the way he jokes; still rude, but I'll take this over his usual pure malice.

My phone alarm vibrates. "I need to get back and study," I tell him.

"You set an alarm to study?"

"I set an alarm for a lot of things; it's just something I do." I hope he just lets this topic go.

"Well, set an alarm for us to do something fun tomorrow after class," he says.

Who is this and where is the real Hardin?

"I don't think my idea of fun is the same as yours." I can't even imagine what "fun" is to Hardin.

"Well, we'll only sacrifice a *few* cats, burn down only a *few* buildings . . ."

I can't stop the giggle from escaping and he smiles back.

"Really, though, you could use some fun, and since we are new friends, we should do something fun."

I need a few moments to contemplate whether I should be

alone with Hardin before I answer him. But before I can answer, he turns to walk away. "Good, I'm glad you're aboard. See you to-morrow."

And he's gone.

I don't say anything; I just sit back down on the curb. My head is spinning from the last twenty minutes. First, he basically offered me sex, telling me I have no idea how good he could make me feel; then, a few minutes later, he was agreeing to try to be nice to me; then we were laughing and joking and it was nice. There are still so many questions I have about him, but I think I can be friends with Hardin, like Steph is. Okay, not like Steph is, but like Nate or one of their other friends who hang out with him.

This is really the best thing. No more kissing, no more sexual advances from him. Just friends.

But as I walk back to my room, past all the other kids going about without any knowledge of Hardin or his ways, I can't quite manage to shake the fear that I just walked into another one of his traps.

chapter twenty-four

I try to study when I get back to my room but can't seem to focus. After staring at my notes for a couple of hours but not having really read anything, I decide a shower might help. When they're crowded, the coed bathrooms still make me uncomfortable, but no one ever messes with me, so I'm getting used to them.

The hot water feels amazing and loosens up my tense muscles. I should be relieved and happy that Hardin and I have reached some sort of truce, but now anger and annoyance have been replaced by nervousness and confusion. I've agreed to spend time with Hardin tomorrow, doing something "fun," and I am terrified. I just hope it goes well; I don't expect to become best friends with him, but I need us to get to a place where we don't scream at each other every time we talk.

The shower feels so good I stay in there for a while, and when I get back to my room, Steph's already come and left. I find a note from her saying Tristan is taking her off campus for dinner. I like Tristan; he seems really nice despite his overuse of eyeliner. If Steph and Tristan continue to see each other then maybe when Noah comes to visit we could all go do something together. Who am I kidding? Noah wouldn't want to hang out with people like them, but I'm aware enough to admit that up until three weeks ago I never would have, either.

I end up calling Noah before bed; we haven't talked all day. He's so polite, he asks about my day as soon as he picks up. I tell him it was good; I should tell him that Hardin and I are going to hang out tomorrow, but I don't. He tells me that his soccer team beat Seattle High by a landslide, even though Seattle's really good. And I'm happy for him, because he seems really happy to have played so well.

THE NEXT DAY GOES BY way too fast. Landon and I walk into Literature class, and Hardin is already in his seat. "Are you ready for our date tonight?" he asks and my mouth falls open. Landon's does, too. I don't know what I feel more conflicted about: Hardin saying it like that, or how it will affect how Landon sees me. Day one of our quest to become friends is not going well so far.

"It's not a date," I say to him, then turn to Landon and roll my eyes and nonchalantly say, "We're hanging out as friends," while ignoring Hardin.

"Same thing," Hardin replies.

I avoid him for the rest of the class . . . which is easy since he doesn't really try to talk to me after that.

After class, as Landon starts putting his stuff into his backpack, he looks at Hardin, then quietly says to me, "Be careful tonight."

"Oh, we're just trying to get along since my roommate is his good friend," I reply, hoping Hardin doesn't hear me.

"I know, you're really a great friend. I'm just not sure Hardin deserves your kindness," he says, purposefully loud, and I look up at him.

"Don't you have something else to do besides bad-mouth me? Get lost, man," Hardin snaps from behind me.

Landon frowns and looks at me again. "Just remember what I said." He walks away, and I worry about how much I've maybe upset him.

"Hey, you don't have to be cruel to him—you guys are practically brothers," I say.

Hardin's eyes go wide. "What did you just say?" he growls.

"You know, your dad and his mom?" Was Landon lying? Or was I not supposed to mention this. Landon said not to bring up Hardin's relationship with his dad, but I didn't think he meant the whole thing.

"That is none of your business." Hardin looks angrily at the door where Landon disappeared. "I don't know why the asshole even told you that. I'm going to have to shut him up, it seems."

"You leave him alone, Hardin. He didn't even want to tell me, but I got it out of him." The idea of Hardin hurting Landon makes me sick. I need to change the subject. "So where are we going today?" I ask, and he glares at me.

"We aren't going anywhere; this was a bad idea," he snaps, turns on his heels, and walks away. I stand there for a minute, waiting to see if Hardin changes his mind and will come back.

What the hell? He really is bipolar, I'm sure of it.

BACK IN MY DORM ROOM, I find Zed, Tristan, and Steph sitting on her bed. Tristan's eyes are focused on Steph and Zed is flicking his thumb across the trigger of a metal lighter. I would usually be annoyed with this many unexpected guests, but I really like Zed and Tristan, and I need the distraction.

"Hey, Tessa! How were classes?" Steph asks and gives me a big smile. I can't help but notice the way Tristan's face lights up when he looks at her.

"They were okay. You?" I put my books on my dresser and she tells me about her professor spilling hot coffee on himself, making them get out early.

"You look nice today, Tessa," Zed tells me, and I say thanks and crowd on Steph's bed with the three of them. The bed really is too small for all of us, but it works. After we've been talking about various weird professors for a few minutes, the door opens and we all turn to see who it is.

It's Hardin. Ugh.

"Geez, man, you could at least knock for once," Steph scolds him and he shrugs. "I could have been naked or something." She laughs, obviously not angry at his lack of manners.

"Nothing I haven't seen before," he jokes, and Tristan's face falls while the other three chuckle. I can't find the humor, either; I hate thinking about Steph and Hardin together.

"Oh, shut up," she says, still laughing, and grabs hold of Tristan's hand. His smile returns and he moves a little closer to her.

"What are you guys up to?" Hardin asks and sits opposite us, on my bed. I want to tell him to get off but I keep quiet. I thought for a second he had come here to apologize, but now I can see he just came to hang out with his friends, and I am not one of them.

Zed smiles. "We were actually going to go to the movies. Tessa, you should come."

Before I can answer, Hardin speaks up quickly. "Actually, Tessa and I have plans." There is a strange edge to his voice.

God, he's so moody.

"What?" Zed and Steph say in unison.

"Yeah, I was just coming to get her." Hardin stands up and puts his hands into his pockets, gesturing toward the door with his body. "You ready or what?"

My mind screams, *No!* but I nod and slip off Steph's bed.

"Well, see you all later!" Hardin announces and practically pushes me out the door. Outside, he leads me to his car and, surprising me, opens the passenger door for me. I stand still with my arms crossed, looking at him.

"Well, I'll remember not to ever open a door for you again . . ."

I shake my head. "What the hell was that? I know full well

you didn't come here to get me—you just got done telling me that you didn't want to hang out with me!" I yell.

And we are back to yelling at each other. He makes me crazy, literally.

"Yes, I did. Now get in the car."

"No! If you don't admit that you didn't come here to see me, I will go back in there and go to the movies with Zed," I say, which makes him clench his jaw.

I knew it. I don't know how to feel about this revelation, but somehow I knew Hardin didn't want me to go to the movies with Zed and that that's the only reason he's trying to hang out with me now.

"Admit it, Hardin, or I am gone."

"Okay, fine. I admit it. Now get in the damned car. I won't ask again," he says and walks around to the driver's side.

Against my better judgment, I get in, too.

Hardin still looks angry as he pulls out of the parking lot. He turns the screeching music up way too loud. I reach down and shut it off.

"Don't touch my radio," he scolds.

"If you're going to be a jerk the whole time, I don't want to hang out with you." And I mean it. If he's like this, I don't care where we are, I'll hitchhike back to the dorms or something.

"I'm not. Just don't touch my radio."

My thoughts go back to Hardin tossing my notes into the air, and in turn I want to yank his radio out and throw it out the window. If I knew I could tear it from the dash, I would.

"Why do you care if I go to the movies with Zed anyway? Steph and Tristan were going, too."

"I just don't think Zed has the best intentions," he says quietly, his eyes glued to the road.

I begin to laugh and he frowns. "Oh, and you do? At least Zed is nice to me." I can't stop laughing. The idea of Hardin trying to protect me in some way is hilarious. Zed is a friend, nothing more. Just like Hardin.

Hardin rolls his eyes but doesn't give me an answer. He turns the music back on and its guitars and bass literally hurt my ears.

"Can you *please* turn it down?" I beg.

To my surprise, he does, but leaves it on for background noise.

"That music is terrible."

He laughs and taps the steering wheel. "No, it's not. Though I would love to know your opinion on what *is* good music." When he smiles like this, he looks so carefree, especially with his window down, the breeze blowing through his hair. He reaches one hand up and pushes his hair back. I love the way it looks when it's back like that. I shake the thoughts from my head.

"Well, I like Bon Iver, and the Fray," I finally answer.

"Of course you do," he says, and chuckles.

I defend my two favorite bands. "What is wrong with them? They are insanely talented, and their music is wonderful."

"Yeah . . . they are talented. Talented at putting people to sleep."

When I reach across and playfully swat his shoulder, he mock winces and laughs.

"Well, I love them," I say with a smile. If we could just stay in this playful state, I might actually have a good time. I look out the window for the first time, but I don't really know where we are. "Where are we going?"

"To one of my favorite places."

"Which is where?"

"You really have to know everything that is going on in advance, don't you?"

"Yeah . . . I like to—"

"Control everything?"

I stay quiet. I know he's right, but that's just the way I am.

"Well, I'm not telling you until we get there . . . which will be only about five minutes from now."

I lean back against the leather seat of his car and turn my head to glance at the backseat. A messy stack of textbooks and loose papers rest on one side and a thick black sweatshirt rests on the other.

"See something that you like back there?" Hardin catches me by embarrassed surprise.

"What kind of car is this?" I ask. I need a distraction from both not knowing where we are going and him calling me out for being nosy.

"Ford Capri—a classic," he boasts, obviously proud. He goes on to tell me all about it even though I have no idea what he is talking about. Still, I like to watch his lips as he talks, the way they move slowly as the words are even slower. After looking over at me a few times during the conversation, he pretty harshly says, "I don't like to be stared at," though he does smile a little after.

chapter twenty-five

We start down a gravel road, and Hardin turns the music off so that the only noise is the little stones crunching beneath the tires. I suddenly realize we are out in the middle of nowhere. I get nervous now; we are alone, really alone. There are no cars, no buildings, nothing.

"Don't worry, I didn't bring you out here to kill you," he jokes and I gulp. I doubt he realizes that I'm more afraid of what I might do when alone with him than if he was to actually try to kill me.

After another mile he stops the car. I look out the window and see nothing but grass and trees. There are yellow wildflowers across the landscape and the breeze is perfectly warm. Granted, the place is nice and serene. But why bring me here?

"What are we going to do here?" I ask him as I climb out of the car.

"Well, first, a bit of walking."

I sigh. *So he took me here to exercise?*

Noticing my sour expression, he adds, "Not too much walking," and begins along a part of the grass that looks flattened from being used a number of times.

We're both quiet for most of the walk, save a few rude snips from Hardin about me being too slow. I ignore him and take in my surroundings. I am beginning to understand why he likes this seemingly random place. It's so quiet. Peaceful. I could stay here forever as long as I brought a book with me. He turns off the trail and goes into a wooded area. My natural suspiciousness kicks in, but I follow. A few minutes later we emerge from the woods to a stream, or really more of a river. I have no idea where we are but the water looks pretty deep.

Hardin doesn't say anything as he pulls his black T-shirt over his head. My eyes scan his inked torso. The way the empty branches of the dead tree are drawn into his skin is more appealing than haunting under the bright sun. He then bends down to untie his dirty black boots, glancing up at me, catching me staring at his half-naked body.

"Wait, why are you undressing?" I ask and look at the stream. *Oh no.* "You are going to swim? In that?" I say and point to the water.

"Yeah, and you are, too. I do it all the time." He unbuttons his pants and I have to force myself to not stare at the way the muscles in his bare back move when he bends down and pulls them over his legs.

"I am *not* swimming in that." I don't mind swimming, but not in a random place in the middle of nowhere.

"And why is that?" He gestures toward the river. "It's clean enough that you can see the bottom."

"So . . . there are probably fish and God knows what in there." I realize how ridiculous I sound but I don't care. "Besides, you didn't tell me we were going swimming so I have nothing to swim in." He can't argue with that.

"You're telling me you're the kind of girl who doesn't wear underwear?" He smirks, and I gape at him, and those dimples. "Yeah, so go in your bra and panties."

Wait, so he thought I would come out here and take all my clothes off and swim with him? My insides stir and I get warm thinking about being naked in the water with Hardin. What is he doing to me? I have never, ever had these types of thoughts before him.

"I am not swimming in my underwear, you creep." I sit on the soft grass. "I'll just watch," I tell him.

He frowns. Now only in his boxer briefs, the black material is tight against his body. This is the second time I have seen him shirtless and he looks even better here, under the open sky.

"You're no fun. *And* you're missing out," he says flatly. And jumps into the water.

I keep my eyes on the grass and pluck a few blades out, playing with them between my fingers. I hear Hardin call, "The water is warm, Tess!" from the stream. From my spot on the grass, I can see the drops of water falling from his now-black hair. He is smiling as he pushes his soaked hair back and wipes his face off with one hand.

For a moment I find myself wishing I was someone else, someone braver. Like Steph. If I was Steph, I would strip down and jump into the warm water with Hardin. I would splash around and climb up the bank just to jump back and soak him. I would be fun and carefree.

But I'm not Steph. I'm Tessa.

"This is one beyond-boring friendship so far . . ." Hardin exclaims and swims closer to the bank. I roll my eyes and he chuckles. "At least take your shoes off and put your feet in. It feels amazing and pretty soon it will be too cold to swim in."

Putting my feet in wouldn't be so bad. So I take my shoes off and roll my jeans up enough to dip my feet over the edge and into the water. Hardin was right, the water is warm and clear. I wiggle my toes and can't help but smile.

"It's nice, isn't it?" he asks, and I can't help but nod. "So just come in."

I shake my head and he splashes me with the water. I scoot back and scowl at him.

"If you come in the water, I will answer one of your always-intrusive questions. Any question that you want, but only one," he warns.

Curiosity gets the best of me and I tilt my head in concentration. There are so many mysteries about him, and here's a chance to maybe solve one of them.

"This offer expires in one minute," he says and slips beneath the water. I can see his long body swimming under the clear water. It does look like fun, and Hardin drives a hard bargain. He knows just how to use my curiosity against me.

"Tessa," he says after his head pops back up above the surface, "stop overthinking everything, and just jump in."

"I don't have anything to wear. If I jump in in my clothes, I will have to walk back to the car and ride back soaked," I whine. I almost want to get in the water. Okay, I know I do.

"Wear my shirt," he offers, which shocks me, so I wait a second for him to tell me he was joking, but he doesn't. "Go on, just wear my shirt. It will be long enough for you to wear in here and you can keep your bra and panties on, *if you wish*," he says with a smile. I take his advice and stop thinking.

"Fine, but turn around and do not look at me while I am changing—I mean it!" I try my best to be intimidating, but he just laughs. He turns around and faces the opposite direction, so I lift my shirt over my head and grab his as quickly as I can. Slipping it on, I can tell he was right, since it reaches down to the middle of my thighs. I can't help but admire the way his shirt smells, like faint cologne mixed with a smell I can only describe as Hardin.

"Hurry the hell up or I will turn around," he says, and I wish I had a stick to throw at his head. I unbutton my jeans and step out of them. Folding my jeans and shirt neatly, I put them next to my shoes on the grass. Hardin turns around and I tug at the bottom of his black T-shirt, trying to pull it as far as it will go.

His eyes widen and I watch them rake down my body. He takes his lip ring between his teeth and I notice his cheeks flush. He must be cold, because I know it couldn't possibly be me he is reacting to.

"Um . . . come in the water, yeah?" he says, his voice raspier than usual. I nod and walk slowly to the bank. "Just jump in!"

"I am! I am!" I yell nervously, and he laughs.

"Get a little running start."

"Okay." I step back a little and start to run. I feel foolish, but I am not letting my tendency to overthink ruin this. As I reach my last stride, I look at the water and stop with my feet right on the edge.

"Oh come on! You were off to such a good start!" His head falls back in laughter, and he looks adorable.

Hardin, adorable?

"I can't!" I am not sure what is stopping me; the water is deep enough to jump in, but not too deep. The water in the spot where Hardin is standing goes only to his chest, which means it would reach just under my chin.

"Are you afraid?" His tone is calm but serious.

"No . . . I don't know. Sort of," I admit and he walks through the water toward me.

"Sit on the edge and I'll help you in."

I sit down and close my legs tightly so he doesn't see my panties. Noticing this, he grins as he reaches me. His hands grip my thighs and once again I am on fire. *Why does my body have to respond to him this way?* I'm trying to make us friends, so I need to ignore the fire. He moves his hands to my waist and asks, "Ready?"

As soon as I nod yes, he is lifting me and pulling me into the water, water that's warm and feels amazing against my hot skin. Hardin lets me go too soon and I stand up in the water. We are closer to the bank so it only reaches just below my chest.

"Don't just stand there," he says mockingly, and I ignore him but do walk out a little. The T-shirt bubbles up from the water going under it and I yelp and pull it down. Once it's positioned, it promises to stay put for the most part.

"You could just take it off," he says with a smirk and I splash at him. "Did you just splash me?" He laughs and I nod, splashing at him again. He shakes his wet head and lunges for me under the water. His long arms hook around my waist and pull me under. My hand flies up to plug my nose; I haven't mastered swimming without my nose plugged. When we emerge, Hardin is cracking up, and I can't help but laugh with him. I am actually having fun, real fun, not that average watching-a-good-movie fun.

"I can't decide which is more amusing: the fact that you are actually having a good time or the fact that you have to plug your nose underwater," he says through his laughter.

I get a jolt of bravery and move toward him, ignoring the way the T-shirt floats up again, and I try to push his head underwater. Of course, he is too strong for me and doesn't budge, so he only laughs harder, showing all of his beautiful white teeth. Why can't he be like this all the time?

"I believe you owe me an answer to a question," I remind him.

He looks off toward the bank. "Sure, but only one."

I'm not sure which one to ask, I have so many. Before I can decide, though, I hear my voice making the decision for me: "Who do you love the most in the world?"

Why would I ask him that? I want to know more specific things, like why is he a jerk? Why is he in America?

He looks at me suspiciously, as if he is confused by my question.

"Myself," he answers, and goes back underwater for a few seconds.

He pops back up and I shake my head. "That can't be true," I say in challenge. I know he is arrogant but he has to love someone . . . anyone? "What about your parents?" I ask and immediately regret it.

His face twists and his eyes lose the softness I was becoming fond of. "Do not speak of my parents again, got it?" he snaps, and I want to smack myself for ruining the good time we were having.

"I'm sorry, I was just curious. You said you would answer a question," I remind him quietly. His face softens a little and he steps toward me, the water around us rippling. "I really am sorry, Hardin, I won't mention them again," I promise. I really don't want to fight with him out here; he would probably leave me out here alone if I upset him too much.

He takes me by surprise when he grabs my waist and lifts me into the air. I kick my legs and flail my arms, screaming at him to put me down, but he only obliges me by laughing and tossing me into the water. I land a few feet away and when I come above water his eyes are bright with glee.

"You're going to pay for that!" I yell. He fake-yawns in response, so I swim at him, and he grabs me again—but this time I wrap my thighs around his waist without really realizing it. A shocked gasp falls from his lips.

"Sorry," I mutter and unhook my legs.

But he grabs them and folds them back around his waist. That electricity between us can be felt again, this time more intensely than ever before. *Why does this always happen with him?* I shut my mind off from my thoughts and put my arms around his neck to steady myself.

"What are you doing to me, Tess," he says softly, and rubs his thumb over my bottom lip.

"I don't know . . ." I answer truthfully into his thumb, which still traces over my mouth.

"These lips . . . the things you could do with them," he says slowly, seductively. I feel that burn deep in my stomach that makes me putty in his arms. "Do you want me to stop?" He looks into my eyes; his pupils are so dilated that there is only a slight ring around the now dark green of his eyes.

Before my mind can catch up, I shake my head and press my body against his under the water.

"We can't just be friends, you know that, don't you?" His lips touch my chin, making me tremble. He continues a line of kisses along my jawline and I nod. I know he is right. I have no idea what this is that we are, but I know I will never be able to only be friends with Hardin. As his lips touch the spot just below my ear, I moan, prompting Hardin to do it again, this time sucking the skin.

"Oh, Hardin," I moan and squeeze him with my legs. I bring my hands down his back and graze my nails against his skin. I might explode just from him kissing my neck alone.

"I want to make you moan my name, Tessa, over and over again. Please let me?" His voice is full of desperation.

And I know deep inside there's no way I can say no.

"Say it, Tessa." He takes my earlobe between his teeth. I nod again, harder. "I need you to say it, baby, out loud so I know you really want me to." His hand travels down and under his T-shirt that I am wearing.

"I want to . . ." I rush the words, and he smiles against my neck, his mouth continuing its gentle assault. He doesn't say anything and instead grabs my thighs, lifting me higher onto his torso as he begins to walk out of the water. When he reaches the bank, he lets me go and climbs out. I whine, certainly inflaming his ego even more—but right now I don't care. All I know is that I want him, I need him. He reaches out for my hands and pulls me up onto the bank with him.

Unsure what to do, I just stand on the grass, feeling Hardin's heavy, soaked shirt on my shoulders and thinking he's too far away.

From where he stands, he dips down a little to meet my eyes. "Do you want it to be here? Or my room?"

I shrug nervously. I don't want to go to his room, because it's too far—the drive will give me too much time to overthink what I am about to do.

"Here," I say and look around. There is no one in sight and I pray that no one will come here.

"Eager?" He smiles and I try to roll my eyes, but it probably looks like a desperate flutter. The heat in my body is slowly burning out the longer Hardin's touch is not on me.

"Come here," he says in a low voice and the heat returns.

My feet pad quietly across the soft grass until I'm only inches from Hardin. His hands immediately reach for the hem of the T-shirt and he peels it upward off my body. The way he looks at me alone drives me crazy; my hormones are out of control. My pulse speeds up as he looks my body up and down one more time before taking my hand.

He spreads his shirt on the grass like a blanket of sorts. "Lie down," he says, guiding me to the ground with him. He lays me on the wet fabric and props himself up on his elbow, lying on his side, facing me on my back. No one has ever seen me this exposed before, and Hardin has seen so many girls, girls much better looking than me. My hands move up to cover my body, but Hardin sits up and grabs both of my wrists and pushes them down to my sides.

"Don't ever cover up, not for me," he says and looks into my eyes.

"It's just . . ." I begin to explain, but he cuts me off.

"No, you will not cover up, you have nothing to be ashamed of, Tess." *Does he mean that?* "I mean it, look at you," he continues, seeming to read my mind.

"You've been with so many girls," I blurt out, and he frowns.

"None like you." And I know I could take his answer many different ways, but I choose to let it go.

"Do you have a condom?" I ask him, trying to remember the few things I know about sex.

"A *condom?*" He chuckles. "I'm not going to have sex with you," he says and I begin to panic. *Is this all a game to humiliate me?*

"Oh," is all I say and begin to pull myself up. But he grabs my shoulders and gently pushes me back down. I'm sure I'm flush red, and I don't want to be exposed to his sarcastic eyes like this.

"Where are you going—" he starts, but then realization hits him. "Oh . . . No, Tess, I didn't mean it like that. I just meant that you have never done anything . . . like *at all,* so I am not going to have sex with you." He stares at me for a moment. *"Today,"* he adds, and I feel a little bit of the pressure in my chest dissolve.

"There are many other things I want to do to you first." He climbs on top of me, all of his weight supported on his hands. He is in a push-up position. His wet hair drips water droplets onto my face and I squirm.

"I can't believe no one has fucked you before," he whispers and he shifts his body to lie on his side once again. He brings his hand to my neck and trails it down, touching me only with his fingertips, down the valley of my breasts, down my stomach until he stops just above my underwear. *We are really doing this, me and Hardin. What is he going to do? Will it hurt?* A hundred thoughts race through my mind but disappear as soon as his hand reaches into my panties. I hear him suck a breath through his teeth and he brings his mouth to mine.

His fingers move a little, and it shocks me.

"Does that feel good?" he asks into my mouth.

He's only rubbing me—how does it feel so good? I nod and he slows his fingers down.

"Does it feel better than when you do it?"

What?

"Does it?" he asks again.

"Wh-what?" I manage, even though I have no control of my body or mind right now.

"When you touch yourself? Does it feel like this?"

I'm not sure what to say, and when I just stare at him, something behind his eyes snaps to. "Wait . . . you've never done that, either, have you?" His voice is full of surprise and something else . . . lust? He goes back to kissing me and his fingers keep moving up and down. "You're so responsive to me, so wet," he says and I moan. Why are these filthy words so hot when Hardin says them? I feel a gentle pinch and it sends a shock through my whole body.

"What? Was . . . *that*?" I half ask, half moan. He chuckles and doesn't answer, but I feel him do it again and my back arches off the grass. His mouth travels down to my neck, then my chest. His tongue dips down under the cup of my bra and his hand massages one of my breasts. I feel a pressure building in my stomach— and it is pure bliss. I pinch my eyes closed and bite down on my lip; my back lifts off the grass once again and my legs begin to shake.

"That's right, Tessa, come for me," he says, which makes me feel like I am spiraling out of control. "Look at me, baby," he purrs.

I open my eyes. The sight of his mouth nipping the skin on my chest sends me over the edge and my vision goes white for a few seconds. "Hardin," I say, and then repeat, and I can tell by the way his cheeks flush that he loves it. Slowly, he pulls his hand out and rests it on my stomach as I try to return my breathing to normal. My body had never felt so energized before, and it's never felt so relaxed as this now.

"I'll give you a minute to recover." He laughs to himself and moves away from me.

I frown. I want him to stay close, but I'm also strangely unable to speak. After the best few minutes of my life, I sit up and look toward Hardin. He already has his jeans and shoes on.

"We're leaving already?" The embarrassment is clear in my

voice. I had assumed he would want me to touch him, too; even if I don't really know what to do, he could explain it to me.

"Yeah, you wanted to stay longer?"

"I just thought . . . I don't know. I thought maybe you would want something . . ." I have no idea how to say this. Lucky for me he catches on.

"Oh, no. I am okay, for now," he says and gives me a small smile. Is he going to go back to being mean again? I hope not, not after this. I have just shared the most intimate experience I have ever had with him. I won't be able to stand it if he treats me terribly again. He did say "for now," so he wants something later? I am already starting to regret this. I put my clothes on over my wet bra and panties and try to ignore the soft wetness between my thighs. Hardin picks up his wet shirt and hands it to me.

He takes in my confused expression and tells me "to towel off." His eyes shift to the apex of my thighs.

Oh. I unbutton my pants and he doesn't bother to turn around as I swipe the shirt across my sensitive skin there. I don't miss the way his tongue brushes across his bottom lip while he watches me. He pulls his cell phone from the pocket of his jeans and his thumb slides across the screen repeatedly. I finish doing what he recommended and hand him his shirt back. As I step into my shoes, the air around us has changed from passionate to distant, and I find myself wishing to be as far away from him as possible.

I wait for him to talk to me as we walk back to the car, but he doesn't say anything. My mind is already coming up with every possible worst-case scenario for what happens next. He opens my door for me and I nod to thank him.

"Is something wrong?" he asks me while he drives back down the gravel road.

"I don't know. Why are you being so weird now?" I ask him,

even though I'm afraid of his answer and can't look directly at him.

"I'm not, you are."

"No, you haven't said a word to me since . . . you know."

"Since I gave you your first orgasm?"

My mouth drops and my cheeks flush. *Why am I still surprised by his dirty mouth?*

"Um, yeah. Since that, you haven't said anything. You just got dressed and we left." Honesty seems to be the best option right now, so I add, "It makes me feel like you're using me or something"

"What? Of course I'm not using you. To use someone I would have to be getting something out of it," he says, so offhandedly that I can suddenly feel the tears coming. I do my best to keep them back but one escapes.

"Are you crying? What did I say?" He reaches over and puts his hand on my thigh. To my surprise it soothes me. "I didn't mean it like that—I am sorry. I'm not used to whatever is supposed to happen after messing around with someone, plus I wasn't going to just drop you off at your room and go our separate ways. I thought maybe we could get some dinner or something? I am sure you're starving." He squeezes my thigh gently.

I smile back at him, relieved by his words. I wipe away the tear that escaped prematurely and with it goes my worry.

I don't know what it is about Hardin that makes me so emotional, in every way possible. The idea of him using me makes me more upset than it should. My feelings for Hardin are so confusing. I hate him one minute and want to kiss him the next. He makes me feel things I never knew I could, and not just sexually. He makes me laugh and cry, yell and scream, but most of all he makes me feel alive.

chapter twenty-six

Hardin's hand is still on my thigh and I hope he never removes it. I take a quick opportunity to study some of the tattoos covering his arms. The infinity symbol above his wrist catches my eye again, and I can't help but wonder if it means something to him. It feels personal, inked there, just above the bare skin on his hand. I check his other wrist for a matching symbol but there isn't one. The infinity symbol is common enough, mostly among women, but the way the two loops on the ends are hearts makes me even more curious.

"So what type of food do you like?" he asks.

What a refreshingly normal question for him to ask me. I pull my matted, almost dry hair into a bun and think for a second about what I want to eat. "Well, I like anything, really, as long as I know what it is—and it doesn't involve ketchup."

He laughs. "You don't like ketchup? Aren't all Americans supposed to be wild for the stuff?" he teases.

"I have no idea, but it's disgusting."

We both laugh and I look over at Hardin, who says, "Let's just stick with a plain diner then?"

I nod and he reaches to turn the music up but stops and puts his hand back on me. "So what do you plan on doing after college?" he asks; it's something he's already asked me before, in his room.

"I'm going to move to Seattle immediately, and I hope to work at a publishing house or be a writer. I know it's silly," I say, suddenly embarrassed by my high ambitions. "But you already asked me that before, remember?"

"No, it's not. I know someone over at Vance Publishing House; it's a bit of a drive, but maybe you should apply there for an internship. I could talk to him."

"What? You would do that for me?" My voice goes high because I'm pretty surprised; even if he has been nice for the last hour, this isn't quite what I expected.

"Yeah, it's not a big deal." He seems a little embarrassed. I am sure he isn't used to doing nice things.

"Wow, thank you. Really. I need to get a job or internship soon anyway, and that would literally be a dream come true!" I clap my hands.

He chuckles and shakes his head. "You're welcome."

We pull into a small parking lot next to an old brick building.

"The food here is amazing," he says and climbs out of the car. Walking around to the trunk, he opens it . . . and pulls out another plain-black T-shirt. He really must have an endless supply. I was enjoying him being shirtless so much that I forgot he would eventually have to put one back on.

When we get inside we seat ourselves in the fairly deserted place. An old woman walks to the table and goes to hand us our menus, but he waves them off, ordering a hamburger and fries, gesturing like I should do the same. I trust him on this one and order it—minus ketchup, of course.

While we wait, I tell Hardin about growing up in Richland, which, being from England, he's never heard of. He isn't missing out on much; the town is small and everyone does the same things and no one ever leaves. Everyone except me: I will never move back there. He doesn't offer me much information about his past, but I'm hopeful and patient. He seems very curious about my life as a child and he frowns when I tell him about my dad's drinking. I had mentioned it to him before, while we were fighting, but this time I went into a little more detail.

During a pause in the conversation, the waitress reappears with our food, which looks delicious.

"Good, huh?" Hardin asks as I take my first bite. I nod and wipe my mouth off. The food is amazing and we both clear our plates, me being more hungry than I've ever been before.

THE DRIVE BACK TO THE DORMS is relaxed. His long fingers rub circles on my leg, and I'm disappointed to see the WCU sign when we finally hit campus and the student parking lot.

"Did you have a nice time?" I ask him. I feel so much closer to him now than I did a few hours ago. He can be really good when he tries to be.

"Yeah, I did, actually." He seems surprised. "Listen, I would walk you to your room, but I don't want to play twenty questions with Steph . . ." He smiles and turns his body sideways to face me.

"It's fine. I'll just see you tomorrow," I tell him. I'm not sure if I should try to kiss him goodbye or not, so I'm relieved when his fingers tug on a few loose strands of my hair and tuck them behind my ear. I rest my face in his palm and he leans over and touches his lips to mine. It starts as a simple and gentle kiss, but I feel it warm my entire body and I need more. Hardin grabs my arm and pulls it to gesture for me to climb over the middle divider. I quickly oblige and straddle his lap, my back hitting the steering wheel. I feel the seat recline slightly, giving us more room as I lift his shirt a little to slide my hands under it. His stomach is hard and his skin is hot. I trace my fingers along the ink there.

His tongue massages mine and he wraps his arms around me tightly. The feeling is almost painful, but it's a pain I will gladly endure to be this close to him. He moans into my mouth as I put my hands farther up his shirt. I love that I can make him moan, too, that I have this effect on him. I'm really about to get lost in the sensation again when we are interrupted by my phone ringing.

"Another alarm?" he teases as I pull back and reach into my purse.

Smiling, I open my mouth to say something smart back at him, but when I look at the screen and see it's Noah, I stop. Looking at Hardin, I can tell he's figured it out. His expression changes, and fearing that I'm losing him, this mood, I hit the ignore button and toss my phone back onto the passenger seat. I am not thinking about Noah right now. I push him to the back corner of my mind and lock that door.

I lean back in to continue kissing Hardin, but he stops me.

"I think I better go." His tone is clipped, and sends worry through me. When I draw back to look at him, his gaze is distant and ice immediately replaces the fire in my body.

"Hardin, I ignored it. I am going to talk to him about all this. I just don't know how or when—but it will be soon, though, I promise." I knew somewhere in the back of my mind that I would have to break up with Noah the moment I kissed Hardin that first time. I can't date him if I've already betrayed him. It would always hang over my head like a dark cloud of guilt, and neither of us wants that. The way I feel about Hardin is another reason I can't be with Noah anymore. I love Noah, but if I really loved him the way he deserves to be loved, I wouldn't be having these feelings for Hardin. I don't want to hurt Noah, but there is no turning back now.

"Talk to him about what?" he snaps.

"All of this." I wave my hands around. "Us."

"Us? You're not trying to tell me you're going to break up with him . . . for me, are you?"

My head starts to spin. I know I should climb off his lap but I am frozen.

"You don't . . . want me to?" My voice comes out as a whisper.

"No, why would you? I mean, yeah, if you want to dump him, go for it, but don't do it on my behalf."

"I just . . . I thought . . ." I start to fumble my words.

"I already told you that I don't date, Theresa," he says.

My body wants to freeze like a deer in headlights; the only thing that makes it possible for me to climb off him is the fact that I refuse to let him see me cry, again.

"You're disgusting," I say bitterly and grab my stuff from the floorboards and my phone from the seat. Hardin looks like he wants to say something, but he doesn't. "Stay away from me from now on—I mean it!" I shout, and he closes his eyes.

I walk as fast as I can to my building, to my room, somehow managing to hold in my tears until I get inside and shut the door. I am so grateful Steph's gone as I slide down the door and break into sobs. How could I be so stupid? I knew how he was when I agreed to be alone with him, yet I practically jumped at the opportunity. Just because he was nice to me today, I got it into my head that *what*—that he would be my *boyfriend*? I laugh through my sobs at how stupid and naïve I am. I really can't even be angry with Hardin. He told me he doesn't date, but today we had such a nice time. He was actually pleasant and playful, and I thought we were really building a relationship of some kind.

But it was all an act, just so he could get into my pants. And I let him.

chapter twenty-seven

My tears dry, and I am showered and somewhat mentally stable by the time Steph returns from the movies.

"So, how was your . . . hangout with Hardin?" she asks and grabs her pajamas out of her dresser.

"It was okay, he was his normal . . . charming self," I tell her and manage a laugh. I want to tell her about what we did, but I'm too ashamed. I know she wouldn't judge me, and despite wanting to be able to tell *someone,* I also really don't want anyone to know.

Steph looks at me with concern evident in her eyes, and I have to look away. "Just be careful, okay; you're too nice for someone like Hardin."

I want to hug her and cry into her shoulder but instead ask, "How was the movie?" to change the subject. She tells me how Tristan kept feeding her popcorn and that she is really starting to like him. I want to gag, but I know I am just jealous because Tristan actually likes her in a way Hardin doesn't like me. But I remind myself that I do have someone who loves me and that I need to start treating him better and stay away from Hardin—for real this time.

THE NEXT MORNING I'm drained. I have no energy and feel like I could cry at any moment. My eyes are red and puffy from crying last night, so I walk over to Steph's dresser and grab her makeup bag. I pull out brown eyeliner and draw a thin line under my eyes and on my eyelid. It makes my eyes look much better. I put a little powder under my eyes to give my skin a little color. A few swipes of mascara and I look like a new person. Pleased with the way I look, I put on my tight jeans and a tank top. Still feeling naked, I grab a white cardigan out of my closet. This is the most effort I have made in my appearance for a regular school day since picture day my senior year of high school.

Landon texts me that we'll have to meet in class, so when I stop by the coffeehouse I grab him a drink, too. I'm still pretty early to class, so I walk slower than usual.

"Hey, Tessa, right?" I hear a guy's voice say. I look over and see a preppy boy coming my way.

"Yeah, Logan, right?" I ask him, and he nods.

"You coming over again this weekend?" he asks. He must be part of the frat; of course he is, he's preppy and gorgeous.

"Oh, no, not this weekend." I laugh and he joins in.

"Bummer, you were fun. Well, if you change your mind, you know where it is. I gotta go, but I'll see you around." Giving me a fake little tip of the hat, he walks away.

In class, Landon is already seated and thanks me repeatedly for bringing him coffee. "You look different today," he says as I sit down.

"I put makeup on," I joke and he smiles. He doesn't ask about my night with Hardin and I am grateful. I'm not sure what I would say to him.

Just as the day gets pleasant, and I begin to stop thinking about Hardin, it's time for Literature.

HARDIN SITS IN HIS NORMAL SEAT in the front. He's wearing a white T-shirt for once and it's thin enough that his tattoos are visible underneath it. It amazes me how attractive I find his tattoos and piercings when I've never cared for either before. I look away quickly, sit down in my usual seat next to him, and pull out my notes. I'm not giving up my great seat because of one rude boy. Still, I hope Landon arrives soon so I won't feel so alone with Hardin.

"Tess?" Hardin whispers as the class begins to fill up.

No. Don't answer him. Ignore him, I repeat to myself.

"Tess?" he says again, this time louder.

"Do not speak to me, Hardin," I say through my teeth. I avoid looking at him. I will not fall back into his trap.

"Oh come on," he says, and I can tell he thinks this is all funny.

My tone is harsh but I don't care: "I mean it, Hardin, leave me alone."

"Fine, have it your way," he says equally harshly, and I sigh.

Landon walks in and I am so grateful. Seeing the tension between Hardin and me, he asks in his kind tone, "You okay?"

"Yeah, I'm fine," I lie, and class begins.

HARDIN AND I continue ignoring each other all week, and each day that passes without talking to him makes it a little easier to not think about him so much. Steph and Tristan have been hanging out all week, so I've had our room mostly to myself, which has been both good and bad. Good because I get a lot of studying done, but bad because I am left alone with my thoughts about Hardin. All week I have been wearing a little bit more makeup, but still my baggy and conservative clothes. By Friday morning, I feel like I am really over this whole mess with Hardin. That is, until everyone keeps talking about partying at the frat house. Seriously, there is a party there every Friday—and usually Saturday, too—so why they feel the need to get excited about it every weekend blows my mind.

After being asked by at least ten people if I will be at the party, I decide to do the only thing that I know will keep me from going. I call Noah.

"Hey, Tessa!" he chirps into the phone. It has been a few days since we've actually talked, and I've missed his voice.

"Hey, do you think you could come visit me?" I ask.

"Sure, yeah. Maybe I can come next weekend?"

I groan. "No, I mean like today. Like now, could you leave right now?" I know he likes to plan things just like I do, but I need him to come now.

"Tessa, I have practice after school. I am still at school now, just at lunch," he explains.

"Please, Noah, I really miss you. Can't you just leave now and come here for the weekend? *Please?*" I know I'm begging, but I don't care.

"Um . . . yeah, sure, Tessa. I'll come now. Is everything okay?"

Happiness floods me—I'm really surprised that squeaky-clean Noah is agreeing to this, but I am so glad he is. "Yeah, I just really miss you. I haven't seen you in almost two weeks," I remind him.

He laughs. "I miss you, too. I am going to get a slip and leave in a few minutes, so I will see you in about three hours. I love you, Tessa."

"I love you, too," I say and hang up. Well, that settles that. Any chance that I might have ended up at that party is now gone.

A NEWFOUND SENSE OF RELIEF fills me as I walk to Literature, and into the gorgeous old brick building the class is in. That sense of relief vanishes when I walk into the classroom and see Hardin hovering over Landon's desk.

What the hell?

I rush over just as Hardin slams his hand on the desk and growls, "Don't ever say some shit like that again, you prick."

Landon moves to stand up, but he would be insane to try to fight Hardin. Landon is muscular and all, but he's so kind I can't imagine him hitting anyone.

I grab hold of Hardin's arm and pull him back away from Landon. His other hand rises into the air and I flinch, but once he realizes it's me, he drops his hand and curses under his breath.

"Leave him alone, Hardin!" I yell and turn to Landon. He looks just as mad as Hardin does but he sits down.

"You need to mind your own business, Theresa," Hardin snidely says and moves to his seat. He really should sit in the back somewhere.

Sitting between them, I lean over and whisper to Landon, "Are you okay? What was that about?"

He looks toward Hardin and sighs. "He is just an asshole. That pretty much sums it up," he says loudly and puts on a chipper grin.

I giggle a little and straighten up. I can hear Hardin's ragged breathing next to me and I get an idea. A childish idea, but I do it anyway.

"I have some good news!" I tell Landon in my best mock-cheery voice.

"Really? What's that?"

"Noah's coming to visit today, and he'll be here all weekend!" I say and smile while clapping my hands together. I know I am overdoing it, but I feel Hardin's eyes on me and I know he heard me.

"Really? That *is* great news!" Landon says earnestly.

Class begins and ends without Hardin saying a word to me. This is how it will be from now on and it's fine with me. I wish Landon a nice weekend and walk back to my room to touch up my makeup and grab something to eat before Noah gets here. I laugh at myself a little while doing my makeup. *Since when am I the type of girl who has to "touch up her makeup" before her boy-*

friend comes? I sense that it's since that day at the stream with Hardin, an experience that changed me, though the way he hurt me after changed me even more. The makeup is only a slight change, but I know it is there.

I eat and straighten my room up a little, folding Steph's clothes and putting them away; I hope she won't mind. Noah finally texts that he's here, and I jump off the bed where I was resting and rush outside to greet him. He looks better than ever in navy blue pants, a cream cardigan, and a white shirt underneath. He really does wear a lot of cardigans, but I love them. His welcoming smile warms my heart and he wraps his arms around me and tells me how nice it is to see me.

As we walk back to my room, he looks at me for a moment and asks, "Are you wearing makeup?"

"Yeah, a little. It's just something I have been experimenting with," I explain.

He smiles. "It looks nice," he says, and kisses my forehead.

IN MY ROOM, we end up browsing through the romantic comedies section on Netflix to pick a movie. Steph texts me and says she is with Tristan and won't be back tonight, so I turn the lights off and we sit back against my headboard, Noah's arm around my shoulder and my head on his chest.

This is me, I think, *not some wild girl swimming in a punk boy's T-shirt.*

We start up a movie that I've never heard of before, and not five minutes into it the door bursts opens. I immediately figure that maybe Steph has forgotten something she needs.

But of course it's Hardin. His eyes go straight to where Noah and I are cuddled on the bed, illuminated by the TV light. I flush; he has come here to tell Noah, I know it. Panic takes over my body, and I scoot away from my boyfriend, making it seem like I just made a surprised little jump.

"What are you doing here?" I snap. "You can't just barge in here!"

Hardin smiles. "I'm meeting Steph," he answers and sits down. "Hey, Noah, nice to see you again." He smirks and Noah looks uncomfortable. He is probably wondering why Hardin has a key to the room and doesn't bother to knock.

"She's with Tristan, probably already at your house," I tell him slowly, silently pleading for him to leave. If he tells Noah now, I have no idea how I could recover.

"Oh?" he says. I can tell by his smirk that he came here just to torment me. He will probably stay until I come clean to Noah myself. "Are you two coming to the party?"

"No . . . we aren't. We're trying to watch a movie," I tell him, and Noah reaches over and takes my hand. Even in the dark, I can see Hardin's eyes focus on where Noah's hand touches mine.

"That's too bad. I better go . . ." He turns toward the door, and I feel some relief. But then he twists back. "Oh, and, Noah," he begins, making my heart drop. "That's a nice cardigan you're wearing."

I let out a breath I didn't know I was holding.

"Thanks. It's from the Gap," Noah says. He is clueless and unaware that Hardin is making fun of him.

"I can see that. You two have fun," Hardin says and leaves the room.

chapter twenty-eight

He's not so bad, I guess," Noah says when the door closes.
I laugh nervously. "What?" And when he raises his eyebrow at me, I continue: "Nothing, I am just surprised to hear you say that." I lie back onto his chest. The electricity that filled the room moments ago has dissolved.

"I'm not saying I would want to hang out with the guy, but he was friendly enough."

"Hardin is nothing even close to friendly," I say, and Noah chuckles and wraps his arm around me. If he only knew the things that happened between Hardin and me, the way we kissed, the way I moaned his name while he—*God, Tessa, just stop.* I lean my head up and kiss Noah's jaw, making him smile. I want Noah to make me feel the way Hardin does. I sit up and turn to face him. I take his face between my hands and press my lips against his. His mouth opens and he kisses me back. His lips are soft . . . just like his kiss. It's not enough. I need the fire, I need the passion. I wrap my hands around his neck and pull myself onto his lap.

"Whoa, Tessa, what are you doing?" he asks and tries to push me off gently.

"What? Nothing, I just . . . I want to make out, I guess," I say and look down. I am usually not embarrassed in front of Noah, but this isn't something we usually talk about.

"Okay?" he says, and I kiss him again. I feel warmth from him, but not the fire. I start to rock my hips, hoping to light it somehow. His hands go down to my waist but he pushes them against me, stopping my movements. I know we agreed to wait until marriage, but we're just kissing here. I grab his hands and pull them away and continue to rock against him. No matter how many times I try to kiss him harder, his mouth stays soft and timid. I can feel him getting turned on, but he won't act on it.

I know I am doing this for all the wrong reasons, but I don't care at the moment—I just need to know that Noah can do to me what Hardin does. *It isn't actually Hardin that I want, it's the feeling . . . isn't it?*

I stop kissing Noah and slide off his lap.

"That was nice, Tessa." He smiles and I give him one back. It was "nice." He is so careful, too careful, but I love him. I press play on the movie and within minutes I feel myself drifting off.

"I should go," Hardin says. His green eyes looking down at me. "Go where?" I don't want him to go. "I am going to stay at a hotel close by; I'll come back in the morning," he says, and after I stare at him a moment, his face fades into Noah's.

I jolt up and wipe my eyes. Noah, it is Noah. It was never Hardin.

"You're obviously really sleepy, and I can't stay the night here," Noah says gently and brushes my cheek.

I want him to stay, but now I'm afraid of what I will see or say in my sleepy state. Noah clearly doesn't think it's decent for him to stay in my room anyway. Hardin and Noah are polar opposites. In every way.

"Okay, thank you again for coming," I mumble and he kisses me lightly on the cheek before sliding out from under me.

"I love you," he says. I nod, bury my head back into my pillow, and descend into dreams I don't remember.

THE NEXT MORNING, I wake up to Noah calling on the phone. He tells me he is on his way, so I roll out of bed and rush to the showers, wondering what Noah and I should do today. There isn't much to do around here unless we go into town; maybe I should text Landon and ask what there is to do around here besides party at a frat house. He seems to be my only friend who would know.

Having decided to wear my gray pleated skirt and a plain blue shirt, I ignore Hardin's voice in the back of my head telling me that it's ugly, and dress in the stall.

Noah is in the hall waiting by my door as I return with the towel still in my hair. "You look lovely," he says with a smile, and puts his arm over my shoulder as I open the door.

"I just need to do my hair and put a little makeup on," I tell him and grab Steph's makeup bag, which I'm glad she didn't take with her. I will need to get some of my own now that I know I like the way it looks.

Noah sits patiently on my bed as I dry my hair and curl the ends. I stop and give him a kiss on the cheek before I apply my makeup. "What do you want to do today?" I finish with mascara and fluff my hair.

"College really suits you, Tessa. You have never looked better," Noah says. "I don't know, maybe we can go to a park or something, then dinner?"

I look at the clock. How is it already 1 p.m.? I text Steph and tell her I will be out most of the day and she responds saying she will be gone until tomorrow. She basically lives at Hardin's fraternity house on the weekends.

Noah opens the passenger door of his Toyota. His parents made sure he had the safest car, the newest model. The interior is spotless, no stacks of books, no dirty clothing. We drive around to find a park, which only takes a little bit. It's a small, quiet space with half-green, half-yellowing grass and a few trees.

As we pull into a spot, Noah asks, "Hey, when are you going to start looking for a car?"

"I think this week, actually. I am going to apply for jobs this week, too." I don't mention the internship at Vance Publishing that Hardin dangled in front of me. I don't know if I can still get it, or how I'd tell Noah if I did.

"That is great news. Let me know if you need any help with either of those," he says.

We walk around the park once and then sit at a picnic table. Noah talks most of the time and I nod along. I find myself zoning in and out of the conversation but he doesn't seem to notice. We end up walking a little more and come to a small stream. I snort at the irony and Noah looks at me quizzically.

"Do you want to swim?" I ask, not quite sure why I push this moment further.

"In there? No way," he says, laughing, and as I deflate a little, I mentally smack myself. I need to stop comparing Noah to Hardin.

"I was just joking," I lie, and drag him along down the trail.

IT IS SEVEN before we leave the park, so we decide to order pizza when we get back to my room and watch a classic: Meg Ryan falling in love with Tom Hanks through a radio show. I am starving by the time the pizza comes so I eat almost half of it myself. In my defense, I haven't eaten all day.

Halfway through the movie my phone rings and Noah reaches over to grab it for me. "Who's Landon?" he asks. There is no suspicion in his voice, only curiosity. He has never been the jealous type; he never needed to be.

Until now, my subconscious reminds me.

"He's a friend from school," I say and answer. Why would Landon be calling me so late? He's never called me for anything other than to compare notes.

"Tessa?" Landon says loudly.

"Yeah, is everything okay?"

"Um, well, no, actually. I know Noah is there but . . ." He hesitates.

"What's wrong, Landon?" My heart starts to race. "Are you okay?"

"Yeah, it's not me. It's Hardin."

Panic overtakes me. "H-Hardin?" I stutter.

"Yeah, if I give you an address can you come here, please?" I hear something crash in the background. I jump off my bed and I have my shoes on before my mind catches up. Noah stands up, too, almost as if in sympathy.

"Landon, is Hardin trying to hurt you?" My mind can't make sense of what else could be going on.

"No, no," he says.

"Text me the address," I tell him and then hear another crash.

I turn to Noah. "Noah, I need your car."

His head turns sideways. "What is going on?"

"I don't know . . . it's Hardin. Give me your keys," I demand.

He reaches into his pocket and pulls them out, but says insistently, "I'm coming with you."

But I snatch the keys from his hands and shake my head. "No, you . . . I need to go alone."

My words hurt him. He *looks* hurt. And I know it's wrong to leave him here, but right now the only thing I can think about is getting to Hardin.

chapter twenty-nine

Landon's text reads 2875 Cornell Rd, which I copy and paste into my maps program, which says the drive is fifteen minutes. What could be going on there that Landon could possibly need me?

I'm just as confused when I arrive at the address as I was when I left my room. Noah has called twice, both of which I've ignored; I need the navigation to stay on the screen and, honestly, the confused look on his face when I left him there is haunting me.

The houses on the street are all large and look like mansions. This house in particular is at least three times larger than my mother's. It's an old-fashioned brick house with a sloped yard that makes it appear to be sitting on a hill. Even under the streetlights, it's beautiful. I'm guessing this must be Hardin's father's house, since this doesn't belong to a college kid and it's the only reason why Landon would be here as well. I take a deep breath, get out, and walk up the steps from the sidewalk. I knock hard on the dark mahogany door, and it opens within seconds.

"Tessa, thank you for coming. I'm sorry, I know you have company. Is Noah with you?" Landon asks and looks out to the car while gesturing me inside.

"No, he's back at the dorms. What's going on? Where's Hardin?"

"The backyard. He is out of control." He sighs.

"And I am here because . . . ?" I ask as nicely as I can. *What does Hardin being out of control have to do with me?*

"I don't know, I know you hate him, but you do talk to him. He's really drunk, completely belligerent. He showed up here and opened a bottle of his father's scotch. He drank over half the bottle! And then he started breaking things: all my mother's dishes, a glass cabinet, basically everything he could get his hands on."

"What? Why?" Hardin told me he doesn't drink—was that a lie, too?

"His dad just told him that he and my mother are getting married . . ."

"Okay?" I'm still confused. "So Hardin doesn't want them to get married?" I ask as Landon leads me through the large kitchen, where I gasp as I take in the huge mess Hardin has made. Broken dishes are scattered across the floor, and a large wooden cabinet has been knocked over, its glass panels shattered.

"No, but it's a long story. Right after his dad called and told him, they left town for the weekend to celebrate. I think that's why Hardin came here, to confront his dad. He never comes here," he explains and opens the back door.

I see a shadow sitting at a small table on the patio. Hardin.

"I don't know what you think I can do, but I'll try."

Landon nods. He leans down and puts his hand on my shoulder. "He was calling out for you," he tells me quietly, and my heart stops.

I walk toward Hardin and he looks up at me. His eyes are bloodshot, and his hair is hidden under a gray beanie. His eyes go wide, then darken, and I want to step back. He looks almost scary under the dim patio light.

"*How did you get here*—" Hardin says loudly and stands up.

"Landon . . . he . . ." I answer, then wish I hadn't.

"You fucking called her?" he yells toward Landon, who for his part walks back inside.

"You leave him alone, Hardin—he is worried about you," I scold.

He sits back down, gesturing for me to take a seat, too. I sit across from him and watch as he grabs the mostly empty bottle of dark liquor and puts it to his mouth. I watch his Adam's apple move as he gulps it down. When he's finished, he slams the bottle down onto the glass of the patio table and it makes me jump, thinking either the bottle or the table or both might break.

"Aww, aren't you two something. You both are so predictable. Poor Hardin is upset, so you gang up on me and try to make me feel bad for breaking some shitty china," he drawls with a sick smirk.

"I thought you don't drink?" I ask him and cross my arms.

"I don't. Until now, I guess. Don't try to patronize me; you're no better than me." He points a finger at me, then grabs the bottle for another swig.

And it's scary, but I can't deny that being near him, even in his drunken state, breathes life into me. I have missed the feeling Hardin gives me.

"I never said I was better than you. I just want to know what made you drink now?"

"What does it matter to you? Where's your *boyfriend*?" His eyes blaze into mine and the emotion behind them is so strong that I am forced to look away. If only I knew what that emotion was; hatred, I suppose.

"He's back in my room. I just want to help you, Hardin." I lean a little over the table to reach for his hand, but he recoils from my touch.

"Help me?" he cackles. I want to ask him why he was calling out for me if he is going to continue to be hateful, but I don't want to throw Landon under the bus again. "If you want to help me, then leave."

"Why won't you just tell me what's going on?" I look down at my hands and pick at my fingernails.

He sighs and pulls his beanie off and runs his hand through

his hair before pulling it back on. "My father decided to tell me *just now* that he is marrying Karen—and the wedding's next month. He should have told me long ago, and not over the phone. I'm sure perfect little Landon's known for a while."

Oh. I hadn't actually expected him to tell me, so I am not sure what to say. "I am sure he had his reasons not to tell you."

"You don't know him; he doesn't give a shit about me. You know how many times I have talked to him in the last year? Maybe ten! All he cares about is his big house, his new soon-to-be wife, and his new, perfect son." Hardin slurs and takes another drink. I stay quiet while he continues. "You should see the dump that my mum lives in in England. She says she likes it there, but I know she doesn't. It's smaller than my dad's bedroom here! My mum practically forced me to come here for university, to be closer to him—and we see how that worked out!"

With this little bit of information he has given me I feel like I can understand him so much better. Hardin's hurt; that's why he is the way he is.

"How old were you when he left?" I ask him.

He eyes me warily but answers. "Ten. But even before he left, he was never around. He was at a different bar every night. Now he's Mr. Perfect and he has all this shit," Hardin says and waves his hand toward the house.

Hardin's dad left when he was ten, just like mine, and they were both drunks. We have more in common than I thought. This wounded and drunk Hardin seems so much younger, so much more fragile than the powerful person I've known so far.

"I'm sorry that he left you guys, but—"

"No, I don't need your pity," he interrupts.

"It's not pity. I'm just trying to—"

"Trying to what?"

"Help you. Be here for you," I say softly.

And he smiles. It's a beautifully haunting smile, and makes

me hopeful that I can help him through this, but I know what is really about to happen.

"You are so pathetic. Don't you see that I don't want you here? I don't want you to be here for me. Just because I messed around with you doesn't mean I want anything to do with you. Yet here you are, leaving your *nice* boyfriend—who can actually stand to be around you—to come here and try to 'help' me. That, Theresa, is the definition of *pathetic*," he says, punctuating it with air quotes.

His voice is full of venom, just like I knew it would be, but I ignore the pain in my chest and look at him. "You don't mean that." I think back to a week ago when he was laughing and tossing me into the water. I can't decide if he is a great actor, or a great liar.

"I do, though; go home," he tells me and raises the bottle to take another drink. Reaching across the table, I snatch it from him and toss it into the yard.

"What the hell?" he yells, but I ignore him and walk toward the back door.

I hear him scramble and then he steps in front of me. "Where are you going?" His face is inches from mine.

"I am going to help Landon clean up the mess you made and then I am going home." My voice comes out much calmer than I feel.

"Why would you help *him*?" The disgust in his voice is clear.

"Because he, unlike you, deserves for someone to help him," I say and his face falls. I should be saying much more to Hardin. I should scream at him for the hurtful things he just said to me, but I know that is what he wants. This is what he does: he hurts everyone near him and he gets a kick out of the chaos that comes out of that.

Hardin quietly steps out of my way.

When I go inside, I find Landon crouched over, pulling the cabinet upright.

"Where's the broom?" I ask when he's done. Landon looks at me with a thankful smile.

"Right over there," he says, motioning to the broom. "Thank you for everything."

I nod and begin sweeping up the smashed dishes. There are just so many. I feel terrible that when Landon's mom comes back she'll find all of her dishes gone. I hope they didn't have any sentimental value to her.

"Ouch!" I gasp when a small piece of glass digs into my finger. Droplets of blood fall onto the wooden floor, and I jump up to reach the sink.

"Are you okay?" Landon asks, worried.

"Yeah, it's just a little piece, I don't know why there is so much blood." It really doesn't hurt that bad. I close my eyes as the cold water runs over my finger, and after a couple of minutes I hear the back door open. I snap my eyes open and turn to see Hardin standing in the doorway.

"Tessa, can I talk to you, please?" he asks.

I know I should say no, but something about the redness around his eyes makes me nod. His eyes look to my hand and then the blood on the floor.

He walks over to me quickly. "Are you okay? What happened?"

"It's nothing, just a little glass," I tell him.

He reaches for my hand and pulls it out from under the water. And when he touches my arm, I feel the electricity. Looking at my finger, he frowns, then lets it go, walking over to Landon. *He was just calling me pathetic, now he is acting all concerned about my health?* He is going to make me crazy, literally crazy, as in locked in a padded room.

"Where are the Band-Aids?" he practically demands of Landon, and Landon tells him they're in the bathroom. Within a minute Hardin is back and he grabs my hand again. First he squeezes some antibacterial gel onto my cut, then he wraps a Band-Aid around my finger gently. I stay quiet, as confused by Hardin's actions as Landon looks.

"Can I talk to you, please?" he asks again, and thought I know I shouldn't, since when do I do what I should when Hardin is involved?

I nod, and he wraps his fingers around my wrist and leads me outside.

chapter thirty

Back at the patio table, Hardin lets go of my wrist and pulls out the chair for me. Feeling like my skin is literally burning from his touch, I rub my fingers over it as he grabs the other chair and drags it across the concrete to sit directly in front of me. When he sits, he's so close that his knees are almost touching mine.

"What could you possibly want to talk about, Hardin?" I ask him in the harshest tone I can muster.

He takes a deep breath and pulls his beanie off again and places it on the table. I watch as his long fingers run through his thick hair and he looks into my eyes.

"I am sorry," he says with an intensity that makes me look away and focus on the large tree in the backyard. He leans in close. "Did you hear me?" he asks.

"Yeah, I heard you," I snap and stare back at him. He is crazier than I thought if he thinks he can just say sorry and I will forget the horrible things he continues to do to me on an almost daily basis.

"You're so damned difficult to deal with," he says and sits back on his chair. The bottle I tossed into the yard is now in his hand, and he takes another drink from it. How is he not passed out yet?

"*I* am difficult? You have to be kidding me! What do you expect me to do, Hardin? You are cruel to me—so cruel," I say and pull my bottom lip between my teeth. I will not cry in front of him again. Noah has never made me cry; we have been in a few fights over the years, but I have never been upset enough to cry.

His voice is low and almost feels like it's part of the night air "I don't mean to be."

"*Yes,* you do, and you know it. You do it purposefully. I have never been treated this poorly by anyone in my entire life." I bite my lip harder. I can feel the knot in my throat. If I cry, he wins. That's what he wants.

"Then why do you keep coming around? Why not just give up?"

"If I . . . I don't know. But I can assure you that after tonight I am not going to. I am going to drop Literature and just take it next semester." I hadn't planned on doing that until now, but it is exactly what I should do.

"Don't, please don't do that."

"Why would you care? You don't want to be forced to be around someone as pathetic as me, right?" My blood is boiling. If I knew what to say to hurt him as bad as he always hurts me, I would.

"I didn't mean that . . . I'm the pathetic one."

I look straight at him. "Well, I won't argue with that."

He takes another drink, and when I reach for the bottle, he pulls it away.

"So you're the only one who can get drunk?" I ask, and a wry smile appears on his face. The patio light shines off his eyebrow ring as he hands me the bottle.

"I thought you were going to toss it again."

I should, but instead I put the bottle to my lips. The liquor is warm and tastes like burnt licorice dipped in rubbing alcohol. I gag and Hardin chuckles.

"How often do *you* drink? You implied before it was never," I say. I need to get back to being angry with him after he answers.

"Before tonight it has been about six months." His eyes fall to the floor like he is ashamed.

"Well, you shouldn't drink at all. It makes you an even worse person than usual."

Still staring at the ground, his face is serious. "You think I am a bad person?"

What, is he *that* drunk that he would ever consider himself *good*?

"Yes."

"I'm not. Well, maybe I am. I want you to . . ." he starts, but then stops, straightens up, and leans back on the chair.

"You want me to *what*?" I have to know what he was going to say. I hand him back the bottle, but he sets it on the table. I don't want to drink; the one was bad enough, given the terrible judgment I have around Hardin as it is.

"Nothing," he says, lying.

Why am I even here? Noah is back in my room waiting for me, and here I am wasting even more time on Hardin. "I should go." I stand up and head for the back door.

"Don't go," his voice says softly. And my feet stop in their tracks at the pleading tone. I turn around to find Hardin less than a foot from me.

"Why not? Do you have more insults to throw in my face?" I shout and turn away. His hand wraps around my arm and jerks me back.

"Don't turn your back on me!" he shouts even louder than I did.

"I should have turned my back on you a long time ago!" I scream and push against his chest. "I don't know why I am even here! I came all the way here the second Landon called me! I left my boyfriend—who, like you said, is the only one who can stand to be around me—to come here for you! You know what? You're right, Hardin, I *am* pathetic. I am pathetic for coming here, I am pathetic for even trying—"

But I'm cut off by his lips against mine. I push at his chest to stop him, but he doesn't budge. Every part of me wants to kiss him back, but I stop myself. I feel his tongue trying to pry its way in between my lips and his strong arms wrap around me, pulling me closer to him despite my attempts to push away. It's no use; he is stronger than me.

"Kiss me, Tessa," he says against my lips.

I shake my head and he grunts in frustration. "Please, just kiss me. I need you"

His words unravel me. This indecent, drunken, terrible man just said he needs me, and somehow it sounds like poetry to my ears. Hardin is like a drug; each time I take the tiniest bit of him, I crave more and more. He consumes my thoughts and invades my dreams.

The second my lips part, his mouth is on mine again, but this time I don't resist. I can't. I know this isn't the answer to my problems and that I'm just digging myself deeper, but that doesn't matter right now. All that matters is his words, and how he said them: *I need you.*

Could Hardin possibly need me the way I desperately need him? I doubt it, but for right now I want to pretend that he does. He brings one of his hands to cup my cheek and he runs his tongue along my bottom lip. I shudder and he smiles, his lip ring tickling the corner of my mouth. I hear a rustling noise and pull away. He lets me stop the kiss, but he keeps his arms wrapped tightly around me, his body pressed against mine. I look toward the back door and pray that Landon didn't witness my terrible lapse of judgment. I don't see him, thank God.

"Hardin, I really have to go. We can't keep doing this; it's not good for either of us," I tell him and look down.

"Yes, we can," he says and lifts my chin up, forcing me to look into his green eyes.

"No, we can't. You hate me, and I don't want to be your punching bag anymore. You confuse me. One minute you're telling me how much you can't stand me or humiliating me after my most intimate experience." He opens his mouth to interrupt me and I put my finger against his pink lips and continue. "Then the next minute you're kissing me and telling me you need me. I don't like who I am when I'm with you, and I hate the way I feel after you say terrible things to me."

"Who are you when you are with me?" His green eyes study my face, waiting for my reply.

"Someone I don't want to be, someone who cheats on their boyfriend and cries constantly," I explain.

"You know who I think you are when you're with me?" He runs his thumb along my jawline, and I try to stay focused.

"Who?"

"Yourself. I think this is the real you and that you're just too busy caring what everyone else thinks about you to realize it."

I don't know what I think about this, but he sounds so honest, so sure of his answer that I take a second to really think about his words. "And I know what I did to you after I fingered you." He notices my scowl and continues. "Sorry . . . after our experience, I know it was wrong. I felt terrible after you got out of my car."

"I doubt that," I snap, remembering how much I cried that night.

"It's true, I swear it. I know you think I'm a bad person . . . but you make me—" He draws up short. "Never mind."

Why does he always stop?

"Finish that sentence, Hardin, or I am leaving right now," I tell him. And mean it.

The way his eyes seem to burn when he looks at me, the way his lips part slowly, as if every word will hold something, a lie or a truth, it makes me wait for his response. "You . . . you make me want to be *good,* for you . . . I want to be good for you, Tess."

chapter thirty-one

I try to take a step back from him, but his grip is too strong. I must have heard him wrong. My emotions are getting the best of me, so I turn and look out into the darkness of the backyard, trying to make sense of the meaning behind his words. Hardin wants to be better for me? *In what way?* He couldn't mean it . . . *Could he?*

I look back at him, my eyes hazy. "What?"

He looks unaffected . . . truthful? Hopeful? *What?* "You heard me."

"No. I'm sure I misunderstood."

"No, you didn't. You make me feel . . . something unfamiliar. I don't know how to handle these types of feelings, Tessa, so I do the only thing I know how to do." He pauses and blows out a small breath. "Which is be an asshole."

Once again I find myself in a trance.

"This could never work, Hardin, we are so different. First off, you don't date, remember?"

"We aren't that different—we like the same things; we both love books for example," he says, traces of liquor in his breath.

Even standing here, I can't wrap my mind around the idea of Hardin trying to convince me that we could be good together. "You don't date," I remind him again.

"I know, but we could . . . be friends?"

There it is. We are back to square one. "I thought you said we couldn't be friends? And I won't be friends with you—I know what you mean by that. You want all the benefits of being a boy-friend without actually having to commit."

His body sways and he leans on the table and loosens his grip on me. "Why is that so bad? Why do you need the label?" I'm thankful for the space between us and the fresh, scotch-free air.

"Because, Hardin, even though I've not really had a lot of re-straint lately, I do have self-respect. I will not be your plaything, especially when it involves being treated like dirt." I raise my hands into the air. "And besides, I'm already taken, Hardin."

Hardin's evil dimples come out with his smirk. "And yet, look where you are right now."

Reflexively, I blurt out, "I *love* him and he *loves* me," and then watch Hardin's expression change. He lets go of me and stumbles over the chair.

"Don't say that to me." He slurs his words, which are coming out faster than before. I almost forgot how drunk he was.

"You're only saying this because you're drunk; tomorrow you will go back to hating me."

"I don't hate you." He goes into the lawn a bit.

I wish he didn't have this effect on me. I wish I could just walk away. But instead I stick around and hear him say, "If you can look me in the eyes and tell me that you want me to leave you alone and never speak to you again, I will listen. I swear, from this point on I will never come near you again. Just say the words."

I open my mouth to tell him just that. To tell him to stay far away from me, to tell him I never want to lay eyes on him again.

He turns and comes closer. "Tell me, Tessa, tell me that you never want to see me again." Then he's touching me. He runs his hands along my arms and goose bumps immediately raise on my skin. "Tell me you never want to feel my touch again," he whis-pers, bringing his hand to my neck. His index finger traces along my collarbone and back up and down my neck. I hear my breath-ing quicken as he brings his lips less than an inch from mine.

"That you never want me to kiss you again," he says, and I can smell the scotch and feel the heat off his breath.

"Tell me, Theresa," he coos and I whimper.

"Hardin," I whisper.

"You can't resist me, Tessa, just as I can't resist you." His lips are close to mine; they are almost touching.

"Stay with me tonight?" he asks, and makes me want to do whatever he says.

A movement by the door catches my eye and I jerk away from Hardin. Looking up, I see Landon's face twisted with confusion before he turns away and disappears from the doorway.

I am snapped back into reality.

"I have to go," I say and Hardin curses under his breath.

"Please, please stay. Just stay with me tonight, and if you decide in the morning to tell me you don't want to see me anymore . . . just please stay. I am begging you and I don't beg, Theresa."

I find myself nodding before I can stop myself. "And what will I tell Noah? He is waiting for me and I have his car." *I can't believe I am actually considering doing this.*

"Just tell him that you have to stay because . . . I don't know. Don't tell him anything. What's the worst thing he can do?"

I shudder. He will tell my mother. Without a doubt. Irritation toward Noah fills me; I should not have to worry about my boyfriend telling my mother on me, even if I do something wrong.

"He is probably asleep anyway," Hardin says.

"No, he has no way to get back to his hotel."

"Hotel? Wait—he doesn't stay with you?"

"No, he has a hotel room close by."

"And you stay there with him?"

"No, he stays there," I say sheepishly, "and I stay in my room."

"Is he *straight*?" Hardin asks, his bloodshot eyes dancing in amusement.

My eyes go wide. "Of course he is!"

"Sorry, but something is not right there. If you were mine, I wouldn't be able to stay away from you. I would fuck you every chance I had."

My mouth falls open. Hardin's dirty words have the strangest effect on me. I flush and look away.

"Let's go inside," I hear him say. "The trees are swaying back and forth. I think that is my cue I've had way too much to drink."

"You're staying here?" I had assumed he would go back to his frat house.

"Yeah, and so are you. Let's go." He grabs my hand and we walk toward the back door.

I will have to find Landon and try to explain what he saw through the door. I don't know what's happening myself, so I'm not sure how I will explain it, but I have to make him understand somehow. As we walk through the kitchen, I notice the mess is almost completely cleaned up.

"You need to clean the rest of this tomorrow," I tell him and he nods.

"I will," he promises. Yet another promise I hope he keeps.

My hand in his, he leads me up the grand staircase. I pray that we don't run into Landon in the hallway and I am relieved when we don't.

Hardin opens the door to a pitch-black room and gently pulls me inside.

chapter thirty-two

My eyes adjust to the darkness, but the only light is a small streak of moonlight coming through the bay window. "Hardin?" I whisper.

I hear him curse as he trips over something and I try not to laugh.

"I'm right here," he says and clicks on a desk lamp. I look around the large room, which reminds me of a hotel. A four-poster bed with dark linens is centered against the far wall and looks like a king-size with at least twenty pillows on top. The desk is oversize and made of cherrywood, and the computer sitting on it has a bigger monitor than the television in my dorm room. The bay window has a built-in bench while the other windows are masked with thick navy curtains that don't allow the moon to shine through.

"This is my . . . room," he says and rubs the back of his neck with his hand. He looks almost embarrassed.

"You have a room here?" I ask, but of course he does. It is his father's house and Landon obviously lives here. Landon had mentioned that Hardin never comes here, so maybe that is why it looks so museum-like, untouched and impersonal.

"Yeah . . . I haven't ever actually slept in it . . . until tonight." He sits on the chest placed at the foot of the bed and unties his boots. He pulls his socks off and tucks them into the shoes. My heart swells at the idea that I am part of a first for Hardin.

"Oh. Why is that?" I am taking advantage of his drunken honesty.

"Because I don't want to. I hate it here," he answers quietly and unbuttons his black pants and pulls them down his legs.

"What are you doing?"

"Getting undressed?" he says, stating the obvious.

"I mean, why?" Even though part of me is dying to feel his hands on me again, I hope he doesn't think I'm going to have sex with him.

"Well, I am not sleeping in skinny jeans and boots," he half laughs. His hand sweeps the hair off his forehead, making it stand straight up. Everything he does sends that wild feeling through my body.

"Oh."

He pulls his shirt over his head, and I can't look away. His tattooed stomach is flawless. He tosses the T-shirt at me, but I don't catch it, letting it fall to the ground. I raise one eyebrow at him and he smiles.

"You can sleep in that. I assume you won't want to sleep in just your underwear. But of course, I am perfectly fine with it if you do." He winks and I giggle.

Why am I giggling? I can't sleep in his T-shirt, I will feel too naked.

"I'm fine sleeping in this," I tell him

He eyes my outfit. He hasn't made a single rude comment about my long skirt or loose blue blouse, so I hope he doesn't start now.

"Fine. Suit yourself; if you want to be uncomfortable, go ahead." He moves toward the bed in only his boxers and begins to toss the decorative pillows onto the floor.

I walk over and open the chest, and just as I had thought, it is empty. "Oh, don't throw those down. They go in here," I tell him, but he just laughs and tosses another onto the floor.

Groaning, I gather the pillows and stuff them into the chest. He again chuckles and pulls back the comforter before plopping down onto the bed. He crosses his arms behind his head, then crosses his feet and gives me a smile. The words tattooed on his ribs are stretched because of the position of his arms. His long, lean body looks exquisite.

"You're not going to whine about sleeping in the bed with me, are you?" he asks, and I roll my eyes. I actually wasn't going to. I know it's wrong, but I want to sleep in the bed with Hardin more than I think I have ever wanted anything.

"No, the bed is big enough for both of us," I say with a smile. I don't know if it's Hardin's smile or the fact that he is wearing only boxers, but I'm in a much better mood than before.

"Now that's the Tessa I love," he teases and my heart lurches at his choice of words. I know he doesn't, and would never, mean it that way, but it sounded so nice coming off his lips.

I climb onto the bed and scoot to the edge, as far away from Hardin's body as I can. Any farther and I'll fall off. I hear him chuckle and I roll over on my side to face him. "What is so funny?"

"Nothing," he lies, and bites his lip trying not to laugh. I like this playful Hardin; his humor is contagious.

"Tell me!" I pout and pucker out my bottom lip. His eyes go straight to my mouth and he runs his tongue along his lips before hooking his lip ring between his teeth.

"You've never slept in a bed with a guy before, have you?" He rolls onto his side and moves a little closer to me.

"No," I simply answer, and his smile grows. We are only a couple of feet apart, and before I know what I'm doing, my hand reaches out and pokes the little dimple on his cheek. His eyes dart to mine in surprise. I start to pull my hand away, but he grabs it and puts it back against his cheek, then moves it up and down his cheek slowly.

"I don't know why no one has fucked you yet; all that planning you do must help you put up a really good resistance," he
says, and I gulp.

"I've never really *had* to resist anyone," I admit. Guys in high
school found me attractive and hit on me enough, but no one
ever tried to actually have sex with me. They all knew I was with
Noah; we were well liked and were both voted onto Homecoming
Court every year.

"That's either a lie or you went to an all-blind high school.
Your lips alone are enough to make me hard."

I gasp at his words and he chuckles. He brings my hand to
his mouth and runs it along his wet lips. His breath is hot against
my fingers, and I'm surprised when he bares his teeth and gently
bites the pad of my index finger, somehow making me feel it in
the pit of my stomach. He moves my hand down to his neck and
my fingertips trace the swirl of an ivy branch tattoo on his neck.
He watches me carefully but doesn't stop me.

"You like the way I talk to you, don't you?" His expression is
dark but so sexy. My breathing hitches and he smiles again. "I can
see the blush in your cheeks and I can hear the way your breathing has changed. Answer me, Tessa, put those full lips of yours to
use," he says, and I giggle—I don't know what else to do. I will
never admit the way his words turn something on deep inside
of me.

He lets go of my hand but wraps his fingers around my wrist
and closes the gap between us. I am hot, too hot. I need to cool
down or I will start sweating soon.

"Can you turn the fan on?" I ask and he furrows his brow.
"Please."

He sighs but climbs off the bed. "If you are hot, why don't
you change out of those heavy clothes; that skirt looks itchy
anyway."

I had been waiting on him to tease me for my clothes, but this only makes me smile, since I can see his true motive here.

"You should dress for your body, Tessa. These clothes you wear hide all of your curves. If I hadn't seen you in your bra and panties, I would never know how sexy and curvy your body actually is. That skirt literally looks like a potato sack."

I laugh, even though he is insulting me and somehow managing to compliment me at the same time. "What do you suggest I wear? Fishnets and tube tops?"

"No, well, I might love to see that, but no. You can still cover yourself but wear clothes your size. That shirt hides your chest, too, and your tits are nothing you should be hiding."

"Will you stop using those words!" I scold him and he smiles.

Rejoining me on the bed, he scoots his practically naked body close to mine. I am still hot, but Hardin's odd way of complimenting me has given me a new wave of confidence. I climb out of bed.

"Where are you going?" he slurs, his voice panicked.

"To change," I say, and walk over to grab his T-shirt from the floor. "Now turn around and don't peek." I put my hands on my hips.

"No."

"What do you mean, 'no'?" *How can he be telling me no?*

"I won't turn around. I want to see you."

"Oh, okay." But I just smile, shake my head, and turn the light off.

Hardin whines, and I smile to myself as I unzip my skirt. It pools at my feet when another light clicks on.

"Hardin!" I hurry and pick the skirt back up. Hardin is leaning up on his elbows to look at me, and he isn't shy about his eyes moving up and down my body. He's seen me in less clothing before, and I know he isn't going to listen, so I take a deep breath and pull my shirt over my head. Not that I won't admit that I'm enjoying this little game we have going right now. I know deep down I want him to look at me, that I want him to want me. I'm wearing a plain white bra and white panties, nothing fancy or special, but Hardin's expression makes me feel sexy. I take his T-shirt and pull it over my head. It smells so good, just like Hardin.

"Come here," he whispers from where he lies. I ignore my subconscious telling me to run away as fast as I can, and walk toward the bed.

chapter thirty-three

Hardin's blazing eyes don't leave mine as I make my way to him. I prop my knee up on the bed and push myself onto it. At the same time, Hardin lifts himself up so his back is against the headboard and holds his hand out for mine. The second I place my small hand in his, he wraps his fingers around it and pulls me onto him. My knees go around his sides and I am straddling his lap. I've done this before with him, but never wearing so little clothing. I hold myself up using my knees so we aren't touching, but Hardin isn't having it. He positions his hands on my hips and gently pushes me down. His T-shirt bunches at my sides, baring my thighs completely, and I am suddenly glad that I shaved my legs this morning. The second our bodies touch my stomach begins to stir. I know this happiness that I feel isn't going to last, and I feel like Cinderella, waiting for the clock to strike and end my blissful night.

"Much better," he says and gives me a crooked smile.

I know he's drunk and that's why he is being so nice—well, nice for *him*—but right now I will take it. *If this is truly my last time around him, then this is how I want to spend it.* I keep telling myself that. I can behave however I want tonight with Hardin because when the daylight comes, I am going to tell him never to come near me again, and he will oblige. It's for the best, and I know that is what he will want when he isn't intoxicated. In my defense, I am just as intoxicated by Hardin as he is by the bottle of scotch he consumed. I keep telling myself that, too.

As Hardin continues to stare into my eyes, I begin to feel nervous. What should I do next? I have no idea where he wants to take this and I don't want to make a fool out of myself by trying to do something first.

He seems to notice my uncomfortable expression.

"What's wrong?" he asks, and brings a hand to my face. His finger traces over my cheekbone and my eyes involuntarily close at his surprisingly gentle touch.

"Nothing . . . I just don't know what to do," I admit and look down.

"Do whatever you want to do, Tess. Don't overthink it."

I lean back a little to create about a foot of space between our torsos and bring my hand up to his bare chest. I look at him for permission and he nods. I press both hands against his chest softly and he closes his eyes. My fingers trace the birds on his chest and down to the dead tree on his stomach. His eyelashes flutter as I trace the scripture on his ribs. His expression is so calm, but his chest is moving up and down quicker than it was a few moments ago. I'm unable to control myself as I bring my hand down and run my index finger along the waistband of his boxers. His eyes shoot open and he looks nervous. Hardin, *nervous?*

"Can I . . . um . . . touch you?" I ask with the hope that he gets what I mean without me having to say it. I feel detached from myself. *Who is this girl straddling this punk boy and asking to touch him . . . down there?* I think back to what Hardin said earlier about me being my true self with him. Maybe he is right. I love the way I feel right now. I love the electricity shooting through my body when we're like this.

He nods. "Please."

So I lower my hand, keeping it on top of his boxers, and slowly I reach the slight bulge in the fabric. He sucks in a breath as I graze my hand over him. I don't know what to do, so I just keep touching it, running my fingers up and down. I am too nervous to look up at him, so I keep my eyes on his growing crotch.

"Do you want me to show you what to do?" he asks quietly, his voice shaky. The usual cocky demeanor has shifted into something mysterious.

I nod and he puts his hand over mine, bringing it down to touch him again. He opens my hand and makes my fingers cup around his length. When he sucks a breath between his lips, I look up at him through my lashes. He takes his hand off mine, giving me full control.

"Fuck, Tessa, don't do that," he growls. Confused, I still my hand and am about to jerk it away when he speaks up. "No, no, not that. Keep doing *that*—I mean don't look at me that way."

"What way?"

"That innocent way—that look that makes me want to do so many dirty things to you."

I want to throw myself back onto the bed and let him do whatever he wants. I want to be his—to be freed for a moment from whatever it is that makes me so scared sometimes. I give him a small smile and begin to move my hand again. I want to take his boxers off, but I'm afraid to. A moan escapes his lips and I tighten my grip; I want to hear that sound again. I don't know if I should move my hand faster or not, so I keep my movements slow and tight, and he seems to like it. I lean in and press my lips against the clammy skin of his neck, causing him to moan again.

"Fuck, Tess, your hand feels so good wrapped around me." I give him a little tighter squeeze and he winces. "Not that hard, baby," he says in a voice that's soft and sounds like it could never be the same one that mocked me before.

"Sorry," I say and kiss his neck again. My tongue runs over the skin beneath his ear and his body jumps. His hands go to my chest and he cups my breasts beneath his hands.

"Can I. Take. Off. Your . . . bra?"

His voice is so uncontrolled and raspy; I'm amazed by the effect I am having on him. I nod and his eyes light up in excitement. His hands are shaky as he reaches under the shirt and up my back, unclasping my bra as soon as his fingers touch the strap with a dexterity that makes me think for a minute about how many times he has done this before. I force the thoughts to the back of my mind, and Hardin slides the straps down my arms, making me let go of him. Tossing my bra off the bed, he returns his hands up under my shirt and grabs hold of my breasts again. His fingers lightly pinch my nipples as he leans forward to kiss me. I moan into his mouth and reach down and grab his length again.

"Oh, Tessa, I'm going to come," he says, and I feel the wetness growing in my panties even though he is only touching my chest. I feel like I may come, too, from his moans and his gentle assault against my breasts alone. His legs tense under me and his kiss becomes sloppier. His hands drop down by his sides, and I feel a wetness spread through his boxers and pull my hand away. I have never made anyone else come before. My chest heats, filling with a strange new sense that I'm now one step closer to being a woman. Staring down at the wet spot on Hardin's boxers, I love the control I feel over him. I love that I could bring his body pleasure the way he does mine.

Hardin's head rolls back and he takes a few deep breaths while I sit on his thighs, unsure what to do. After a moment, his eyes open and he lifts his head back up to look at me. A lazy smile crosses his face and he leans forward to kiss me on my forehead.

"I have never come like that before," he says, and I am back to being embarrassed.

"It was that bad?" I ask and try to move off his legs. He stops me.

"What? No, you were that good. It usually takes more than someone just grabbing me through my boxers."

A pang of jealousy hits me. I don't want to think about all the other girls that have made Hardin feel this way. He takes in my silence and cups my cheek, brushing his thumb along my temple. I am comforted by the fact that the others had to do more than I did, but I still wish there *weren't* any others. I don't know why I bother to feel this way; Hardin and I are still unresolved. We are never going to date or be anything other than this, but right now, I just want to live in the moment, just the two of us. I laugh a little as the thought crosses my mind. I am not a "live in the moment" type of person at all.

"What are you thinking?" he asks, but I shake my head. I don't want to tell him about my jealous thoughts. It's not fair, and I don't want that conversation.

"Oh come on, Tessa, just tell me," he says, and I shake my head again. In a very un-Hardin move he grabs hold of my hips and begins to tickle me. I scream with laughter and fall off him and onto the soft bed. He continues to tickle me until I can't breathe. His laughter booms through the room—and it's the most beautiful sound I have ever heard. I have never heard him laugh this way, and something tells me hardly anyone has. Despite his flaws, his many flaws, I consider myself lucky to see him in this moment.

"Okay . . . okay! I will tell you!" I screech and he stops.

"Good choice," he says. But looking down, he adds, "But hold that thought. I need to change my boxers."

I blush.

chapter thirty-four

Hardin goes over to his dresser and opens the top drawer, pulling out a pair of blue-and-white plaid boxers, and holds them up in the air with a disgusted look on his face.

"What?" I ask, and prop my head up on my elbow and look at him.

"These are hideous," he says.

I laugh, but I'm also pleased that the earlier secret about whether or not there were clothes in the dresser is now settled at least. Landon's mother or Hardin's father must have purchased all the clothes in the room for Hardin. Which is sad, really, that they would buy clothes and fill the dresser in hopes that Hardin would come around sometime.

"They aren't so bad," I tell him, and he rolls his eyes. I doubt anything will look as good as Hardin's usual black boxer briefs, but then again I can't imagine anything looking actually *bad* on him.

"Well, beggars can't be choosers. Back in a minute," he says and walks out of the room wearing only his wet boxers.

Oh God, what if Landon sees him? I will be humiliated. I need to find Landon first thing in the morning to explain the turn of events. But, really, what am I going to say? *It's not what it looked like. We were just talking and then I agreed to stay the night, and somehow I ended up in my panties and a T shirt, and then gave him the closest thing to a hand job that I know of?* That sounds terrible.

I lay my head onto the pillows and stare at the ceiling. I consider getting up and checking my phone but decide against it. The last thing I need right now is to read texts from Noah. He is probably panicking, but, honestly, as long as he doesn't tell my mother, I don't care as much as I should. If I'm completely honest with myself, I haven't felt the same about Noah since I kissed Hardin for the first time.

I know I love Noah; I have always loved Noah. But I'm beginning to question whether I really love him as a boyfriend and someone I could spend my life with, or if I love him because he has always been such a stable person in my life. He's always been there for me—and on paper we're perfect for each other—but I can't ignore the way I feel when I'm with Hardin. I've never had these types of feelings before. Not just when we're on top of each other, but the way he gives me butterflies just by looking at me, the way I find myself desperately wanting to see him even when I'm fuming mad at him, and, mostly, the way he always invades my thoughts even when I try to convince myself that I hate him.

Hardin has gotten under my skin no matter how hard I try to deny it. I'm in his bed instead of with Noah. On cue, the door opens and I am snapped from my thoughts. I look up and see Hardin in the clean plaid boxers and giggle. They are a little too big, and much longer than his briefs, but they still look great.

"I like them." I smile and he glares at me before turning out the light and switching on the television. He climbs back onto the bed and lies down close to me.

"So, what were you going to tell me?" he asks, and I cringe. I was hoping he wouldn't bring it up again.

"Don't be shy now, you've just made me come in my boxers," he jokes and then pulls me closer to him. I bury my head in the pillow, and he laughs.

I pull my head up and Hardin tucks my hair behind my ear before giving me a soft kiss on my lips. It's the first time he has kissed me that tenderly, and yet it feels more intimate than when we kiss with tongue. He lays his head back on the pillow and changes the channel. I want him to hold me until I fall asleep, but I get the feeling Hardin is not a cuddling type of guy.

I want to be good for you, Tess. Hardin's words from earlier tonight play in my head and I wonder if he meant them or if he was just really drunk.

"Are you still drunk?" I ask and lay my head on his chest. His body stills but he doesn't push me off.

"No, I think our little screaming match in the yard sobered me up," he says. One of his hands is holding the remote and the other is hanging in the air awkwardly as if he doesn't know what to do with it.

"Oh, well, at least something good came out of it."

He turns his head and looks down at me. "Yeah, I guess so," he says, and finally puts his hand on my back. It's an amazing feeling having him hold me. No matter what terrible thing he says to me tomorrow, he can't take this moment away from me. This is my new favorite place to be, my head on his chest and his arm on my back.

"I think I actually like drunk Hardin better." I yawn.

"Is that so?" he says and turns to look at me again.

"Maybe," I tease and close my eyes.

"You're terrible at distractions; now, tell me."

I might as well just tell him. I know he isn't going to drop it.

"Well, I was just thinking of all the girls you've . . . you know, done things with." I try to hide my face in his chest, but he drops the remote on the bed and tilts my chin up to look at him.

"Why were you thinking about that?"

"I don't know . . . because I have literally no experience and you have a lot. Steph included," I answer. The image of the two of them together makes me nauseous.

"Are you jealous, Tess?" His voice is full of humor.

"No, of course not," I lie.

"So you don't mind if I tell you a few details, then?"

"No! Please don't!" I beg, and he chuckles and wraps his arm a little tighter around me.

He doesn't say anything else about it, and I could not be more relieved. I couldn't bear to hear the details of his flings. I feel my eyes getting heavier and try to focus on the television. I am so comfortable lying here in his arms.

"You're not going to sleep, are you? It's still early," he says, barely breaking through my haze.

"Is it?" It feels like it has to be at least two in the morning. I arrived here around nine.

"Yeah, it's only midnight."

"That isn't early." I yawn again.

"To me it is. Plus, I want to return the favor."

What?

Oh.

My skin is starting to tingle already.

"You want me to, don't you?" he purrs, and I gulp. Of course I do. I look up at him and try to hide my eager smile. He notices and with a swift, delicate motion flips us over so he is hovering above me. He supports his weight with one arm while his other hand reaches lower. I bring my leg up to his side, and when my knee bends he runs his hand from my ankle to the top of my thigh.

"So soft," he says and repeats the motion. He gives my thigh a light squeeze and my skin is covered in goose bumps within seconds. Hardin leans over and places a single kiss on the side of my knee, causing my leg to jerk. He grabs it and laughs, hooking his arm around it.

What is he going to do? The anticipation is driving me crazy.

"I want to taste you, Tessa," he says, eyes locked on mine to gauge my reaction.

My mouth is instantly parched. *Why is he asking to kiss me, when he knows he can do that anytime?* I part my lips and wait for him.

"No. Down *here*," he corrects me, bringing his hand in between my legs. My lack of experience must astound him, but he at least tries to fight his smile. I frown at him and his finger touches me over my panties, causing me to suck in a breath. His finger makes soft strokes over my sex as he continues to look into my eyes.

"You're already wet for me." His voice is raspier than usual. His hot breath stings my ear and he runs his tongue along my earlobe.

"Talk to me, Tessa. Tell me how badly you want it." He smirks and I squirm as he applies more pressure to my sensitive area.

I can't find my voice because my body is on fire from his touch. After a few more seconds he pulls his hand away and I whimper.

"I didn't want you to stop," I whine.

"You didn't say anything," he snaps, and I recoil. I don't want this Hardin. I want the laughing, playful Hardin.

"Couldn't you tell?" I ask him and move to sit up.

He pulls himself up and sits on my thighs, holding his weight on his parted knees. He brushes his fingers across the tops of my thighs and my body instantly reacts, shifting my hips to meet his.

"Say it," Hardin instructs. I know that he is well aware that I do; he just wants to make me say it aloud. I nod and he waves his finger back and forth in front of me.

"No nodding, just tell me what you want, baby," he says, and climbs off of my knees. I mentally weigh the pros and cons of this situation. Is the humiliation of telling Hardin that I want him to . . . kiss me down there worth the feeling I will get from him doing it? If it feels anywhere near as good as what Hardin did to me with his fingers the other day, then I know it's worth it. I reach out and grab his bare shoulder to stop him from moving any farther away from me. I'm overthinking this, I know I am, but my mind won't stop racing.

"I want you to." I move closer to him.

"Want me to what, Theresa?" He has to be kidding me; he knows exactly what he's doing.

"You know . . . to kiss me," I say and his smile grows. He leans over and plants a kiss on my lips. I roll my eyes and he kisses my lips again.

"Is that what you wanted?" he says with a smirk and I swat his arm. He is going to make me beg him.

"Kiss me . . . there." I blush and cover my face with my hands. He pulls them away, laughing, and I frown at him. "You're embarrassing me on purpose." I scowl. His hands are still on mine.

"I'm not meaning to embarrass you. I just want to hear you say what you want from me."

"Never mind, Hardin," I say and sigh loudly. Because I *am* embarrassed and maybe my hormones are going haywire and messing with my emotions but now the moment has passed and I'm annoyed with his ego and constant need to goad me. I roll over and lie on my side, facing away from him, and cover myself with the blanket.

"Hey, I'm sorry," he says, but I ignore him. I know part of me is just annoyed at myself that being around Hardin has turned me into a typical hormonal teenager.

"Good night, Hardin," I snap and hear him sigh. He mutters something under his breath that sounds like "fine," but I don't ask him to repeat it. I force my eyes closed and try to think of anything besides Hardin's tongue or the way his arm just draped across my body as I fall asleep.

chapter thirty-five

I am hot, too hot. I try to pull the covers off me, but they won't budge. When my eyes open, the night before comes flooding into my mind: Hardin screaming at me in the yard, the scotch on his breath, the broken glass in the kitchen, Hardin kissing me, Hardin moaning as I touched him, his wet boxers. I try to lift myself, but he's too heavy, his head lying across my chest and his arm wrapped around my waist, his body cloaking mine. I'm surprised we ended up like this; he must have moved this way in his sleep. I do admit, I don't want to leave this bed, leave Hardin, but I have to. I have to get back to my room. Noah is there. Noah. Noah.

I gently push Hardin off by his shoulder, rolling him onto his back. Then he rolls onto his stomach and groans but doesn't wake.

I hurry to my feet and grab my scattered clothes off the floor. Being the coward that I am, I want to be out of here by the time he wakes. Not that he'll mind; at least he won't have to invest his energy in hurting me on purpose if I leave on my own. This way is better for both of us. Regardless of how we laughed together last night, nothing is the same in the light of day. Hardin will remember how we got along pretty well last night and then will feel the need to be extra hateful to make up for it. It's what he does, and I will not be around this time. For a second last night, the thought had crossed my mind that maybe our night together would change his mind, make him want to have more with me. But I know better, really.

I fold his T-shirt neatly on the dresser and zip my skirt up. My shirt is wrinkled from lying on the floor last night, but that's really the least of my worries at the moment. I slip my feet into my shoes and as I grab hold of the door handle, I think, *One more look back won't hurt.*

I look back to the sleeping Hardin. His messy hair is sprawled onto the pillow, and his arm is now draped over the side of the bed. He looks so peaceful, so beautiful despite the pieces of metal in his face.

I turn back around and turn the door handle.

"Tess?"

My heart drops. I slowly turn back around to Hardin, expecting to see his harsh green eyes glaring at me. But instead, they are closed; a frown is set on his face, but he is still asleep. I can't decide if I'm relieved that he is asleep, or somber that he called out my name. *Is that what he did, or am I hearing things now?*

I jump out of the room and gently close the door behind me. I have no idea how to get out of this house. I walk straight down the hall and I am relieved to find the stairs easily. I pad down the stairs and nearly collide with Landon. My pulse quickens as I try to think of something to say. His eyes scan my face and he stays silent, waiting for an explanation, I assume.

"Landon . . . I . . ." I have no idea what to say.

"Are you okay?" he asks with concern.

"Yeah, I'm fine. I know you must think—"

"I don't think anything. I really do appreciate you coming. I know you don't like Hardin, and it means a lot to me that you would come here to help get him in control."

Oh. He is so nice, too nice. I almost want him to tell me how disgusted he is that I stayed the night with Hardin, that I left my boyfriend alone in my room all night after I took his car and ran to Hardin's rescue, just so I feel as bad as I should.

"So are you and Hardin friends again?" he asks, and I shrug.

"I have no idea what we are. I have no idea what I'm doing. He just . . . he . . ." I break into sobs. Landon wraps his arms around me in a warm and comforting hug.

"It's okay. I know he can be so terrible," Landon says softly. Wait . . . he must think that I'm crying because Hardin did something terrible to me. He would probably never assume that I'm crying because of my feelings for Hardin.

I need to get out of here before I ruin Landon's good opinion of me and before Hardin wakes up. "I have to go. Noah is waiting," I say, and Landon gives me a sympathetic smile before saying goodbye.

I get into Noah's car and drive back to my dorm as fast as I can, crying most of the way there. How will I explain this all to Noah? I know I have to—I can't lie to him. I just can't imagine how much this will hurt him.

I'm a terrible person for doing this to him. Why couldn't I just stay away from Hardin?

I've calmed myself as much as I can before I pull into the student lot. I walk as slow as I can, unsure how I'm going to face Noah.

When I open the door to our room, I find Noah lying back on my small bed, staring at the ceiling. He jumps up when he sees me come in.

"Jesus, Tessa! *Where have you been all night?* I've been calling you nonstop!" he shouts. This is the first time Noah has ever actually raised his voice at me. We've bickered before, but this is a little scary to see.

"I am so, so sorry, Noah. I went to Landon's house because Hardin was drunk and he was breaking things, and the time just got lost, I guess, so by the time we cleaned up, it was really late and my phone was dead," I lie.

I can't believe I'm lying straight to his face—all the times he has been there for me, and here I am lying to him. I know I should tell him but I can't imagine hurting him.

"Why didn't you use someone else's phone?" he says forcefully, but then pauses. "Never mind—Hardin was breaking stuff? Are you okay? Why did you stay there if he was being violent?"

I feel like he is asking me a thousand questions at once, disorienting me.

"He wasn't being violent; he was just drunk. He wouldn't hurt me," I say and cover my mouth, desperately wishing I could push those last words back in.

"What do you mean *he wouldn't hurt you*? You don't even know him, Tessa," he snaps and takes a step toward me.

"I'm just saying that he wouldn't hurt me like physically. I know him well enough to know that. I was just trying to help Landon, who was there, too," I say back.

But Hardin would hurt me, emotionally—he already has, and I'm sure he will try again. And here I am defending him.

"I thought you were going to stop hanging around those type of people? Didn't you promise me and your mom that you would? Tessa, they aren't good for you. You've started drinking and staying out all night, and you left me here all night—I don't know why you even had me come here if you were just going to leave." He sits down on the bed and rests his head on his hands.

"They aren't bad people; you don't know them. When did you become so judgmental?" I ask him. I should be begging for him to forgive me for how badly I've treated him, but I can't help but be irritated by the way he's talking about my friends.

Mostly Hardin, my subconscious reminds me, and I want to slap her.

"I am not judgmental, but you would have never hung out with those Goth people before."

"What? They aren't Gothic, Noah, they're just themselves," I say. I am as surprised by the defiance in my words as Noah is.

"Well, I don't like you hanging out with them—they're changing you. You aren't the same Tessa that I fell in love with." I realize then that his tone hasn't been malicious at all. It's just *sad*.

"Well, Noah—" I begin, and the door flies open. My eyes follow Noah's to an angry Hardin storming into the room.

I look at Hardin, then at Noah, and back to Hardin. There is no way this is going to go well.

chapter thirty-six

"What are you *doing* here?" I ask Hardin, even though I do not want to hear the answer, especially not in front of Noah.

"What do you think? You snuck out on me while I was asleep—what the hell was that?!" he booms. I hold my breath as his voice echoes off the wall. Noah's face flashes with anger and I know that he's beginning to put the puzzle pieces together.

And I'm torn between trying to explain to Noah what is going on and trying to explain to Hardin why I left.

"Answer me!" Hardin yells and stands in front of my face. I'm surprised when Noah steps between us.

"Don't yell at her," he warns Hardin.

I'm frozen in place while Hardin's face twists in anger. Why is he so mad that I left? He was mocking my inexperience last night, and would have kicked me out this morning probably anyway. I need to say something before this all blows up in my face.

"Hardin . . . please don't do this right now," I beg. If he leaves now, I can try to explain to Noah what is going on.

"Do *what*, Theresa?" Hardin asks and walks around Noah. I hope Noah keeps his distance. I don't think Hardin will hesitate to take him down. Noah is pretty buff from soccer, especially compared to Hardin's lean body, but I have no doubt that Hardin can hold his own, and most likely win.

What the hell is happening in my life that I have to worry about Noah and Hardin fighting?

"Hardin, please just go and we will talk about this later," I say, trying to defuse things.

But Noah just shakes his head. "Talk about *what*? What the hell is going on, Tessa?"

Oh God.

"Tell him; go on and tell him," Hardin says.

I can't believe he is doing this. I know how cruel he can be, but this takes it to a whole other level.

"Tell me what, Tessa?" Noah asks, and I can see his stance is an aggressive one, because of Hardin, but it's softening as he wonders about me.

"Nothing, just what you know, that I stayed at Hardin and Landon's last night," I lie. I try to match my gray eyes to Hardin's in hopes that he will stop this now, but he looks away immediately.

"Tell him, Tessa, or I will," Hardin growls.

I know it's all lost. I know there's no hiding anything anymore, and I begin to cry. But I want Noah to hear it from me, not the smirking asshole who's brought us to this point. I'm humiliated—not for myself, but for Noah. He doesn't deserve any of this, and I'm ashamed of the way I've treated him and the confessions I'm going to be forced to make in front of Hardin. "Noah . . . I . . . me and Hardin have been . . ." I start.

"Oh my God," Noah stutters, and his eyes begin to water.

How could I do this to him? What the hell was I thinking? Noah is so kind, and Hardin's cruel enough to break Noah's heart in front of him.

Noah's hands go to his forehead and he shakes his head. "How could you, Tessa? After everything we have been through? When did this start?" Tears stream down his face from his bright blue eyes. I have never felt this terrible   I caused those tears. I look over at Hardin and my hatred for him consumes me so that I shove him instead of answering Noah. Hardin is caught off guard and stumbles backward, but he steadies himself before he falls.

"Noah, I am so sorry. I don't know what I was thinking." I rush over to my boyfriend and try to hug him, but he refuses to let me touch him. And he's probably right to. If I'm being honest, I've not been good to Noah for a while. I don't know what the hell I was thinking. I suppose something crazy like Hardin becoming decent and me breaking up with Noah so I could date him—how stupid can I be? Or that I could just stay away from Hardin and Noah would never know about what happened between us? The problem is that I *can't* stay away from Hardin. I am a moth to his flame, and he never hesitates to burn me. Both were stupid and naïve ideas, but I haven't made one good choice since I've met Hardin.

"I don't know what you were thinking, either," Noah says, with a look of regret and hurt in his eyes. "I don't even know you anymore."

And with that, he walks out the door. Out of my life.

"Noah, please! Wait!" I rush after him, but Hardin grabs my arm and tries to pull me back.

"Don't touch me! I can't believe you! This is low, Hardin, even for you." I scream and jerk my arm out of his grasp. I push him again, hard. I have never pushed anyone in my life before today, and I hate him so much.

"If you go after him, I'm done," he says, and my mouth falls open.

"Done? Done with *what*? Fucking with my emotions? I hate you!" But not wanting him to feed off my rage, I slow down and speak more calmly. "You can't end something that never began."

His hands fall to his sides and his mouth opens but no words come out.

"Noah!" I call and rush out the door. I run down the hall and out across the great lawn, finally catching up to him in the parking lot. He starts walking faster.

"Noah, please listen. I am sorry, so sorry. I was drinking. I know that isn't an excuse, but I . . ." I wipe my eyes and his face softens.

"I can't listen to you anymore . . ." he says. His eyes are red. I reach for his hand, but he pulls away.

"Noah, please, I am so sorry. Please forgive me. Please." I can't lose him. I just can't.

Reaching his car, he runs a hand over his perfectly gelled hair, then turns to face me. "I just need some time, Tessa. I don't know what to think right now."

I sigh in defeat, not knowing what to say to that. He just needs time to get over this and we can go back to normal. He just needs time, I tell myself.

"I love you, Tessa," Noah says, then catches me by surprise when he kisses my forehead before climbing into his car and driving away.

chapter thirty-seven

Being the disgusting person that he is, Hardin is sitting on my bed when I return. Visions of me grabbing the lamp and bashing him in the head flash through my mind, but I don't have the energy to fight with him.

"I'm not going to apologize," Hardin tells me as I walk past him toward Steph's bed. I will not sit on my bed while he's on it.

"I know you aren't," I say and lie back.

I won't let him bait me into this fight, and I don't expect him to apologize. I know him better by now. Well, recent history would say that I don't know him at all. Last night I thought he was just an angry boy whose father left him, and that he held on to that hurt, using the only emotion he could to keep people out. This morning, I see that he is just a terrible, hateful person. There is nothing good about Hardin. At any moment I believed there was, it was only because that is what he tricked me into believing.

"He needed to know," he says.

I bite down on my lip to prevent the tears from returning. I stay quiet until I hear Hardin get up and move toward me. "Just go, Hardin," I say, but when I look up he is standing over me. When he sits down on the bed, I jump up.

"He needed to know," he repeats, and anger boils inside me. I know he just wants to get a rise out of me.

"*Why*, Hardin? *Why* did he need to know? How could hurting him possibly be a good thing? You weren't affected one bit by him not knowing—you could have gone on with your day without telling him. You had no right to do that to him, or me." I feel the tears coming again but this time I can't stop them.

"I would want to know if I was him," he says, his voice steady and cold.

"You aren't him, though, and you never will be. I was stupid to think you could possibly be anything even close to him. And since when do you care about what is right?"

"Don't you dare compare me to him," he snaps. I hate the way he chooses only one of my statements to respond to, and that he usually warps what I'm saying to better provoke himself. He stands up and moves toward me, but I back away to the other side of the bed.

"There is no comparison. Don't you get that by now? You are a cruel and disgusting jerk who doesn't give a shit about anyone but yourself. And he—he loves me. *He* is willing to try to forgive me for my mistakes." I stare into his eyes. "My terrible mistakes," I add.

Hardin takes a step back as if I'd pushed him. "Forgive you?"

"Yeah, he will forgive me for this. I know he will. Because he loves me, so your pathetic plan to get him to break up with me so you can sit back and laugh didn't work. Now get out of my room."

"That wasn't . . . I—" he starts to say, but I cut him off. I've wasted enough time on him already.

"Get out! I know you're probably already plotting your next move against me, but guess what, Hardin? It isn't going to work anymore. Now get the fuck out of my room!" I am surprised at my harsh words, but I don't feel bad for using them against Hardin.

"That isn't what I'm doing, Tess. I thought after last night . . . I don't know, I thought you and I . . ." He seems to be at a loss for words, which is a first. Part of me, a huge part of me, is dying to know what he is going to say, but this is how I got so tangled in his web in the first place. He uses my curiosity against me, like it's all a game to him. I furiously wipe my eyes, thankful I didn't wear makeup yesterday.

"You aren't really expecting me to buy that, are you? That you *feel* something about me?"

I need to stop and he needs to leave before his claws sink deeper into me.

"Of course I do, Tessa. You make me feel so—"

"No! I don't want to hear it, Hardin. I know you're lying, and this is your sick way of getting off. To make me believe that you could possibly feel the same way about me as I do about you, and then will flip the switch. I know how this goes by now, and I won't keep it going."

"Feel the same way you do? Are you saying that you . . . you have feelings for me?" His eyes flash with what appears to be hope. He is a much better actor than I thought.

He knows I do, he has to know that. What other reason could there be for me to keep this unhealthy cycle between us going? With a fear I've never felt before, I realize that though I had barely admitted my feelings for Hardin to myself, I now have put them out there in front of him, giving him easy access to smash them. Worse than he already has.

I feel my walls slowly being torn down by the way Hardin is looking at me and I can't let it happen. "Leave, Hardin. I won't ask again. If you don't leave I will call campus security."

"Tess, please answer me," he begs.

"Don't call me Tess; that name is reserved for family, *friends,* for people who actually care about me—now leave!" I yell, much louder than I had planned. I need him to get out and get away from me. I hate when he calls me Theresa, but I hate when he calls me Tess even more. Something about the way his lips move when he says it makes it sound so intimate, so lovely. Damn it, Tessa. Just stop.

"Please, I need to know if you—"

"What a long weekend, boys and girls—I am exhausted!" Steph says as she bursts into the room, playful exhaustion coloring her words. But when she notices my tearstained cheeks, she stops and her eyes narrow at Hardin.

"What is going on? What did you do?!" she yells at him. "Where is Noah?" she asks and looks at me.

"He left, just like Hardin is about to," I tell her.

"Tessa . . ." Hardin begins.

"Steph, *please* make him leave," I beg and she nods. Hardin's mouth falls open with annoyance at my use of Steph against him. He thought he had me trapped again.

"Let's go, Boy Wonder," she says and grabs his arm, dragging him toward the door.

I stare at the wall until I hear the door shut but immediately hear their voices in the hall.

"What the hell, Hardin? I told you to stay away from her; she is my roommate and she's not like the other girls you mess with. She's nice, innocent, and, honestly, too good for you."

I am pleased and surprised by the way she is sticking up for me. But it still doesn't soothe the pain in my chest. My heart literally hurts. I thought I had experienced heartbreak after my day with Hardin at the stream, but that was nothing compared to how I feel right now. I hate to admit it to myself, but I know that spending the night with Hardin last night made my feelings for him so much stronger than they already were. Hearing him laugh while he tickled me, the way he gently kissed my lips, his tattooed arms wrapping around me, the way his eyes fluttered and closed when I traced my fingers over his bare skin—all of it made me fall deeper for him. Those intimate moments between us that made me care for him more also make this hurt so much more. On top of that, I have hurt Noah in a way that I can only pray he forgives me for.

"It's not like that." In his anger his accent has become thick and his words clipped.

"Bullshit, Hardin, I know you. Find someone else to mess around with; there are plenty of other girls. She isn't the type of girl you need to be doing this with; she has a boyfriend and she can't handle this shit."

I don't like hearing her say that I'm too sensitive, like I'm weak or something, but I guess she is right. I have done nothing but cry since I met Hardin, and now he has tried to ruin my relationship with Noah. I don't have what it takes to be something like friends with benefits, regardless of how he makes me feel. I have more respect for myself than that and I'm too emotional.

"Fine. I will stay away from her. But don't bring her to any more parties at my house," he snaps, and I hear him stomping off. As he goes down the hall, his voice recedes, too, as he yells, "I mean it, I don't want to see her again! And if I do, I will ruin her!"

chapter thirty-eight

Steph walks in and right away wraps her tiny arms around me. It's odd that her frail arms can feel so comforting.

"Thank you for making him leave," I say, sobbing, and she hugs me tighter. My tears really are flowing now and I don't see an end in sight.

"Hardin may be my friend, but so are you, and I don't want him upsetting you. I'm sorry, this is all my fault. I knew I should have given my key to Nate, and I shouldn't have let him come around you all the time. He can be a real dick."

"No, it's not your fault at all. I am sorry, I don't want to come in between your friendship."

"Oh please," she says.

I pull out of her embrace and see the look of concern on her face. I appreciate her being here with me more than she will ever know. I feel completely alone: Noah's taking time to decide whether to break up with me or not, Hardin is an asshole, my mother would lose it if I talked to her about this, and Landon would be disappointed in me if he knew the depth of my situation with Hardin. I literally have no one except this flame-haired, tattooed girl who I never expected would become my friend. But I'm really glad she did.

"Do you want to talk about it?"

I do, actually, I want to get it all off my chest. I tell her everything, from the first time I kissed Hardin, to our day at the stream, to the orgasm I gave him and how he called my name in his sleep, to the way he destroyed every ounce of respect I had for him when he made me tell Noah. Her face goes from concerned to shocked to sad during my story. My shirt is soaked with tears by the time I finish and she is holding my hand.

"Wow, I had no idea that so much happened. You could have told me after the first time. I knew something was up when Hardin showed up here the night we were going to the movies. I had literally just got off the phone with him, then he shows up, so I'd suspected he came here to see you. Listen, Hardin is a good guy, sometimes. I mean, deep down he just doesn't know how to really care for someone the way that you—well, most girls—need to be cared for. If I was you, I would try to make things work with Noah because Hardin isn't capable of being anyone's boyfriend," she says and squeezes my hand.

I know everything she is saying is true and she is right. So why does it hurt so bad?

ON MONDAY MORNING, Landon is leaning against the brick outside the coffeehouse, waiting for me. I wave when I see him, but then I notice he has a blue-purple ring around his left eye. And when I look closer, I see another bruise on his cheek.

"What happened to your eye?!" I exclaim, running up to him. Realization hits me like a truck. "Landon! Did *Hardin* do this?" My voice is shaky.

"Yeah . . ." he admits and I am horrified.

"*Why?* What happened?" I want to kill Hardin for hurting Landon.

"He stormed out of the house after you left and then came back about an hour later. He was so pissed. He started looking around for more stuff to break, so I stopped him. Well, I fought with him. It wasn't so bad, actually. I think both of us got a lot of our anger toward each other out. I got quite a few good hits on him, too," he boasts.

I don't know what to say. I'm surprised at Landon's light tone while talking about fighting with Hardin.

"Are you sure you're okay? Is there anything I can do?" I ask him. I feel like this is my fault. Hardin was mad because of me, but assaulting Landon?

"No, really, I'm okay." He smiles.

While we walk to class he tells me how Hardin's father broke up their fight, luckily arriving home before they killed each other, and how his mother cried when she realized Hardin had broken all her dishes. Though they didn't have any sentimental value, she was hurt that Hardin would do that nonetheless.

"But in other news, much better news, Dakota is coming to visit next weekend. She is coming to the bonfire!" He smiles.

"Bonfire?"

"Yeah, haven't you seen the signs all over campus? It's an annual thing, to start the new year. Everyone goes. I am not usually into stuff like that, but it's actually a pretty good time. Noah should come up again. We can make a double date out of it."

I smile and nod. Maybe inviting Noah would show him I do have some good friends, like Landon. I know Hardin and Landon—I mean, Noah and Landon would get along great, and I really want to meet Dakota.

Now that Landon has mentioned the bonfire, I notice signs littering almost every wall. I guess I was just too distracted all week to notice.

Before I know it, I'm in Literature and begin scanning the room for Hardin, despite my subconscious shouting at me not to. When I don't see him his voice plays in my head: *I will ruin her.*

What could he possibly do that's worse than outing me in front of Noah? I don't know, but I start imagining things until Landon breaks me out of my zone.

"I don't think he's here. I heard him talking to that Zed guy about switching his classes around. Darn, I do wish you could see *his* black eye." Landon smiles at me and my eyes snap to the front of the room.

I want to deny that I was looking for Hardin, but I know I can't. Hardin has a black eye? I hope he is okay; no, I don't, actually. I hope it hurts like hell.

"Oh, okay," I mumble and pick at my skirt.

Landon doesn't mention Hardin for the rest of the class.

THE REST OF THE WEEK is exactly the same way: I don't talk about Hardin to anyone and no one mentions him to me. Tristan has been hanging out in our room all week, but I don't mind. I actually really like him and he makes Steph laugh, and even me, too, sometimes, despite what seems to be the worst week of my life. I've just been wearing whatever is clean and handy and pulling my hair into a bun every day. My short-lived affair with eyeliner has ended and I am back to my normal routine.

Sleep, class, study, eat, sleep, class, study, eat.

By Friday, Steph's clearly making an effort to get this spinster out and about.

"Come on, Tessa, it's Friday. Just come with us and we'll drop you back off before we go to Har . . . I mean the party," she begs, but I shake my head. I don't feel like doing anything. I need to study and call my mother. I've been dodging her calls all week, and I need to call Noah and find out if he's made a decision. I've been giving him his space all week, only sending him a few friendly texts in hopes that he will come around. I really want him to come to the bonfire next Friday.

"I think I will pass . . . I'm looking at cars tomorrow, so I need my rest," I half lie. I really am going to look at cars tomorrow but I know I won't be getting rest sitting here alone with my thoughts about Noah's uncertainty, about how Hardin was obviously serious about staying away from me—which I'm really glad he's done.

I just can't shake him from my thoughts. *I just need more time*, I keep telling myself.

But the way he acted like he wanted something from me the last time I saw him, that got under my skin.

My thoughts drift off to a place where Hardin was pleasant and funny and we got along. A place where we could date, really date, and he would take me out to the movies or to dinner. He would put his arm around me and be proud that I was his; he would drape his jacket over my shoulders if I was cold and kiss me good night, promising me that he would see me tomorrow.

"Tessa?" Steph says and my thoughts disappear like a puff of smoke. They weren't reality and the boy in my daydream would never be Hardin.

"Oh come on, you've been wearing those fuzzy cloud pants all week," Tristan teases and I laugh. These pants are my favorite to wear to bed, especially when I am sick, or going through a breakup, or two. I'm still confused about how Hardin and I ended something that was nothing to begin with.

"Okay. Okay, but you need to drop me off right after dinner because I have to get up early," I warn.

Steph claps and jumps up and down. "Yay! Just please let me do you a favor?" she asks with an innocent smile while she bats her lashes.

"What?" I whine, knowing she is up to no good.

"Let me give you a little makeover? Pleeeaassee!" She draws out the word for dramatic purposes.

"No. Way." I can picture myself with pink hair and pounds of eyeliner, wearing only a bra for a shirt.

"Nothing too dramatic, I just want to make you look . . . like you haven't been hibernating in pajamas all week." She smiles and Tristan tries to stifle his laugh.

And when I give in and say, "Fine," she begins clapping again.

chapter thirty-nine

After Steph has plucked my eyebrows—a procedure that hurt worse than I ever imagined—she turns me around and refuses to let me see myself until she's done putting on my makeup. I fight the nervous feeling in my stomach as she dusts powder onto my face. I remind her over and over not to put too much makeup on me, and she promises over and over that she won't. She brushes my hair and curls it before coating my hair and half of the room with hair spray.

"Makeup and hair: done! Let's get you changed, and then you can see yourself. I have a few things that will fit you." She is obviously proud of her work. I just hope that I don't look like a clown. Following her to the closet, I try to sneak a peek in her small mirror but she yanks me away.

"Here, put this on," she says, pulling a black dress off a hanger. "Out, you!" she shouts at Tristan, and he laughs but graciously leaves the room.

The dress is strapless and looks incredibly short. "I can't wear this!"

"Fine . . . how about this one?" She pulls another black dress out. She must have at least ten. This one looks longer than the last and has two thick straps. The neckline worries me because it's in the shape of a heart and my bust isn't small like hers.

When I take too long looking it over, she sighs. "Just try it, please?"

I oblige and take my comfortable pajamas off and fold them

into a neat pile. She rolls her eyes at me playfully and I smile while stepping into the dress. I pull it up my body and it feels a little snug before it's even zipped. Steph and I aren't that much different in size but she is taller and I'm curvier. The material has a slight shine to it and feels silky. The bottom of the dress reaches halfway down my thigh. It isn't as short as I thought it would be, but it is shorter than anything I would ever wear. I feel almost naked with my legs this exposed. My fingers tug at the material to try to pull it down a little.

"You want some tights?" she asks.

"Yeah, I just feel so . . . naked." I laugh. She digs into her drawer and pulls out two different pairs of tights. "These are plain black, and these have a lace print."

Lace tights are just too much for me, especially given the fact that I probably have ten pounds of makeup on. I grab the plain ones and slide them on my legs while Steph digs through her closet for shoes.

"I can't wear heels!" I remind her. I literally can't; I waddle like an injured penguin in them. "Well, I have low heels or wedges. Tessa, I'm sorry but your Toms just won't work with this dress."

I scowl at her jokingly. I am perfectly fine wearing Toms every day. She pulls out a pair of black heels with silver beading on the front, and I have to admit they catch my eye. I could never wear them, but for once I wish I could.

"You like these?"

I nod. "Yeah, but I can't pull them off," I tell her and she frowns.

"Yes, you can, they strap around your ankle to prevent you from falling."

"Is that what the strap is actually for?" I ask.

She laughs. "No, but it helps with that." She laughs again. "Just try them."

I sit on the bed and stretch my legs out, gesturing for her to put them on me.

She helps me stand up and I take a few steps. The straps really do help with my balance.

"I can't wait any longer! Look at yourself," she says and opens the other closet door. I look in the full-body mirror and gasp.

Who the heck is that? My reflection looks just like me, but a lot better. I was afraid she would go overboard on my makeup, but she didn't. My gray eyes look lighter against the chestnut eye shadow, and the pink blush on my cheeks makes my cheekbones more prominent. My hair looks shiny and is curled into big waves, not the small, stringy curls I was expecting.

"I *am* impressed." I smile and look closer. I poke my cheek to make sure what I'm seeing is real.

"See, you are still you. Just a more sexy, well-kept you." She giggles and calls for Tristan to join us.

He opens the door and his lips part. "Where is Tessa?" he asks and looks around the room playfully. He picks up a pillow and looks under it.

"What do you think?" I ask and tug the dress down again.

"You look great, really great." He smiles and wraps his arm around Steph's waist. She leans in and I look away.

"Oh, one more thing," she says and reaches over to the dresser, pulling out a tube of lip gloss and puckering her lips. I close my eyes and do the same while she rubs the sticky gloss across my lips.

"Ready?" Tristan asks and she nods.

As we head out, I grab my purse and throw a pair of Toms inside, just in case.

DURING THE DRIVE I sit in the back and stare out the window, letting my mind wander. When we arrive at the restaurant, I cringe at the number of motorcycles outside. I had assumed we would be going somewhere like T.G.I. Friday's or Applebee's, not a biker bar and grill. When we walk inside I feel like everyone is staring at me, even though they probably aren't.

Steph grabs a hold of my hand and pulls me along as they walk to a booth in the back. "Nate is coming. That's okay, right?" she asks as we take our seats.

"Yeah, of course," I tell her. As long as it's not Hardin, I don't mind. Besides, some company would be nice, because right now I feel like the third wheel.

A woman with even more tattoos than Steph and Tristan strides over to the table and takes our drink order. Steph and Tristan both order beers. This must be why they like to come here, because they don't card. The woman raises an eyebrow when I order a Coke, but I don't want to drink. I have studying to do when I get back to my room. Minutes later she brings our drinks and I'm taking a big swig when I hear a wolf whistle as Nate and Zed walk toward our table. As they get closer, Molly's pink hair comes into view . . . followed by Hardin.

I spit the Coke back into my cup.

Steph's eyes widen as she lays eyes on Hardin and she looks at me. "I swear I didn't know he was coming. We can leave now if you want," she whispers as Zed slides into the booth next to me. I have to force myself not to look toward Hardin.

"Whoa, Tessa, you look superhot!" Zed proclaims, and I blush. "Really, like wow! I've never seen you like this."

I thank him by way of a small smile. Nate, Molly, and Hardin sit in the booth behind us. I want to ask Steph to trade seats with me so my back will be to Hardin, but I can't bring myself to. I will just avoid eye contact with him the entire time. I can do it.

"You do look smokin', Tessa," Nate says over the divider, and I smile because I'm not used to all this attention. Hardin hasn't commented on my new look, but I didn't expect him to. I'm just glad he isn't insulting me.

Hardin and Molly are sitting right in my line of sight. I can see Hardin's entire face through the space between Steph and Tristan's shoulders.

If I just look once, it couldn't hurt . . . Stealing a peek before I can stop myself, I instantly regret it. Hardin's arm is hooked around Molly's shoulders.

Jealousy tears through me—my punishment for looking at him when I shouldn't be. Of course they are probably messing around again. Or still. They probably never stopped. I remember how comfortable she was straddling him at the party, and I swallow down the bile rising in my throat. Hardin is free to do whatever or whoever he pleases.

"She does look great, doesn't she?" Steph encourages them and they all nod.

I can feel Hardin's eyes on me but I can't look over at him again. He is wearing a white T-shirt that I'm sure lets his tattoos show through, and his hair is perfectly messed up, but I don't care. I don't care how good he looks or how skanky Molly is dressed.

She's so irritating, with her stupid pink hair and her skanky clothes. She is a slut. I'm surprised by my thoughts and my anger toward her, but it's true. And I really don't like her. I don't think I've actually ever called anyone a slut, even in my head.

So of course she picks right now to compliment me. "You do look good, girl, better than ever before!" she says and then leans into Hardin's chest.

I make eye contact with her and fake a smile.

"Mind if I have a sip?" Zed asks, but grabs my cup before I really answer.

I let him drink out of my glass, which I'm usually against, but

I am so uncomfortable right now that I can't think straight. He gulps down half my Coke and I nudge him.

"Sorry, babe, I'll order you another," he says smoothly. He really is very attractive and looks more like a model than a college student. If he didn't have so many tattoos, he probably *would* be a model.

A noise comes from the other booth, and my eyes dart to Hardin. He clears his throat loudly, staring at me with blazing eyes. I want to look away, but I can't. I'm caught in his gaze as Zed lifts his arm up and rests it on the back of the booth, directly behind me.

Hardin's eyes narrow and I decide to have a little fun.

Remembering that he was pretty adamant about me not hanging out with Zed before, I lean into Zed ever so slightly. Hardin's eyes go wide, but he quickly recovers. I know how immature and ridiculous this whole thing is, but I don't care. If I have to be around him, I want him to be as uncomfortable as I am.

The biker woman returns and takes everyone's food order. I go with a burger and fries, minus the ketchup, and everyone else orders hot wings. She brings Hardin a Coke and the rest of them another round of beers. I am still waiting on my Coke but I don't want to be rude by pointing that out to the woman.

"They have the best wings here," Zed informs me and I smile at him.

"So are you going to the bonfire next weekend?" I ask him.

"I don't know, it's not really my scene." He takes a drink of his beer and brings his arm down from the booth to rest fully over my shoulder. "Are you going?"

I don't look his way, but I imagine Hardin's irritation at this. Truth is, I do feel guilty flirting with him this way, and I've never really tried to flirt with anyone before, so I'm sure I am terrible at it. "Yeah, with Landon."

Everyone bursts into laughter. "Landon *Gibson*?" Zed asks, still laughing.

"Yeah, he's my friend," I snap. I don't like the way they are all laughing at him.

"He would go to the bonfire! He is such a lame," Molly says, and I glare at her.

"No, he isn't, actually. He is really cool," I say in his defense. I understand that my definition of cool is not the same as theirs, but mine is better.

"*Landon Gibson* and *cool* do not belong in the same sentence," Molly says and brushes Hardin's hair back off his forehead.

I hate her.

"Well, sorry if he isn't cool enough to hang out with you guys, but he is . . ." I start to shout and sit up straighter in the booth, knocking Zed's arm off my shoulders.

"Whoa, Tessa, calm down. We are just teasing," Nate says and Molly smirks at me. I get the feeling she doesn't care for me much, either.

"Well, I don't like when people tease my friends, especially when he isn't here to defend himself." I need to calm down . . . My emotions are running wild from being around Hardin and the way he's hanging all over Molly in front of me.

"Okay, okay, I'm sorry. Besides, I do gotta give him some credit for that black eye he gave Hardin," Zed says and wraps his arm back around me. Everyone excerpt Hardin laughs, even me.

"Yeah, good thing that professor broke the fight up, or Hardin would have gotten beat even worse by the loser—" Nate says and then looks at me. "Sorry, it slipped," he says and gives me an apologetic smile.

A professor? Their fight wasn't broken up by a professor—it was broken up by Hardin's dad. Either Landon lied, or . . . wait, I wonder if these guys even know Hardin and Landon are soon to be stepbrothers. I look at Hardin, who now looks worried. He lied to them. I should call him out on it right now in front of everyone.

But I can't. I'm not like him. I find it harder to hurt people than he does.

Except Noah, my subconscious reminds me, and I push her back.

"Well, I think the bonfire will be fun," I say.

Zed looks at me with interest. "Maybe I will make an appearance after all."

"I'm going," Hardin adds randomly from the other booth.

Everyone turns to look at him, and Molly laughs. "Yeah, sure you are." She rolls her eyes and laughs again.

"No, really, it won't be so bad," Hardin softly insists, earning another eye-rolling from Molly.

Hardin going because Zed said he was? Maybe I'm a better flirt than I thought.

The server brings out our food and hands me my burger. It looks great, except for the ketchup dripping off the side. My nose scrunches up and I try to wipe some of it off with a napkin. I hate sending food back, and I'm already having a hard enough time tonight. The last thing I need is to draw even more attention to myself.

Talk of the party tonight circles the booths while everyone digs into their wings and I pick at my fries. Eventually the server stops back and asks if we need anything else.

"No, I think we're good," Tristan starts to say, and she begins to walk away.

"Wait. She ordered her burger with no ketchup," Hardin says loudly, and I drop a fry onto the plate.

The waitress looks at me with concern. "I'm sorry about that. Do you want me to take it back?"

I'm so embarrassed, all I can do is shake my head.

"Yeah. She does," Hardin answers for me.

What the hell is he doing? And how did he even know it had ketchup? He is just trying to make me uncomfortable.

"Here, honey, give me your plate." She smiles and holds her hand out. "I'll bring you a new one." I hand it to her and look down while I thank her.

"What was that?" I hear Molly ask Hardin. She should really work on her whispering voice.

"Nothing, she doesn't like ketchup," he simply says and she huffs before taking a drink of her beer.

"So?" Molly says and Hardin glares at her.

"So, nothing. Just drop it."

At least I know I am not the only one he is rude to.

My new food sans ketchup arrives, and I eat most of it despite my lack of appetite. Zed ends up paying for my meal, which is both nice and awkward at the same time. Hardin's annoyance seems to grow as Zed puts his arm around me yet again on the walk outside.

"Logan says the party is already *packed!*" Nate says, reading a text.

"You should ride with me there," Zed offers, then frowns when I shake my head.

"Oh, I am not going to the party. Tristan is going to take me back."

"I can take her back to her room since I drove," Hardin says.

I almost trip over my feet at this, but fortunately Steph grabs hold of me and smiles at Hardin. "No, Tristan and I will take her. Zed can ride with us, too."

If looks could kill, Steph would be collapsing on the floor right now.

Hardin turns to Tristan. "You don't want to drive drunk on campus; the police are going to be looking for people to give tickets to because it's Friday."

Steph looks at me, waiting for me to speak up, but I don't know what to say. I don't want to be in the car with Hardin alone, but I don't want to drive with Tristan when he has been drinking. I shrug and lean into Zed while they settle this among themselves.

"Great, let's drop her off and then go have some fun," Molly tells Hardin, but he shakes his head.

"No, you ride with Tristan and Steph," he says forcefully and Molly shrinks.

"For God's sake can we just get in the cars and go!" Nate whines and pulls his keys out.

"Yeah, let's go, Tessa," Hardin says and I look up at Zed and then at Steph.

"Tessa!" Hardin barks again as he unlocks his car door. He looks back at me and I get the feeling that if I don't follow he will drag me to the car. But why would he even want to be around me if he told Steph that I had better not come around? He disappears inside the car and starts the engine.

"It'll be okay, just text me as soon as you get back to the room," Steph says, and I nod and walk to Hardin's car. My curiosity gets the best of me, and I have to know what his intentions are. I just have to.

chapter forty

No matter how hard I tried to avoid seeing him all week, I somehow end up in his car with him. He doesn't look at me as I get in or while I buckle my seat belt. I tug at the dress again, trying to pull it over my thighs. We sit in silence for a moment and then he pulls out of the parking lot. One saving grace is his not allowing Molly to ride with us—I would have rather walked home than watch her fawn all over him.

"What's with the new look?" he finally asks once we're on the freeway.

"Um . . . well, Steph wanted to try something new with me, I guess." I keep my eyes fixed on the buildings passing by outside the window. His usual aggressive music is playing quietly through the car.

"It's a little over-the-top, don't you think?" he asks and I ball my fists on my lap. So this is his plan today, to insult me the whole way back to my room.

"You didn't have to drive me home, you know." I lean my head against the window, trying to create as much space between us as possible.

"Don't get so defensive; all I am saying is your little makeover is a little extreme."

"Well, good thing I don't care what you think, but considering your distaste for my usual appearance, I'm surprised you don't think I look better like this," I snap and close my eyes. I am already exhausted from being around him and he is sucking the little bit of energy that remained from me.

I hear him chuckle quietly and he turns the radio off completely. "I never said there was anything wrong with your appearance. Your clothes, yes, but I'd much rather see the hideous long skirts than these clothes."

He's trying to explain but his answer doesn't really make sense. He seems to like when Molly dresses this way, only much skankier, so why not me?

"Did you hear me, Tessa?" he asks when I don't respond, and I feel his hand touch my thigh. I jerk away from his touch and open my eyes.

"Yes, I did. I just don't have anything to say about it. If you don't like the way I'm dressed, then don't look at me." One good thing that comes from talking to Hardin is that for once in my life I can say exactly what comes to my mind without worrying about hurting his feelings, seeing as how he has none.

"That is precisely the problem here, isn't it? That I can't stop looking at you." The words leave his mouth and I consider opening the car door and hurling myself onto the freeway.

"Oh! Please!" I laugh. I know he will say just enough nice, yet cryptic, things to make it more painful when he takes them back and throws more insults at me later.

"What? It's true. I approve of the new clothes, but you don't need all this makeup. Regular girls wear tons of makeup to look as good as you do without it."

What? He must have forgotten that we aren't speaking, that he tried to ruin my life less than a week ago, and that we despise each other.

"You don't expect me to thank you, do you?" I half-laugh. He is so confusing; he is brooding and angry one minute and telling me he can't stop looking at me the next.

"Why didn't you tell them the truth about Landon and me?" he asks, changing the subject.

"Because you obviously didn't want them to know."

"Still, why would you keep my secrets?"

"Because they are not mine to tell."

He looks over to me with hooded eyes and a slight smile. "I wouldn't have blamed you if you did, considering what I did with Noah."

"Yeah, well, I am not you."

"No, no you're not," he says, his voice much quieter. And after that he remains silent for the rest of the drive, as do I. I have nothing to say to him.

We finally pull onto campus and he parks in the farthest possible spot from my room. Of course.

I reach for the door handle and Hardin's hand touches my thigh again. "You're not going to thank me?" He smiles and I shake my head.

"Thanks for the ride," I say sarcastically. "Hurry back— Molly's waiting," I add as I climb out. I hope he didn't hear me; I am not sure why I even said that.

"Yeah . . . I better. She sure is fun when she's drunk," he says with a smirk.

Trying to hide the fact that I feel like he just punched me in the stomach, I lean down to look at him through the passenger window and Hardin rolls it down. "Yeah, I am sure she is. Noah's coming soon, anyway," I lie and watch his eyes narrow.

"He is?" Hardin picks at his fingernails, a nervous habit, I assume.

"Yep, see you around." I smile and walk off.

I hear him get out of his car and shut the door. "Wait!" he says and I turn around. "I . . . never mind, I thought you, um, dropped something but you didn't." His cheeks flush. He's clearly lying, and I want to know what he was going to say, but I need to walk away now, so I do just that.

"Bye, Hardin." The words mean more than I let on. I don't look back to see if he is coming after me because I know he isn't.

I TAKE THE HEELS OFF before I even get to my room and walk barefoot the rest of the way through campus. The second I get into the room I put my fuzzy pajamas back on and call Noah. He answers on the second ring.

"Hey," I squeak. My voice sounds too high-pitched. *It's only Noah, why am I so nervous?*

"Hey, Tessa, how was your day today?" he asks softly. He doesn't sound like the same distant Noah that I've gotten all week. I sigh in relief.

"It was okay, actually, I am just hanging out in my room tonight. What are you doing?" I purposely leave out my dinner with Steph and everyone, including Hardin. That will not help my "please forgive me" campaign.

"I just got out of practice. I'm thinking I'll study tonight because I'm helping the new neighbors cut a tree down tomorrow."

He is always helping everyone. He is too good for me.

"I'm just studying tonight, too."

"I wish we could study together," he says, and I smile while picking at the tiny lint balls on my fuzzy socks.

"You do?"

"Yeah, of course, Tessa. I still love you and I miss you. But I have to know that nothing like this will ever happen again. I'm willing to try to put this past us, but you have to promise me you will stay away from him," he says. He doesn't have to say his name.

"Of course I will, I swear—I love you!" Part of me knows that I am desperate to have Noah forgive me only because I don't want to be completely alone and fawning over Hardin, but I ignore it.

After exchanging more "I love you's" with Noah, he agrees to accompany me to the bonfire next weekend and we get off the phone. I look online for the closest car dealerships to campus, and lucky for me there appears to be a good number of used-car lots ready to rip off college students. After noting the addresses of a few, I dig through Steph's makeup bag and finally find the wipes to remove all my makeup. It takes forever, and this obnoxious process alone makes me never want to wear it again, regardless of how good it looked.

chapter forty-one

I take out my notes and textbooks and dive into my studies. I am working on next week's assignments. I like to stay ahead one week at least so there is no chance I fall behind. But my thoughts drift to Hardin and his moodiness, so I'm not really paying attention to the essay I'm supposed to be writing. It has been only two hours since I got off the phone with Noah, but it seems like four.

I decide to find a movie and lie in bed until I fall asleep, settling on *The Vow* despite the fact that I have seen it numerous times. Less than ten minutes into the movie I hear someone cursing outside in the hall. I turn the volume up on my laptop and ignore the cursing; it's Friday, which means drunk people all over the dorms tonight. A few minutes later, I hear the cursing again—a male voice, then a female voice joins in. The guy shouts louder, and then I recognize the accent. It's Hardin.

I jump off my bed and swing open the door to find him sitting on the floor with his back against the wall outside my room. An angry girl with bleach-blond hair is standing over him, scowling with her hands on her hips.

"Hardin?" I say, and he looks up.

A huge grins slides over his face. "Theresa . . ." he says and begins to stand.

"Can you please tell your boyfriend to get away from my door—he spilled vodka all over the floor!" the girl yells.

I look at Hardin. "He's not my . . ." I start to say, but Hardin grabs my hand and pulls me toward my door.

"Sorry for the spill," he says and rolls his eyes at the blonde. She huffs and storms into her room, slamming her door.

"What are you doing here, Hardin?" I ask him. He tries to walk past me and into my room but I block the entrance.

"Why can't I come in, Tessa? I will be nice to your grandpa." He laughs and I roll my eyes. I know he is making fun of Noah.

"He isn't here."

"Why not? Okay, so let me in then," he says, slurring his words.

"No, are you drunk?" My eyes scan his face. His eyes are red, and his smirk gives it all away. He takes his lip between his teeth and puts his hands into his pockets.

"I thought you didn't drink, but now you have been drinking a lot."

"It's only been twice. Chill out," he says, and pushes past me and flops down on my bed. "So why didn't Noah come?"

"I don't know," I lie.

He nods several times, like he's considering this seriously. "Sure. The Gap probably had a sale on cardigans, so he canceled on you." He bursts out laughing, and the energy in the room is such that I can't help but join him.

"So where is Molly?" I ask. "At a Skanks 'R' Us sale?"

Hardin stops for a second and then laughs harder. "That was a terrible attempt at a comeback, Theresa," he jokes, and I kick my foot at where his shins dangle over the bed.

"Either way, you can't stay here. Noah and I are back together, officially."

I notice his smile fade and he rubs his hands against his knees. "Nice pajamas," he says, and I look down.

Why is he being so cavalier? We haven't resolved anything, and the last time I checked we were both staying away from each other.

"Hardin, you have to go."

"Let me guess: one of Noah's conditions for reconciliation was that you have to stay away from me?" His tone is more serious now.

"Yeah, and the last time I checked you and I weren't friends or even speaking. Why did you drop Literature and why did you hit Landon?"

"Why do you always ask so many questions?" he whines. "I don't want to talk about any of that! What were you and your cool pajamas doing before I came in—and why is your light off?" Hardin is much more playful when he has been drinking but I am beginning to wonder why he's begun drinking when he didn't before.

"I was watching a movie," I tell him; maybe if I am nice to him he will answer some of my questions.

"What movie?"

"The Vow," I answer and look at him. I expect him to laugh at me and after a few seconds he does.

"You would like that sappy movie. That is so unrealistic."

"It's based on a true story," I correct him.

"It still seems stupid."

"Have you even seen it?" I ask him, and he shakes his head.

"I don't have to see it to know it's stupid. I can tell you how it ends right now: she gets her memory back and they live happily ever after," he says in a high-pitched voice.

"No, actually that isn't how it ends," I laugh. Hardin makes me insane most of the time, but it's the rare occasions like this when he makes me forget how terrible he can be. I forget that I am supposed to hate him and instead find myself tossing one of Steph's pillows at him. He lets it hit him, even though he could easily block it, and then yelps as if he is actually wounded, so we both laugh again.

"Let me stay and watch it with you," he half-asks, half-demands.

"I don't think that is a good idea," I tell him and he shrugs.

"The worst ideas are often the best ideas. Besides, you wouldn't want me to drive back drunk, would you?" He smiles, and I can't resist even though I know I should.

"Fine, but you are sitting on the floor or Steph's bed."

He pouts but I hold my ground. God knows what will happen if we are both on my small bed. I flush at the possibilities and then scold myself for thinking that way when I *just* promised Noah I would stay away from Hardin. It sounds like such a simple promise to make, but somehow I always find my way to Hardin. Or, like tonight, he finds his way to me.

Hardin slides down to the floor and I take a moment to admire how hot he looks in a plain white T-shirt. The contrast of his black ink and white shirt is perfect and I love the way the ivy branches along the bottom of his neck peak out from under the collar and the black ink can be seen under the material.

I press play and immediately he asks, "Got any popcorn?"

"No, you should have brought your own," I tease and turn the screen so he can see it better from the floor.

"I could always go for another type of snack," he says and I smack his head lightheartedly.

"Watch the movie, and no more talking, or I'll kick you out."

Hardin pretends to zip his lips and hand me a key, which makes me giggle as I pretend to toss it behind me. As Hardin lays his head back against the bed, I feel more calm and at peace than I have all week.

Hardin watches me more than the movie, but I don't care. I notice the way he smiles when I laugh at a funny line, the way he frowns when I sob over Paige losing her memory, and the way he too sighs with relief when Paige and Leo end up together again in the end.

"So what did you think?" I ask him as I scroll through to find another movie.

"Utter rubbish." But he smiles, and I ruffle my hand through his hair before I realize what I'm doing. I sit myself up and he turns toward the wall.

Way to make it awkward, Tessa.

"Let me choose the next movie," he says and reaches for my laptop.

"Who said you could stay for another?" I ask and he rolls his eyes.

"Can't drive. Still drunk," he says with a mischievous grin.

I know he is lying. He's mostly sobered up, but he's right. He should stay. I will deal with whatever Hardin decides to do to me tomorrow, just to be able to spend time with him. I really am pathetic, just like he said. And at the moment, I don't care.

I want to ask him why he came here and why he isn't at his own frat party, but I decide to wait until the movie is over because I know he will turn sour once I begin to question him. Hardin chooses some Batman film that I haven't seen and swears it is the best movie of all time. I laugh at his enthusiasm as he tries to explain the previous movies in the trilogy, but I have no idea what he is talking about. Noah and I always watch movies together, but I have never enjoyed it as much as I do with Hardin. Noah stares at the screen in silence, whereas Hardin banters along, adding hilarious sarcastic entertainment.

"My ass is numb from your hard floor," Hardin complains as soon as the movie begins.

"Steph's bed is nice and soft," I say, and he frowns.

"I won't be able to see the screen from over there. Come on, Tessa, I will keep my hands to myself."

"Fine," I groan and scoot over.

He smiles and lies next to me on his stomach mimicking me, bending his knees and putting his feet in the air. Hardin lays his head on his folded hands, which takes away all his rough edges and leaves him looking adorable. The movie is much better than

I expected, and I must've been more into it than Hardin, because when the credits roll and I look over at him, he's fast asleep.

He looks so perfect, so peaceful in his sleep. I love the way his eyelids flutter and the way his chest moves up and down and the lovely sigh that leaves his full lips. I want to reach over and touch his face, but I don't. Despite the fact that I should wake him and make him leave, I cover him with my blanket and go lock the door before lying down on Steph's bed. I glance over at him again and admire the way the dim light from the television illuminates his face. He looks younger and much happier in his sleep.

As I drift to sleep, I realize that I've spent the night with Hardin a couple of times now, and never with Noah. My subconscious helpfully reminds me that I've done *a lot* of things with Hardin that I've never done with Noah.

chapter forty-two

The faint sound of buzzing floats through my dream in a steady pattern. Why won't it stop? I roll over, not wanting to wake up, but the obnoxious sound insists that I do. I'm disoriented, and forget where I am. And then when I realize I'm in Steph's bed, I still almost forget Hardin is in my room.

How do we always end up together? And more important, where is that annoying noise coming from? In the dim light provided by streetlights just outside the window, I follow the noise and it leads to Hardin's pocket. I feel as if the noise is calling to me in my dreamy state. I debate whether or not to reach into his pocket, my eyes focused on the imprint of the phone in the front pocket of his tight jeans. It stops as I reach my bed so I steal another opportunity to take in how peaceful Hardin looks in his sleep. There is no soft crinkle in his forehead from his constant frowning, and there is no purse to his pink lips. I sigh and turn around only to have the buzzing start again. I'm just going to grab it, he won't wake up. I dip my hand down and struggle to reach into Hardin's pocket. If his pants weren't so tight, I would be able to pull the phone from his pocket . . . but I have no such luck.

"What are you doing?" he groans.

I jolt a few feet away from my bed. "Your phone is going off and it woke me up," I whisper, despite the fact that we are the only people in the room.

I watch silently as he digs into his pocket, his large hand

struggling to pull out his phone. "What?" He snaps into the mouthpiece when he does get it out, only to swipe his hand over his forehead at whatever response he received.

"I am not coming back there tonight. I am at a friend's house."

Are we friends? Of course not, I'm just a convenient excuse for why he isn't returning to the party. I stand awkwardly and shift my weight from one leg to the other.

"No, you can't go into my room. You know this. I'm going back to sleep now, so don't wake me up again. And my door is locked, so don't waste your time trying." He hangs up, and I instinctively back away. His bad mood is palpable, and I don't want to be on the receiving end of his venom. I crawl onto Steph's bed and pull the blanket to me.

"Sorry that my phone woke you," he says quietly. "It was Molly."

"Oh." I sigh and lie down on my side, facing my bed across the room. Hardin gives me a small smile, as if he knows what I'm thinking about Molly. I can't ignore the small bubble of excitement that comes from him being here instead of with Molly, even though his actions make no sense to me.

"You don't like her, do you?" He rolls fully onto his side, his hair messy and everywhere on my pillow.

I shake my head. "Not really, but please don't tell her. I don't want any drama," I beg. I know I can't trust him, but hopefully he will forget to stir up controversy with this information.

"I won't. I don't care for her, either," he murmurs.

"Yeah, you really seem to dislike her," I say just as sarcastically as I can manage.

"I don't. I mean, she is fun and all, but she is quite annoying," he admits, making that bubble grow a little more.

"Well, maybe you should stop messing around with her," I suggest and roll onto my back so he can't see my face.

"Is there a reason I shouldn't mess around with her?"

"No. I mean, if you think she is annoying, then why keep doing it?" I know I don't want the answer to this, but can't help it.

"To keep me occupied, I guess."

I close my eyes and take a deep breath. Talking about Hardin messing around with Molly hurts me worse than it should.

His smooth voice interrupts my jealous thoughts. "Come lie with me."

"No."

"Come on, just lie with me. I sleep better when you're near me," he says like it's a confession.

I sit up and look at him. *"What?"* I can't hide my surprise at his words. Whether he means them or not, they make my insides melt.

"I sleep better when you're with me." He breaks eye contact and looks down. "Last weekend I slept better than I have in a while."

"It was probably the scotch, not me." I try to make light of his confession. I don't know what else to do or say.

"No, it was you."

"Good night, Hardin." I turn over. If he keeps saying these things and I keep listening, I will be putty in his hands yet again.

"Why don't you believe me?" he almost whispers.

"Because you always do this: you say a few nice things and then you flip the switch and I end up crying."

"I make you cry?"

How doesn't he know that? He has seen me cry more than anyone else I know.

"Yeah, often," I say, gripping Steph's blanket tight.

I hear his bed squeak lightly and I close my eyes, out of fear, out of something else, too. Hardin's fingers graze my arm as he sits on the edge of Steph's bed, and I tell myself it's too late— well, early—for this at 4 a.m.

"I don't mean to make you cry."

I open my eyes and look up at him. "Yes. Yes, you do. That's your *exact* intention every time you say hurtful things to me. And when you forced me to tell Noah about us. And when you humiliated me in your bed last week because I couldn't say exactly what you wanted me to. Tonight you tell me you sleep better when I am around, but if I was to lie with you, the second we woke up you would just tell me I am ugly, or that you can't stand me. After we went to the stream, I thought that . . . never mind. There are only so many times I can have this talk with you." I take in a couple of deep breaths, panicked at my unloading on him.

"I'm listening this time." His eyes are unreadable, but they make me want to continue.

"I just don't know why you love this cat-and-mouse game you play with me so much. You're nice, then mean. You tell Steph you'll 'ruin' me if I come around you, then you want to drive me home. You are just all over the place."

"I didn't mean that. That I would ruin you, I just . . . I don't know. I just say things sometimes," he says, running his hands through his hair.

"Why did you drop Literature?" I finally ask.

"Because you want me to stay away from you, and I need to stay away from you."

"So why don't you, then?" I am slightly aware of the shift in energy around us. Somehow we have moved closer, our bodies only inches apart.

"I don't know," he huffs. He rubs his hands together, then rests them on his knees.

I want to say something—anything—but I can't without telling Hardin that I *don't* want him to stay away, that I think about him every second of every day.

Finally, he breaks the silence. "Can I ask you something and you will be completely honest?"

I nod.

"Did you . . . did you miss me this week?"

That was the last thing I expected him to ask me. I blink a few times to clear my frantic mind. I told him I would answer truthfully, but I'm afraid to.

"Well?"

"Yeah," I mumble and hide my face in my hands, only to have him pull them away, his touch on my wrists setting fire to my skin.

"Yeah, what?" His voice is strained, like he is desperate for my answer.

"I missed you," I gulp, expecting the worst.

What I did not expect is his sigh of relief, and the smile that stretches across his beautiful face. I want to ask him if he missed me, but he begins to speak before I get the chance.

"Really?" he asks, almost like he doesn't believe me.

I nod in reply and he gives me a shy smile. Hardin *shy*? More likely he's pleased by my admittance because it tells him he has me wrapped around his finger.

"Now can I go back to sleep?" I whine. I know he isn't going to reciprocate my confession with one of his own, and it is really late.

"Only if you sleep with me. As in, in the same bed, of course." He smiles.

I sigh and mumble, "Oh, Hardin, can we just go to sleep?" as I roll over, careful not to touch him. But a sudden yank on my legs makes me yelp in surprise, and I quickly find Hardin lifting me off the bed and throwing me over his shoulder. He ignores my kicking and pleas to put me down until he reaches my bed, rests one knee on it, and lays me down gently on the side against the wall before lying down next to me. I glare at him silently, afraid that if I fight him too hard he'll leave, which I know I don't want.

He reaches down and picks up the pillow that I tossed at him earlier and places it between us as a barrier with a smirk on his face. "There, now you can sleep, safe and secure."

I smile back at him. I can't help it. "Good night," I half-giggle.

"Night, Tessa." He laughs back and I roll over on my side.

But suddenly I'm not anywhere near tired, so I just stare at the wall, hoping this electricity will dissipate and I can sleep. Well, half-hoping.

A few minutes later I feel the pillow move and then Hardin's arm wraps around my waist and he pulls me to his chest. I don't move it or call attention to his actions. I am enjoying the feeling too much.

"I missed you, too," he whispers against my hair. I smile knowing that he can't see me. I feel the light pressure of his lips against the back of my head and my stomach flips. As much as I love it, I am left more confused than ever as I drift off to sleep.

chapter forty-three

My alarm goes off too early and I roll over. I lift my hand, smacking at it to stop the hideous beeping assaulting my ears. My hand smacks against a soft, warm surface, and I blink my eyes open to find Hardin staring down at me. I reach for my pillow to cover my embarrassment but Hardin yanks it away.

"Good morning to you, too," he says with a smile, rubbing at his arm.

I stare back, working an apology in my mind. *How long has be been watching me?*

"You're cute when you're asleep," he teases and I sit up as quick as I can, sure I look fairly hideous, like usual in the morning.

He hands me my phone. "What's the alarm for?"

I switch it off and climb off the bed. "I'm going to look for a car today, so you can leave whenever," I tell him and he frowns.

"You're obviously not a morning person."

I pull my hair back into a tail, in an effort to keep it from looking like a bird's nest. "I am . . . I just don't want to keep you." I feel a little guilty for being rude, but I had expected him to be rude himself, to be honest.

"You're not. Can I come with you?"

I search around my room, wondering if I heard him correctly. Finally I turn to him with suspicion in my eyes. "To look at a car? Why would you want to do that?"

"Why do I have to have a reason? You act like I'm plotting to kill you or something." He laughs and stands up, ruffling his hair.

"Well, I'm just a little taken aback by your cheerful mood this morning . . . and you wanting to go somewhere with me . . . and you not insulting me," I admit.

I turn away from him and gather my clothes and bathroom kit. I need to take a shower before I go anywhere.

Unfazed by my honesty, Hardin presses some more. "It'll be fun, I promise. Just let me show you that we could . . . that I could be nice. It's just one day."

His smile is beautiful and convincing. But Noah will surely break up with me and never speak to me again if he knows that Hardin stayed the night with me, in my bed, holding me as we slept. I don't know what it is that keeps me constantly afraid of losing Noah; maybe it's my fear of my mother's reaction if we broke up, or maybe that my old self is so tied to Noah. He has always been there for me, and I feel like I owe it to myself and him to continue our relationship. But I think the biggest reason is that I know Hardin can't and won't give me the type of relationship I need and honestly want from him.

While I am lost in my thoughts it finally seems okay for me to admit that listening to Hardin's steady breathing in my ear while he slept was worth never speaking to Noah again.

"Earth to Tessa!" Hardin calls from across the room and I snap to. I have been frozen standing here debating with myself and completely forgot Hardin was even in my room.

"Is something wrong?" he asks and steps toward me.

Oh, nothing, just that I am finally admitting to myself that I have feelings for you and want more from you, yet know you will never care about anyone, especially me.

"Just trying to figure out what to wear," I lie.

His eyes move down to the clothes in my hands, and he tilts

his head but only says, "So, can I come? It will be easier for you, anyway—so you don't have to take the bus."

Well, it might be fun. And it would be easier. "Yeah, okay," I say. "Just let me get ready." I walk toward the door and he follows me.

"What are you doing?" I ask him.

"Coming with you."

"Um, I'm going to take a shower." I dangle my toiletry bag in front of him and he snatches it from me.

"What a coincidence—me, too!"

Damn coed bathrooms. He walks past me and opens the door without looking back. I rush to catch up with him and grab hold of his shirt.

"Nice of you to join me," he jokes and I roll my eyes.

"We haven't even begun the day and you're already annoying me," I tease back.

A group of girls walks by us and into the bathrooms; they don't even try to be subtle about staring at Hardin.

"Ladies," Hardin greets them, and they giggle like schoolgirls. Well, technically they *are* schoolgirls, but they are also adults, so they should act like it.

chapter forty-four

After a stop to use the toilet, I come out and don't see or hear Hardin in the showers, so my mind of course starts worrying that he went off somewhere with those girls. He didn't even bring any clothes with him, so if he does shower, he would just be putting on dirty clothes. Hardin could wear clothes matted with mud and still look better than any guy I have ever seen. *Except Noah,* I remind myself.

After a quick shower, I dry off and pull my clothes on and make my way back to my room, where I'm relieved to find Hardin sitting on my bed. *Take that, schoolgirls,* part of me yells. He is shirtless and the water has made his dark hair blacker yet. I close my mouth to make sure my tongue isn't hanging out.

"Took you long enough," he says and leans back. His muscles constrict as he lifts his arms behind his head to brace him against the wall.

"You're supposed to be nice to me, remember," I say and walk over to Steph's closet and open the door to use the mirror. Grabbing Steph's makeup bag, I sit myself down and cross my legs in front of it.

"This *is* me being nice."

I stay quiet as I try to apply a little makeup. After three attempts of making a straight line on my top eyelid, I chuck the eyeliner at the mirror and Hardin laughs.

"You don't need that, anyway," he tells me.

"I like it," I say, and he rolls his eyes.

"Fine, we can just sit here all day while you try to color on your face," he says. So much for nice Hardin.

He catches himself and gives me a quick, "Sorry, sorry," while I wipe my eyes off. But I give up the makeup routine. It's a little hard to do with someone like Hardin watching me.

"I'm ready," I tell him and he jumps up. "Are you going to put a shirt on?" I ask him.

"Yeah, I have one in my trunk."

I was right: he must have an endless supply in there. I don't want to think about the reasons behind that.

TRUE TO HIS WORD, Hardin pulls a plain black T-shirt out of his trunk and finishes getting dressed in the parking lot.

"Stop staring and get in the car," he teases me. I stutter a denial and oblige.

"I like you in the white shirts," I say when we're both inside, the words just popping out before I can process them.

Cocking his head sideways, he gives me a smug grin. "Is that so?" He raises his eyebrow. "Well, I like you in those jeans. They show off your ass wonderfully," he says and my mouth drops. Hardin and his dirty words.

I swat at him playfully and he laughs, but I mentally pat myself on the back for wearing these pants. I want Hardin to look at me even though I would never admit it, and I am flattered by his strange way of complimenting me.

"So where to?" he asks, and I pull out my phone. I read him the list of used-car dealers within a five-mile radius and tell him about a few of the reviews on each.

"You plan things way too much. We aren't going to any of those places."

"Yes, we are. I already have this planned; there is a Prius that

I want to see at Bob's Super Cars," I tell him and cringe at the cheesy name.

"A *Prius*?" he says in disgust.

"Yeah? They have the best gas mileage and they are safe and—"

"Boring. I knew somehow you would want a Prius. You just scream, 'Lady with a planner in her Prius!'" he says in a fake woman's voice and then cackles.

"Tease me all you want but I will save hundreds on gas every year," I remind him, laughing, when he leans over and pokes my cheek. I look over at him, shocked by his doing such a small but adorable thing; he looks as surprised at what he did as I do.

"You're cute sometimes," he tells me.

I look forward again. "Gee, thanks."

"I mean that in a nice way, like sometimes you do cute things," he mutters. The words seem uncomfortable on his tongue and I know he isn't used to saying things like this.

"Okay . . ." I say and look out the side window.

Every second I spend with Hardin increases my feelings for him, and I know it's dangerous for me to allow these small, seemingly meaningless moments to occur, but I don't have control of myself when Hardin is involved. I become merely a passerby in this storm.

HARDIN ENDS UP DRIVING TO BOB'S, and I thank him. Bob ends up being a short, sweaty, and overgelled man who smells like nicotine and leather and whose smile is punctuated with a gold tooth. While he talks to me, Hardin stands nearby, making faces when he isn't looking. The little man seems to be intimidated by Hardin's harsh appearance, but I don't blame him. I take one look at the condition of the used Prius and decide against it. I have a feeling the moment I drove off the lot it would have broken down, and Bob has a strict no-return policy.

We visit a few more lots and they are all equally as trashy. After a morning of countless balding men, I decide to suspend my search for a car. I will have to go farther away from campus for a decent car and I just don't feel like it today. We decide to get some lunch at a drive-through, and while we eat in the car Hardin surprisingly tells me a story about when Zed got arrested for puking all over the floor of a Wendy's last year. The day is going better than I could have imagined, and for once I feel like we could both make it through this semester without killing each other.

On our way back to campus, we pass a cute little frozen yogurt bar and I beg Hardin to stop. He groans and acts like he doesn't want to, but I see the hint of a smile hiding behind his sour features. Hardin tells me to find a spot and he goes and gets our yogurt for us, piling on every candy and cookie imaginable. It looks disgusting, but he convinces me it's the only way to get your money's worth. As gross as it looks, it's delicious. I can't even finish half of mine, but Hardin happily clears his cup and the remainder of mine.

"Hardin?" a man's voice says.

Hardin's head snaps up and his eyes narrow. *Was that an accent I heard?* The stranger is holding a bag and a drink carrier full of yogurt cups.

"Um . . . hey," Hardin says, and I know instinctively that this is his father. The man is tall and lean, like Hardin, and has the same-shaped eyes, only his are a deep brown instead of green. Other than that, they are polar opposites. His father is wearing gray dress pants and a sweater vest. His brown hair has some gray scattered on its sides and his demeanor is coldly professional. Until he smiles, that is, and shows a warmth similar to Hardin's, when he isn't putting so much effort into being a jerk.

"Hi, I'm Tessa," I politely say and reach my hand out. Hardin glares at me but I ignore him. It's not like he was going to introduce me.

"Hello, Tessa. I am Ken, Hardin's father," he says and shakes my hand.

"Hardin, you never told me you had a girlfriend—you two should come over for dinner tonight. Karen will make a nice meal for everyone. She's an excellent cook."

I want to keep Hardin's anger in check and tell his father that I'm not his girlfriend, but Hardin speaks first.

"We can't tonight. I have a party to go to and she doesn't want to come," he snaps. A gasp escapes my lips at the way Hardin speaks to his father. Ken's face drops and I feel terrible for him.

"Actually, I would love to. I'm also a friend of Landon; we have classes together," I interject, and Ken's friendly smile reappears.

"You are? Well, that is great. Landon is a nice kid. I would be happy to have you over tonight," Ken says and I smile.

I feel Hardin's eyes blazing at me as I ask, "What time should we be there?"

"'We'?" his father asks and I nod. "Okay . . . let's do seven. I need to give Karen a bit of a warning or she will have my head," he jokes and I smile. Hardin stares angrily out the glass wall.

"Sounds great! We'll see you tonight!"

He says goodbye to Hardin, who rudely ignores him despite me kicking his foot under the table. A minute after his dad leaves the store, Hardin stands abruptly and slams his chair into the table. It topples over and he kicks it partway across the room before rushing out the door and leaving me alone to deal with everyone's stares. Not sure what to do, I leave my yogurt where it is, stammer an apology under my breath, and clumsily upright the chair before running out after him.

chapter forty-five

I call out Hardin's name, but he ignores me. When he gets half-way to the car, he spins around so quickly that I almost crash into him.

"*What the hell,* Tessa! What *the fuck* was *that?*" he screams at me. People walking by start to stare, but he continues. "What kind of game are you trying to play here?" He moves toward me. He is angry—beyond angry.

"There's no game here, Hardin—didn't you see how much he wanted you to come over? He was trying to reach out to you, and you were so *disrespectful!*" I'm really not sure why I'm yelling, but I'm not going to just let him shout at me.

"*Reach out to me?* Are you fucking kidding me? Maybe he should have reached out to me back when he was abandoning his family!" The veins in his neck strain under his skin.

"Stop swearing at me! Maybe he is trying to make up for lost time! People make mistakes, Hardin, and he obviously cares about you. He has that room for you at his house, full of clothes just in case—"

"You don't know *shit* about him, Tessa!" he screams and shudders with anger. "He lives in a fucking mansion with his new family while my mum works her ass off, fifty hours a week to pay her bills! So don't try to lecture me—mind your own damn business!"

He gets in the car, slamming his door closed. I scramble in, afraid that he might leave me here, he's so mad. So much for our argument-free day.

He's fuming mad but thankfully silent as we pull onto the main road. If I could keep it this quiet the rest of the ride, I'd be happy. But part of me insists that Hardin needs to understand that I will not be yelled at; that is one redeeming quality I give my mother credit for. She showed me exactly how not to be treated by a man.

"Fine," I say, feigning calm. "I will mind my own business, but I'm accepting the invitation to dinner tonight whether you go or not."

Like a wild animal who's been riled up, he turns in my direction. "Oh no you're not!"

Retaining my fake calm, I say, "You have no say in what I do, Hardin, and in case you didn't notice, I was invited. Maybe I should see if Zed wants to join me?"

"What did you just say!?" The dirt and dust start flying all over as Hardin jerks the steering wheel and pulls onto the shoulder of the busy road.

I know I pushed him too far, but I really am just as angry as he is by this point and yell, "What the hell is wrong with you? Pulling off the road like this!"

"What the hell is wrong with *you* is the question! You tell my dad I will go to his house for dinner, then you have the audacity to mention bringing Zed?"

"Oh, yeah, sorry, your cool friends don't know that Landon is your stepbrother and you're afraid they will find out?" I say and laugh at how ridiculous he is.

"He is not my stepbrother, for one. And two, you know that isn't why I don't want Zed there." His voice is much lower now, yet still thick with anger.

But through the chaos in the car, that bubble of hope grows again at Hardin's jealousy. I know his feelings are more of a competition thing than actual concern over my being with him, but it still makes my stomach flutter.

"Well, if you won't go with me, I will have to invite him." I would never actually do it, but Hardin doesn't know that.

Hardin stares straight out onto the street for a few seconds and then sighs, deflating some of the tension. "Tessa, I really don't want to go. I don't want to sit around with my dad's perfect family. I avoid them for a reason."

I lighten my tone as well. "Well, I don't want to force you to go if it will hurt you, but I would really like if you could come with me. I am going either way."

We went from eating yogurt to screaming at each other and now we are calm again. My head is spinning at least as much as my heart.

"Hurt me?" He sounds incredulous.

"Yeah, if it will bother you that much to be there, I won't try to make you come," I answer. I know that I could never make Hardin do anything he doesn't want to do; he has no history of ever being cooperative.

"Why would you care if it hurt me?" His eyes meet mine and I try to look away, but once again I am under his spell.

"Of course I would care; why wouldn't I?"

"Why *would* you is the question."

The look in his eyes is a pleading one, like he wants me to say the words, but I can't. He will use them against me and then probably never want to hang out with me again. I will become the annoying girl who likes him, the kind of girls Steph told me about.

"I care about how you feel," I say and I hope this answer can be good enough for him.

Interrupting our moment in the car, my phone rings. I pull it out of my purse and see it's Noah. Without thinking, I hit ignore before I realize what I'm doing.

"Who is it?" Hardin is so nosy.

"Noah."

"You're not going to answer?" He looks surprised.

"No, we're talking." *And I would rather talk to you,* my sub-conscious adds.

"Oh" is all he says, but his smile is evident.

"So are you going to come with me? It's been a while since I've had a home-cooked meal, so I am *not* passing it up." I smile; the mood in the car is lighter but tense all the same.

"No. I have plans, anyway," he mutters. I don't want to know if those plans involve Molly.

"Oh, okay. Are you going to be mad at me if I go?" It's sort of strange for me to just go to Hardin's father's house, but Landon is my friend, too, and I *was* invited.

"I'm always mad at you, Tess," he says, amusement in his eyes when he looks over at me.

I laugh. "I'm always mad at you, too," I tell him and he chuckles.

"Can we go back now? If a cop comes along, we'll get a ticket."

He nods, putting the car into drive and pulling back onto the road. The fight with Hardin blew over more quickly than I expected. I suppose he's much more used to constant conflict than I am; I would much rather spend time with him without fighting.

I promised myself that I wouldn't ask but I have to know . . . "So, what are your . . . um . . . plans today?"

"Why are you asking?" I can feel his eyes on me but I stare out the window.

"I'm just wondering, you said you had plans anyway so I was just wondering."

"We have a party again. That is basically what I do every Friday and Saturday, except last night and last Saturday . . ."

I trace a circle on the window with one finger. "Doesn't it get old? Just doing the same thing every weekend with the same drunk people?" I hope that doesn't offend him.

"Yeah . . . I guess it does. But we're in college, and I'm in a fraternity; what else is there to do?"

"I don't know . . . it just seems tedious, to clean up everyone's mess, every weekend especially when you don't even drink."

"It is, but I haven't found anything better to do with my time so—" He stops. I know he is still looking at me, but I keep my eyes away from him.

The rest of the drive is quiet. Not awkward, just quiet.

WALKING ALONE from the lot to my dorm, I'm flustered. My emotions are in overdrive. I just spent the night and most of the afternoon with Hardin and we got along, mostly. It was actually fun, a lot of fun. Why can't I have a great time like that with someone who actually likes me? Like Noah. I know I should call him back, but I want to revel in the way I feel right now.

When I get back to my room, I'm surprised to see Steph there; she usually stays gone all weekend.

"Where have you been, young lady?" she teases and shoves a handful of cheese popcorn into her mouth.

I laugh and take my shoes off before plopping onto the bed. "I was looking for a car."

"Find one?" she asks, and I dive into telling her about the run-down lots I visited, leaving out Hardin's involvement in the afternoon. After a few minutes, there's a knock at the door and Steph gets up to answer.

"What are you doing here, Hardin?" she growls.

Hardin. I glance up nervously and he walks over to my bed. He has his hands in his pockets and he rocks back on his heels.

"Did I forget something in your car?" I ask, and hear Steph gasp. I will have to explain to her later, though I'm not sure how we ended up hanging out, either.

"Ermm . . . no. Um, well, I thought maybe I could drive you to my dad's house tonight. You know, since you didn't find a car," he spits out, not seeming to notice or care that Steph is standing in the room with her jaw practically on the floor. "If not . . . that's okay, too. I just thought I would offer."

I sit up and he pulls his lip ring between his teeth. I love when he does that. I am so surprised by his offer, I almost forget to actually answer him. "Yeah . . . that would be great. Thank you."

I smile and he smiles back, warm and seemingly relieved. He pulls one hand out of his pocket and sweeps it through his hair before stuffing it back in.

"Okay . . . I'll come by about six thirty, so you can get there on time."

"Thank you, Hardin."

"Tessa," he says calmly and walks out the door, pulling it shut behind him.

"What the hell was that?!" Steph squeals.

"I don't know, actually," I admit. As soon as I think Hardin could not get more confusing, he does something like this.

"I cannot believe that just happened! I mean, Hardin . . . the way he came in here, like he was nervous or something! Oh my God! And he offered to drive you to his dad's . . . Wait, why are you going to his dad's house? And you thought you left something in his car? How do I miss so much! I need details!" She practically shouts and bounds onto the foot of my bed.

So I go through the whole thing, explaining to her how he showed up here last night and we watched a movie and he fell asleep, how we went to look at cars today—and how I didn't mention him being there before because I figured that if I insisted she help me keep him away, it would feel odd to admit I'd hung out with him. I don't say much about his dad except that I am going there for dinner, but she seems more interested in last night anyway.

"I can't believe he stayed here—that is a huge deal. Like Hardin doesn't just stay places, ever. And he never lets anyone stay with him. I heard he has nightmares or something, I don't know.

But seriously—what have you done to him? I wish I would have recorded the way he looked when he just came here!" she yells and laughs. "I still don't think this is a good idea, but you do seem to handle him better than most. Just be careful," she warns again.

What have I done to him? Nothing, surely. He just isn't used to being nice, but for some reason he's being nice to me. Maybe it's a way to beat me at some game, or prove a point that he can fake manners? I am not sure and it hurts my head to try to figure it out.

I bring up Tristan, and Steph takes the conversation from there. I try to pay attention to her stories from last night's party: how Molly ended up shirtless (go figure) and Logan beat Nate in a drunken arm-wrestling match (she swears it was one of those things that are much funnier when you're there). My thoughts drift back to Hardin, of course, and I check the clock to make sure I have enough time to get ready for tonight. It is four o'clock now, so I should start getting ready at five.

Steph talks until five thirty and is ecstatic when I ask her to do my hair and makeup. I am not sure why I am putting such effort into looking okay for a family dinner that I really shouldn't be going to, but I do anyway. She applies the makeup lightly so you can barely tell it's there, but it looks great. Natural but pretty. Then she curls my hair the way she did before. I decide to wear my favorite maroon dress, despite Steph's attempts to have me wear something from her closet. My maroon dress is nice and conservative, perfect for a family dinner.

"At least wear the lace tights underneath, or let me cut the sleeves off it," she says with a groan.

"Fine, give me the lace tights, I guess. This isn't that bad, though—it's formfitting," I rebut.

"I know, it's just . . . boring." She crinkles her nose. She looks more pleased when I put on the tights and agree to high heels. I still have a pair of Toms tucked in my purse from yesterday, just in case.

As six thirty approaches, I realize I am more nervous about the ride to dinner than the actual dinner. I fidget with the tights and practice walking around the room a few times before Hardin finally knocks on the door. Steph gives me a strange smile and I pull the door open.

"Wow, Tessa, you . . . um . . . look nice," he mumbles and I smile. Since when does he say "um" in every sentence?

Steph escorts us out the door, winks, and exclaims like a proud parent, "You two have fun!"

Hardin flips her off, and she returns the vulgar gesture as he closes the door in her face.

chapter forty-six

The drive to Hardin's father's house is nice. The low music in the background of his car feels like a distraction, and I notice the way his hands are gripping the steering wheel a little too hard. He seems on edge during the drive, but I know if he wants to talk about something, he would have no problem calling it out.

I climb out of the car and walk up the steps from the sidewalk. With the sun still in the sky, I can see some old vines creeping up the sides of the house and the small white flowers that join them. Unexpectedly, I hear Hardin's door open and close, and then his boots on the sidewalk. I turn around to see him a few steps behind me.

"What are you doing?" I ask him.

"Coming with you, obviously." He rolls his eyes and takes one long stride to join me at the top of the steps.

"Really? It seemed like you weren't—"

"Yeah. Now let's go inside and have the worst night of our lives."

His face twists into the fakest smile I have ever seen. I elbow him and ring the doorbell. "I don't ring doorbells," he tells me and turns the knob. I suppose it's okay because it's his father's house, but I still feel a little uncomfortable.

We walk inside and through the foyer before his father appears. The surprise is evident on his face, but he smiles his charming smile and goes to hug his son. Hardin, however, dodges his gesture and walks right past him. The embarrassment flashes on Mr. Scott's handsome features, but I look away before he realizes that I saw his subtle gesture.

"Thank you so much for having us, Mr. Scott," I say as we pass through the doorway.

"Thank you so much for coming, Tessa. Landon has told me some about you. He seems very fond of you. And please, call me Ken." He smiles and I follow him into the living room.

Landon is sitting on the couch with his Literature book on his lap as I enter. His face lights up and he closes the book as I walk over and sit down next to him. I'm not sure where Hardin went to, but he'll appear sooner or later.

"So you and Hardin are giving your friendship another try?" Landon asks with a slight frown. I want to explain what is going on between Hardin and me, but I honestly have no idea myself.

"It's complicated." I try to smile but I feel it falter.

"You're still with Noah, right? Because Ken seems to think you and Hardin are dating." He laughs. I hope my laugh doesn't sound as fake as it feels. "I didn't have the heart to tell him otherwise, but I am sure Hardin will," he says.

I shift uncomfortably, unsure what to say. "Yeah, I'm still with Noah, it's just—"

"You must be Tessa!" A woman's voice rings through the room. Landon's mom walks toward me and I stand up to shake her hand. Her eyes are bright and her smile is lovely. She is wearing a turquoise dress, similar to my maroon dress, with an apron printed with small strawberries and bananas over the top of it.

"It's so nice to meet you; thank you for having me. Your home is beautiful," I tell her. Her smile covers her face and she squeezes my hand.

"You are so welcome, dear, it's my pleasure," she says, beaming. A timer goes off from the kitchen and she jumps a little. "Well, I'm going to finish up in the kitchen, but I'll see you all in the dining room in a few minutes."

"What are you working on?" I ask Landon and he pulls out a folder.

"Next week's assignments. That essay on Tolstoy is going to kill me."

I laugh and nod; that essay took me hours to write. "Yeah, it was a killer. I just finished it a few days ago."

"Well, if you two nerds are done comparing notes, I would love to eat dinner sometime in the next year," Hardin says. I glare at him, but Landon just laughs and puts his book down before walking to the dining room. It seems their fight was good for them after all.

I follow them both to the large dining room. There, a long table is decorated beautifully with full place settings and multiple platters of food in the center. Karen really went all out for this; Hardin had better behave or I will kill him.

"Tessa, you and Hardin will sit on this side," Karen instructs us and gestures to the left of the table. Landon sits across from Hardin. Ken and Karen take their seats on the other side of Landon.

I thank her and sit down next to Hardin, who is quiet and seems uncomfortable. I watch as Karen makes Ken's plate for him and he thanks her with a brief kiss on her cheek. It is such a sweet gesture, I have to look away. I fill my plate with roast beef, potatoes, and squash, then pile a roll on top of it. Hardin chuckles quietly at the mound of food.

"What? I'm hungry," I whisper.

"Nothing. Hungry girls are the best." He laughs again and piles his plate even higher than mine.

"So, Tessa, how are you liking Washington Central so far?" Ken asks.

I chew my food quickly so I can answer. "I really enjoy it. It's only my first semester, though, so ask me again in a few months," I joke and everyone laughs, except Hardin.

"Well, that's great. Are you in any clubs on campus?" Karen asks and wipes her mouth with her napkin.

"Not yet, I plan on joining the Literary Club next semester."

"Really? Hardin used to be a member," Ken adds and I look at Hardin. His eyes are narrowed and he looks annoyed.

"So how do you like living near WCU?" I ask to divert attention from Hardin. His eyes soften and I imagine that's his way of thanking me.

"We enjoy it. When Ken first became chancellor, we lived in a much smaller place until we found this house and we fell in love with it immediately."

My fork drops against the glass plate. "Chancellor? Of WCU?" I gasp.

"Yes. Hardin never mentioned it?" Ken asks, looking over at his son.

"No . . . I didn't."

Karen and Landon follow Ken's eyes to Hardin and he shifts nervously.

For his part, Hardin looks back at his father with a glaring hatred. He launches to his feet, shouting, "No! Okay, no, I didn't tell her—I don't know why it fucking matters. I don't need to use your name or position!" As he storms away from the table, Karen looks like she might cry, and Ken's face is red.

"I am so sorry, I didn't know he . . ." I start.

"No, don't apologize for his poor behavior," Ken tells me.

I hear the back door slam. "Excuse me," I say, and stand up from the table to go find Hardin.

chapter forty-seven

I rush out the back door and see Hardin pacing back and forth on the deck. I'm not sure what I can do to help the situation, but I know I would rather be out here with Hardin than face his family in the dining room after that outburst. I feel responsible for this whole thing anyway, since I agreed to come here when Hardin didn't want to. If he started suddenly hanging out with my mother, I know I would feel weird about it.

Ha, like she would ever let that happen, my subconscious points out.

As if he heard my thoughts, Hardin shoots me an annoyed look. When I approach him he turns away from me.

"Hardin . . ."

"No, Tessa, don't," he says sharply. "I know you're going to say that I need to go back in there and apologize to them. But there is no way in hell that is happening, so don't waste your breath! Why don't you just go back in there and enjoy your dinner and leave me the hell alone."

I take a step closer, but all I can manage to say is "I don't want to go back in there."

"Why not? You fit in perfectly with their prudish and boring personalities."

Ouch! Why am I here again? Oh, yeah, that's right: to be Hardin's punching bag.

"You know what? *Fine!* I will leave—I don't know why I *just can't stop trying with you!*" I shout, but hope they can't hear me inside.

"Because you just can't take a hint, I guess." As the words leave his mouth, I feel the lump growing in my throat.

"The hint is well-taken." I stare at the stone patio and try to swallow the sting from his words, but it's impossible. When I look up at Hardin, his cold eyes meet mine.

"That's it? That's your defense?" He laughs and rakes his hands through his hair.

"You don't *deserve* any more of my time. You don't deserve for me to even *speak to you,* or those nice people in there to spend their time setting up this dinner to have you ruin it! *That's what you do: ruin things, everything!* And I am *done* being one of those things." My tears soak my face as Hardin steps toward me. I back away, my feet tripping on something. Hardin reaches out to steady me, but I grab hold of a patio chair instead. I don't want or need his help.

Looking up, I see that his expression is one of exhaustion. His voice is, too, when he says softly, "You're right."

"I know I am." I turn away from him.

Faster than I could have imagined, he snakes his fingers around my wrist and pulls me to his chest. I lean into him without hesitation, wanting to touch him so badly. But I know better: I can hear the warning in the thump of my heart, rapid beneath my chest. I wonder if Hardin can hear it, too, or feel the pounding of my pulse under his grip. His eyes are full of anger and I know mine mirror his.

I have no warning before he crashes his lips down on mine, the force of his mouth almost painful. His action is so full of desperation and hunger that I am lost. Lost in Hardin. Lost in the salty taste of my tears on both our lips, lost in his fingers threaded through my hair. His hands move from my head to my waist and he lifts me onto the railing. My legs part for him and he moves between them, never losing contact with my mouth. We are all heat and gasps, tangled in each other. My teeth graze over his bottom lip, causing him to groan and pull me even closer.

The back door creaks open, breaking the spell. Turning to look, I am horrified as Landon's soft eyes meet mine. His face is red, and his eyes wide. I push Hardin away from me and jump down from the rail, adjusting my dress as my feet hit the deck.

"Landon, I . . ." I begin.

He holds up his hand to silence me and steps toward us. Hardin's breathing is so loud that I swear it echoes between the house and the trees. His cheeks are flamed, his eyes wild.

"I don't understand. I thought you guys hated each other, and here you are . . . You have a boyfriend, Tessa, I didn't think you were like that." Landon's words are harsh but his tone is soft.

"I'm not . . . I don't know what this is." I motion between me and Hardin. Hardin stays silent, for which I am glad. "Noah knows, well, about before. I was going to tell you, I just don't want you to think differently of me," I say, almost apologetically.

"I don't know what to think . . ." Landon says and walks back toward the door.

Then, like something out of a movie, a clash of thunder rolls through the air.

"It looks like it might storm," Hardin says, his eyes scanning the darkening sky. Despite his flushed appearance, his voice is calm.

"A storm? Landon just caught us . . . kissing," I say, feeling the fire slowly burning out between us.

"He'll be okay."

I look up at him, expecting to see a smug expression, but it's not there. He puts his hand on my back and rubs gently.

"Do you want to go back inside or do you want me to take you home?" he asks.

It's astounding how abruptly his mood can change from angry to lustful to calm.

"I would like to go back inside and finish dinner. What do you want to do?"

"I suppose we can go back in; the food is pretty good," he says, smiling, and I giggle. "That's a lovely sound," he tells me and I meet his gaze.

"You're in a much better mood," I say and he smiles again.

He rubs the back of his neck like he always does. "I don't understand it, either."

So he is just as confused as I am? I wish my feelings for him weren't so strong; then I could deal with him much better. When he says things like this it makes me care for him that much more. I only wish he could feel the same, but I have been warned by Steph and Hardin himself that it will never happen.

Thunder rolls again and Hardin takes my hand. "Let's go inside before it rains."

I nod and he leads me inside. He doesn't remove his hand from mine as we walk back into the dining room. Landon's eyes dart down to note this, but he says nothing. As much as I don't want Landon to see it, I love the way Hardin's hand feels over mine. I love it too much to pull away. Landon focuses back on his plate as we retake our seats. Letting go of my hand, Hardin looks up at his father and Karen.

"I am sorry for yelling at you that way," he mutters.

The surprise on everyone's face is evident and Hardin looks down at the table. "I hope I didn't ruin the dinner that you put so much effort into," he continues.

I can't help myself. I reach under the table and put my hand over Hardin's, giving it a light squeeze.

"It's okay, Hardin, we understand. Let's not let the night be ruined; we can still enjoy the dinner." Karen smiles and Hardin looks at her. He gives her a small smile, which I know takes a lot of effort from him. Ken doesn't say anything, but he nods in agreement with the sentiment.

I slowly pull my hand away, but Hardin laces his fingers through mine and looks sideways at me. I hope I don't wear the giddy expression I feel inside. For what seems like the first time in my life, I don't overthink things, like why I am holding his hand when I'm dating Noah.

Dinner continues well, but I find myself a little intimidated by Ken now that I know he's the chancellor. That is a huge deal. He tells us about when he moved from England, and how he loves America, and the state of Washington in particular. Hardin is still holding my hand as we both struggle to eat using one hand, but neither of us seems to mind.

"The weather could be better, but it's beautiful here," Ken muses, and I nod in agreement.

"What are your plans after college?" Karen asks me as everyone finishes eating.

"I'm going to move to Seattle, and hopefully work in publishing while I work on my first book," I say with confidence.

"Publishing? Do you have any houses in mind?" Ken asks.

"Not exactly. I will take any opportunity I can get to get my foot in the door."

"That's great. I happen to have some pretty good connections at Vance. Have you heard of it?" he asks and I look at Hardin. He had mentioned knowing someone there before.

"Yes, I've heard great things about it." I smile.

"I can make a call for you if you would like, to see about an internship. It would be a great opportunity for you. You seem like a very bright young woman, and I'd love to help out."

I take my hand out of Hardin's and clasp it with my other just under my chin. "Really? That would be so nice of you! I really appreciate it!"

Ken tells me that he will call whoever it is that he knows on

Monday, and I thank him repeatedly. He assures me it's nothing and that he loves to help anytime he can. I put my hand back under the table, but Hardin has moved his hand away, and when Karen stands and begins to clear the table, he excuses himself and walks off upstairs.

chapter forty-eight

Karen smiled appreciatively when I offered to help with the cleanup, and seemed a little surprised I would. I load the dishwasher while she washes the large serving plates. I realize the plates all look really new, and remember how much damage Hardin caused that night. He can be so cruel.

"If you don't mind me asking, how long have you and Hardin been seeing each other?" She blushes at her own question, but I give her a warm smile.

Figuring it best just to dodge the dating question, I say, "Well, we have only known each other about a month; he is friends with my roommate, Steph."

"We have only met a few of Hardin's friends. You are . . . well, you are different from the ones that I have come across."

"Yeah, we're very different."

Lightning flashes and the rain begins to pound against the windows. "Wow, it's really coming down out there," she says and pushes the small window in front of the sink closed.

"Hardin isn't as bad as he seems," she tells me, though really it feels sort of like she's reminding herself. "He's just hurt. I would love to believe that he won't always be this way. I must say I was very surprised that he came tonight, and I can only believe that's your influence on him."

Taking me by surprise, she wraps her arms around me and pulls me into a hug. Unsure what to say, I hug her back. She pulls away but keeps her well-manicured hands on my shoulders.

"Really, thank you," she says, then blots her eyes with a tissue from her apron before returning to the dishes.

She is too kind for me to tell her that I don't have any influence on Hardin. He came tonight only because he wanted to annoy me. After I finish loading the dishwasher, I stare out the window watching the raindrops trickle down the glass. It is remarkable that Hardin, who hates everyone except himself, and maybe his mother, has all these people who care about him yet refuses to let himself care for them. He is lucky to have them, us. I know I am one of those people. I would do anything for Hardin; even though I would deny it, I know it to be true. I have no one, except Noah and my mother, and both of them together don't care about me the way Hardin's soon-to-be stepmother does him.

"I'm going to go check on Ken. Make yourself at home, dear," Karen says to me. I nod and decide to go find Hardin, or Landon, whichever one of them appears first.

Landon is nowhere to be found downstairs, so I make my way up to Hardin's room. If he's not up here, I figure, I'll just go sit downstairs alone. I turn the handle, but the door is locked.

"Hardin?" I try to speak quietly so no one hears me. I tap my knuckles against the door but hear nothing. Just as I start to turn away, the door clicks and he opens it.

"Can I come in?" I ask him and he nods once and pulls the door open just enough for me. There is a breeze in the room and I can smell the cool scent of the rain coming through the bay window. He walks over and sits down on the built-in bench surrounding the window and raises his knees up. He stares out the window but doesn't say a word to me. I sit across from him and wait as the constant drumming of the rain creates a calming rhythm.

"What happened?" I finally ask. When he looks at me with a confused expression, I explain: "I mean downstairs. You were holding my hand and then . . . why did you pull away?" I am embarrassed by the desperation in my voice. I sound too needy, but the words have already been delivered.

"Was it the internship—do you not want me to take it for some reason? You offered to help me before?"

"That's just it, Tessa," he says, and looks out the window again. "I want to be the one to help you, not him."

"Why? It's not a competition, and you were the one who offered first, so thank you." I want to ease his mind on this, even though I don't understand why it matters.

He lets out an exasperated sigh and hugs his knees. Silence hangs between us as we both stare out the window. The wind has picked up, swaying the trees back and forth, and the lightning is more frequent now.

"Do you want me to leave now? I can call Steph and see if Tristan can pick me up," I whisper. I don't want to leave but sitting in silence with Hardin is driving me insane.

"*Leave?* How do you get that I want you to leave from me saying I want to help you?" He raises his voice.

"I-I don't know. You aren't speaking to me and the storm is getting worse . . ." I stutter.

"You are maddening, absolutely maddening, Theresa."

"How?" I squeak.

"I try to tell you that I . . . that I want to help you and I hold your hand but that doesn't do anything . . . you still don't get it. I don't know what else to do." He puts his face in his hands. *He can't possibly mean what I think he does?*

"Get what? I don't get what, Hardin?"

"That I want you. More than I have ever wanted anyone or anything in my entire life." He looks away from me.

My stomach flips over and over and my head starts to spin. The air between us has once again shifted. Hardin's unguarded admission hits me hard. Because I want him, too. More than anything.

"I know you don't . . . you don't feel that way, but I . . ." he begins and this time I am the one to cut him off.

I move his hands off his knees and pull them, bringing him to me. He hovers over me, uncertainty clear in his green eyes. I hook my finger into the collar of his shirt and pull him down to me. Eye to eye. He rests his knee beside my thighs on the bench and I look up at him again. He takes a few breaths, his eyes shifting from my lips back to my eyes. His tongue swipes over his lower lip and I inch closer. I expected him to kiss me by now.

"Kiss me," I beg.

And he moves his head closer, leaning into me. He snakes his arm around my back and guides me down so my back is lying flat on the cushioned bench. I open my legs for him, for the second time today, and he lays his body between them. His face is inches away from mine when I lift my head up to kiss him. I can't wait any longer. As our lips brush, he gently pulls away, nuzzles his head in my neck, planting a small kiss there, then slowly brings his lips back up. He kisses the corner of my mouth, then my jaw, sending shivers of pleasure through me. His lips brush over mine once more and he runs his tongue over my bottom lip before closing his lips around mine and opening them again. The kiss is gentle and slow, as he laps his tongue around mine. One of his hands rests on my hip, fisted around the material of my dress where it has bunched up at my thighs. The other hand caresses my cheek as he kisses me; my arms wrap around his back, hugging him tightly to me. Every fiber of me wants to bite his lip, to pull his shirt over his head, but the soft and gentle way he is kissing me feels even better than the usual burn of fire.

Hardin's lips mold to mine, and my hands travel up his back. His narrow hips grind down on mine, and a whimper escapes my lips. He swallows my gasps as his lips trace mine, movement for movement.

"Oh, Tessa, the things you do to me . . . the way you make

me feel," he whispers into my mouth. His words unravel me and I reach for the hem of his shirt. His hand travels down from my cheek, to my chest, and down my stomach, where goose bumps are forming on my skin. His hand moves to the small space between our bodies where my legs are parted, and I gasp as he rubs gently over the lace of my tights. He applies a little more pressure and I groan and arch my back off the bench.

No matter how angry or upset he makes me, one touch from him and I am under his control. But his calm and control seem to be faltering; he is trying to hold on to them, but I can see his resolve crumbling. He brushes his nose against my cheek as I pull his shirt up and over his head. It strains to get over his hair, but he reaches one hand up and tugs it as he lifts off me. He tosses the shirt and immediately dips his head back down and finds my lips once more. I grab his hand and move it back between my thighs; a small chuckle vibrates through him and he looks down at me.

"What do you want to do, Tessa?" His voice is hoarse.

"Anything," I tell him and mean it. I will do anything with him, and I don't care about the consequences that might come tomorrow. He said he wants me, and I am his to take. I have been since I kissed him that first time.

"Don't say *anything,* because there are a lot of things I can do to you," he groans and pushes his thumb against my tights and panties. My imagination runs wild with ideas.

"You decide," I moan as he moves his thumb in a circle.

"You're so wet for me I can feel you through the tights." He licks his lips and I moan again. "Let's get these tights off, okay?" he asks, but before I answer he moves off me. His hands slide up my dress and grab the tights, pulling them down, along with my panties at the same time. The cool air hits me and I buck my hips involuntarily.

"Fuck," he mutters as his eyes rake my body and stop between my legs. Unable to stop himself, he reaches down and slides his finger down my spot. Then he brings his finger to his lips and he sucks on it with hooded eyes. Oh. Watching him sends heat through my whole body.

"Remember when I said I wanted to taste you?" he asks, and I nod. "Well, I want to now. Okay?" His expression is eager. I am a little embarrassed by the idea, but if it feels as good as him rubbing me at the stream, I want him to. He licks his lips again and bores his eyes into mine. The last time I was going to let him do this, we ended up fighting because he was being cruel. I hope he doesn't ruin it again.

"Do you want me to?" he asks, and I groan.

"Please, Hardin, don't make me say it," I beg.

He brings his hand back down to me and runs his fingers along my hips in wide circles. "I won't," he promises. I am relieved. I nod my head and he lets out a breath.

"We should move to the bed so you have more room," he suggests and reaches for my hand. I pull my dress down once I stand up and he smirks at me. He walks to the side of the bay window and pulls a string, setting free thick blue curtains, making the room much darker.

"Take it off," he demands quietly and I do as I am told. The dress pools at my feet and I am left in just my bra. My bra is plain white, with a small bow on the dip between the cups. His eyes go wide and loiter on my chest, and he reaches out and takes the small bow between his long fingers.

"Cute." He smiles and I cringe. I need to invest in some new underthings if Hardin is going to keep seeing me in them. I try to cover my naked body from him. I am more comfortable with Hardin than I have ever been with anyone, but I am still shy standing here clad in only a bra. I glance toward the door and he pads over to make sure it's locked.

"Are you smirking at me?" I scold and he shakes his head.

"Never." He chuckles and leads me to the bed. "Lie down at

the edge of the bed, with your feet on the ground so I can kneel in front of you," he instructs.

I lay back on the large bed and he slides me down by my thighs. My feet dangle but don't reach the floor.

"I never realized how tall the bed is," he says and laughs. "So maybe lie toward the top." I scoot toward the top of the bed and Hardin follows behind. He hooks his arms around my thighs and bends his knees slightly so he is crouched in front of me, between my legs. The anticipation of how this will feel is driving me wild. I wish I had more experience so I would know what to expect.

Hardin's curls tickle my thighs as he lowers his head.

"I'm going to make you feel so good," he mutters against my stomach. My pulse is thrumming through my ears, and I temporarily forget we're in the house with other people.

"Spread your legs, baby," he whispers and I oblige. He gives me a dazed smile and brings his mouth down and kisses just under my belly button. His tongue swirls around my creamy skin and my eyes flutter closed. He nips at the soft skin covering my hip and I yelp in surprise. He sucks the skin between his lips. It stings, but there is something so sensual about it that I don't mind the pain.

"Hardin, please," I breathe. I need some sort of relief from his slow, teasing torture.

Then, without warning his tongue presses flat against my center, making me cry out in pleasure. He makes small strokes with his tongue, and my hands grip the comforter on the bed. I wriggle underneath his skillful tongue and he wraps his arms tighter, holding me in place. I feel Hardin's finger rubbing along with his tongue's caresses and the burn begins to build in my stomach. I feel the cool metal of his lip ring, which adds a different texture and temperature to the sensation.

Without my permission, Hardin slowly slides a finger inside

me, gently easing it in. I clench my eyes closed, waiting for the uncomfortable sting to go away.

"Are you okay?" He lifts his head up slightly, his plump lips glistening from me. I nod, unable to find the words, and he withdraws his finger slowly and slides it back in. It feels incredible in combination with his tongue. I groan and move a hand to his soft hair, threading my fingers through and tugging. His finger keeps entering me and drawing out slowly. Thunder booms throughout the house, echoing off the walls and all around, but I am too distracted to care.

"Hardin," I moan as his tongue finds that overly sensitive spot and he gently sucks. I never knew that anything could feel this way, this good. My body is overtaken by sensation and pleasure, and I sneak a peek down at Hardin, who looks incredibly sexy between my legs, the hard muscles under his skin contracting as he pumps his finger in and out.

"Should I make you come this way?" he asks. I whimper at the loss of his tongue and nod frantically. He smirks and touches his tongue to me again, this time in flicking motions against that spot that I have come to love, literally.

"Oh, Hardin," I breathe and he groans against me, sending the vibrations straight through my center. My legs stiffen, and I mutter his name repeatedly while I come undone. My vision blurs and I screw my eyes shut. Hardin holds me and flicks his tongue faster. I take one hand from his hair and cover my mouth with it, biting down to ensure I won't scream. Seconds later, my head hits the pillow and my chest is heaving up and down as I try to catch my breath. My body is still tingling from the euphoric state I was just in.

I am barely aware of Hardin's body moving up on the bed and lying next to me. He props himself on his elbow and brings his thumb up to caress my cheek. He lets me come back to reality before trying to make me speak.

"How was that?" he asks, his voice holding a hint of uncertainty as I roll my head to look at him.

"Mmm-hmm." I nod and he chuckles. It was incredible, beyond incredible. Now I know why everyone does this type of stuff.

"That sedated, huh?" he teases. The pad of his thumb brushes my lower lip. I bring my tongue out to wet my lips, and it touches Hardin's thumb.

"Thank you." I smile shyly. I don't know why I feel shy after what we just did, but I do. Hardin has seen me in my most vulnerable state, a state that no one else has, and that terrifies me as much as it excites me.

"I should have warned you before using my fingers. I tried to be gentle," he says in apology.

I shake my head. "It's okay, it felt good." I blush.

He smiles and tucks my hair behind my ear. A small shiver runs down my spine, and Hardin's brows lower. "Are you cold?" he asks and I nod. He surprises me by pulling the side of the comforter over and covering my almost naked body.

Bravery brings me to scoot closer to him. His eyes regard me carefully as I curl my body and lay my head against the hard surface of his stomach. His skin is colder than I expected, though the breeze is still floating through the room from the storm. I pull the sheets up and cover his chest, hiding my head underneath. He lifts them up, revealing my face, and I duck away from him, laughing lightly at our little game of hide-and-seek.

I wish I could just lay here with him for hours, feeling his heartbeat against my cheek. "How much longer until we have to go back downstairs?" I ask.

He shrugs. "We should probably go down now before they think we are fucking up here," he jokes and we both laugh a little. I'm getting more and more used to his foul mouth, but it's still a little shocking to hear him say those words so casually. The thing that shocks me the most is the way my skin tingles when he says them.

I groan and climb out of bed. I feel Hardin's eyes on me as I bend down to retrieve my clothes. I toss him his shirt and he pulls it over his head, then ruffles his messy hair. I step into my panties and shimmy them on under his gaze. The tights are next and I almost trip over them as I step into them.

"Stop watching me; it's making me nervous," I tell him, and he smiles, his dimples as prominent as ever.

His hands slide into his pocket and he looks up at the ceiling. I giggle and finally get the tights up.

"Can you zip my dress once I get it on?" I ask him. His eyes scan my body and I can see his pupils dilate from three feet away. I glance down and I see why. My breasts are spilling out of my bra and the lace tights hang just above my hips; I suddenly feel like a pinup girl.

"Y-yeah. I. Will help," he says, gulping. It is astounding that someone as handsome—well, as sexy—as Hardin would be as affected by me as he is. I know I'm considered attractive, but I am nothing like the girls he usually messes with. I have no tattoos, no piercings, and I dress conservatively.

I put the dress on and turn away from him, exposing my back to him, waiting for him to zip it up. I lift my hair up and hold it above my head. His finger grazes along my spine, skipping over my bra strap before he zips the dress. I shiver and lean back against him. I purposely push my behind against him and hear him suck in a breath. His hands move down to my hips and he squeezes gently. I feel him hardening against me, sending electricity through me for what feels like the hundredth time today.

"Hardin?" Karen's voice calls from the hall as a delicate tapping hits the door, and I become extremely thankful we're both dressed.

Hardin rolls his eyes and brings his lips to my ear. "Later," he promises and walks to the door. He switches on the light before opening it, revealing Karen.

"I am so sorry for intruding, but I made some desserts as well, and thought maybe you two would like some?" she offers sweetly. Hardin doesn't answer her but he looks back at me, waiting for my reply.

"Yes, that would be lovely," I say with a smile and she grins back.

"Great! I will see you downstairs," she tells us and turns to walk away.

"I've already had my dessert," Hardin says mischievously, and I swat his arm.

chapter forty-nine

Karen has made lots of sweets for us to eat. I eat a few while she and I discuss her love for baking. Landon doesn't join us in the dining room but it doesn't seem to cause any suspicion. I look over to where he just sits on the couch with his book on his lap and remind myself that I need to make sure I talk to him soon. I don't want to lose his friendship.

"I love baking as well, I am just no good at it," I tell Karen, and she laughs.

"I would love to teach you," she says. Hope is evident in her brown eyes and I nod.

"That would be great." I don't have the heart to say no. I feel for her; she is really trying to make an effort to get to know me. She believes me to be Hardin's girlfriend and I can't tell her otherwise. Hardin has made no move to tell her or his father, either, which gives me a swell of hope. I wish this night was how my life could always be, enjoying spending time with Hardin, his eyes constantly meeting mine as I converse with his father and future stepmother. He is being nice, for the last hour at least, and his thumb rubs over my knuckles in a gentle gesture that gives me a constant string of butterflies. The rain continues to pour outside and the wind howls.

After we finish the desserts, Hardin gets up from the table. I look at him questionably and he leans down to whisper in my ear.

"Be right back, just going to the loo," he says, and I watch him disappear down the hall.

"We both cannot thank you enough. It is so wonderful having Hardin here, even if it's only one dinner," Karen says and Ken takes her hand above the table.

"She's right. It is wonderful, as his father, to see my only son in love. I had always worried he wouldn't be capable . . . he was an . . . angry child," Ken mutters and looks at me. He must notice how I shift uncomfortably in my seat, because he follows up with "I'm sorry, I don't mean to make you uncomfortable, we just love to see him happy."

Happy? Love? I choke on my breath and break into a heap of coughs; the cool water in my glass slides down my throat, calming it, and I look back at them. They think Hardin is in love with me? It would be incredibly rude to laugh at them, but he obviously doesn't know his son.

Before I can respond, Hardin returns and I thank the heavens that I didn't have to respond to their sweet, but false, assumptions. Hardin doesn't sit down, but rather stands behind me with his hands on the back of the chair.

"We really should get going. I have to take Tessa back to the dorms," he says.

"Oh, don't be silly. You two should stay tonight. It's storming outside and we have plenty of room. Right, Ken?"

Hardin's father nods. "Of course, you're both welcome to stay."

Hardin looks at me. I want to stay. To extend my time with Hardin in what feels like a world away from the world, especially when he is in such a good mood.

"I don't mind," I answer. But I don't want to upset him by wanting to stay here any longer. His eyes are unreadable, but he doesn't seem to be angry.

"Great! Then it's settled. I'll show Tessa to a room . . . unless you'll be staying with Hardin in his?" she asks. There is no judgment behind her voice, only kindness.

"No, I'd like my own room, please. If that's okay?"

Hardin glares at me.

So he wanted me in his room with him? The thought excites me, but I don't feel comfortable with them knowing Hardin and I are at that point yet. My snarky subconscious reminds me that we aren't dating at all, or even close to it, so being at a "point" isn't possible. That I have a boyfriend who is not Hardin. I ignore her as usual and follow Karen upstairs. I wonder why she's sending us straight to bed, but I'm not comfortable enough to ask.

She shows me to a room directly across from Hardin's. It isn't quite as large, but it's decorated just as beautifully. The bed is a little smaller and sits on a white frame against the wall. There are pictures of boats and anchors scattered through the room. I thank her multiple times and she hugs me again before leaving me to my room.

I walk around the room and find myself at the window. The backyard is much bigger than I had thought; I had only seen the deck and the trees on the left side. On the right side there is a small building that looks like a greenhouse, but I can't tell through the heavy rain.

As I stare at the rain, my thoughts begin to run wild. Today has been the best time I have ever had with Hardin, despite his multiple outbursts. He has held my hand, which he never does; he put his hand on my back as we walked, and he did his best to comfort me when I was worried about Landon. This is the furthest we have gone in our . . . friendship, or whatever this is. That's the confusing part: I know we can't and never will actually date, but maybe whatever we are doing now will be good enough? I have never imagined being someone's friend with benefits, but I know I won't be able to stay away from him. I have tried many times now, and it never works.

A light knock on the door brings me out of my thoughts. I expect to see Karen or Hardin, but instead I find Landon when I open the door. His hands are in his pockets, and his handsome face holds a small, awkward smile.

"Hey," he says and I smile.

"Hey, do you want to come in?" I ask him, and he nods.

I walk over and sit on the bed; he pulls the chair out from the small table in the corner and takes a seat.

"I—" we both say at the same time and laugh.

"You first," he suggests.

"Okay, I am so sorry that you found out about Hardin and me that way. I didn't go out there with that intention. I was just making sure he was okay; this whole dinner with his father was really getting to him and somehow we just ended up . . . kissing. I know how terrible it is of me, and I know I am horrible for cheating on Noah, but I am just so confused, and I tried to stay away from Hardin. I really did."

"I'm not judging you, Tessa. I was just surprised to see you two making out on the deck. I thought when I walked out I would find you yelling at each other." He laughs and continues. "I knew something was up with you two when you had that fight in the middle of Literature and then when you stayed last weekend, and then when he came back and started a fight with me. The signs were all there, but I thought you would tell me, though I do understand why you didn't."

I feel a huge weight lift off my shoulders. "You're not mad at me? Or think any different of me?" I ask him and he shakes his head.

"No, of course not. I *am* worried about you and Hardin, though. I don't want him to hurt you, and I believe he will. I am sorry for saying that, but as your friend I need you to know that he will."

I want to get defensive and even angry, but part of me knows he is right. I just hope somehow he isn't.

"So what are you going to do about Noah?"

I groan. "I have no idea. I am afraid that if I break up with him I will regret it, but what I am doing to him isn't fair. I just need a little time to decide what to do."

He nods.

"Landon, I'm so relieved that you aren't mad at me. I was being a jerk earlier. I just didn't know what to say. I am sorry."

"Me, too, I completely understand." We both stand up and he hugs me. A warm and comforting hug as the door opens.

"Um . . . am I interrupting something?" Hardin's voice travels through the room.

"No, come in," I tell him and he rolls his eyes. I hope he is still in a decent mood.

"I brought you some clothes to sleep in," he tells me. He places a small pile on the bed and goes to walk out.

"Thank you, but you can stay." I don't want him to leave.

He looks at Landon and snaps, "No, I'm good," before leaving the room.

"He is so moody!" I whine and plop down on the bed.

Landon chuckles and sits back down. "Yeah, *moody* is one word for it."

We both burst into laughter and then Landon begins to talk about Dakota and how he can't wait for her to come visit next weekend. I almost forgot about the bonfire. Noah is coming. Maybe I should tell him not to. What if this change between Hardin and me is all in my head? I feel like something has changed between us today, and he did tell me he wants me more than he has ever wanted anyone. But he didn't exactly say he has feelings for me, only that he wants me. After an hour of Landon and I talking about everything from Tolstoy to the Seattle skyline, he tells me good night and retreats to his room, leaving me alone to my thoughts and the sound of the rain.

chapter fifty

I pick up the clothes Hardin brought me to wear: one of his signa-
ture black T-shirts, a pair of red-and-gray plaid pants, and some
large black socks. I laugh at the idea of Hardin actually wearing
those, but then I realize these are likely from the dresser of un-
worn clothes. I lift the shirt up and it smells like him. He has worn
this one, and recently. The smell is intoxicating, minty and indescribable, but it is my newly acquired favorite scent in the entire
world. I change into the clothes, finding the pants much too big
but very comfortable.

I lie down on the bed and pull the blanket up to my chest, my
eyes fixated on the ceiling as I relive the whole day in my mind. I
feel myself drifting off to sleep, to dream of green eyes and black
T-shirts.

"NO!!" Hardin's voice jolts me awake. *Am I hearing things?*

"Please!" he yells again. I jump out of bed and run across the
hall. My hands find the cold metal of the doorknob to Hardin's
room and, thank God, it opens.

"NO! Please . . ." he yells again. I didn't think this through; if
someone is hurting him, I have no idea what I will do. I fumble
around for the lamp and switch it on. Hardin is shirtless and tangled in the thick comforter, thrashing and tossing. Without thinking, I sit on the bed and reach for his shoulder. His skin is hot,
too hot.

"Hardin!" I say quietly, trying to wake him. His head snaps to
the side, and he whimpers but doesn't wake.

"Hardin, wake up!" I cry and shake him harder while my body moves to sit astride his. Both of my hands go to his shoulders once more and I shake him again.

His eyes fly open; terror fills them for a brief moment before confusion, then relief. Beads of sweat cover his forehead.

"Tess," he chokes. The way he says my name breaks my heart, then heals it. Within seconds he untangles his arms and brings them to my back, pushing me forward to lie on his chest. The wetness of his chest startles me, but I stay put. I can hear his heart beating, pumping rapidly against my cheek. Poor Hardin. I put both of my hands on his sides, hugging him. He strokes my hair as he repeats my name over and over, as if I am his talisman in the dark.

"Hardin, are you okay?" My words are lower than a whisper.

"No," he confesses. His chest is rising and falling slower than it was, but his breathing is still shallow. I don't want to push him to discuss what terror he has just dreamed.

I don't ask him if he wants me to stay; somehow I know he does. When I lift up to turn the lamp off his body stills.

"I was going to switch the light off, or do you want it on?" I ask him. Once he realizes my intentions he relaxes, letting me reach farther to the lamp.

"Off, please," he begs. Once the room returns to darkness, I lay my head back on his chest. I would imagine lying this way, straddling his body would be difficult, but it is comforting to him and me both. Hearing his heart beat under the hard surface of his chest is calming, more calming than the patter of the rain on the roof. I would do anything, give anything, to be able to spend every night with Hardin, to lie this way with him, to have his arms wrapped around me and his breathing slow in my ear.

I WAKE UP to Hardin shifting below me. I am still lying on top of him, my knees astride him. I lift my head from where it rests on his chest and encounter his dazzling green eyes. In the light of day I am not sure if I am wanted the way I was last night. I can't read his expression, which leaves my nerves to take over. I move to climb off him, since my neck feels sore from sleeping on his hard chest, and I need to stretch my legs out anyway.

"Good morning." He gives me a dimpled smile, soothing my fear.

"Good morning."

"Where are you going?" he asks.

"My neck hurts," I say, and he brings me to lie next to him, my back pressed against his front. He startles me by bringing his hand to my neck, causing me to jump. I recover quickly as his hand begins to rub my neck. My eyes close and I wince a little at his contact with the ache, but the pain slowly disappears as he massages.

He speaks before me. "Thank you."

I turn my head to look at him. "For what?" *Maybe he is telling me to thank him for the neck rub?*

"For . . . coming in here. For staying." His cheeks flush and his eyes dart away from mine. He is embarrassed. Hardin embarrassed; he never ceases to amaze and confuse me.

"You don't have to thank me. Do you want to talk about it?" I hope he does. I want to know what he dreams about.

"No," he states plainly, and I nod. I want to push it further, but I know what will happen if I do.

"I will talk about how incredibly sexy you look wearing my shirt, though," he coos in my ear. He nudges my head with his and brings his lips to my skin. My eyes close in response to his plump lips wrapping around my earlobe, gently tugging. I can feel him hardening against me, making me feel drowsy in an incredible way. This type of mood swing is one that I can enjoy.

"Hardin," I chirp and he chuckles against my neck. His hands travel down my body; he brings his thumb along the waistband of the oversize plaid pajamas. My pulse begins to quicken and I gasp as his hand slides down the front of the pants. He always has the same effect on me; within seconds I feel myself pooling in my panties. His other hand cups my breast and he hisses as he flicks his thumb over my sensitive nipple, making me glad I decided not to sleep in my bra.

"I can't get enough of you, Tess." His raspy voice is even deeper, filled with lust. His hand cups me over my panties and he pulls me as close to him as possible. His erection presses against me. I reach down and take his hand, removing it from my pants. When I turn to face him, a frown covers his face.

"I . . . I want to do something for you," I whisper slowly, embarrassed.

A smile overtakes the frown and he takes my chin in between his fingers, forcing me to look at him.

"What do you want to do?" he asks. I don't know, exactly; I just know I want to make him feel as good as he does me. I want to see him lose control like I did in this same room.

"I don't know . . . what do you want me to do?" My lack of experience is evident in my tone.

Hardin puts my hands in his and slides them down to the bulge in his pants. "I really want those plump lips wrapped around me."

I gasp at his words, and feel the pressure in between my thighs.

"Is that something you want?" he asks, his hands moving circles over his crotch. His dark eyes regard me, gauging my reaction.

I nod and gulp, earning a smile from him. He sits up and pulls me to join him. Nervousness and want both flood my body. The loud jingle of his ringtone echoes through the room and he groans before snatching his phone off the table. His eyes meet the screen and he sighs.

"I'll be right back," he informs me and disappears out of the room. He returns a few minutes later and his mood has changed once more.

"Karen is making breakfast. It's almost finished." He pulls open the dresser and grabs a T-shirt, tossing it over his head without looking in my direction.

"Okay." I stand up and go to the door, needing to put a bra on before I go see his family.

"See you downstairs." His tone is emotionless.

I swallow the lump rising in my throat. Guarded Hardin is my least favorite Hardin, even less liked than angry Hardin. *Who called him, and why did it make him so distant? Why can't he just stay in a good mood?*

I nod and walk across the hall, smelling bacon that causes my stomach to grumble.

I put my bra on, and pull the drawstring on the plaid pants as tight as it will go. I contemplate putting my dress back on, but I really don't want to be uncomfortable this early in the morning. Checking the large mirror on the wall, I run my fingers through my unruly hair and wipe the sleep from my eyes.

As I close the bedroom door, Hardin opens his. Instead of looking at him, I focus on the wallpaper and walk forward down the hall. I can hear his steps behind me, and when I reach the staircase his hand wraps around my elbow, pulling me gently.

"What's wrong?" he asks, worry clouding his features.

"Nothing, Hardin," I snap. I am overly emotional and I haven't even had breakfast yet.

"Tell me," he demands, dipping his head so that his face is in full view.

I give in. "Who called you?"

"No one."

He lies. "Was it Molly?" I don't want to know the answer.

He doesn't say anything, but his expression gives away that I'm right. He left the room as I was about to . . . do that to

him . . . to answer a phone call from Molly? I should be more surprised than I am.

"Tessa, it's not . . ." he begins. I pull my arm from his grip and
he clenches his jaw.

"Hey, guys." Landon appears in the hall, and I smile. His hair
is sticking up slightly and he wears plaid pants similar to mine. He
looks adorable and sleepy. I pass Hardin and move toward Landon.
I refuse to let Hardin know how embarrassed and hurt I am by him
answering Molly's call while we were together like that.

"How did you sleep last night?" Landon asks and I follow him
down the stairs, leaving a frustrated Hardin to himself.

Karen has gone all out on breakfast, like I could have pre-
dicted she would. Hardin joins us at the table a few minutes later,
but I've already piled eggs, bacon, toast, a waffle, and a few grapes
on my plate.

"Thank you so much for making this breakfast for us," I tell
Karen on mine and Hardin's behalf; I know he won't be bothered
with thanking her.

"It's my pleasure, dear—how did you sleep? I hope the storm
didn't keep you awake." She smiles.

Hardin tenses beside me, probably worried I will mention his
nightmare. He should know by now I would never do that, so his
lack of trust only bothers me more.

"I slept great, actually. I sure didn't miss my bed in my dorm!"
I laugh and everyone joins me, everyone except Hardin, of course.
He takes a drink of his orange juice and keeps his eyes focused on
the wall. Mindless breakfast chatter fills the dining room as Ken
and Landon banter about some football game.

AFTER BREAKFAST, I help Karen clean up the kitchen once more.
Hardin hovers in the doorway, not offering to help but just watching me.

"If you don't mind me asking, is that a greenhouse in the backyard?" I ask Karen.

"Why yes, it is. I haven't done much with it this year, but I absolutely love gardening. You should have seen it last summer," she says. "Do you like to garden?"

"Oh, yes, my mother has a greenhouse out back as well and it was where I spent most of my free time as a child."

"Really? Well, maybe if you two come around more often, we could make something out of mine," she says. She is so kind, and loving. Everything I wish I had in a mother.

I smile. "That would be lovely."

Hardin disappears momentarily, and when he returns he clears his throat loudly. We both turn to look at him.

"We should get going soon," he says and I frown. He has my clothes and purse in his hands, holding out my Toms. It's a little weird he doesn't give me a moment to change out of the pajamas, and a little discomforting that he went through my things, but I overlook it. We say our goodbyes and I hug Karen and Ken while Hardin waits impatiently by the door.

I promise them that we will return soon, and hope that it will come true. I knew my time here would end, but it has been such a nice departure from my normal life, no lists, no alarms, no obligations. I am not ready for it to end.

chapter fifty-one

The car ride is awkward. I hold my clothes on my lap and stare out the window, waiting to see if Hardin is going to break the silence that hangs between us. He makes no move to speak so I pull my phone out of my purse. It's off; it must have died last night. I try to turn it on anyway and the screen comes to life. I am relieved to find that I have no new voicemails or texts. The only noise in the car is the light rain and the slow screech of the windshield wipers.

"Are you still mad?" he finally asks as he pulls onto campus.

"No," I lie. I am not exactly mad, just hurt.

"It sure seems like you are. Don't act like a child."

"Well, I am not. I couldn't care less if you want to drop me off so you can go hook up with Molly." The words tumble from my mouth before I can stop them. I hate the way I feel about him and Molly. It makes me sick to my stomach to think of them together. What is it about her, anyway? Her pink hair? Her tattoos?

"That's not what I am doing. Not that it's your business," he scoffs.

"Yeah, well, you jumped to answer your phone when I was about to . . . well, you know," I mutter. I should have just stayed quiet. I don't want to fight with Hardin right now. Especially when I don't know when I will see him again. I really wish he hadn't dropped Literature. He just pushes my buttons, every single one.

"It isn't like that, Theresa," he says.

So we are back to Theresa?

"Really, Hardin? It seems like it is to me. I don't really give a crap anyway. I knew it wouldn't last," I finally admit to him and myself. The reason I didn't want to leave his father's house is that I knew once it was just Hardin and me, it would go back to this. It always does.

"What wouldn't last?"

"This . . . us. You being decent to me." I don't dare to look at him; that's how he gets me to turn to putty every time.

"So what then? You're going to avoid me for another week? We both know that by this weekend you'll be back in my bed," he snaps.

He surely did not just say that.

"Ex-*cuse me*?!" I shout. I am at a loss for words. No one has ever talked to me the way he has—no one has ever been so disrespectful. Tears brim over my eyes as the car slows to park.

Before he can respond, I open the door, grab my things, and bolt toward my room. I cut across the soaking grass and curse at myself for not taking the sidewalk, but I just need to get as far away from Hardin as possible. When he said he wants me, he meant *sexually*. I knew this but it hurts to let it soak in.

"Tessa!" I hear him call. One of Steph's heels drops and falls to the ground but I keep running. I will get her a new pair.

"Damn it, Tessa! Stop!" he yells again. I hadn't expected him to follow me. I push myself to run faster, and finally I reach my building and run down the hall. By the time I reach my dorm room, I am full-on sobbing. I yank the door open, then slam it shut behind me. My tears mix with the rain and I turn to look for my bath towel to clean off with—

And am frozen in place when I see Noah sitting on my bed.

Oh God, not now. Hardin will be crashing through the door any second.

Noah gets up and rushes toward me. "Tessa, what is wrong?

Where have you been?" His hand tries to cup my cheek, but I turn my head. Pain flashes in his eyes as I turn away from his touch.

"It's . . . I am so sorry, Noah," I cry as Hardin yanks the door open, the hinges squeaking and cracking from his might.

Noah's eyes widen and narrow as his gaze meets Hardin's. He backs away from me with a horrified expression. Hardin tosses the high heel that I left behind and walks farther into the room without acknowledging Noah's presence at all.

"I didn't mean that, what I just said," he says.

Noah looks at me, hatred laced through his voice as he exclaims, "That's where you were? You were with him all night? Are those his clothes? I tried to call you and text you all night and all morning—I left you *countless* voicemails and you were with *him*?"

"What? I—" I start, but then turn to Hardin. "You went through my phone, didn't you? You deleted the messages!" I shout at him. My head tells me to answer Noah, but my heart is focused only on Hardin.

"Yeah . . . I did," he admits.

"Why the hell would you do that? You can answer Molly's calls, but you delete my messages from my boyfriend?!"

He winces as I call Noah my boyfriend.

"How dare you play these games with me, Hardin!" I scream, sobbing again.

Noah grabs my wrist and turns me to face him, which only prompts Hardin to shove Noah back by his shoulders.

"Do not touch her," he growls.

This is not happening. I watch as the daytime soap opera that has become my life unfolds in front of me.

"You don't tell me what to do with my girlfriend, you prick," Noah says angrily, and shoves Hardin.

Hardin advances toward Noah once more, but I grab his shirt

and pull him back. Maybe I should let them fight each other. Hardin deserves a good punch in the jaw.

"Stop it! Hardin, just go!" I wipe my tears.

Hardin glares at Noah again and moves to stand in front of me. I reach over and gently place my palm against Hardin's back, hoping it may help calm him.

"No, I'm not leaving this time, Tessa. I have already done that too many times." He sighs and runs his fingers through his hair.

"Tessa, make him leave!" Noah begs, but I ignore him. I have to know what Hardin will say.

"I didn't mean what I said in the car, and I don't know why I took Molly's phone call. It's a habit, I guess—please just give me another chance. I know you have already given me too many chances, but I just need one more. Please, Tess." He lets out a big breath. He sounds exhausted.

"Why should I, Hardin? I have continued to give you chances to be my friend over and over," I tell him. "I don't think I have it in me to try again." I am faintly aware of Noah gaping at us, but at the moment I don't care. I know this is wrong—I'm wrong—but I've never wanted anything so much in my life.

"I don't just want to be friends . . . I want more." His words knock the wind right out of me.

"No, you don't." *Hardin doesn't date,* my subconscious warns.

"Yes, I do. I do."

"You said you don't date and that I wasn't your type," I remind him. My mind still can't wrap itself around the fact that I am having this conversation with Hardin, in front of Noah, at that.

"You aren't my type, just the way that I am not yours. But that's why we are good for each other—we are so different, yet we're the same. You told me once that I bring out the worst in you. Well, you bring out the best in me. I know you feel it, too, Tessa. And yes, I didn't date, until you. You make me want to

date, you make me want to be better. I want you to think I am
worthy of you; I want you to want me the way I do you. I want to
fight with you, even scream at each other until one of us admits
we are wrong. I want to make you laugh, and listen to you ramble
about classic novels. I just . . . I need you. I know I am cruel at
times . . . well, all the time, but that's only because I don't know
how else to be." His voice becomes a half whisper, his eyes wild.
"This has been me for so long, I have never wanted to be any
other way. Until now, until you."

I am dumbfounded. He's said everything I wanted him to say
but never imagined that he actually would. This is not the Hardin
I know, but the way his words came out in a rushed string, and
the heavy breathing that accompanied them, somehow make it all
the more true and natural.

I am not sure how I am still standing after his declaration.

"What the *hell*? *Tessa?*" Noah says frantically.

"You should go," I whisper, not breaking eye contact with
Hardin.

Noah steps forward and crows with victory. "*Thank* you! I
thought that was never going to end."

Hardin looks heartbroken, absolutely crushed.

"Noah, I said *you should go*," I repeat.

Both men suck in a sharp breath. Relief washes over Hardin
and I reach for his hands, threading my small fingers through his
trembling ones.

"*What?*" Noah shouts. "You can't be serious, Tessa! We have
known each other so long—this guy is just using you. He will toss
you aside as soon as he is done with you, and I *love* you! Don't
make this mistake, Tessa," he begs.

I feel for him, and it hurts me to do this to him, but I know I
can't be with Noah. I want Hardin. More than anything I've ever
wanted in my life.

And Hardin wants me. More with me.

My heart flutters again and I look at Noah, who opens his mouth to say something.

"I would stop talking. Now," Hardin warns him.

"I am so sorry that it happened this way, I really am," I say.

He doesn't say anything else. He looks broken as he picks up the backpack he brought and leaves my room.

"Tessa . . . I . . . You really do feel the same way?" Hardin gasps and I nod.

How could he not know this by now?

"No nodding, please say it." Desperation fuels his words.

"Yeah, Hardin I do," I say. I don't have a beautiful or meaningful speech like he did, but those simple words seem to be enough for him.

The smile I receive heals some of the pain I feel from breaking Noah's heart.

"So what do we do now?" he asks. "I'm new at this." He flushes.

"Kiss me," I say and he pulls me to his chest, his hand fisting the loose fabric of his shirt on my back. His lips are cool and his tongue is warm as it slips into my mouth. Despite the chaos that just occurred in my small room, I feel calm. This feels like a dream. I somehow know it is the calm before the storm, but right now Hardin is my anchor. I just pray that he doesn't pull me under.

chapter fifty-two

When Hardin finally breaks our kiss, he sits on my bed and I join him.

We're quiet for a few minutes, so I begin to feel nervous, like there is some way I should be behaving now that we are . . . more, but I have no clue what way that is.

"What do you have planned for the rest of the day?" he asks.

"Nothing, just studying," I say.

"Cool." He clicks his tongue onto the roof of his mouth. He seems nervous, too, and I am glad it isn't just me.

"Come here." Hardin beckons me and opens his arms.

The moment I sit on his lap, the door opens and he groans. Steph, Tristan, and Nate all pour in and then stare at us as I climb off Hardin and sit on the other side of the bed.

"So are you guys like fuck buddies now?" Nate says plainly.

"No! We aren't!" I squeak. I don't know what I should tell them, so I just wait for Hardin to say something. He stays quiet as Tristan and Nate begin to talk to him about the party last night.

"It seems I didn't miss much," Hardin says to them, and Nate shrugs.

"Until Molly gave us a strip show; she got completely naked, you should have been there," Nate replies. I cringe and look toward Steph, who is staring at Tristan, probably hoping he isn't going to comment on Molly being naked.

Hardin smiles. "Nothing I haven't seen before."

I gasp, then try to conceal it as a cough. *He did not just say that.*

His face falls, seeming to understand what he just did.

Maybe this was a terrible idea; it is already sort of awkward, and now that everyone is in the room it's magnified. Why didn't he tell them we were dating? *Are we dating?* I don't really understand, myself. I thought after his confession that we were, but we never actually said it. *Maybe we don't need to?* This uncertainty is already driving me crazy; the entire time I have been with Noah I have never had to worry about his feelings for me. I never had to deal with ex-friends with benefits—I am the only girl Noah has ever kissed in his life, and honestly I like it that way. I wish Hardin had never done anything with another girl, or at least had done things with fewer of them.

"We're going bowling after I change. Do you want to come?" Steph asks and I shake my head.

"I have to catch up on my studying. I have barely gotten any done this weekend," I tell her and look away as the memories of this weekend flood through my mind.

"You should come, it will be fun," Hardin says, but I shake my head. I really need to stay in, and I was sort of hoping he would stay with me. Steph steps into the closet and returns a few minutes later with different clothes on.

"Ready, guys? You're sure you don't want to come?" she asks me.

I nod. "I'm sure."

They all get up to leave, and Hardin gives me a wave and a small smile before exiting the room. I'm disappointed with Hardin's goodbye, and hope that he'd made these plans before this weekend together and the drama today.

But what did I expect? For him to rush over and kiss me, tell me he would miss me? I laugh at the thought. I don't know if anything will even change between Hardin and me besides us actively trying to avoid one another. I am too used to how things are with Noah, so I have no idea how this is going to be, and I hate not having control over every situation.

After an hour of studying and attempting to take a nap, I grab my phone to text Hardin. *Wait, I don't even have his number.* I had never thought about it before; we have never talked on the phone or texted before. We never needed to; we couldn't stand each other. This is going to be more complicated than I thought.

I call my mother to catch up with her, and mostly to see if Noah has told her what happened yet. He would be arriving back home soon from the two-hour drive, and I am sure he won't waste any time telling her everything. She answers with a simple hello, so I know she has no clue yet. I tell her about my failed attempt to get a car, and the possible internship with Vance. Of course, she reminds me that I have been at college over a month and I still haven't found a car. I roll my eyes and let her continue to ramble on about what she has been doing the last week. My phone lights up while I am listening to her. I place her on speakerphone and read the text.

You should have come with us, with me, the message reads. My heart swells; it's Hardin.

Pretending to listen to my mother, I mumble "Hmm . . . oh . . ." a few times while I text him back.

You should have stayed, I send. I stare at the screen, waiting for him to reply.

I am coming to pick you up, he replies after what seems like forever.

What? No, I don't want to go bowling, you're already there. Just stay.

I already left. Be ready. Boy, he's demanding, even through text messages.

My mother is still talking and I have no idea what about. I stopped listening once Hardin texted me. "Mom, I will call you back," I interrupt.

"Why?" she asks with surprise and disdain.

"I . . . um . . . well, I spilled coffee on my notes. I gotta go."

I hang up and hastily go into the closet, pulling Hardin's pajamas off and grabbing my new jeans and a plain purple top. I brush out my hair, which looks decent considering it hasn't been washed. I check the time and go down to the bathroom to brush my teeth, and when I return Hardin is waiting on my bed.

"Where were you?" he asks.

"Brushing my teeth," I tell him and put my toiletry bag away.

"Ready?" He stands up and walks toward me. I half expect him to hug me, but he doesn't. He just moves to the door.

I nod and grab my purse and phone.

When we get to his car, he keeps the radio down as he drives. I really don't want to go to the bowling alley. I hate bowling, but I want to spend time with him. I don't like how codependent I already feel.

"How long do you think we will be there?" I ask after a few minutes of silence.

"I don't know . . . why?" He looks sideways at me.

"I don't know . . . I don't really care for bowling."

"It won't be too bad. Everyone's there," he assures me. I hope everyone doesn't include part-time ho Molly.

"I guess," I mumble and look out the window.

"You don't want to go?" His voice is quiet.

"Not really, that's why I said no the first time." I laugh a little nonlaugh.

"Let's go somewhere else, then?"

"Where?" I am irritated with him, but I'm not sure why.

"My house," he suggests and I smile and nod. His smile grows, showing the dimples that I have grown so fond of. "My house it is, then." He reaches over and puts his hand on my thigh. My skin warms, and I put my hand over his.

Fifteen minutes later we are pulling up to the large frater-nity house. I haven't been here since Hardin and I fought and I walked back to the dorms. As he leads me up the stairs, none of the guys bothers to look twice at us; they must be used to see-ing Hardin bring a girl home. My stomach pings at the thought. I need to stop thinking this way, because it's going to drive me in-sane and there is nothing I can do to change it.

"Here we are," Hardin says and unlocks his door. I follow him inside and he turns the light on, kicking his boots off his feet and onto the floor. He moves over to his bed and pats the spot next to him.

As I walk toward him, my curiosity gets the best of me. "Was Molly there? At the bowling alley?" I look out his window as I ask him.

"Yeah, of course she was," he answers casually. "Why?"

I sit down on the soft bed and Hardin pulls me by my an-kles closer to him. I laugh and slide closer, my back flat against the bed, putting my knees up and my feet on the other side of his legs.

"I was just wondering . . ." I tell him and he grins.

"She is always going to be around; she's a part of our group."

I know it's silly of me to be this jealous of her, but she just bothers me. She acts like she likes me, when I know she doesn't, and I know she likes Hardin. Now that we are . . . whatever we are, I don't want her near him.

"You aren't like worried that I will fuck her, are you?"

I swat his arm at his use of words. I love the way dirty words sound coming off his lips, but not when she's involved.

"No, well, I . . . maybe. I just know you have before, and I don't want you to again," I say. I am sure he is going to mock my jealousy, so I turn my head sideways.

His hand goes to my knee and he squeezes gently. "I wouldn't do that . . . not now. Don't worry about her, okay?" His words are gentle, and I believe him.

"Why didn't you tell anyone about us?" I know I should just shut my mouth, but it has been bothering me.

"I don't know . . . I wasn't sure if you wanted me to. Besides, what we do is our business. Not theirs," he explains. His answer is much better than what was going through my mind.

"I guess you're right. I thought maybe you were embarrassed or something?" I say and he laughs.

"Why would I possibly be embarrassed by you? Look at you." His eyes darken and he moves his hand to my stomach. His fingers tug up my shirt and he draws circles on my bare skin with his digits. Goose bumps raise my skin and he smiles.

"I love the way your body responds to me," he breathes. I know what is coming next, and I can't wait.

chapter fifty-three

Hardin's fingers trail farther up my shirt, causing my breath to quicken. A smile creeps onto his beautiful face as he becomes aware.

"One touch and you're already panting," his raspy voice whispers. He leans over, moving my feet off his lap so that he can bring his mouth to my neck. His tongue makes a flat stripe down my neck and I quiver. My fingers thread into his curls and I tug as he nips at my skin. One of his hands slides down in between my legs but I grab his wrist to stop him.

"What's wrong?" he asks.

"Nothing . . . I just thought that I would do something for you this time?"

I look away, but his fingers cup my chin so I am forced to make eye contact with him. He tries to hide his smirk, but I catch him.

"And what would you like to do for me?"

"Well . . . I thought I could, you know, what you said the other day?" I don't know why I am so shy with words when Hardin says anything and everything he is thinking, but the words "blow job" are not in my vocabulary.

"You want to suck my cock?" he asks, clearly surprised.

I am officially horrified. Yet somehow turned on. "Um . . . yeah. I mean if you want me to?" I hope as our relationship progresses I will be able to say these things to him. I would love to be comfortable enough with Hardin to be able to feel that sort of bravery, to tell him exactly what I want to do to him.

"Of course I want you to. I've wanted your lips around me since I first saw you." I'm oddly flattered by his crude remark, but then he asks, "Are you sure, though? Have you ever . . . even seen a dick before?"

I'm sure he knows the answer to that; maybe he's just trying to get me to say it?

"Of course I have. Not a real one, but pictures, and I once walked in on the neighbor watching a naughty movie," I tell him and he stifles a laugh. "Stop laughing at me, Hardin," I warn him.

"I'm not, baby, I'm sorry. It's just I have never met anyone who has such little experience. It's a good thing, though, I swear. Sometimes your innocence just throws me off a bit. But with that being said, it's a huge turn-on that I am the only one who has ever made you come, yourself included." He doesn't laugh this time, which makes me feel better.

"Okay . . . so let's get started."

He smiles and runs his thumb along my cheek. "So sassy, I like it," he says and stands up.

"Where are you going?" I ask him and he smiles.

"Nowhere, I am just taking my pants off."

"I wanted to do that," I say with a pout and he chuckles and tugs his pants back up.

"Here ya go, babe." He puts his hands on his hips.

I smile and move forward, pulling his pants down. Should I pull down his boxers, too? Hardin takes a step back and puts his heels against his bed before sitting down. I drop to my knees in front of him and he takes a deep breath.

"Come closer, babe."

I scoot closer and place my hands on his bent knees.

"Are you okay?" he asks carefully.

I nod and he pulls me up by my elbows.

"Let's just kiss for a minute, okay?" he suggests and pulls me on top of him.

I have to admit I'm relieved. I still want to do this, I just need a minute to process, and kissing will make me more comfortable. He kisses me, slowly at first, but within seconds the electricity builds and takes over me. I grip his arms hard under my finger- tips and rock back and forth on his lap. The bulge in his thin box- ers grows and I tug gently on his hair. *I wish I would have worn a skirt so I could lift it up and feel him against me . . .* I'm shocked by my own thoughts as I reach down and palm him through his boxers.

"Fuck, Tessa. If you keep doing that, I *will* come in my box- ers again," he moans and I stop, climbing off him. I move to get on my knees again.

"Take your jeans off," he instructs, and I nod before unbut- toning them and sliding them down my legs. Feeling brave, I pull my shirt over my head and toss it aside. Hardin takes his lip be- tween his teeth as I move back down in front of him. My fingers grip the waistband of his boxers and tug as he lifts off the bed enough for me to pull them down.

I can feel my eyes widen and hear my own gasp as Hardin's manhood comes into view. Wow, it's big. Much bigger than I ex- pected. *How am I going to even get it into my mouth?*

I stare for a few seconds until I reach out and touch it with my index finger. Hardin chuckles as it moves slightly but bounces right back.

"How . . . I mean . . . what should I do first?" I stutter. I am intimidated by the size of him, but I want to do this.

"I'll show you. Here . . . wrap your fingers like last time . . ."

My fingers go around him and I wiggle them a little. The skin covering him is much softer than I expected. I know I'm poking it and examining it like a science project, but this is so new to me, it almost feels like one.

I grip it lightly and move my hand up and down slowly. "Like this?" I ask, and Hardin nods, his chest rising and falling.

"Now . . . just put your mouth around it. Not all of it, well, if you can . . . but just put as much as you can."

I take a deep breath and lean down. Opening my mouth, I take him in, only about halfway. He hisses and his hands move to my shoulders. I pull back slightly and taste something salty. Is that come already? The taste goes away and I move my head up and down. Some instinct that I wasn't aware of tells me to move my tongue up and down his shaft as I move.

"Holy fuck. Yeah, like that," Hardin groans and I repeat the action. His grip on my shoulders tightens, and his hips rock upward to meet my mouth. I push myself farther, taking almost all of him in, and look up at him. His eyes are rolled to the back of his head and he looks heavenly. The lean muscle underneath his tattooed skin is pulling, making the script across his ribs move slowly. I turn my focus back to sucking and move a little faster.

"Use your hand on . . . on the rest . . ." he gasps and I oblige. My hand moves up and down on the bottom of him as my mouth works the top. I suck my cheeks in and he groans again.

"Fuck . . . fuck. Tessa. I am . . . I am so close," he says, straining. "If you don't want it in your mouth . . . then . . . you . . . have to stop."

I look up at him, keeping him in my mouth. I love the way he is losing control because of me.

"Shit . . . keep looking . . . at me." His body tenses as he watches me. I bat my eyelashes, giving the full effect. Hardin curses my name repeatedly, beautifully, and I feel a slight jerk in my mouth and a warm, salty liquid shoots down my throat in short spurts. I gag and pull back. It didn't taste as bad as I thought it would, but it definitely doesn't taste good. His hands move from my shoulders to my cheeks.

He's out of breath and dazed. "How . . . was it?"

I climb off my knees and sit next to him on the bed. His arms wrap around me and he lays his head on my shoulder. "I thought it was nice," I say, and he laughs.

"Nice?"

"It was fun, sort of. To see you that way. And it didn't taste as bad as I thought," I confess. I should be embarrassed that I just admitted to liking it, but I'm not. "How was it for you?" I ask nervously.

"I was so very pleasantly surprised—the best head I have ever gotten."

I blush at his words. "Sure it was." I laugh. I appreciate him trying to make me feel better about my lack of experience.

"No, really. The way you are so . . . pure, it does something to me. And fuck, when you looked up at me—"

"Okay! Okay!" I cut him off and wave my hand at him. I don't want to relive every detail of my first time doing this. He chuckles and gently pushes me back against the mattress.

"Now let me make you feel as good as you did me," he growls in my ear and sucks the skin on my neck. His fingers hook into my panties and tug them down. "Do you want my finger or my tongue?" he whispers seductively.

"Both," I answer and he smiles.

"As you wish." He dips his head down. I whimper and tug at his hair again. I do that a lot to him, but he seems to like it. My back arches off the bed, and within minutes I'm in a completely euphoric state, calling Hardin's name as I come undone.

AFTER MY BREATHING SLOWS, I sit up and bring my fingers to trace the dark ink on his chest. He watches me carefully but doesn't stop me. He stays quiet as he lies down next to me, letting me enjoy my sedated state.

"No one has ever touched me this way," he says, and I swallow all the questions I want to ask him. Instead of interrogating him, I give him a small smile and a quick kiss on his chest.

"Stay with me tonight?" he asks and I shake my head.

"I can't; tomorrow is Monday and we have classes." I want to stay with him but not on a Sunday.

His look is soft. "Please."

"I don't have any clothes to wear tomorrow."

"Wear those; please stay with me. Just one night. I promise you will make it to your classes on time."

"I don't know . . ."

"I will even make sure you get there fifteen minutes early and have enough time to stop by the coffeehouse and meet Landon," he says and my lips part.

"How do you know I do that?"

"I watch you . . . I mean not all the time. But I notice you more than you think," he tells me and my heart swells. I'm falling for him, hard and fast.

"I'll stay," I tell him but hold my hand up to continue. "On one condition."

"What's that?"

"Come back to Literature," I ask, and he raises his eyebrow.

"Done."

I smile at his simple answer and he pulls me closer to his chest.

chapter fifty-four

After lying in Hardin's arms for a few minutes, I begin to think about my agreement to stay with Hardin tonight.

"What about my shower in the morning?" I remind him.

"You can take one here, down the hall." His lips meet my jaw, trailing kisses up and down. His lips on my skin cause my judgment to cloud; he knows exactly what he is doing.

"In a frat house? Who knows who will come in."

"One, the door locks, and two, I would accompany you, obviously," he says between kisses.

I scowl at his tone but decide to ignore it. "Fine. But I'd like to take a shower now, before it gets too late."

He nods and stands up and reaches for his jeans. I climb off the bed and do the same, leaving my panties off.

"No panties?" He smirks.

Ignoring him, I roll my eyes and say, "Do you have shampoo? I don't even have a hairbrush." I am starting to get anxious thinking of all the things that I don't have with me. "And Q-tips? Dental floss?" I continue.

"Relax, we have Q-tips and floss. We probably even have an extra toothbrush, and I know there is a hairbrush or two in there. There are probably even extra panties in every size lying about somewhere, if you want some," he informs me.

"Panties?" I ask before I realize he means they were left by other girls. "Never mind," I say and he laughs. I hope Hardin doesn't have some weird collection of underwear from girls he has slept with.

He leads me to the bathroom. I feel more comfortable in here than I imagined, only because I have been in this bathroom quite a few times.

Hardin turns on the water and pulls his shirt over his head.

"What are you doing?" I ask.

"Taking a shower?"

"Oh, I thought I was taking one first."

"Take one with me," he says casually.

"Um . . . no! I won't." I laugh. I can't take a shower with him.

"Why not? I've already seen you, you have seen me. What's the big deal?" he groans.

"I don't know . . . I just don't want to." I know he has already seen me naked but this just seems so intimate. More intimate even than what we just did.

"Fine. You go first, then," he says, but his voice has picked up a slight edge.

I smile sweetly and ignore his sour tone and undress. His eyes scan my body and then look away. My hand reaches behind the curtain to check the temperature of the water and I step in.

Hardin stays silent while I wet my hair. Too silent. "Hardin?" I call. Did he leave the bathroom?

"Yeah?"

"I thought maybe you left."

He pulls back the curtain a little and pops his wavy head in. "Nope, still here."

"Is something wrong?" I ask him, frowning sympathetically. He shakes his head in response but doesn't say anything. Is he really pouting like a child because I won't take a shower with him? I almost want to tell him to join me, but I want him to get the point that he can't just get his way all the time. His head disappears from the shower and I hear him sit down on the toilet.

The shampoo and body wash are both strong musky scents. I miss my vanilla shampoo, but this is fine for one night. It probably would have made more sense for Hardin to stay with me in my room, but Steph would be in there, and it would be awkward to explain everything, and I don't imagine Hardin would be as affectionate if she was around. The thought bothers me, but I push it back.

"Could you hand me a towel?" I ask him and shut off the water. "Or two, if you have enough." I like to have one for my hair and one for my body.

His hand pushes through the curtain holding two towels. I thank him, and he mutters something that I don't understand.

He pulls his jeans down as I dry off and turns the water back on. His long arms pull back the curtain and I can't help but stare at his naked body. The more I get to see him this way, the more beautiful the designs printed on his skin are to me. I continue to stare as he steps into the shower. The water sprays onto his dark hair and he closes the curtain. I should have taken one with him, not because he is pouting, but because now I really want to.

"I'm going to go back to your room," I tell him, figuring he's ignoring me anyway.

He jerks the curtain back, causing the rings to scrape against the rod. "No, you're not."

"Okay, what is your problem?" I snap.

"Nothing, you're just not going back by yourself. There are thirty guys living here, so you don't need to be wandering the halls."

"No, there's something else; you have been pouting since I said you couldn't take a shower with me."

"No . . . I haven't."

"Tell me why or I will go out there in this towel," I threaten, knowing I would never actually do it. His eyes narrow and he reaches out for my arm to stop me, splashing water on the floor.

"I just don't like being told no." His voice is low but much softer than it was moments ago.

I imagine that when it comes to girls Hardin hardly, if ever, hears the word *no*. My mind tells me to tell him to get used to it, but I haven't told him no until this point, either. As soon as he touches me, I do whatever he wants.

"Well, I am not like the other girls, Hardin," I snap, my jealousy coming forward.

A small smile plays on his lips as the water runs over his face. "I know, Tess. I know." He closes the curtain and I pull my clothes on and he turns the water off.

"You can wear some of my clothes to bed," he tells me and I nod. I barely hear him because I am too focused on his glistening body in front of me. He rubs the white towel against his hair, leaving it sticking up all over his head, then wraps the towel around his waist. The towel hangs so low on his hips he looks like pure sex. It feels like the temperature in the bathroom has risen twenty degrees. Bending down to open a cabinet, he pulls out a hairbrush and places it into my hand.

"Come," he says and I shake my head, trying to clear the dirty thoughts from my mind. We walk down the hall and turn the corner as a tall blond guy almost runs into me . . . I look up at his face and my bones chill.

"Haven't seen you in a while," he purrs and I feel nauseous.

"Hardin," I squeak and he turns around; it takes him only a moment to remember this is the same guy who tried to make a move on me before.

"Get away from her, Neil," he barks and Neil pales. He must not have seen Hardin before he turned the corner. His mistake.

"My bad, Scott," he says and walks away.

"Thanks," I whisper to Hardin. He wraps his hand over mine and unlocks his door.

"I should just beat the shit out of him, yeah?" Hardin says as I take a seat on the bed.

"No! You shouldn't!" I beg. I can't tell if he is serious, but I don't want to find out. He grabs the remote off his dresser and switches the television on before opening the drawer and tossing me a T-shirt and a pair of boxers.

I remove my jeans and pull the boxers on, rolling them a few times at the top.

"Could I maybe wear the shirt you wore today?" I don't realize how weird it sounds until the words are out.

"What?" He grins.

"I . . . well . . . never mind. I don't know what I was saying," I lie. *I want to wear your dirty shirt because it smells good?* That sounds strange and crazy. He chuckles and picks the shirt off the floor and walks over to me.

"Here, babe," he says and hands it to me. I am glad he didn't embarrass me further, but I still feel a little silly.

"Thanks," I chirp and pull my own shirt off and remove my bra, then slip his shirt on. I inhale and find it smells just as amazing as I knew it would.

Catching this, his eyes soften as he looks at me. "You are beautiful," he says and looks away. I get the feeling he didn't mean to say the words out loud, which makes my heart swell even more. I smile at him and take a step toward him.

"So are you."

"Enough of that," he says with a laugh as his cheeks flush. "What time do you need to be up in the morning?" he asks and sits on the bed, browsing through the channels.

"Five, but I will set my own alarm."

"Five? Five in the morning? Your first class is at what, nine? Why do you get up so early?"

"I don't know, just to be prepared, I guess?" I rake the hair-brush through my hair.

"Well, let's get up at seven; my body doesn't function before seven," he tells me and I groan. Hardin and I are so different.

"Six thirty?" I try to compromise.

"Fine, six thirty," he agrees.

We spend the rest of the evening watching random television shows before Hardin falls asleep with his head on my lap, my fingers running through his hair. I slide down and lie next to him, trying not to wake him.

"Tess?" He groans and his hands move in front of him as if he is reaching for me.

"Here," I whisper from behind him. He turns to his other side and wraps his arm around me before falling back to sleep. He says that he sleeps better when I am around, and I think that's true for me as well.

THE NEXT MORNING, my alarm goes off at six thirty and I rush around to try to put yesterday's clothes on and get Hardin up and dressed. He's so hard to wake up. I feel flustered and unprepared, but we make it to my room by seven fifteen, giving me plenty of time to change and brush my hair and teeth again. Steph sleeps through it all, and I prevent Hardin from pouring a glass of water on her head to wake her. I'm also really happy that Hardin doesn't make any rude comments as I pull on one of my long skirts and a plain blue shirt.

"See, it's only eight; we have twenty minutes before we have to leave to walk to the coffeehouse," Hardin brags.

"We?"

"Yeah, I thought I would walk with you? If not, that's cool, too," he says and looks away.

"Yeah, of course it's fine." I am just not used to whatever this is that has changed between Hardin and me. It will be nice not to have to avoid him, or worry about running into him. *What will Landon think? Will we even tell Landon?*

"What should we do with our twenty minutes?" I smile.

"I have a few ideas." His lips turn to a smirk and he pulls me onto him.

"Steph is here," I remind him as he sucks the skin under my ear.

"I know, we are only kissing," he says, laughing, and he presses his lips to mine.

We leave before Steph wakes, and Hardin offers to carry my bag, which is a nice but unexpected gesture.

"Where are your books?" I ask him.

"I don't bring them. I just borrow one every day, in every class. Keeps me from having to carry one of these," he says and gestures to my bag on his shoulder. I roll my eyes and laugh at him.

When we reach the coffeehouse Landon is leaning against the brick and seems surprised to see Hardin and me together. I give him an "I will explain everything later" look and he smiles.

"Well, I better get going, I have classes to sleep through," Hardin says and I nod. *What should I do, hug him?*

But before I can decide, he drops my bag and hooks his arm around my waist, pulling me to his chest before kissing me. I didn't see this coming. I kiss him back and he releases me.

"See you later," he says with a grin and looks at Landon. This couldn't be more awkward. Landon's jaw is practically on the floor and I find myself embarrassed by Hardin's bold move.

"Um . . . sorry about that." I don't really care for public displays of affection. Noah and I have never done anything like that, except when I tried to kiss him at the mall to get Hardin off my mind.

"I have a lot to tell you," I tell Landon, who picks up my bag.

chapter fifty-five

andon stays quiet during most of my explanation of my breakup with Noah and my question about what to call my relationship with Hardin, since I think we're dating but we haven't exactly discussed it with technical terms.

"I know I have already warned you, so I won't do it again. But please just be careful with him. Though I will admit he seems as infatuated with you as someone like him can be," Landon says as we take our seats.

It means a lot to me that despite his dislike of Hardin he is doing his best to be understanding and supportive.

As I walk into my third class, my Sociology professor waves me over to his podium.

"I just got a call that you should report to the chancellor's office," he tells me.

What? Why? A million fears seize hold of my mind, and then I remember that Hardin's father is the chancellor. I relax a little, only to have my nerves take over for different reasons. What could he possibly need? I know college doesn't work the same way as high school, but I feel as if I am getting called down to the principal's office, only the principal happens to be my . . . *boyfriend's?* . . . dad.

I pull my bag onto my shoulder and make my way across campus to the administration building. It's a long walk and takes me over a half hour. I give the secretary at the front desk my name and she quickly picks up the phone. I can't hear anything except "Dr. Scott."

"He is ready for you," she says with a professional smile and points to the wooden door across the hall.

I go over, but before I can knock, the door creaks open and Ken greets me with a smile. "Tessa, thank you for coming," he says, guiding me inside, then gestures for me to sit down. He takes a seat in the large swivel chair behind an oversize cherry-wood desk. I feel much more intimidated by him in this office than I ever did at his home.

"Sorry for calling you out of class. I didn't know how else to reach you and you know reaching Hardin can be . . . difficult."

"It's okay, really. Is something wrong?" I ask nervously.

"No, not at all. I have a few things to discuss with you. Let's start with the internship." He leans forward and puts his hands on the desk. "I'm happy to say that I talked to my friend at Vance, and he would love to meet with you, the sooner the better. If you're free tomorrow, that would be best," he says.

"Really!" I shriek, my excitement bringing me to my feet. Feeling awkward to be standing, I hastily sit back down. "That's so great, thank you so much! You have no idea how much I appreciate it!" I tell him. This is such great news, I can't believe he would do this for me.

"It really is my pleasure, Tessa." He raises his eyebrows with interest. "So, shall I tell him you will come tomorrow?"

I really don't want to miss any classes, but this is worth it and I am ahead anyway. "Yes, that will be great. Thank you again. Wow," I say and he laughs.

"Now for the second thing, and if you say no, that is perfectly fine. It is more of a personal request, or favor, I suppose. Your internship at Vance will not be affected in any way if you decline," he says and I grow nervous. I nod and he continues. "I am not sure if Hardin has told you that Karen and I are to be married next weekend."

"I knew the wedding was coming up. Oh, and congratulations," I tell him. I didn't know it was that close. My thoughts travel to when Hardin crashed their home and drank almost an entire bottle of scotch.

He smiles kindly. "Thank you very much. What I was wondering was if there is any way . . . that you could possibly . . . convince Hardin to come." His eyes leave mine and he stares at the wall. "I know this is overstepping my boundaries here, but I would hate for him not to be there. And honestly, I believe you are the only one who could convince him to show up. I have asked him a few times and he said no immediately." He lets out a frustrated breath.

I have no idea what to say to him. I would love to get Hardin to his father's wedding, but I doubt he will listen to me. Why does everyone seem to think he will? I remember when Ken told me he believes Hardin is in love with me—a thought that's as absurd as it is untrue.

"I will certainly talk to him. I would love if he went," I tell him in all honesty.

"Really? Thank you so much, Tessa. I hope you don't feel pressured to say yes, though I look forward hopefully to seeing you both there."

A *wedding with Hardin?* The idea sounds so lovely, but Hardin will be hard to convince.

"Karen is very fond of you, and she really enjoyed having you over this weekend. You're welcome anytime."

"I really enjoyed being there. Maybe I can get in touch with her about those baking lessons she offered." I laugh and he chuckles, too. He looks so much like Hardin when he smiles that it makes my heart warm. Hardin's father is so desperate to have a relationship with his angry, broken son that it makes my heart ache for him. If I can do anything to help Ken, I certainly will.

"She would love that! Come by anytime," he booms, and I stand up.

"Thank you again for helping me with the internship. It means so much to me."

"I have looked over your application and transcript, and they are very impressive. Hardin could learn a lot from you," he says with hope in his green eyes.

I feel my cheeks heat up as I smile and say goodbye. By the time I get back across campus to the Literature building, I have only five minutes until class begins. Hardin occupies his old seat and I can't help the smile on my face.

"You held up your end of the deal; so did I," he says and smiles back. I greet Landon and take my seat between them.

"Why were you so late?" Hardin whispers as the professor begins class.

"I'll tell you after class." I know if I bring this up now, he will cause a scene in the middle of class.

"Tell me."

"I said I'll tell you after class. It's no big deal," I promise him. He sighs but lets it go.

When class ends, Hardin and Landon both stand up and I am not sure which one to talk to. I usually talk to Landon after class and we walk out together, but now that Hardin is back, I'm unsure.

"Are you still coming to the bonfire with Dakota and me on Friday? I was thinking you should come over for dinner first. I know my mom would love it," Landon says before Hardin can speak.

"Yeah, of course I am still coming. Dinner sounds great; just let me know the details and I'll be there." I can't wait to meet Dakota. She makes Landon happy and for that I already love her.

"I'll text you," he says and walks away.

"*I'll text you,*" Hardin mocks and I roll my eyes.

"Don't make fun of him," I warn.

"Oh yeah, I forgot how angry you get. I recall you almost jumping over that booth at Molly when she did." He laughs and I give his shoulder a shove.

"I mean it, Hardin, leave him alone," I say, then add, "Please," to soften the mood.

"He's living with my dad. I have earned the right to make fun of him." He smiles at me and I laugh. As we walk out of the building, I decide it's now or never.

"Speaking of your dad . . ." I look over and find Hardin has already tensed up. His eyes are leery as they wait for what I'll say next. "That's where I was today. In his office. He set up an interview at Vance for me tomorrow. Isn't that great?"

"He *what*?" he scoffs.

Here we go.

"He set up an interview for me. It's a great opportunity, Hardin." I plead for his understanding.

"Fine," he sighs.

"There's more."

"Of course there is . . ."

"He invited me to the wedding next weekend . . . well, us. He invited *us* to the wedding." I barely manage to get it out for the glare he's giving me.

"No, not going. End of discussion." He turns to walk away from me.

"Wait, just hear me out. Please?" I reach for his wrist but he jerks away.

"No. You really need to stay out of this, Tessa. I am not kidding. Mind your own damn business for once," he snaps.

"Hardin . . ." I say once more, but he ignores me.

He walks off into the parking lot. My feet have become cement, keeping me from following after him. I watch as his white
car peels out of the parking lot. He is overreacting, and I am not
going to feed into it. He needs some time to cool off before we
speak again. I knew he wouldn't want to go, but I had hoped he
would at least discuss it.

Who am I kidding? We only started this "more" thing two days
ago. I don't know why I keep expecting things to be so much different. They are, in some ways: Hardin is nicer to me mostly, and
he kissed me in public, which was really surprising. However,
Hardin is still essentially Hardin, and he is stubborn and has an
attitude problem. Sighing, I hook my bag over my shoulder and
walk back to my room.

Steph is sitting cross-legged on the floor staring up at her
television when I enter the room. "Where were you last night? It's
not like you to stay out on a school night, young lady," she teases
and I roll my eyes playfully.

"I . . . was out," I tell her. I don't know if I should tell her that
I stayed with Hardin.

"With Hardin," she adds for me, and I look away. "I know
you were; he asked me for your number, then he left the bowling
alley and never came back." Her smile is massive and full of glee
for me.

"Don't tell anyone. I don't exactly know what is going on myself," I say.

Steph promises to stay mute, and we spend the rest of the afternoon talking about her and Tristan before he arrives to pick her
up to take her to dinner. He kisses her as soon as she opens the
door, holds her hand while she gathers her things, and smiles at
her the entire time. Why can't Hardin be that way with me?

I haven't heard anything from Hardin in a few hours, but
I don't want to be the one to text him first. Petty, I know, but I

don't care. When Steph and Tristan leave, I finish up my studying and have gathered my things to go take a shower when my phone buzzes. My heart leaps as soon as I see Hardin's name.

Stay with me tonight? the text reads. He hasn't spoken to me in hours but he wants me to stay with him? Again?

Why? So you can be a jerk to me? I respond. I want to see him, but I'm still annoyed.

I'm on my way, be ready. I roll my eyes at his bossy tone but can't help but feel excited to see him.

I rush down and take a shower so I don't have to take one at his frat house again. By the time I finish, I barely have enough time to gather my clothes for tomorrow. I dread taking the bus all the way to Vance, when it's only a thirty-minute drive, so I renew my resolve to go car shopping again. I am folding my clothes neatly into my bag when Hardin opens the door—without knocking, of course.

"Ready?" he asks and grabs my purse off the dresser. I nod and put my bag over my shoulder and follow him out. We walk to his car in silence, and I find myself repeating a small prayer that the rest of the night doesn't go this way.

chapter fifty-six

I stare out the passenger window, not wanting to speak first. After a couple of blocks, Hardin turns the radio on and then turns it up too loud. I roll my eyes but try to ignore it—until I can't. I hate his taste in music and it gives me an instant headache. Without asking, I turn the knob down and Hardin looks over at me.

"What?" I snap.

"Whoa, someone is in a pissy mood," he says.

"No, I just didn't want to listen to that, and if anyone is in a bad mood, it is you. You were being rude earlier, then you text me and ask me to stay; I don't get it."

"I was pissed because you brought up the wedding. Now that it's settled that we aren't going there is no need for me to be pissed." His tone is calm and sure.

"It is *not* settled—we didn't even talk about it."

"Yes, we did. I told you I'm not going, so drop it, Theresa."

"Well, you may not be going but I am. And I am going over to your dad's house to learn to bake with Karen this week," I tell him.

He clenches his jaw and glares at me. "You're not going to the wedding, and what—are you and Karen like best friends now? You barely even know her."

"So what if I barely know her? I barely know *you*," I tell him. His face falls, and I feel bad, but it is true.

"Why are you being so difficult?" he says through gritted teeth.

"Because you aren't going to tell me what to do, Hardin. It's not happening. If I want to go to the wedding, I will, and I really would like you to come with me. It could be fun—you may even have a nice time. It would mean a lot to your father and Karen, not that you care about that."

He doesn't say anything. He lets out a large breath and I stare back out the window. The rest of the ride is spent in silence, both of us too angry to speak. When we pull up to the fraternity house, Hardin grabs my bag out of the backseat and puts it over his shoulder.

"Why are you part of a frat, anyway?" I ask him. I have been wanting to know the answer since I discovered his room the first time.

He takes a deep breath as we walk up the steps. "Because, by the time I agreed to come here, the dorms were full—and I sure as hell wasn't going to live with my father—so this was one of the few options I had."

"But why stay in it?"

"Because I don't want to live with my father, Tessa. Besides, look at this house; it's nice, and I did get the biggest room." He smirks a little, and I'm glad to see his anger is dying down.

"I mean, why don't you live off campus?" I ask him and he shrugs. Maybe he doesn't want to have to get a job.

I follow him quietly up to his room and wait as he unlocks the door. What is it with him and his obsession over no one going into his room?

"Why won't you let anyone in your room?" I ask and he rolls his eyes. He puts my bag down on the floor.

"Why do you always ask so many questions?" he groans and sits on the chair.

"I don't know, why won't you answer them?" I ask, but of course he ignores me. "Can I hang up my outfit for tomorrow? I don't want it to get too wrinkled from being in my bag."

He seems to think about it for a second before he nods and stands to retrieve a hanger from his closet. I grab the skirt and blouse out and put them on the hanger, ignoring his sour expression at my clothing.

"I have to get up earlier than usual tomorrow so I can be at the bus station by eight forty-five; the stop three streets over is on the route that gets me two blocks away from Vance," I inform him.

"What? You're going there tomorrow? Why didn't you tell me?"

"I did . . . you were too busy sulking to pay attention," I fire back.

"I will drive you there; you don't need to take, what's it, like an hour-long bus ride."

I want to decline his offer just to annoy him but I decide against it. Hardin's car is a much better way to get there than a crowded bus.

"I am going to get a car soon; I can't last any longer without one. If I get the internship, I would have to take the bus there three days a week."

"I would drive you," he says, his voice almost a whisper.

"I'll just get my own car," I tell him. "The last thing I need is for you to be mad at me and not pick me up."

"I would never do that." His tone is serious.

"Yeah, you would. Then I would be stuck trying to find a bus route. No, thanks," I half-joke. I honestly feel like I could depend on him, but I don't want to take any chances. He is just too moody.

Hardin turns on the television and stands up to change his clothes, so I home in on what he's doing. No matter how annoyed with him I am, I would never turn down a chance to watch him undress. His shirt is pulled over his head first, then I watch his muscles contract under his skin as he unbuttons and pulls down his tight black jeans. Just as I think he is going to wear only boxers, he pulls a pair of thin cotton pants out of his dresser and puts them on. He stays shirtless, lucky for me.

"Here," he mumbles and hands me the shirt he just removed. I can't help the smile on my face as I take it in my hands. This must be our thing now; he must like me wearing his shirt to bed as much as I love the smell of him on the fabric. Hardin focuses on the television as I follow his lead and change into his shirt and a pair of yoga pants. The pants are more like spandex leggings, but they are comfortable. After I fold up my bra and clothes Hardin finally looks at me again. He clears his throat and his eyes rake my body.

"Those . . . um . . . are really sexy."

I flush. "Thanks."

"Much better than your fuzzy cloud pants," he teases, and I laugh while taking a seat on the floor. I feel oddly comfortable in his room. Maybe it's the books, or Hardin, I am not sure.

"Did you mean it in the car when you said you barely know me?" he asks quietly. His question is very unexpected.

"Sort of. You aren't the easiest person to get to know."

"I feel like I know you," he says, his eyes locked onto mine.

"Yeah, because I let you. I tell you things about myself."

"I tell you things, too. It may not seem that way, but you know me better than anyone else does." He looks down at the floor, then back into my eyes. He looks sad and vulnerable, such a difference from his usual angry intensity, but equally as captivating.

I am not sure what to say to his confession; I feel like I do know Hardin on a very personal level, like somehow we connect much deeper than just knowing minuscule bits of information about each other, but it doesn't feel like nearly enough. I need to know more.

"You know me better than anyone, too," I tell him. He knows me, the real Tessa. Not the Tessa that I have to pretend to be around my mother, or even Noah. I have told Hardin things about my father leaving, my mother's criticism, and my fears that I never told anyone else. Hardin seems very pleased with this information; a smile covers his beautiful face as he stands from the chair and moves over to me. He takes my hands into his and pulls me up.

"What do you want to know, Tessa?" he asks, and my heart warms. Hardin is finally willing to tell me more about himself. I am this much closer to figuring out this complicated and angry, yet sometimes lovely, man.

Hardin and I both lie back on the bed, eyes on the ceiling as I ask him at least a hundred questions. He talks about the place he grew up, Hampstead, and how nice it was living there. He talks about the scar on his knee from the first time he learned to ride a bike with no training wheels, and how his mother passed out from the blood. His father was at the bar that day—all day long—so his mother was the one who taught him. He tells me about grade school and how he spent most of his time reading. He was never very social, and as he got older, his dad drank more and more and his parents fought more and more. He tells me about how he got kicked out of secondary school for fighting but his mother begged them to let him back. He began getting tattoos at sixteen; his friend would do them in his basement. His first tattoo was a star, and once he got one he wanted more and more. He tells me he doesn't have a specific reason why he hasn't tattooed his back; he just hasn't gotten around to it yet. He hates birds, despite the two inked above his collarbones, and loves classic cars. The best day of his life was when he learned to drive, and the worst was when his parents divorced. His father stopped drinking when he was fourteen and has been trying to make up for all the terrible years, but Hardin isn't having it.

My head is swimming with all of this new information and I feel like I finally understand him. There are still many more things I would love to know about him, but he falls asleep while telling me about the playhouse made from cardboard boxes that he and his mother and her friend made when he was eight. As I watch him sleep, he appears so much younger now that I know about his childhood, which seems like it was mostly happy until his father's alcoholism poisoned it, creating the angry Hardin of today. I lean over and give the proud rebel a kiss on his cheek before crawling into bed to sleep, too.

I don't want to wake him, so I pull the comforter sideways to cover myself up. That night, my dreams are clouded by a curly-haired little boy falling off a bicycle.

"STOP!"

I jolt awake at the pained sound of Hardin's voice. I look around for him, then peer over the bed to see his body jerking on the floor. I hurry out of the bed to get down to him and gently shake his shoulders to try to wake him. I remember how difficult it was the last time, so I lean down on him and wrap my small arms around his shoulders as he tries to thrash away from me. A whimper escapes his perfect lips and then his eyes shoot open.

"Tess," he gasps and wraps his arms around me. He is panting, sweating. I should have asked him about the nightmares, but I didn't want to be greedy; he told me much, much more than I had expected him to.

"I'm here, I'm here," I say to comfort him. I pull his arm, gesturing for him to get up and come to bed. When his eyes meet mine, the confusion and fear slowly fade out of them.

"I thought you left," he whispers. We lie down and he pulls me as close to him as possible. I run my fingers through his damp and unruly hair, and his eyes flutter closed.

I don't say anything. I just continue to rub his scalp to calm him.

"Don't ever leave me, Tess," he whispers and falls back into sleep. My heart nearly explodes at his plea, and I know that as long as he wants me here, I'm here.

chapter fifty-seven

The next morning I wake up before Hardin and manage to roll him off me and untangle our legs without waking him. The memory of him saying my name in relief and all the secrets about himself he disclosed makes my stomach flutter. He was so unguarded and open last night, it made me care for him even more. The depth of my feelings for him scares me and I feel like I can tell they're there, but I'm not really ready to face them yet. I get my curling iron and the small bag of Steph's makeup I borrowed, with her permission, of course, and walk down to the bathroom.

The hallway is empty, and no one knocks on the door while I get ready. I'm not as lucky as I make my way back to Hardin's room. Three guys come down the hall in my direction, one of them Logan.

"Hey, Tessa!" he chirps and flashes me his perfect smile.

"Hey, how are you?" I feel awkward with the three of them staring at me.

"Good, just on our way out. Are you like moving in here or something?" he says, and laughs.

"No, definitely not. Just . . . um . . . visiting." I have no clue what to say. The tall guy bends down and whispers something into Logan's ear. I can't make out what he says, but I look away. "Well, I will see you guys later," I say.

"Yeah, see you tonight at the party," Logan says and walks away.

What party? Why wouldn't Hardin mention a party to me?

Maybe he doesn't plan on being there? *Or maybe he doesn't want you to come,* my subconscious adds. Who throws a party on a Tuesday, anyway?

When I reach Hardin's door, it opens before I reach the handle.

"Where were you?" he says and opens it wide enough for me to walk in.

"Doing my hair. I wanted to let you sleep," I tell him.

"I told you not to be wandering the halls, Tessa," he scolds.

"And I told you not to boss me around, Hardin," I add sarcastically, and his features soften.

"Touché." He laughs and steps closer to me. He places one of his hands on the small of my back and puts the other beneath my shirt and on my stomach. His fingers are rough with calluses but glide gently on my skin, moving higher and higher on my stomach.

"However, you really should wear a bra when you're roaming the halls of a fraternity house, Theresa." He brings his mouth to my ear at the exact moment that his fingers find my breasts. He rubs over the sensitive area with his thumbs, making them harden under his touch. He sucks in a sharp breath, and I am frozen but my heart is racing. "You never know what kind of perverts are lurking in the halls," he says softly into my ear.

His thumbs swirl around my nipples, before he pinches them lightly. My head falls to his chest and I am unable to control my moans as his fingers continue their gentle assault.

"I bet I could make you come just by doing this," he says and applies more pressure.

I had no idea that this could feel this . . . good. I nod and Hardin chuckles, his mouth against my ear. "Do you want me to do that? Make you come?" he asks and I nod again. Does he even have to ask? My heavy breathing and shaky knees should give it away.

"Good girl, now let's move to the—" he begins when the alarm on my cell phone goes off.

I snap to attention. "Oh God! We have to leave in ten minutes, Hardin, and you're not even dressed. I'm not even dressed!"

I pull away, but he shakes his head and pulls me back to him, this time pulling my pants and panties down my legs. He reaches over and shuts my phone off.

"I only need two minutes; that leaves eight to get dressed." He lifts me off the floor, taking me over to the bed. He sits me down on it, kneels in front of me, and pulls me by my ankles to the edge. "Spread your legs, baby," he coos, and I oblige.

I know this wasn't on my schedule for this morning, but I can't think of a better way to start my day. His long finger traces up my thighs and he holds me down with one hand. His head dips down and he licks up and down my core once before puckering his lips and sucking. It's that spot again, oh Lord. My hips buck off the bed and he pushes me back down and continues to hold me down. Using his other hand, he inserts a finger into me, pumping faster than ever before. I can't decide if his hands or his sucking feels better, but the combination is mind-blowing. Within seconds I feel that burn in the pit of my stomach and he pumps his finger faster.

"I'm going to try two, okay?" he says and I moan in approval. The feeling is strange and a little uncomfortable, like the first time he slipped his one finger inside me, but when he places his lips back on me and sucks again, I forget about the subtle pain. I whimper as Hardin removes his mouth once more.

"Shit, you're so tight, baby." His words alone are going to send me over the edge. "You okay?" he asks.

I grab him by his curls and push his face down. He chuckles and then attaches his lips again. I moan his name and pull his hair as I experience my strongest orgasm ever. Not that I have had many, but this one was definitely the quickest and strongest. Hardin places a small kiss on my hipbone before standing and walking to the closet. I lift my head and try to catch my breath. He walks back over and wipes me off with a T-shirt, which might be more embarrassing if I were fully coherent.

"I'll be right back. I'm going to brush my teeth." He smiles and exits the room. I stand up and get myself dressed and check the time. We have three minutes until we have to leave. When Hardin returns, he quickly gets dressed and we're gone.

"Do you know how to get there?" I ask as he pulls out of the driveway.

"Yeah, my father's best mate from university is Christian Vance," he tells me. "I've been there a couple of times."

"Oh . . . wow." I knew Ken had a connection there, but I didn't know the CEO was his best friend.

"Don't worry, he's a nice guy. A bit of a square but nice; you'll fit right in." His smile is contagious. "You look lovely, by the way."

"Thank you. You seem to be in a good mood this morning," I say teasingly.

"Yeah, having my head between your thighs this early in the morning seems like an omen for a good day." He laughs and takes my hand in his.

"Hardin!" I scold him, but he only laughs once more.

The drive goes quickly, and in no time we're pulling around back of a six-story building with mirrored glass sides and a large *V* placed on the front.

"I'm nervous," I admit as I check my makeup in the mirror.

"Don't be; you will do fine. You are *so* smart, and he'll see that," Hardin assures me.

God, I love when he is nice like this.

"Thank you," I say and lean across to kiss him. It is a sweet and simple kiss.

"I'll be in the car waiting for you," he says and kisses me again.

The inside of the building is just as elegant as the outside.

When I reach the front desk, I am given a day pass and instructed to go to the sixth floor. I reach the desk on the sixth floor and give the young man my name.

He flashes his perfect white smile at me before walking me to a large office and saying, "Mr. Vance, Theresa Young is here," to a middle-aged man with light patches of facial hair I can see through the doorway.

Mr. Vance waves me in and walks toward me to shake my hand. His green eyes can be seen from across the room and his smile is comforting and relaxes me as he tells me to have a seat.

"It's very nice to meet you, Theresa. Thank you for coming," he says.

"Tessa, call me Tessa. Thank you for having me," I say with a smile.

"So, Tessa, you are a freshman English major?" he asks.

"Yes, sir," I say, nodding.

"Ken Scott gave you a great recommendation, says I would be missing out if I didn't give you an internship."

"Ken is a very kind man," I say and he nods, rubbing his beard with his fingers.

He asks me to tell him what I've been reading of late and who are my favorite and least favorite authors, and to explain why I feel that way. He nods and hmms through my explanation, and when I finish, he smiles.

"Well, Tessa, when can you begin? Ken says with your courses it's easy enough to condense your schedule so you can be here two days a week and take classes on campus the other three," he says and my mouth falls open.

"Really?" is all I can say. This is beyond my expectations. I had assumed I would have to take night classes and come here during the day, *if* I got the offer.

"Yes, and you will also receive credit hours toward your degree for your time spent here."

"Thank you so much. This is such an amazing opportunity, thank you, thank you again." I can't believe how lucky I am.

"We will discuss your pay Monday when you start."

"Pay?" I had assumed it would be an unpaid internship.

"Yes, of course you will be paid for your time." He smiles.

I just nod, afraid that if I open my mouth I will thank him for the thousandth time.

I PRACTICALLY RUN to the car and Hardin climbs out as I near it.

"Well?" he asks and I squeal.

"I got it! It's paid and I will be here two days a week and in school three days—and I get college credit—and he was so nice—and your dad is wonderful for doing this for me—and you are, too, of course. I am just so excited and I . . . well . . . I guess that's it." I laugh and he wraps his arms around me, squeezing me tight and lifting me into the air.

"I'm so happy for you," he says and I bury my fingers in his hair.

"Thank you," I say and he puts me down. "Really, thank you for driving me and waiting in the car."

He assures me that it's no problem, and as we both climb into the car he asks, "What do you want to do for the rest of the afternoon?"

"Go back to school, of course; we can still make it to Literature."

"Really? I bet we could find something much more fun to do."

"No, I've already missed too many classes this week; I don't want to miss any more. I'm going to Literature, and so should you." I smile.

He rolls his eyes but nods in agreement.

We make it just in time for class and I gush to Landon about the internship. He congratulates me and gives me a tight hug.

Hardin rudely makes gagging noises behind us and I kick back at his leg.

After class Hardin walks out with Landon and me as we discuss the details of the bonfire this Friday. I agree to meet Landon at his house at five for dinner and then we'll go to the bonfire at seven. Hardin stays quiet during our discussion, and I wonder if he will accompany me. He said at one point he would go, but I'm pretty sure that was only to compete with Zed. Landon says his goodbyes as we reach the parking lot and walks off, whistling.

"Scott!" someone calls. We both turn around to see Nate and Molly walking toward us. Great, Molly. She is wearing a tank top and a red leather skirt. It's only Tuesday and she's already almost used up her skank quota for the week. She should save that stuff for the weekends.

"Hey," Hardin says and takes a step away from me.

"Hey, Tessa," Molly says in return.

I return her greeting and stand awkwardly as Hardin and Nate exchange hellos.

"You're ready, right?" Nate asks him, and it becomes clear that Hardin told them to meet him here. I don't know why I had assumed we would hang out again; it's not like we can spend every day together, but he could have said something.

"Yeah, I'm ready," Hardin tells them and looks at me. "See you around, Tessa," he casually says and walks off with them. Molly looks back at me with a smirk on her makeup-covered face as she climbs into the passenger seat of Hardin's car and Nate gets in back.

And I stand on the pavement and wonder what the hell just happened.

chapter fifty-eight

During my walk back to my room I realize how foolish I have been, expecting Hardin to be different than before. I should have known better. I should have known that this was too good to be true. Hardin kissing me in front of Landon, Hardin being nice and wanting "more." Hardin telling me about his childhood. I should have known that as soon as his friends came along he would go right back to the Hardin that up until two weeks ago I despised.

"Hey, girl! You coming tonight?" Steph asks as I walk into our room. Tristan is sitting on her bed staring at her in the adoring way I wish Hardin would stare at me.

"No, I'm going to study," I say. It's nice to know that everyone was invited, yet Hardin didn't see fit to even mention the party to me. Probably so he could hang out with Molly without any distractions.

"Oh come on! It will be fun. Hardin will be there." She smiles and I force one back to her.

"Really, it's okay. I need to call my mother and catch up with her and plan my assignments for next week."

"Laaaame!" Steph teases and grabs her purse. "Suit yourself. I'll be out all night, so if you need anything let me know," she says and hugs me goodbye.

I call my mother and tell her about my internship, and of course she is beyond pleased by my amazing opportunity. I leave

Hardin out of the explanation, but I do mention Ken, though I say he is Landon's soon-to-be stepfather, which is true. She asks about Noah and me, but I dodge her questions. I'm surprised and grateful to find that Noah hasn't told my mother everything. He doesn't owe me anything, but I'm thankful for his omission. After listening to her talk for far too long about her new coworker, who she believes is having an affair with her boss, I finally tell her I really need to study and I get off the phone. Immediately, my mind goes back to Hardin, as always. My life was much more simple before I met Hardin, and now after . . . it is complicated and stressful, and I am either extremely happy or there is this burning in my chest when I think of him with Molly.

I will go insane if I just sit here, and it's only six o'clock by the time I give up trying to study. Maybe I should go for a walk? I really need some more friends. I grab my phone and call Landon.

"Hey, Tessa!" His voice is friendly and soothes some of my anxiety.

"Hey, Landon, are you busy?" I ask him.

"No, just watching the game. Why, is something wrong?"

"No, I was just wondering if maybe I could come over and hang out . . . or maybe if your mom doesn't mind I could take her up on those baking lessons." I let out a weak laugh.

"Yeah, of course. She would love that—I'll let her know you're coming."

"Okay, the next bus isn't for thirty minutes, but I will be there as soon as I can," I tell him.

"Bus? Oh yeah, I forgot you haven't found a car. I will come get you."

"No, really, it's okay. I don't mind, I don't want you to go out of your way."

"Tessa, it's less than ten miles. I'll leave now," he says and I finally agree.

I grab my purse and check my phone one last time. Of course Hardin hasn't texted or called me. I hate the way I feel dependent on him, especially when I obviously can't depend on him.

Determined to be independent, I turn my phone off. If I leave it on, I will go crazy checking it every few minutes. Figuring that I really should just leave it here, I put it in the top drawer of my dresser before I go out to wait for Landon to pick me up.

Minutes later he pulls up and honks lightly. I jump off the curb in surprise and we both laugh as I climb into the car.

"My mother is going insane in the kitchen right now, so be prepared for a very detailed baking lesson," he says.

"Really? I love the details!"

"I know you do—we're alike that way," he says and turns on the radio.

I hear the familiar sound of one of my favorite songs. "Can I turn this up?" I ask and he nods.

"You like the Fray?" he asks in a surprised tone.

"Yes! They're my favorite band—I love them. Do you like them?"

"Yes! Who doesn't?" He laughs. I almost tell him Hardin doesn't, but then decide against it.

When we arrive at the house, Ken greets us at the door with a friendly smile. I hope he wasn't expecting Hardin to be with me, but seeing no disappointment on his face, I smile back.

"Karen is in the kitchen; enter at your own risk," he says mischievously.

He wasn't joking. Karen has the entire large island covered in pans, mixing bowls, and a lot of other things I don't recognize.

"Tessa! I'm just getting everything ready!" She's beaming as she makes a hand gesture to highlight all the strange equipment.

"Is there anything I can help you with?"

"No, not at the moment. I am almost finished. . . . There, I'm done."

"I hope it wasn't too late notice for me to come by," I say.

"Oh no, dear, you are always welcome here," she assures me and I can tell she means it.

She hands me an apron to wear and I tie my hair up into a bun. Landon sits on the bench and talks to us for a few minutes while Karen shows me all the ingredients used to make cupcakes from scratch. I pour them into the mixer and turn it on low speed.

"I already feel like a professional baker." I laugh and Landon leans across, wiping his hand across my cheek.

"Sorry, you have some flour on your face." His cheeks flush and I smile.

I start pouring my cupcake batter into the baking pan. When we put them in the oven and start talking about school and home, Landon leaves the "girl talk" and goes to the other room to finish watching a football game he's recorded.

We get lost in conversation while our creations bake and cool, and when she says it's time to ice the cupcakes, I look at them and am really pleased with the way mine turned out. Karen shows me how to use the piping bag to make an L on the top of one of them, and I set it aside for Landon. Karen expertly pipes flowers and green blades of grass onto her cupcakes while I do the best I can with mine.

"I think it's cookies next time." She smiles and places the cupcakes in a serving case.

"Sounds good to me," I tell her and take a bite of one of my cupcakes.

As Karen adjusts the case of sweets, she asks, "And where's Hardin tonight?"

I chew my cake slowly, trying to discern a motive behind her asking. "He's at his house," I answer simply. She frowns slightly but doesn't push it.

Landon wanders back into the kitchen and Karen leaves the room to take a few cupcakes to Ken.

"Is this cupcake for me?" Landon asks and holds up the cupcake with the squiggly *L* written in icing.

"Yeah, I have to work on my piping skills."

He takes a big bite. "The important part is it tastes good," he says with a full mouth. I giggle and he wipes his mouth.

I eat another cupcake and Landon talks about the game, which I don't really care about, but he's nice, so I pretend to listen. My mind travels to Hardin again and I stare out the window.

"Are you okay?" Landon pulls me out of my thoughts.

"Yeah, I'm sorry. I was paying attention . . . at first." I smile apologetically.

"It's all right. Is it Hardin?"

"Yeah . . . how'd you know?" I ask.

"Where is he?"

"The frat house. There's some party tonight . . ." I start, and then decide to confide in him. "And he didn't tell me about it. He had his friends meet him and he just said, 'See you around, Tessa.' I feel like an idiot even repeating this, I know how stupid I sound, but it's driving me crazy. That girl Molly, he used to mess around with her all the time and she's with him now, and he didn't tell them we are . . . whatever we are." I let out a heavy sigh.

"Aren't you two supposed to be dating?" Landon asks.

"Yeah . . . well, I thought so but I don't know now."

"Why don't you try to talk to him? Or go to the party?"

I just look at him. "I can't just go to the party."

"Why not? You've been to their parties before, and you and Hardin are sort of dating, or whatever this is, and your roommate will be there. I would go if I was you."

"Really? Steph did invite me . . . I don't know."

I want to go just to see if Hardin is with Molly but I feel stupid just showing up there.

"I think you should."

"Will you come with me?" I ask.

"Oh no, no. Sorry, Tessa. We are friends but no-ho-ho."

I knew he wouldn't but it was worth asking. "I think I will go. At least to talk to him."

"Good. Just wipe the flour off your face first."

He laughs and I gently push his arm. I stay a little while longer to hang out with Landon; I don't want him to think I was just using him for a roundabout ride to the party, even though I know he doesn't think that.

"GOOD LUCK; CALL ME if you need me," he says as I get out of the car in front of the frat house. After he drives away I think of the irony of my leaving my phone in my room to avoid worrying about Hardin, and yet here I am showing up at his house.

A group of scantily clad girls are standing in the yard, causing me to look down at my outfit: jeans and a cardigan. I barely have any makeup on and my hair is in a bun on top of my head. *What the hell was I thinking coming here?*

I swallow my anxiety and walk inside. I don't see any familiar faces except Logan, who's doing a body shot off a girl wearing only a bra and panties. I walk through the kitchen and someone hands me a red cup full of alcohol, which I put to my lips. If I am going to confront Hardin, I need alcohol. I push my way through the crowded living room to the couch that their group usually hangs out on. Between bodies and over shoulders, Molly's pink hair comes into view . . .

And I feel sick as I notice she isn't sitting on the couch, but on Hardin's lap. His hand is on her thigh and she leans back against him, laughing among her friends like this is the most normal thing in the world.

How did I get myself in this situation with Hardin? I should have stayed away from him. I knew it then and I am slapped in the face with it now. I should just leave. I don't belong here, and

I don't want to cry in front of these people again. I am sick of crying over Hardin, and I am done trying to make him something he isn't. Every time I think I feel as low as I can, he does something else that makes me realize I previously had no idea of the real pain that unrequited feelings can cause. I watch as Molly puts her hand over Hardin's; he moves his away, only to put it on her hip, giving her a playful squeeze and she giggles. I try to force myself to move, to back up, to run, to crawl, to do anything to get me out of here, but my eyes are locked on the boy I was falling for while his eyes are locked on her.

"Tessa!" someone calls. Hardin's head snaps up and his green eyes meet mine. They are wide with shock, and Molly looks my way, then leans farther onto Hardin. His lips part as if he is going to say something, but he doesn't.

Zed appears at my side and I finally force my eyes from Hardin's. I try to muster a smile for him, but all of my energy is being used to prevent myself from bursting into tears.

"Do you want a drink?" Zed asks and I look down. *I was holding a cup of beer, wasn't I?*

At my feet is my cup, the beer spilled across the carpet. I take a step away from it; I normally would clean it up and apologize, but right now I would rather just pretend it wasn't mine. It's so crowded in here, nobody will know.

I have two options: I can run out of here in tears and let Hardin know he got the best of me, or I can put on a brave face and act like I don't care about him and the way he is still holding Molly on his lap.

I decide to go with option two.

"Yes, please. I'd love a drink," I say, my voice strained.

chapter fifty-nine

I follow Zed to the kitchen, mentally psyching myself up so I can get through this party. I wanted to go over and curse Hardin out, tell him to never speak to me again, slap him and rip Molly's pink hair out of her head. However, he would probably just smirk the whole time, so instead I decide to gulp down the entire cherry vodka sour that Zed makes me and ask for another. Hardin has ruined too many of my nights, and I refuse to be that girl.

Zed makes me another sour, but when I hold my cup out again a couple of minutes later, he laughs and holds up his hands. "Whoa, slow down, killer. You already drank two!"

"It just tastes really good." I laugh and lick the remaining cherry flavor off my lips.

"Well, let's just take it slow on this one, yeah?"

When I agree, he mixes me up another one and then says, "I think we are about to play another round of Truth or Dare."

What is with these guys and their annoying games of Truth or Dare? I thought people stopped playing those ridiculous games when they were in high school. The pain in my chest returns as my mind goes over all the things Hardin and Molly may have already been dared to do tonight.

"What did I miss during the last round?" I ask him with the best flirty smile I can manage. I probably look insane, but he smiles back, so it seems to work.

"Just some drunk people sucking face, the usual." He shrugs. The lump in my throat rises but I swallow it back down with my drink. I give a fake laugh and continue to drink out of my cup as we make our way back to the others. Zed takes a seat on the floor diagonally from Hardin and Molly's spot on the couch, and I sit down next to him, closer than I usually would, but that's the point. Part of me had assumed Hardin would have gotten Molly off his lap by now, but he hasn't. So I lean in a little closer yet to Zed.

Hardin's eyes draw to slits, but I ignore him. Molly is still perched on his lap like the whore she is, and Steph gives me a sympathetic smile and glances toward Hardin. The vodka is beginning to take its effect as Nate's turn comes around.

"Truth or dare?" Steph asks.

"Truth," he answers, and she rolls her eyes.

"Pussy." Her colorful language never ceases to surprise me. "Okay . . . Is it true that you pissed in Tristan's closet last weekend?" she asks and they all start laughing except me. I have no clue what they are talking about.

"No! I already told you guys *that wasn't me!*" he groans, making everyone laugh harder. Zed looks over and winks at me in the middle of the uproar.

I hadn't really noticed before, but, *Geez, he is hot. Really hot.*

"Tessa, you playing?" Steph asks and I nod. I look up at Hardin, who is staring at me. I smile at him, then look back at Zed. The frown on Hardin's face takes a little pressure off my chest. He should feel as terrible as I do.

"Okay, truth or dare?" Molly asks.

Of course she would be the one to ask me.

"Dare," I bravely say. God knows what she will have me do.

"I dare you to kiss Zed." A few gasps and chuckles are heard.

"We already know how she feels about kissing people; pick something else," Hardin says through his teeth.

"Actually, it's fine." He wants to play, we can play.

"I don't think—" Hardin starts to say.

"Shut up, Hardin," Steph says and gives me an encouraging smile.

I can't believe I agreed to kiss Zed, even if he's one of the most attractive people I have ever seen. I have only really kissed Noah and Hardin; I figure Johnny from elementary school doesn't count, especially since he tasted like glue.

"You sure?" Zed asks. He's trying to act concerned but I can see the excitement in his perfect features.

"Yeah, I am sure." I take another drink, forcing myself not to look up at Hardin, lest I change my mind. Everyone's eyes are on us as Zed licks his lips and leans in to kiss me. His lips are cold from his drink and I can taste the sweetness of the cherry juice on his tongue. His lips are soft, yet hard against mine, and his tongue moves expertly with mine. I feel the heat rising in my stomach, not nearly as hot as with Hardin, but it feels so good that when Zed's hands move to my waist, we both move up to our knees—

"Okay . . . damn. She said kiss, not fuck in front of everyone," Hardin says and Molly tells him to shut up.

I let my eyes go over to Hardin, and he looks mad, beyond mad. But he brought this upon himself.

I pull away from Zed and feel my cheeks flush as everyone stares at us. Steph gives me a thumbs-up, but I look at the ground. Zed looks very pleased and I feel embarrassed but thrilled with Hardin's reaction.

"Tessa, your turn to ask Tristan," Zed says. Tristan chooses dare, so I give him the least creative dare and have him take a shot.

"Zed, truth or dare?" Tristan asks as he chases his shot.

I down the rest of my drink, and the more I drink, the more numb my emotions become.

"Dare," Zed answers, and Steph whispers something in Tristan's ear that makes him grin.

"I dare you to take Tessa upstairs for ten minutes," Tristan says, and I choke on my breath. This is too much.

"That's a good one!" Molly says and laughs at my expense.

Zed looks at me as if asking me if I'm okay with it. Without thinking, I stand up and grab Zed's hand. He looks as surprised as everyone else, but he stands up, too.

"This isn't part of Truth or Dare, this is . . . um . . . well, it's fucking dumb," Hardin says.

"Why does it matter? They are both single and it's all in good fun, so why do you care?" Molly asks him.

"I . . . I don't care. I just think it's stupid," Hardin answers and my chest hurts again. He obviously had no plan to tell any of his friends that we are . . . were . . . whatever we were. He has been using me this entire time, I am just another girl to him and I was foolish, beyond foolish, to think otherwise.

"Well, good thing it's none of your business, Hardin," I snap and pull Zed by the hand.

"Burn!" "Damn!" I hear a few voices say, and Hardin swears at them as Zed and I walk away. We find a random bedroom at the top of the stairs and Zed pulls the door open and turns the light on.

Now that I am away from Hardin, I begin to feel much more nervous being alone with Zed. No matter how angry I am, I don't want to mess around with Zed. Well, I wouldn't say I don't want to, but I know I shouldn't. I'm not that type of girl.

"So what do you want to do?" I squeak.

He chuckles a little and leads me to the bed. *Oh Lord.*

"Let's just talk, yeah?" he says and I nod and look down at the floor. "Not that I wouldn't love to do many other things with you, but you're intoxicated and I don't want to take advantage of you."

I gasp.

"Surprised?" He beams and I laugh.

"A little," I admit.

"Why? I'm not a jerk, like Hardin," he says and I look away again. "You know, I thought you and Hardin had something going on for a little bit."

"No . . . we are just . . . well, we were friends, but not any-more." I don't want to admit how stupid I was for believing Hardin's lies.

"So are you still seeing your boyfriend from high school?" he asks.

Relieved not to be talking about Hardin, I relax and say, "No, we broke up."

"Oh, that's too bad. He was a lucky guy," he says with a sweet smile.

Zed is so charming. I find myself staring into his caramel eyes; his eyelashes are fuller than mine. "Thanks."

"Maybe I could take you out sometime? On a proper date? Like, not into a bedroom at a frat party," he says, then chuckles nervously.

"Um . . ." I don't know what to say.

"How about I ask again tomorrow when you're sober?" He is much nicer than I thought he would be. Usually guys as attractive as him are jerks . . . like Hardin.

"Deal."

He takes my hand again. "All right then! Let's go back down."

When we walk back downstairs, Hardin and Molly are still on the couch, but Hardin now has a drink and Molly has moved so her legs are draped over him from the side. When Hardin's eyes dart down to where my hand is intertwined with Zed's, I jerk away without thinking, but then grab it again quickly. Hardin clenches his jaw and I look away into the crowd of partiers.

"How was it?" Molly smirks.

"Fun," I answer and Zed stays quiet. I will thank him later for not correcting me.

"It's Molly's turn," Nate announces as we sit back on the floor.

"Truth or dare?" Hardin asks her.

"Dare, of course."

And Hardin looks right into my eyes and says, "I dare you to kiss me."

My heart stops, literally. It stops beating; he is a bigger ass-hole than I ever imagined. My ears are swimming and my heart is pounding as Molly shoots a boastful glance my way before she latches herself to Hardin. All the anger I feel toward Hardin is washed away and replaced by hurt, all-consuming hurt and the feel of hot tears on my face. I can't watch anymore, I just can't.

Within seconds, I'm on my feet and pushing through the drunk crowd. I hear Zed and Steph both call after me, but the room feels like it's spinning and when I close my eyes all I can see is Molly and Hardin. Knocking into people and not looking back, I finally reach the door and the fresh air outside fills my lungs and brings me back to reality.

How could he be so cruel? I run down the stairs on the side-walk. I have to get away from here. I wish I had never met him, I wish I had had a different roommate. I even wish I had never come to WCU.

"Tessa!" I hear and I turn around, convinced I am imagining it until I see Hardin running after me.

chapter sixty

I have never been very athletic, but my adrenaline is in full effect and I push my legs to go faster. I reach the end of the street, but begin to tire. Where the hell am I going to go? I don't remember the path that I walked back to my dorm last time, and I stupidly left my phone in my room. To prove a point. About my independence from Hardin. Hardin, who's chasing me and yelling, "Tessa, stop!"

And I do stop. I stop dead in my tracks. *Why am I even running from him? He* needs to explain why he keeps playing games with *me.*

"What did Zed say to you?"

What? When I turn around to face him, he is only a few feet away and has a shocked expression; he didn't actually expect I would stop.

"*What,* Hardin! *What could you possibly want from me?*" I scream. My heart is pounding from running, and from his breaking it.

"I . . ." He seems to be at a loss for words for once. "Did Zed say something to you?"

"No . . . why would he?" I take another step forward so I am face-to-face with him, my anger rolling off me in waves.

"I'm sorry, okay?" he says quietly. He looks into my eyes and reaches his hand out to take mine, but I swat it away. He ignores my question about Zed but I am too mad to care.

"You're sorry? You're sorry?" I repeat, my voice coming out in a laugh.

"Yeah, I am."

"Go to hell, Hardin." I begin to walk away, but he grabs my arm again. My anger boils over and my hand flies up and smacks him, hard. I am as surprised by my own violence as he is, and I almost want to apologize for hitting him, but the pain he has caused me is so much more than a cuff on the cheek.

His hand moves to his face, slowly rubbing over the red skin of his cheek. He looks at me, anger and confusion stirring behind his eyes.

"What the hell is your problem? You were the one kissing Zed!" he yells. A car passes and the driver stares but I ignore him. I don't care about causing a scene right now.

"You're not seriously trying to blame me! You lied to me and played me like a fool, Hardin! Just when I thought I could trust you, you humiliate me! If you wanted to be with Molly, why not just tell me to leave you alone? No, instead, you feed me that bullshit about wanting more and beg me to stay the night with you just so you can use me! What was the point—what did you get out of it—oh, besides a blow job?" I scream. The word tastes odd coming out of my mouth.

"What? You think that's what I am doing? You think I'm using you?" he shouts.

"No, that's not what I *think,* Hardin—that's what I *know*. But guess what? I'm done, I am so beyond done. I will change dorms if I have to so I don't have to see you again!" I say, and mean it. I don't need any of these people making my life worse.

"You're overreacting," he says flatly, and it takes everything in me not to slap him again.

"I'm overreacting? You didn't tell your friends about us—you didn't tell me about this party, and then you left me standing in the parking lot like a dumbass while you left with Molly, of all people! Then I show up here to find Molly on your lap, and then you kiss her. Right in front of me, Hardin. I'd say my reaction is *quite* justified," I say, my voice drawing to a whisper at the end, exhausted. I wipe fresh tears from my face and blink up at the night sky.

"You kissed Zed right in front of me! And I didn't tell you about the party because *I don't have to*! You wouldn't have wanted to come anyway—you would have been too busy studying or watching the damn paint dry," he barks.

I look at his blurry form through my watery eyes and ask him simply, "So why even waste your time with me? Why even follow me out here, Hardin?" When he doesn't say anything, I have my answer. "That's what I thought. You thought you could come out here and say sorry and I would accept and stay a secret, your boring little hidden girlfriend. You're wrong; you took my kindness for weakness and you were sadly mistaken."

"Girlfriend? You thought you were my *girlfriend*?" he howls.

The pain in my chest is magnified by a thousand and I can barely stand. "No . . . I," I start to say. I don't know what to say.

"You did, didn't you?" he says, laughing.

"You know . . . I did," I admit. I am already humiliated, so I have nothing to lose. "You fed me that bullshit about wanting more, and I believed you. I believed all the shit you said to me, all the things you claimed to never tell anyone, but I'm sure that was all bullshit, too. I'm sure none of that even happened." I shrug, giving up completely. "But you know what? I'm not even mad at you; I'm mad at myself for believing it. I knew how you were before I started to fall for you. I knew you would hurt me. What were your words, *You'll destroy me*? No, *ruin*, you'll ruin me. Well, congratulations, Hardin, you won," I sob.

Pain flashes in his eyes . . . well, what looks like pain. It is probably humor.

I no longer care about winning or losing or playing these exhausting games. I turn away from him again and begin to walk back toward the house, figuring I'll find someone's phone to use to call Landon or somehow get a ride back to the dorms.

"Where are you going?" he asks. It hurts that he doesn't have anything to say, that he has offered me no explanation. He has only confirmed what I already knew, that he is heartless.

I walk faster, ignoring him. He trails behind me, calling my name a couple more times, but I refuse to let myself be charmed by his voice again.

When I get back to the house's front steps, of course I spot Molly's pink hair outside. "Aww, look, she is waiting for you. You two really are perfect for each other," I call over my shoulder to Hardin.

"It's not like that and you know it," he grumbles.

"I don't know anything, obviously," I snap and climb two steps at a time.

Zed appears in the doorway, and I rush to his side. "Can I use your phone? Please?" I beg and he nods.

"Are you okay? I tried to go after you, but you were long gone," he says and I nod.

Hardin stands in front of Zed and me while I call Landon and ask him to pick me up. Zed and Hardin stare at each other for a second when they hear me say Landon's name, then Zed looks away and back down at me. "Is he coming?" he asks, his voice full of concern.

"Yeah, he will be here in a few minutes. Thank you for letting me use your phone," I tell him, ignoring Hardin.

"No problem. Do you want me to wait with you?" he asks.

"No, I will wait with her," Hardin injects, his voice full of venom.

"I would love it if you could wait with me, Zed," I say and walk back down the steps with him. Hardin, being the asshole that he is, follows us and stands behind us awkwardly. Steph, Tristan, and Molly trickle down, too.

"Are you okay?" Steph asks.

"Yeah," I say, nodding. "I'm leaving, though. I shouldn't have even come here."

When Steph hugs me, Molly mutters under her breath, "You got that right."

My head snaps around at the sound of her voice. I hate confrontation usually, but I hate Molly even more. "You're right! I *shouldn't* be here. I'm not as adept as you at getting drunk and hanging all over every guy in the place."

"Excuse me?" she says.

"You heard me."

"What's your problem? Mad that I kissed Hardin? Because, guess what, sweetie, I kiss Hardin *all the time*," she brags.

I feel the blood draining from my face. I look at Hardin, who doesn't say anything. So he's been messing with Molly the entire time? This doesn't surprise me as much as it should. I don't even have a comeback for her. I try to think of something to say back, anything really, but I can't. I'm sure as soon as I walk away I will think of ten replies, but right now I have nothing.

"Let's go inside . . ." Tristan suggests and grabs Molly and Steph by their arms. I try to give him a thankful smile as they start to go.

"You too, Hardin. Get away from me," I say and stare at the street.

"I haven't kissed her, I mean lately. Except for tonight. I swear," he says.

Why is he saying this in front of them?

Molly turns around.

"I don't really give a shit who you kiss. Now get away from me," I repeat.

A huge wave of relief washes over me as I see Landon's car pull up. "Thanks again," I tell Zed.

"No problem, don't forget what we talked about," he says hopefully, reminding me of our supposed "date."

"Tessa . . ." Hardin calls as I step toward the car. When I ignore him, he calls louder. "Tessa!"

"I have said everything I have to say to you, Hardin. I am done listening to you and your bullshit—now leave me the fuck alone!" I scream, turning around to face him. I am aware everyone's eyes are on us, but I have had enough.

"I . . . Tessa, I . . ."

"You *what*? You *what*, Hardin?" I scream even louder.

"I . . . I love you!" he yells.

And all the air disappears from my lungs.

And Molly sounds like she is choking.

And Steph looks like she has seen a ghost.

And for a few moments everyone just stands there, like something alien has passed by us and left us frozen. When at last I can speak, I say quietly, "You're sick, Hardin, you're really fucking sick."

Despite the fact that I know this is part of his game, it still awakens something inside me to hear those words come off his lips. I grab for the door handle on Landon's car but I am yanked away by Hardin.

"It's true, I do. I know you won't believe me, but I do. I love you." His eyes brim with tears. His lips press in a hard line and he covers his face with his hands. He takes a step back, then another forward, and when he takes his hands away, his green eyes appear sincere, full of panic.

Hardin . . . he's a better actor than I thought. I can't believe he is doing this in front of everyone.

I shove him backward and open the car door, locking it before Hardin regains his balance. As Landon drives off, Hardin bangs his hands against the window, and I put my hands over my face so he doesn't see me cry.

chapter sixty-one

After I finally stop sobbing, Landon quietly asks, "Did I hear him say that he loves you?"

"Yeah . . . I don't know . . . He was just trying to cause a scene or something," I say, and almost start crying again.

"Do you think . . . don't get mad at me . . . but do you think that maybe he does? You know, love you?"

"What? Of course not. I am not even sure if he even likes me. I mean, when we're alone he is so different, and I think maybe he does care about me. But I know he doesn't love me. He isn't capable of loving anyone other than himself," I explain.

"I'm on your side, Tessa, I am," Landon replies. "But the look on his face as we drove away, he looked heartbroken. And you can't be heartbroken if you aren't in love."

That can't be true. I felt my heart shatter when he kissed Molly, but I don't love him.

"Do you love him?" he asks simply.

My voice comes out strained and my words too quick. "No. I don't love him . . . he is . . . well . . . he's a jerk. I have known him less than two months, and half of that . . . actually all of that time we have spent fighting. You can't love someone you only met two months ago. Besides, he's a jerk."

"You already said that," Landon says and I notice the hint of a smile on his lips as he tries to keep his expression neutral.

I don't like the pressure that I feel in my chest as we talk about me loving Hardin. It makes me feel nauseous and the space in the car feels much smaller. I roll down the window a crack and lean my head against it, feeling the little stream of air slip across me.

"Do you want to come back to our house, or go to your dorm?" he asks.

I want to go to my dorm and curl into a ball on my bed, but I am afraid that Steph or Hardin will show up. The chance of Hardin coming to his father's house is so slim, that seems to me the better option.

"Your house, but can we go by my room so I can grab some clothes? I'm sorry for asking you to drive me all over."

"Tessa, the drive is short and you're my friend; stop thanking and apologizing to me," he says sternly, but his sweet smile makes me laugh.

He is the best person I have met here and I am so lucky to have him.

"Well, let me thank you one last time for being such a great friend to me," I say, and he frowns playfully.

"You're welcome. Now let's move on."

I RUSH AROUND MY ROOM gathering my clothes and books. I feel like I never stay in my room anymore. This will be the first night in days that I will be sleeping without Hardin. I was beginning to get used to it, how foolish of me. I grab my phone out of my drawer and walk back to Landon's car.

When we get to his house it's after eleven. I'm exhausted, and thankful that Ken and Karen are asleep when we arrive. Landon puts a pizza in the oven for us and I eat another one of my cupcakes from earlier. Baking with Karen seems like weeks ago, not hours. I have had such a long day, and it started so well with my morning with Hardin and the internship, and then he ruined it, just like he always does. After we eat the pizza, Landon and I walk upstairs and he shows me to the guest room that I stayed in last time. Well, I didn't quite *stay* in there, since I was woken up by a screaming Hardin. Time hasn't made sense since I met him; everything has happened so quickly, and it makes me dizzy to think about the better times we've had and how they're spaced out between a lot of arguing. I thank Landon again and he rolls his eyes at me before leaving me and going into his room. I turn on my phone to find many texts from Hardin, Steph, and my mother. I delete all but my mother's message without reading them. I already know what they will say and I have had enough of it today. I turn my ringtone and text notifications off, put my pajamas on, and climb into the bed.

It's one in the morning, and I have to wake up in a few hours. Tomorrow is going to be a long day. If I hadn't missed my morning classes today, I would just stay home, well, here. Or go back to my dorm. Why did I convince Hardin to come back to Literature? After tossing and turning, I roll over to check the time: almost three. Despite the fact that today has been one of the best, and then worst, days of my life, I am too exhausted to even sleep.

Before I realize what I'm doing, I'm standing in front of Hardin's bedroom door. And then I enter it. With no one around but myself to judge me, I open the second drawer and grab a white T-shirt. I can tell that it has never been worn but I don't care. I pull my own shirt off and replace it. I lie down on the bed and bury my head in the pillow. Hardin's minty scent fills my nostrils and I finally fall asleep.

chapter sixty-two

When I wake up, it takes me a moment to remember that I am not in bed with Hardin. The sun is peacefully shining through the bay window and as I look over, I catch sight of a figure and sit up quickly, orienting myself. As my eyes adjust I am convinced that I am going mad.

"Hardin?" I say quietly and wipe my eyes.

"Hey," he says from where he sits in a wingback chair, his elbows on his knees.

"What the hell are you doing here?" I snap. My heart aches already.

"Tessa, we need to talk," he says, the bags under his eyes prominent.

"Have you just been watching me sleep?" I ask.

"No, of course not. I came in here a few minutes ago," he says. I wonder if he had nightmares without me in bed with him. If I hadn't witnessed them myself, I would think those were part of his games as well, but I remember holding his sweaty face between my hands and seeing the real fear in his green eyes.

I stay silent. I don't want to fight with him. I just want him to go away. I hate that I don't actually want him to go away but know that he has to.

"We need to talk," he repeats. When I shake my head no, he runs both hands through his hair and takes a deep breath.

"I have to go to class," I tell him.

"Landon already left. I turned your alarm off. It's eleven already."

"You what!"

"You were up late and I thought you—" he begins.

"How dare you even . . . Just go." The pain from his actions yesterday is still fresh, and actually overshadows the anger I feel at missing my morning classes, but I can't show any weakness or he will pounce on it. He always does.

"You're in my room," he points out.

I climb out of the bed, not caring if I am only in a T-shirt, his T-shirt. "You're right. I'll go," I say, the lump in my throat growing and tears threatening to spill out.

"No, I meant . . . I meant: you are in my room . . . Why?" His voice is bleak.

"I don't know . . . I just . . . I couldn't sleep . . ." I admit. I need to stop talking. "It's not really your room anyway. I've slept here just as many times as you have. Actually more now," I point out.

"Your own shirt didn't fit?" he asks, his eyes focused on the white shirt. Of course he is making fun of me.

"Go ahead, tease me," I say, the tears pooling at the bottom of my eyes. He makes eye contact with me but I look away.

"I wasn't teasing you." He stands up from the chair and takes a step toward me. I back away and raise my hands to block him and he stops. "Just hear me out, okay?"

"What else could you possibly have to say, Hardin? We always do this. We have the same fight over and over, only worse each time. I can't do it anymore. I can't."

"I said I was sorry for kissing her," he says.

"That isn't what this is about. Well, that's part of it, but there is so much more. The fact that you don't get that proves that we are wasting our time. You will never be who I need you to be, and

I am not who you want me to be." I wipe my eyes as he looks out the window.

"But you are who I want you to be," he says.

I wish I could believe him. I wish he wasn't so incapable of feelings.

"You're not," is all I can say. I didn't want to cry in front of him, but I can't seem to stop myself. I have cried so many times since I met him, and if I get tangled back into his web, this is how it will always be.

"I'm not what?"

"Who I want you to be; you do nothing but hurt me." I walk past him and cross the hall to the guest room. I hastily pull my pants up my legs and gather my things, Hardin's eyes following my every move.

"Didn't you hear what I told you yesterday?" he finally says.

I was hoping he wouldn't bring this up.

"Answer me," he says.

"Yeah . . . I heard you," I tell him, avoiding looking in his direction.

His voice becomes hostile. "And you have nothing to say about it?"

"No," I lie. He steps in front of me. "Move," I beg.

He is dangerously close to me and I know what he is going to do as he moves in to kiss me. I try to back away from him, but his strong hands pull me closer, holding me in place. His lips touch mine, and his tongue tries to push through my lips but I refuse.

He eases his head back slightly. "Kiss me back, Tess," he demands.

"No." I push at his chest.

"Tell me you don't feel the same, and I will go." His face is inches from mine, his breath hot on my face.

"I don't." It hurts to say the words but he has to go.

"Yes, you do," he says, his tone desperate. "I know you do."

"I don't, Hardin, and neither do you. You can't possibly think that I bought that?"

He lets go of me. "You don't believe that I love you?"

"Of course not, how stupid do you think I am?"

He stares at me for a second before he opens his mouth and closes it again. "You're right," he says.

"What?"

He shrugs. "You're right, I don't. I don't love you, I was just adding to the drama of the whole thing." He laughs lightly. I know he didn't mean it, but that doesn't make his honesty hurt any less. A part of me, a larger part than I want to accept, hopes that he actually did.

He stands against the wall as I walk out of the room, my bag in hand.

As I reach the stairs, Karen smiles up at me. "Tessa, sweetheart, I didn't know you were here!" Her smile fades as she notices my distressed state. "Are you okay? Did something happen?"

"No, I'm good. I was locked out of my room last night and I . . ."

"Karen," Hardin's voice says from behind me.

"Hardin!" Her smile slightly returns. "Would you two like something to eat, some breakfast? Well, lunch, it's noon."

"No, thank you, I was just going back to the dorms," I tell her as I descend.

"I could eat," Hardin says behind me.

She seems surprised as she looks at me and then back at him. "Okay, great! I will be in the kitchen!"

After she disappears, I head for the door.

"Where are you going?" He grabs my wrist. I struggle for a second before he releases it.

"The dorms, like I just said."

"You're just going to walk?"

"What is wrong with you? You act like nothing is happening,

like we haven't just been fighting, like you haven't done anything. You are seriously insane, Hardin—I'm talking mental institution, medicated, padded-walls insane. You say horrible things to me and then try to offer me a ride?" I can't keep up with him.

"I didn't say anything horrible, actually; all I said was that I don't love you, which you claim you already knew. And secondly, I wasn't offering you a ride. I was simply asking if you were going to walk back."

His smug expression makes me dizzy. Why would he even come here to find me if he doesn't care about me? Doesn't he have anything better to do than torture me?

"What did I do?" I finally ask. I have been wanting to ask this for a while, but I've always been afraid of his answer.

"What?"

"What did I do to make you hate me?" I ask, trying to keep my voice down so Karen doesn't hear me. "You can have practically any girl you want and you continue to waste your time—and mine—to find new ways to hurt me. What's the point? Do you dislike me that much?"

"No, it's not that. I don't dislike you, Tessa. You just made yourself an easy target—it's all about the chase, right?" he says boastfully. Before he can say anything else, Karen calls his name and asks if he wants pickles on his sandwich.

He walks to the kitchen and answers her; I walk out the door.

On the way to the bus stop, I figure that I've already missed so many classes lately I might as well miss the rest of the day and get a car. Luckily, the bus pulls up minutes later and I find a seat in the very back.

As I slump down in the seat, I think back to what Landon said about heartbreak, that if you don't love the person, they can't break your heart. Hardin repeatedly breaks my heart, even when I don't think there are any more pieces to break.

And I love him. I love Hardin.

chapter sixty-three

The salesman is a creep and smells like stale cigarettes, but I can't be picky any longer. After an hour of negotiating, I write him a check for the down payment and he gives me the keys to a decent 2010 Corolla. The white paint is chipped in a few places, but I managed to talk him down low enough that I can let it slide. I call my mother before I drive out of the lot to tell her, and of course she says I should have gotten a bigger car and lists the reasons why. I end up pretending to lose service and shut my phone off.

It feels amazing to drive my own car. I no longer have to depend on public transportation and now I can drive myself to my internship. I hope my cutting ties with Hardin doesn't affect it. I don't think it can, but what if he is bored with just simply making me cry and does something to ruin it? Maybe I should talk to Ken and try to explain that Hardin and I are no longer . . . dating? He thinks we are dating, so I will have to come up with something besides "Your son is the cruelest person in the world and he is toxic to me so I can no longer be around him."

I turn the radio on and turn it up louder than I usually would, but it does what I need it to. It drowns out my thoughts and I focus on every lyric to every song. I ignore the fact that every song seems to remind me of Hardin.

Before heading back to campus, I decide to go buy some more clothes. It's getting colder, so I need some more jeans, and besides, I'm growing tired of wearing my long skirts all the time.

I end up buying a few new outfits to wear to Vance, some plain shirts and cardigans, and a couple of pairs of jeans. They are tighter than usual but they look good on me.

Steph isn't in the room when I return, which is good. I really think I may need to look into changing rooms. I do like Steph, but we can't continue to live together if Hardin is around. Depending on how much I will be making at my internship, I could get my own apartment and live off campus. My mother would lose it but it isn't up to her.

I fold my new clothes and put them away before grabbing my toiletry bag and heading to the showers. When I return, Steph and Zed are sitting on her bed, looking at her computer.

Great.

She looks up sleepily. "Hey, Tessa, did Hardin ever find you last night?" When I nod, she asks, "So did you work it out?"

"No. Well, yeah, I guess. I am done with him," I tell her. Her eyes go wide; she must have assumed he would sink his claws back into me.

"Well, I for one am glad." Zed smiles and Steph swats his arm. Her phone beeps and she looks down.

"Tristan is here, we gotta go. Wanna come?" she asks.

"No, thanks. I'm gonna stay here—but I did get a car today!" I tell her and she squeals.

"Really! That's awesome!" she says and I nod. "You'll have to show me it when I get back," she says and they head for the door. Steph walks out but Zed lingers in the doorway.

"Tessa?" His voice is as smooth as velvet. I look up and he smiles at me. "Did you think about our date?" he asks, staring into my eyes.

"I . . ." I am about to reject him, but why? He's very attractive and seems sweet. He didn't take advantage of me when he easily could have. I know he would be better company than Hardin; anyone would be, honestly. "Sure." I smile.

"Sure as in you will let me take you out?" His smile grows.

"Yeah, why not?" I reply.

"Tonight, then?"

"Yeah, tonight is good." I don't think tonight is a good idea, seeing as I have studying to make up for, but I'm still ahead of the course despite having missed a few classes this week.

"Awesome, I'll be here at seven, yeah?"

"Okay."

He brings his lower lip between his perfect teeth. "See you tonight, beautiful," he says and I flush, waving goodbye as he leaves the room.

It is four now, so I have three hours. I blow-dry my hair and curl the ends, and to my surprise it looks really good. I apply light makeup and put on one of my new outfits, a pair of dark jeans, a white tank top, and a long brown cardigan. My nerves are getting the best of me as I stare into the mirror. *Maybe I should change?* I switch to a blue tank top and a button-up shirt. I can't believe I am going on a date with Zed. I've had one boyfriend in my entire life, and now I am going on a date with Zed after all this mess with Hardin. Maybe guys with tattoos and piercings are my new type?

I pull out my old copy of *Pride and Prejudice* and begin to read to pass the time. But my mind wanders, and thoughts of Noah continue to preoccupy me. Should I call him? I reach for my phone and scroll through the names until I reach his. I stare at the screen; my guilt and my common sense fight it out until I toss my phone back onto my bed.

WHAT SEEMS LIKE just minutes later, there is a knock at the door. I know it must be Zed because Hardin wouldn't knock. He would rudely barge in and throw my stuff all over the place.

When I open the door I can't help but gape. Zed is dressed in tight black jeans, white sneakers, and a T-shirt with a cutoff jean jacket over it. He looks so hot.

"You look beautiful, Tessa," he says, and then hands me a flower.

A *flower?* I'm both surprised and flattered by Zed's thoughtful gift.

"Thank you." I smile and bring the white lily to my nose.

"Are you ready?" he asks politely.

"Yes, where are you taking me?" I ask him as we walk outside.

"I figured we'd just go to dinner and a movie, something casual, no pressure." He beams.

I reach for the passenger door handle but he stops me. "Allow me," he says with humor in his voice.

"Oh. Thanks."

I'm still nervous, but Zed's so nice it makes it easy to start to relax. When we get into the car he keeps the radio off and makes small talk, asking about my family and my plans after college. He tells me how he is going to WCU for environmental science, which surprises but intrigues me.

We arrive at a casual café-style restaurant and sit out on the patio. After ordering our meals, we continue chatting until the food comes. Zed eats all of his food and begins to steal fries off my plate.

I lift my fork menacingly. "If you take another fry, I'll have to kill you," I tease.

He gives me a mock-innocent look and laughs with his tongue between his teeth. I find myself laughing for what seems like ages, and it feels great.

"You have an adorable laugh," he says, and I roll my eyes.

We end up going to see a cheesy comedy that fails to entertain either of us. But that's okay, because we entertain ourselves with small jokes to each other during the movie, and toward the end he puts his hand over mine. It's not uncomfortable, like I had assumed that it would be, but it doesn't feel the same as when Hardin does it. And right then it occurs to me that I made it hours without even thinking of Hardin, which is a refreshing change from him consuming my thoughts every day, all day.

When Zed gets me back to campus, it's almost eleven. I'm glad it's Wednesday—only two more days until the weekend, when I can catch up on my sleep.

He gets out of the car and walks over to me as I adjust my purse on my hip. "I had a really nice time; thank you for agreeing to come out with me," he says.

"I had a nice time, too." I smile.

"I was thinking . . . remember when you asked if I was going to the bonfire?" When I nod, he asks, "Do you mind if I come along?"

"Sure, that would be fine. I'll be going with Landon and his girlfriend, though." I don't recall Zed joining in on the group teasing Landon, but I just want to make sure he knows that it is not okay.

"That's fine, he seems nice," he says and I smile.

"Well, it's settled, then. Meet you there?" I suggest. There is no way I am taking him to dinner at Landon's house.

"Sounds good. Thanks again for tonight." He takes a step closer.

Is he going to kiss me? I start to panic. But instead he wraps his hand over mine and brings it up to his mouth. Placing one single kiss on the top of my hand, his lips are soft against my hot skin and his gesture is very sweet.

"Have a good night, Tessa," he says and gets back into his car.

I let out a deep breath, relieved that he didn't try to really kiss me. He's cute, and was a good kisser during Truth or Dare, but the timing just doesn't feel right.

* * *

THE NEXT MORNING Landon is waiting at the coffeehouse for me and I tell him about Zed.

Annoyingly, the first thing he says is "Does Hardin know about this?"

"No, and he doesn't need to. It's none of his business." I realize my tone was a little too harsh, so I add, "I'm sorry, it's just a touchy subject."

"Obviously. Just be careful," he warns me sweetly and I promise him that I will.

The rest of the day zooms by and Landon doesn't bring up Hardin or Zed again. Finally it's time for Literature, and I hold my breath as Landon and I walk into the room, where Hardin is sitting in his usual seat. My chest aches at the sight of him. He glances over at me but then turns back to the front of the room.

"So you went out with Zed last night?" he asks as I sit down. I was praying that he wouldn't talk to me.

"That's none of your concern," I reply quietly.

He turns in his seat and brings his face close to mine. "Word travels quickly in our group, Tessa, remember that."

Is he trying to threaten to tell his friends about all the things we did together? The thought makes my bile rise.

I turn away from him and focus my attention to the professor, who clears his throat and says, "Okay, everyone, let's start where we left off yesterday discussing *Wuthering Heights*."

My stomach drops. We aren't supposed to be discussing *Wuthering Heights* until next week—this is what I get for missing class. I feel Hardin's eyes on me. Perhaps, like me, he is thinking about the first time I was in his bedroom and he caught me reading his copy of the novel.

Our teacher paces before us, his hands clasped behind his back. "So, as we know, Catherine and Heathcliff had a very passionate relationship, their passion being such a force in the novel that it ruined essentially every other character's life in its wake.

Some argue that they were terrible for each other, and some argue that they should have married one another instead of fighting their love from the beginning." He pauses, looking out at all of us. "So, what do you think?" he asks.

Usually, I would raise my hand immediately, proud to show off my expert knowledge on classic novels, but this one hits too close to home.

A voice from the back of the room answers, "I think they were terrible for one another; they fought constantly and Catherine refused to admit her love for Heathcliff. She married Edgar, even though she knew she was in love with Heathcliff the entire time. If they would have just been together in the beginning, everyone would have been a lot less miserable."

Hardin looks at me, and I feel my cheeks heat up. "I think Catherine was a selfish, pompous bitch," he lets out. Gasps fill the room and the professor glowers at Hardin, but he continues. "Sorry, but she thought she was too good for Heathcliff—and maybe she was, but she knew Edgar could never compare to Heathcliff and yet she married him anyway. Catherine and Heathcliff were just so similar that it was hard for them to get along, but if Catherine wasn't so stubborn they could have lived a long and happy life together."

I feel foolish as I, too, begin to compare Hardin and myself to the characters in the novel. The difference is that Heathcliff loved Catherine tremendously, so much so that he sat by idly as she married another man before he finally married someone else. Hardin does not love me that way—or at all—so he has no right to compare himself to Heathcliff.

The entire class seems to be looking at me, waiting for my reply. They are probably hoping for an argument like last time, but I stay quiet. I know Hardin is trying to bait me, and I will not fall for it.

chapter sixty-four

After class I say goodbye to Landon and walk straight to the professor to explain my absences. He congratulates me on my internship and explains that he rearranged the syllabus a little. I keep our conversation going until Hardin exits the room.

I make my way back to my room, where I lay out all my notes and textbooks on my bed. I try to study but feel on edge waiting for Steph, Hardin, or one of the many other people who are always in and out of my room, to show up. I pack my study materials into my bag and head to my car. I will find a place to study off campus, maybe a coffee shop.

Driving toward town, I spy a small library on the corner of a busy street. Only a few cars are in the lot, so I pull in. I walk all the way to the back of the library and sit next to the window, pulling all of my books and notes out so I can get to work. For the first time, I can study in peace, no distractions. This will be my new sanctuary, the perfect place to study.

"MISS, WE ARE CLOSING in five minutes," an elderly librarian comes over to inform me.

Closing? Looking out the window, I see that it *is* dark out. I didn't even notice the sun going down. I was so engrossed in my books, hours passed and I didn't even notice. I will definitely have to come here more often.

"Oh, okay, thank you," I reply and pack up my things. Checking my phone, I see a new text from Zed.

I just wanted to tell you goodnight, I can't wait for Friday.

He really is very nice, so I reply, That is very sweet, thank you. I am looking forward to it too.

Back in the room, Steph is still gone, so I change into my pajamas and grab *Wuthering Heights*. I fall asleep quickly, dreaming of Heathcliff and the moors.

WHEN I WAKE UP ON FRIDAY, I have a text message from Landon telling me that he won't be on campus at all today because Dakota is arriving earlier than he thought. Skipping Literature crosses my mind momentarily, but I decide against it. I can't let Hardin ruin anything else I like.

I take a little more time to get ready today and braid the front of my hair back before curling it. It's supposed to be warm, so I wear a purple sleeveless fleece jacket and jeans. When I go to the coffeehouse before class, Logan ends up in front of me in line. Before I can walk away unnoticed, he turns around.

"Hey, Tessa," he says.

"Hey, Logan. How are you?" I ask politely.

"I'm good, you coming tonight?"

"To the bonfire?"

"No, the party. The bonfire is going to be lame, it always is."

"Oh well, I'm going to the bonfire." I laugh lightly and he chuckles.

"Well, if you get bored, you can always stop by," he says and grabs his coffee.

I thank him as he walks away, relieved that Hardin's group seems uninterested in the bonfire, which means I won't have to deal with any of them tonight.

When it's time for Literature, I walk right to my seat without a single glance in Hardin's direction. The discussion continues on *Wuthering Heights,* but Hardin stays silent. As soon as we are dismissed, I gather my things and practically bolt to the door.

"Tessa!" I hear Hardin call behind me, but I just walk faster. Without Landon here I feel more vulnerable. When I reach the sidewalk, I feel a light touch on my arm. I know it's him from the way my skin tingles.

"What!" I shout.

He takes a step back and holds out a notebook. "You dropped this."

Relief and disappointment battle inside me. I wish this ache in my chest would go away. Instead of shrinking, it seems to get larger every moment of every day. I shouldn't have admitted to myself that I love him—if I would have kept ignoring the truth, maybe it would hurt less.

"Oh, thanks," I mumble and grab the notebook from him. His eyes catch mine and we just stare at one another until after a few seconds I remember that we are standing on a crowded sidewalk and I look around at everyone passing by us. Hardin shakes his hair out and pushes it back before he turns and walks away.

I HEAD TO MY CAR and drive straight to Landon's. I wasn't going to go until five; it's only three, but I can't sit alone in my room. I really have gone mental since Hardin came into my life.

When I arrive, Karen answers the door with a huge smile and invites me in.

"It's only me here right now. Dakota and Landon are at the store fetching a few things for me," she says as she brings me into the kitchen.

"That's okay, sorry for coming so early."

"Oh, don't be sorry. You can help me cook!" She hands me a

cutting board and a few onions and potatoes to chop and we talk about the weather and the upcoming winter.

"Tessa, did you still want to help me get the greenhouse going? It's climate controlled, so we don't have to worry about the winter."

"Yes, of course! I would love to."

"Great, maybe tomorrow? Next weekend I will be a *little busy*," she jokes.

Her wedding. I'd almost forgotten. I try to smile back at her. "Yeah, I'd say so." I wish I could've gotten Hardin to agree to go, but it was impossible then and it's even more impossible now.

Karen puts the chicken in the oven and gathers plates and silverware so we can set the table. "Is Hardin coming to dinner tonight?" she asks as we start laying things out. She's clearly trying to sound nonchalant, but I can see she's a little nervous about the question.

"No, he won't be coming," I tell her and look down.

She stops what she's doing. "Are you guys okay? I don't mean to be nosy."

"That's all right." I might as well tell her. "I don't think we're okay."

"Oh, honey, I'm sorry to hear that. You two really had something, I thought. But I know it's really hard to be with someone who is afraid to show their feelings."

This line of conversation makes me feel a little weird. I can't even talk to my own mother about stuff like this, but something about Karen's openness makes me more able to discuss this sort of thing. "What do you mean?"

"Well, I don't know Hardin as well as I wish I did, but I know he is very closed off emotionally. Ken used to stay awake nights worrying about him. He has always been an unhappy child." Her eyes go glossy. "He wouldn't even tell his mom he loved her."

"What?" I say again.

"He just won't say it. I am not sure why. Ken can't recall a single time when Hardin said he loved either of them. It's truly sad, not only for Ken, but for Hardin as well." She blots her eyes.

For someone who refuses to tell anyone, even his own parents, that he loves them, he sure was quick to use the words against me in a hateful way. "He is . . . He's very difficult to understand," is all I can think to say.

"Yes, yes, he is. But, Tessa, I hope you'll still come around even if you two don't work things out."

"Of course," I tell her.

PERHAPS SENSING MY MOOD, Karen switches to talk of the greenhouse while we wait for the food to finish cooking and then put everything out on the table. Midway through a sentence, Karen stops and puts on a wide smile. I turn to find Landon walking into the kitchen followed by a beautiful girl with curly hair. I knew she would be gorgeous, but she is even more so than I could have imagined.

"Hi, you must be Tessa," she says even as Landon opens his mouth to introduce us. She immediately comes over and hugs me, and I immediately like her.

"Dakota, I have heard so much about you—it's nice to finally meet you!" I say, and she smiles. Landon's eyes follow her as she walks past and hugs Karen, then takes a seat at the counter.

"We passed Ken on our way here. He was getting gas, so he should be here any minute," Landon tells his mom.

"Great, Tessa and I have already set the table."

Landon goes over to where Dakota sits, puts his arm around her waist, and leads her to the table. I take my seat across from them and glance over at the empty place setting next to me, which Karen had set up for "purposes of symmetry," but it just makes me a little sad. In another life Hardin would be sitting next to me, holding my hand the way Landon is Dakota's, and I could lean into him without fear of being rejected. I'm beginning to wish I had invited Zed even though it would have been extremely awkward; having dinner with two deeply in-love couples may prove worse.

Ken enters, saving me from my thoughts. He walks over and kisses Karen on her cheek before sitting down.

"Dinner looks great, honey," he says and playfully places a napkin on his lap. "Dakota, you get more beautiful each time I see you." He smiles at her, then turns to me. "And Tessa, congratulations on your internship at Vance. Christian called me and told me. You made a wonderful first impression on him."

"Thank you again for calling him; it's such an amazing opportunity." I smile and the table's silent for a moment while we all try Karen's chicken, which is *delicious*.

"Sorry I'm late," I hear from behind me and my fork falls out of my hand onto my plate.

"Hardin! I didn't know you were coming!" Karen says nicely, then looks at me. I look away. My pulse is already quickening.

"Yeah, remember we discussed it last week, Tessa?" He smiles his menacing smile and takes the seat next to me.

What is wrong with him? Why can't he just leave me alone? I know it is partly my fault for letting him get to me, but he really enjoys playing cat-and-mouse. Everyone's eyes are on me, so I nod and pick up my fork. Dakota looks confused and Landon looks worried.

"You must be Delilah?" Hardin says to her.

"Oh, Dakota, actually," she corrects him sweetly.

"Yeah, Dakota. Same thing," he mutters and I kick him under the table.

Landon glares at him, but Hardin doesn't seem to notice. Ken and Karen go into conversation between themselves, as do Dakota and Landon. I stay focused on my food and think of an exit strategy.

"So, how's your evening so far?" Hardin asks in a casual tone. He knows that I won't cause a scene, so he is trying to annoy me.

"Fine," I answer quietly.

"You're not going to ask me how mine is?" He smirks.

"Nope," I mumble and take another bite.

"Tessa, was that your car outside?" Ken asks and I nod.

"Oh yeah, I finally got my own car!" I say, with a little extra excitement in the hopes that everyone else will join in so I'm not stuck talking to just Hardin.

Hardin raises his eyebrow at me. "When?"

"The other day," I answer. *You know, the day that you told me that it's all about the chase?*

"Oh. Where did you get it?"

"A used-car lot," I answer and watch Dakota and Karen both try to hide their smiles. Sensing an opportunity to direct the attention off me, I say, "So, Dakota, Landon told me you were thinking of going to New York for a ballet school?" She tells us all about her plans to move to New York, and Landon looks genuinely happy for her despite the distance that will stay between them.

When she finishes, Landon looks at his phone and says, "Well, we should get going soon. That bonfire waits for no man."

"What?" Karen says. "Okay, but at least take some of the dessert with you!"

Landon nods and helps her put some into a Tupperware container.

"Are you going to ride with me?" Hardin says. I look around like I'm confused about whom he's addressing.

"I'm talking to you," he states.

"What? No, you're not going," I tell him.

"Yes, I am. And you can't stop me from going, so you might as well ride with me." He smiles and tries to put his hand on my thigh.

"What the hell is wrong with you?" I say under my breath.

"Can we talk outside?" he asks and looks toward his father.

"No," I say quietly—every time Hardin and I "talk," I end up crying.

But Hardin stands up quickly and grabs my hand, pulling me to my feet. "We'll be outside," he announces, and pulls me through the living room and out the front door.

Once we're outside, I yank my arm away and warn him, "Stop touching me!"

He shrugs. "Sorry, but you weren't going to come with me."

"Because I didn't *want* to."

"I am sorry. For everything, okay?" His fingers play with his lip ring and I avoid focusing on his mouth. I stare at the way his eyes search my face.

"You're *sorry*? You're not sorry, Hardin—you just want to mess with me. Just *stop*. I am exhausted and drained from fighting with you all the time. I can't do it anymore. Isn't there anyone else that you can mess with? Heck, I'll even help you find someone, some poor innocent girl for you to torture as long as it isn't me."

"That's not what I am doing. I know I am back and forth a lot with you, and I don't know why I do it. But if you give me one chance, one more chance, I will stop. I tried to stay away from you but I can't. I need you . . . ." He looks down at the deck, rubbing the tips of his boots together.

The audacity of what he's saying helps me keep my tears in check this time; his ego has seen quite enough of them. "*Stop!* Just *stop*. Aren't you tired of this? If you needed me you wouldn't treat me the way you do. You told me yourself it was *all about the chase,* remember? You can't just show up here after everything and act like nothing happened."

"I didn't mean that. You know I didn't."

"So you admit you just said it to hurt me?" I glare at him, trying to keep my guard up.

"Yeah . . ." He looks down.

I'm so confused by him; he says he wants more, then he kisses Molly, then he tells me he loves me and takes it back, and now he is apologizing again? "Why should I forgive you—you just admitted that you did something solely to hurt me."

"One more chance? Please, Tess. I'll tell you everything," he pleads. I almost believe the pain in his eyes as he looks down at me.

"I can't, I have to go."

"Why can't I come with you?" he asks.

"Because . . . because I am meeting Zed there."

I watch as his expression changes and seems to crumple before me. It takes everything in me not to comfort him. But Hardin did this to himself. Even if he actually does care, it's too late.

"Zed? So are you guys, what . . . dating now?" His tone is full of disgust.

"No, we haven't even talked about it. We are just . . . I don't know, spending time together, I guess."

"You haven't talked about it? So if he asked you, you *would*?"

"I don't know . . ." And I honestly don't know. "He is nice and polite and he treats me well." *Why am I even explaining myself to this boy?*

"Tessa, you don't even know him, you don't know—"

The front door shoots open and an exuberant Landon asks, "Ready?"

His eyes dart to Hardin, who for once looks unguarded and even . . . heartbroken.

I force my feet toward my car and follow Landon as he pulls out of the driveway. I can't help but look back at Hardin, who is still on the porch, still staring back at me as I drive away.

chapter sixty-five

Pulling into the spot next to Landon, I text Zed to tell him that I have arrived. He writes back immediately with a note to meet him at the far left corner of the field.

I tell Landon where he'll be as he and Dakota walk up.

"Sounds good," he says, but he seems less than thrilled.

"Who's Zed?" Dakota asks.

"He's my . . . friend." He is just my friend.

"Hardin's your boyfriend, right?" she asks.

I look over at her. She doesn't seem to be implying anything, she just seems confused. *Welcome to the club.*

"No, babe." Landon laughs. "Neither of them are."

I laugh, too. "It's not as bad as it sounds."

Right as we get to where everyone is, the school band begins to play and the field becomes more and more crowded. I'm relieved when I spot Zed leaning against the fence. I point him out, and we head over there.

"Oh," Dakota squeals as we get close. I can't tell if she's surprised by his tattoos and piercings, or his good looks. Maybe both.

"Hey, beautiful," Zed says, beaming, and hugs me. I smile at him, returning the hug.

"Hi, I'm Zed. It's nice to meet you both." He nods toward Landon and Dakota. I know he's met Landon before, so maybe he's just trying to be polite.

"Have you been here long?" I ask.

"Only about ten minutes. A lot more people here than I expected."

Landon leads the way to a less crowded area near the enormous mound of wood, and we all sit on the grass. Dakota sits between Landon's legs and leans back against his chest. The sun is going down and the breeze is picking up. I should have worn long sleeves.

"Yeah, have you been to one of these before?" I ask Zed, who shakes his head.

"No, this isn't my typical scene," he says with a laugh before adding, "But I'm glad to be here tonight."

I smile at his compliment and right then someone walks up to the central bandstand and gives us all a warm welcome on behalf of the school and the band. After a couple of minutes of rambling on, they finally count down to the lighting of the fire, and three, two, one . . . the fire ignites and swallows the mound of wood fiercely. It's actually quite beautiful being this close to the flames, and I can tell I'll be warm enough after all.

"So how long are you here?" Zed asks Dakota.

She frowns. "Only the weekend. I wish I could come back for the wedding next weekend."

"What wedding?" Zed asks.

I look at Landon, who answers, "My mother's."

"Oh . . ." He pauses and looks down, as if thinking about something.

"What?" I ask him.

"Nothing. I'm just trying to remember who else said something about a wedding next weekend . . . Oh yeah—Hardin, I think. He was asking us what he should wear to a wedding."

My heart stops. I hope I don't show it on my face. So Hardin definitely still hasn't told any of his friends that his father is the chancellor, or that he's marrying Landon's mother.

"Bit of a coincidence, right?" he asks.

"No, they are—" Dakota begins, but I interrupt: "Quite a co-incidence, but, then, in a town this size, there are probably a few every weekend."

Zed nods in agreement, and Landon whispers something in Dakota's ear.

Hardin is actually considering going to the wedding?

Zed chuckles. "I can't imagine Hardin at a wedding anyway."

"Why not?" My tone is a little harsher than I meant it to be.

"I don't know, because he's Hardin. The only way to get him to go to a wedding would be if he knew he could have sex with the bridesmaids. *All* of them," he says and rolls his eyes.

"I thought you and Hardin are friends?" I say.

"We are. I'm not saying anything bad about him—that's just how Hardin is. He has sex with a different girl every weekend, sometimes more than one."

My ears are buzzing and the fire feels too hot on my skin. I stand up before I realize what I am doing.

"Where are you going? What's wrong?" Zed asks.

"Nothing, I just . . . I need some air. Some fresh air," I mumble. I know how stupid that sounds but I don't care. "Be right back, I just need a second." I march away quickly before any of them can follow me.

What is wrong with me? Zed is sweet and he actually likes me, he enjoys my company, and yet all it takes is a mention of Hardin and I can't stop thinking about him. I take a quick stroll around the stands and few deep breaths before walking back over to them.

"Sorry, the fire was just . . . too hot," I lie and sit back down.

Zed has his phone out and turns the screen away from me as he slides it back into his pocket. He tells me it's fine and we make small talk with Landon and Dakota for the next hour.

"I'm getting sort of tired, I had an early flight," Dakota finally tells Landon, who nods.

"Yeah, I'm tired, too. We're going to get going." Landon stands up and helps Dakota to her feet.

"Do you want to go, too?" Zed asks me.

"No, I'm okay. Unless you want to?"

He shakes his head. "I'm cool." We say goodbye to Landon and Dakota and watch as they disappear into the crowd.

"So what's the reason behind the bonfire?" I ask Zed, unsure that he really knows.

"I think it's like to celebrate the end of the football season," he tells me. "Or the middle of it, or something . . . ?" I look around and notice for the first time that a lot of people are wearing jerseys.

"Oh." I look over at Zed. "I see it now," I say and laugh.

"Yeah," he says and then squints. "Is that Hardin?"

I snap my head in the direction he's looking. Sure enough, Hardin is walking toward us with a short brunette wearing a skirt.

I scoot closer to Zed. This is exactly why I didn't listen to Hardin on the porch—he's already found some girl to bring here just to spite me.

"Hey, Zed," the girl says in a high-pitched voice.

"Hey, Emma." Zed hooks his arm around my shoulder. Hardin glares at him but takes a seat with us.

I know I am being rude by not introducing myself to this girl, but I can't help but dislike her already.

"How's the bonfire so far?" Hardin asks.

"Warm. And almost over, I think," Zed replies.

There is tension between the two of them. I can feel it. I don't know why there would be—Hardin made it clear to his friends that he doesn't give a shit about me.

"Do they have food here?" the girl says in her annoying voice.

"Yeah, they have a concession stand," I tell her.

"Hardin, come with me to get some food," she demands. He rolls his eyes but stands up.

"Bring me back a pretzel, yeah?" Zed yells, smiling, and Hardin clenches his jaw.

What is up with them?

As soon as Hardin and Emma disappear I turn to Zed. "Hey, can we go? I don't really want to hang out with Hardin; we sort of hate each other, in case you forgot." I try to force out a playful laugh, but it doesn't happen.

"Yeah, sure, sure," he says. We both stand up and he reaches for my hand. We hold hands as we walk, and I find myself looking around for Hardin and hoping he won't see.

"Do you want to go to the party?" Zed asks as we reach the parking lot.

"No, I don't really want to go there, either." That is the *last* place I want to go.

"Okay, well, we can just hang out another . . ." he begins.

"No, I still want to hang out. I just don't want to be here or at that frat house," I say quickly.

He looks surprised as his eyes meet mine. "Okay . . . well, we can go to my place? If you want; if not, we can go somewhere else? I actually don't really know where else to go in this town." He laughs and I join him.

"Your place is fine. I'll follow you there," I tell him.

During the drive, I can't help but picture Hardin's face when he returns to find us gone. *He* brought a girl there with him, so he has no right to be upset, but it doesn't really ease the pang in my stomach to justify it like that.

Zed's apartment is right off campus and is small but clean. He offers me a drink, but I decline since I plan on driving back to my room tonight.

I plop down on the couch, and he hands me the remote before going back to the kitchen to make himself a drink. "You can be in control; I don't know what you like to watch."

"Do you live alone?" I ask him and he nods. I feel a little awkward as he sits next to me and puts his arm around my waist, but I hide my nervousness with a smile. Zed's phone buzzes in his pocket and he stands up to answer it. Holding a finger up to tell me he will be back, he wanders into his small kitchen area.

"We left," I hear him say. "So . . ." "Fair." "Too bad." The few snippets of conversation that I catch make no sense to me . . . except the "we left."

Is that Hardin on the phone? I stand up and walk toward the kitchen as Zed hangs up.

"Who was that?" I ask.

"No one important," he assures me and leads me back to the couch. "I am really glad we are getting to know each other; you're different from the rest of the girls here," he says sweetly.

"Me, too," I tell him. "Do you know Emma?" I can't help but ask.

"Yeah, her girlfriend is Nate's cousin."

"Girlfriend?"

"Yeah, they have been together awhile. Emma's pretty cool."

So Hardin wasn't there with her, not in that way at least. Maybe he actually came there to try to talk to me again, instead of trying to hurt me with another girl.

I look over to Zed just as he leans in to kiss me. His lips are cool from his drink and taste like vodka. His hands are careful and smooth against my arms, then my waist. Hardin's heartbroken face from earlier pops into my mind, the way he begged for one more chance and I didn't believe him, the way he watched me drive away, the outburst in class about Catherine and Heathcliff, the way he always shows up when I don't want him to, the way he never tells his mother that he loves her, the way he said he loved me in front of everyone, the hurtful way he took it back, the way he breaks things when he's angry, the way he came to his father's house tonight even though he hates it there, and the way he asked his friends what to wear to the wedding—it all makes perfect sense, but no sense, at the same time.

Hardin loves me. In his own damaged way, he does love me. The realization of this hits me like a truck.

"What?" Zed says and pulls away from our kiss.

"What?" I repeat his word.

"You just said Hardin."

"No, I didn't," I defend.

"Yes, yes, you did." He stands up and steps away from the couch.

"I have to go . . . I am sorry," I say and grab my purse and rush out of the door before he can say anything else.

chapter sixty-six

I take a second to think about what I am doing. I left Zed to go find Hardin, but I really need to think about what will happen next. Hardin will either say terrible things to me, curse at me, and make me leave, or he will admit that he has feelings for me and that all these games he has been playing are just his way of not being able to deal with and express his feelings in a normal way. If the first scenario happens, and I mostly expect it to, I will be in no worse a state than I am in now. But, if it's the second, am I ready to forgive him for all the terrible things he has said and done to me? If we both admit the way we feel about each other, will everything change? Will *he* change? Is he capable of caring for me the way I need him to, and, if so, am I capable of putting up with his mood swings?

The problem is, I can't answer any of these questions on my own, not a single one. I hate the way he clouds my thoughts and makes me feel unsure about myself. I hate not knowing what he will do or say.

I pull up to the damned fraternity house that I have spent way too much time in. I hate this house. I hate a lot of things right now, and my anger toward Hardin is almost to its boiling point. I park at the curb and rush up the steps and into the crowded house. I head straight for the old couch Hardin is usually perched on, but, not spotting his mop of hair, I duck behind a heavyset guy before Steph or anyone else can spot me.

Rushing up the stairs to his room, I bang my fist against the door, annoyed that once again he has it locked.

"Hardin! It's me, open the door!" I yell desperately and continue to pound, but there's no answer. *Where the hell is he?* I don't want to call him to find out, even though that is obviously easier, but I'm angry and I feel like I need to stay angry so I can say what I mean—what I *need* to say—and not feel bad about it.

I call Landon to see if Hardin is at his father's, but he isn't. The only other place that I know to look is the bonfire, but I doubt he would still be there. Still, I don't have any other options right now.

So I drive back to the stadium and park my car, repeating the angry words I have saved for Hardin over and over to make sure I don't forget anything in case he actually is here. Approaching the field, I can see that almost everyone has left already and the fire is almost out. I walk around and squint in the dying light and stare at couples to see if they are Hardin and Emma, without luck.

Just as I decide to stop looking, I finally do see Hardin leaning against the fence by the goalpost. He is alone, and doesn't seem to notice me walking toward him as he takes a seat on the grass, wiping his mouth. When he removes his hand, it looks red. *Is he bleeding?*

Suddenly Hardin's head snaps up as if he can sense my presence, and, yes, the corner of his mouth is bleeding and the shadow of a bruise is already forming on his cheek.

"What the hell—" I say and kneel down in front of him. "What happened to you?" I ask.

He looks up at me and his eyes are so haunted, my anger dissolves like sugar on my tongue.

"Why do you care? Where's your *date*?" he growls.

I click my tongue gently and move his hand away from his

mouth, examining his busted lip. He jerks away from me but I bite my tongue. "Tell me what happened," I demand.

He sighs and runs his hand over his hair. His knuckles are busted and bloody. The cut on his index finger looks deep and very painful.

"Did you get in a fight?"

"What gave you that idea?" he snaps.

"With who? Are you okay?"

"Yeah, I am fine, now leave me alone."

"I came here to find you," I tell him and stand up, wiping the dead grass off my jeans.

"Okay. And you found me, so go."

"You don't have to be such an asshole," I say. "I think you should go home and get cleaned up. You might need stitches on that knuckle."

Hardin doesn't respond but stands up and walks past me. I came here to yell at him for being such an idiot and tell him how I feel, and he's making it very hard—I knew he would.

"Where are you going?" I ask, following him like a lost puppy.

"Home. Well, I'm going to call Emma and see if she will come back and pick me up."

"She left you here?" I don't like her at all.

"No. Well, technically, but I told her to."

"Let me take you," I say and grab his jacket. He shrugs me off, and I want to slap him. My anger is returning and I am more pissed-off than before. The tables have turned; our . . . whatever this is has shifted. I am usually the one running from him.

"*Stop walking away from me!*" I yell and he turns around, eyes blazing. "I said *let me take you home!*" I scream.

He almost smiles but frowns instead and sighs. "Fine. Where's your car?"

* * *

HARDIN'S SCENT IMMEDIATELY fills the car, only now there is a hint of metal mixed in; it's still my favorite smell in the entire world. I turn the heat on and rub my arms to warm up.

"Why did you come here?" he asks as I pull out of the parking lot.

"To find you." I try to remember everything I had planned to say, but my mind is blank and all I can think about is kissing his busted mouth.

"For what reason?" he asks quietly.

"To talk to you, we have so much to talk about." I feel like crying and laughing at the same time and I have no idea why.

"I thought you said we didn't have anything to talk about," he says and turns to look out the window with a coolness I suddenly find beyond irritating.

"Do you love me?" The words come out rushed and strangled. I had not planned on saying them.

His head snaps to the side to look at me. "What?" His tone is one of shock.

"Do you?" I repeat, worrying that my heart might pop right out of my chest.

He focuses forward. "You are not seriously asking me this while we are driving down the street."

"What does it matter where or when I am asking, just tell me," I practically beg.

"I . . . I don't know . . . No, I don't." He looks around, almost like he needs to escape. "And you can't just ask someone if they love you when they are trapped in a car with you—what the hell is wrong with you?" he says loudly.

Ouch. "Okay," is all I can manage to say.

"Why do you even want to know?"

"It doesn't matter." I'm confused now, so confused, and my plan to talk out our problems has crashed and burned in front of me, along with any dignity I still held.

"Tell me why you asked me that, now," he demands.

"Don't tell me what to do!" I shout back.

I pull up to his house and he looks out at the crowded lawn. "Take me to my dad's," he says.

"What? I am not a damn taxi."

"Just take me there, I will get my car in the morning."

If his car is here, why doesn't he just drive himself? I don't want our conversation to end yet, though, so I roll my eyes, and head off toward his father's house.

"I thought you hated it there," I say.

"I do. But I don't feel like being around a lot of people right now," he says quietly. Then, louder, he goes on: "Are you going to tell me why you asked that? Does this have something to do with Zed? Did he say something to you?"

He seems really nervous. Why does he always ask if Zed said something to me?

"No . . . It has nothing to do with Zed. I just wanted to know." It doesn't really have to do with Zed; it has to do with the fact that I love him and thought for a second, he might love me, too. The longer I am around him, the more ridiculous that possibility seems.

"Where did you and Zed go when you left the bonfire?" he asks as I pull into his father's driveway.

"Back to his apartment," I say.

Hardin's body tenses and his bloody fists clench, tearing the skin on his knuckles further. "Did you sleep with him?" he asks and my mouth falls open.

"What? Why the hell would you assume that? You should know me better than that by now! And who do you think you are to even ask such a personal question? You made it clear that you don't care about me so, what if I *did*?" I shout.

"So you didn't?" he asks again, his eyes like stone.

"God, Hardin! No! He kissed me, but I wouldn't have sex with someone I barely know!"

He leans over and turns my car off, clenching his bloody hand over the keys and pulling them out of the ignition.

"You kissed him back?" His eyes are hooded as he seems to look straight past me.

"Yeah . . . well, I don't know, I think I did." I don't remember anything except Hardin's face in my mind.

"How do you not know? Have you been drinking?" His voice is louder now.

"No, I just . . ."

"You what!" he shouts and turns his body to face me. I can't read the energy between us, and for a moment I sit there, trying to get a handle on it.

"I-I just kept thinking of you!" I finally admit.

His stone features soften tremendously and he brings his eyes to mine. "Let's go inside," he says and opens the passenger door.

chapter sixty-seven

K aren and Ken are sitting on the couch in the living room and both look up when we walk in.

"Hardin! What happened?" his father asks, panicked. He jumps up and comes over to us, but Hardin brushes him off.

"I'm fine," Hardin grumbles.

"What happened to him?" Ken turns to me.

"He got in a fight, but he hasn't told me with who or why."

"I am standing right here—and I just said I am *fucking fine*," Hardin says angrily.

"Don't talk to your father like that!" I scold him and his eyes widen. Instead of screaming at me, he takes my wrist in his busted hand and pulls me out of the room. Ken and Karen discuss Hardin's bloody appearance as he drags me upstairs, and I hear his dad openly wonder why Hardin keeps coming here when he never used to before.

Once we reach his room, he turns me around, pinning both of my wrists to the wall and steps up close, leaving only a few inches between us.

"Don't ever do that again," he says through his teeth.

"Do what? Let go of me, right now," I tell him.

He rolls his eyes but does let me go and walks over to his bed. I stay close to the door.

"Don't tell me how to talk to my father. Worry about your own relationship with *your own father* before trying to meddle with mine."

As soon as the words come out of his mouth, Hardin registers what he says, and he immediately looks apologetic. "I'm sorry . . . I didn't mean it like that . . . It just came out." He takes a step toward me with outstretched arms, but I take a step backward into the doorway.

"Yeah—it always just 'comes out,' doesn't it?" I can't help the tears pricking my eyes. Bringing my father into this is just way too much, even for Hardin.

"Tess, I . . ." he begins but stops himself when I hold up one hand.

What am I doing here? Why do I keep thinking he will stop the endless string of insults long enough to have an actual conversation with me? Because I am an idiot, that's why.

"It's fine, really. That's who you are; that's what you do. You find people's weakness and you exploit it. You use it to your advantage. How long have you been waiting to say something about my father? *You've probably been waiting for an opening since you met me!*" I shout.

"Damn it! No I haven't! I wasn't thinking when I said that! You are not innocent here—you provoke me on purpose!" he yells, even louder than I did.

"Provoke you? I provoke you! Please, do enlighten me!" I know everyone in the house can hear. But, for once, I don't care.

"You always push my buttons! You constantly fight with me! You go on dates with Zed—I mean, fuck! You think I like being this way? Do you think I like you having this control over me? I hate the way you get under my skin. I loathe the way I can't seem to stop thinking about you! I hate you . . . I really do! You're such a pretentious little . . ." He stops and looks at me. I force myself to look back at him, putting on the charade that he didn't just tear me apart with every syllable.

"This is what I am talking about!" He runs his hands over his hair as he paces back and forth across the room. "You . . . you make me crazy, literally fucking mental! And then you have the nerve to ask if I love you? Why would you even ask that? Because I said that one time, by accident? I told you already that I didn't mean it, so why would you ask again? You like rejection—don't you? That's why you keep coming around me, isn't it?"

All I want to do is run, run out of this room and never, ever look back. I need to run, I need to *flee*.

I try to stop it, but he has me in such a rage, I yell the thing I know will get to him, break his control: "No, I keep coming around *because I love you!*"

I cover my mouth immediately, wishing I could push the words back in. He couldn't possibly hurt me worse than he has, and I don't want to be left wondering years from now what he would have said if I told him. I am okay with him not loving me. I got myself into this knowing how he was all along.

He looks astonished. "You *what*?" He blinks rapidly as if trying to process the words.

"Go on, tell me how much you hate me again. Go ahead and tell me how stupid I am for loving someone who can't stand me," I say, my voice coming out foreign and almost in a whine. I wipe my eyes and look at him again, feeling as if I've been gravely defeated and need to leave the scene to bandage my wounds. "I'll be going now."

As I go to turn, he takes one long stride to close the gap between us. I refuse to look at him as he puts his hand on my shoulder. "Damn it, don't go," he says, his voice full of emotion.

Which emotion is the question.

"You love me?" he whispers and puts his busted hand under my chin to tilt my head to him. I dart my eyes away from his and nod slowly, waiting for him to laugh in my face.

"Why?" His breath comes in a hot burst against my face.

I finally bring my eyes to his and he looks . . . *afraid?* "What?" I ask softly.

"Why do you love . . . how could you possibly love me?" His voice cracks and he stares at me, and I feel like the words I say next will determine my fate more than anything I've ever done before.

"How could you not know that I love you?" I ask instead of answering him.

He doesn't think I could love him? I have no explanation except that I just do. He drives me crazy, makes me angrier than I have ever been, but somehow I fell for him, hard.

"You told me you didn't. And you went out with Zed. You always leave me; you left me on the porch earlier when I begged you for another chance. I told you I loved you, and you rejected me. Do you know how hard that was for me?" he says.

I must be imagining the tears welling in the corners of his eyes, though I am too aware of his callused fingers under my chin.

"You took it back before I could even process what you said. You've done a lot of things to hurt me, Hardin," I tell him and he nods.

"I know . . . I'm sorry. Let me make it up to you? I know I don't deserve you. I don't have the right to even be asking this . . . but please, just one chance. I am not promising not to fight with you, or get mad at you, but I am promising to give myself to you, completely. Please, just let me try to be what you need." He sounds so unsure of himself, it turns my insides to liquid.

"I want to think this can work, but I just don't know how it could, so much damage has already been done."

But my eyes betray me as the tears fall. Hardin brings his fingers up from my chin and captures them, even as a single tear escapes down his own cheek.

"Do you remember when you asked me who I love the most in the world?" he asks, his lips inches from mine.

I nod, though it seems so long ago, and I didn't think he was even paying attention.

"It's you. You're the person that I love most in the world."

His words surprise me and dissolve the ache and the anger in my chest.

Before I will let myself believe him and turn me to putty in his arms, I ask, "This isn't part of your sick game, is it?"

"No, Tessa. I'm done with the games. I just want you. I want to be with you, in a real relationship. You'll have to teach me what in the hell that even means, of course." He laughs nervously and I join him with earnest laughter of my own.

"I have missed your laugh. I haven't heard it enough. I want to be the one to make you laugh, not cry. I know I am a lot to handle—"

I cut him off by pressing my lips against his. His kisses are rushed and I can taste blood from his cut. My knees want to buckle from the electricity shooting through me, it seems so long ago that I last felt his mouth on mine. I love this damaged, self-loathing asshole so much that I'm afraid it will crush me. He lifts me up and I wrap my thighs around him, tangling my fingers into his hair. He moans into my mouth and I gasp, pulling harder. My tongue runs over his bottom lip and when he winces, I pull away.

"Who did you get in a fight with?" I ask and he laughs.

"You're asking that now?"

"Yeah, I want to know." I smile.

"You always have so many questions. Can't I answer them later?" He pouts.

"No, tell me."

"Only if you'll stay." He holds me against him tighter. "Please?" he begs.

"Okay," I say and kiss him again, completely forgetting about my question.

chapter sixty-eight

ventually we stop kissing and I go to sit at the foot of the bed,
and Hardin follows me, sitting up by the headboard.

"Okay, now tell me who you fought with; was it Zed?" I ask,
afraid of his answer.

"No. It was just a few random guys."

I'm relieved it wasn't Zed, but then I register what he actually
said. "Wait, a few? How many?"

"Three . . . or four. I am not really sure." He laughs.

"It's not funny—why were you fighting, anyway?"

"I don't know . . ." He shrugs. "I was pissed that you left with
Zed and it seemed like a good idea at the time."

"Well, it's *not* a good idea, and now look how busted up you
are." I frown and he cocks his head to the side with a puzzled expression. "What?"

"Nothing . . . come here," he says and holds his arms out to
me. I move across the bed and lean back on him between his legs.

"I am sorry for the way I treated . . . well, *treat* you," he says
quietly into my ear.

A shiver runs through my body from his breath in my ear and
his unforced apology. "It's okay. Well, it's not okay. But I am going
to give you one more chance."

I hope he doesn't make me regret it. I don't think I can handle any more hot and cold from him.

"Thank you, I know I don't deserve it. But I am selfish enough
to take it," he says, his mouth against my hair. He wraps his arms

around me, and sitting with him like this feels foreign and nostalgic at the same time.

When I stay silent he turns my shoulders slightly to have me look at him. "What's wrong?" he asks.

"Nothing. I'm just afraid that you'll change your mind again," I say. I want to dive into this headfirst but am desperately afraid I will hit the bottom.

"I won't. I have never changed my mind. I've just fought my feelings for you. I know you can't trust my words alone, but I want to earn your trust. I won't hurt you again," he promises and leans his forehead against mine.

"Please don't," I beg. I don't care how pathetic I sound.

"I love you, Tessa," he says and my heart leaps out of my chest. The words sound perfect coming off his lips and I would do anything to be able to hear them again.

"I love you, Hardin." This is the first time we have both openly said the words, and I fight down my urge to panic over the possibility that he could take them back again. Even if he does, I will always have the memory of how they sounded, how they made me feel.

"Say it again," he whispers and turns me around to face him. In his eyes I see more vulnerability than I had thought possible for him. I move to my knees and take his face in my hands, rubbing my thumbs over the light stubble on his perfect face. I can tell by his expression that he needs me to say it, over and over again. I will say it as many times as I have to until he believes that he is worthy of someone loving him.

"I love you," I repeat and cover his lips with my own. He hmms in appreciation as his tongue grazes gently over mine. Kissing Hardin feels new and different each time, and he is like a drug that I can't get enough of. His hands press against the small of my back, bringing our chests together. My mind is telling me to take it slow, to kiss him gently and to savor each second of this

gentle calm between us. But my body is telling me to grab a fist-
ful of his hair and pull his shirt over his head. His lips travel down
my jaw and attach themselves to my neck.

That does it. I can't control myself anymore. This is us, all
anger and passion and now love. An involuntary moan escapes my
lips and he groans against my neck, grabbing my waist and flipping us over so he is hovering over me.

"I . . . have . . . missed you . . . so much," he says in between
sucking the skin on my neck. I can't keep my eyes open; it feels
too good. He unzips my jacket and looks down at me with hungry
eyes. He doesn't ask for my permission before tugging at the fabric, pulling my tank top up and over my head, and he sucks in a
sharp breath as I arch my back so he can unclasp my bra.

"I have missed your body . . . the way you fit perfectly in
my hand," he growls as he palms my breasts. I moan again and
he presses his lower body against mine so I can feel his arousal
pressed against my lower stomach. Our breathing is rapid and uncontrolled, and I have never wanted him more. It seems the admission of our feelings hasn't lessened the overwhelming passion
between us. I am glad. His hand glides down over my bare stomach and pops open the button on my jeans. As his fingers slide
into my panties he gasps into my mouth. "I have missed how wet
you always are for me."

His words do wicked things to me, and I lift my hips again,
begging for contact.

"What do you want, Tessa?" He breathes heavily into the
crook of my neck.

"You," I answer before my mind can process what I just said.
But I know it's true: I want Hardin in the most primal, deep way
possible. His finger slides easily into me and my head falls back
against the pillow as he slips in and out.

"I love to watch you, to see how good I make you feel," he
says and I moan in response. My hands fist his T-shirt at his back.

He has too many clothes on, but I can't form a coherent sentence to demand their removal. How do we go from "I hate you" to "I love you" to this? I don't care for the answer, though—all I care about is the way he is making me feel, the way he always makes me feel. His body slides down mine and he removes his hand from my pants. I whine from the loss of contact and he smiles.

As he pulls down my jeans and panties, I gesture at his fully clothed body. "Undress," I say, and he chuckles.

"Yes, ma'am." He smirks and pulls his shirt over his head, revealing his inked skin. I want to run my tongue along every single line on every single tattoo. I love the way the infinity symbol above his wrist is so out of place among the flames inked below it.

"Why did you get this?" I ask, running the pad of my index finger over the mark.

"What?" He's distracted, his eyes and hands focused on my breasts.

"This tattoo. It's so different than the rest. So much . . . softer, and sort of feminine?"

His fingers roam across both breasts and he leans in, pressing his arousal against my leg. "Feminine, huh?" He smiles and traces his lips across mine before pulling away and cocking a brow.

I no longer have interest in his tattoo or why he got it. I just want to touch him, to feel his mouth on mine.

Before either of us can ruin the moment with more words, I grab hold of his hair and pull his face to mine. I kiss him briefly on his lips before moving to his neck. From my experience in pleasuring Hardin, I know that the spot on his neck just above his collarbone drives him crazy. I plant wet and warm kisses against there, feeling his body jerk and tense as I lift my hips to him again. The feeling of his bare body on top of mine is exquisite. All of our bare skin is already starting to shine a little with perspiration. If one small movement is made, this will be taken to another level. A level that I had never been ready to reach until now. The flexing of Hardin's hard muscles as he slowly rubs himself against me, moaning, is too much for me to resist.

"Hardin . . ." I moan as he glides against me again.

"Yes, baby?" He stops moving. I bring my heels to his thighs and force him to move again. His eyes flutter closed. "Fuck," he moans.

"I want to . . ." I say.

"You want to what?" His breath is hot and heavy against my clammy skin.

"I want to . . . you know . . ." I say, finding myself suddenly embarrassed despite our intimate position.

"Oh," he says. He stops moving again and stares into my eyes. He seems to be wagering some internal battle with himself. "I . . . I don't know if that's a good idea . . ."

What? "Why?" I push him off me. Here we go again.

"No . . . no, baby. I just mean for tonight." He wraps his arms around me and puts me on my side, lying next to me. I can't look at him, I'm too humiliated.

"Listen, look at me," he says, tilting my chin. "I want to, fuck do I want to. More than anything, trust me. I have wanted to feel you around me since I met you, but I . . . I just think after everything today and . . . I just want you to be ready. I mean all the way ready, because once we do this, it's done. You can't take it back."

My humiliation eases and I look at him. I know he is right, I know I need to think about this more, but I have a hard time believing that my answer will be any different tomorrow. I should think about it when I'm not under the influence of his naked body grinding against mine. He's worse than alcohol running through my veins.

"Don't be upset with me, please, just think about it for a little while, and if you're sure that's what you want to do, I will gladly fuck you. Over and over, when and where you want. I want to—"

"Okay! Okay!" I bring my hand up to cover his mouth. He

laughs against my palm and shrugs his shoulders as if to say, "Just saying."

When I remove my hand from his mouth, he playfully bites my palm and pulls me to him. "I guess I should put some clothes on so you aren't so tempted," he teases and I blush.

I can't decide which aspect of this is more surprising: the fact that I just suggested we have sex, or the fact that he actually has enough respect for me to turn me down.

"But first, let me make you feel good," he mutters and flips me onto my back in one swift motion. His mouth ducks down between my legs, and within minutes my legs are shaking and I'm covering my mouth with my hand to keep from screaming his name for everyone to hear.

chapter sixty-nine

I wake up to Hardin snoring lightly, his lips pressed to my ear. My back is tight against his chest and his legs are hooked around mine. Memories from last night bring a smile to my lips, before the euphoric feeling is replaced by panic.

Will he feel the same in the light of day? Or will he torture and taunt me for offering myself to him? I roll over slowly to face him, to examine his perfect features while his permanent frown is smoothed by sleep. I reach out and run my index finger over his eyebrow ring, then down to the bruise on his cheek. His lip looks better, as do his knuckles, since he finally agreed to let me help him wash them off last night.

His eyes snap open as my finger greedily traces his lips. "What are you doing?" he asks. I can't decipher his tone, which makes me uneasy.

"Sorry . . . I was just . . ." I don't know what to say. I don't know what type of mood he will be in after we fall asleep in each other's arms.

"Don't stop," he whispers and closes his eyes again. Half of the weight on my chest disappears and I smile before tracing over the shape of his plump lips again, careful to avoid his injury.

"What are your plans for today?" he asks a few minutes later, reopening his eyes.

"I actually have plans with Karen to work on her greenhouse out back," I tell him and he sits up.

"Really?" He must be mad. I know he doesn't like Karen, even though she is one of the sweetest people I have ever met.

"Yeah," I mumble.

"Well, I guess I don't have to worry about my family liking you. I think they probably like you better than they do me." He chuckles and runs the pad of his thumb across my cheek, sending a shiver down my spine. "The problem with that is, if I keep hanging out here my dad may start to believe I actually like him," he says, his tone light but his eyes dark.

"Maybe you and your dad could hang out or something while Karen and I are outside?" I suggest.

"No, definitely not," he growls. "I'll go back to my house, my real house, and wait for you to be done."

"I wanted you to stay here, though; it may take a while. Her greenhouse is in pretty bad shape," I say.

He seems to be at a loss for words, which makes my heart warm at the thought that he doesn't want to be away from me for very long. "I . . . I don't know, Tessa. My father probably doesn't want to hang out with me anyway," he mumbles.

"Of course he does. When is the last time you two were even in the same room alone together?"

He shrugs. "I don't know . . . years. I don't know if this is a good idea," he says, running his hands over his head.

"If you get uncomfortable, you can always join Karen and me outside," I assure him. Frankly, I'm astonished that he is considering spending time with his father.

"Fine . . . but I am only doing this because the thought of leaving you, even for a little while . . ." He stops. I know he isn't good at expressing how he feels, so I stay quiet, giving him time to collect himself. "Well, let's just say it's worse than hanging out with my prick of a father."

I smile, despite the harsh words against his dad. The father that Hardin knows from his childhood is not the same man that is downstairs, and I hope Hardin can come around to see that. After I climb out of bed, I remember that I have no clothes with me, no toothbrush, nothing.

"I need to go by my room and grab some things," I tell him and he tenses.

"Why?"

"Because I don't have any clothes, and I need to brush my teeth," I say. When I look at him he has a small smile on his face but it doesn't reach his eyes. "What's wrong?" I ask, afraid of the answer.

"Nothing . . . How long will you be gone?"

"Well, I was assuming you would come with me?" As the words leave my mouth, he visibly relaxes. *What is with him?*

"Oh."

"Are you going to tell me why you are being weird?" I ask with my hands on my hips.

"I'm not . . . I just thought you were trying to leave. Leave me." His voice is so small and unlike him that I get the urge to walk over and cradle him. Instead, I gesture for him to come to me and he nods before getting up and standing in front of me.

"I'm not going anywhere. I just need some clothes," I tell him again.

"I know . . . it's just going to take a little getting used to. I'm used to you running away from me, not leaving and coming back."

"Well, I'm used to you pushing me away from you, so we both just have some adjusting to do." I smile and lay my head on his chest. I feel oddly comforted by his worry. I had been terrified that he would change his mind this morning and it feels good to know he was just as afraid.

"Yeah, I guess we do. I love you," he says, and it hits me just as hard as it did the first time, and the twentieth, last night.

"And I love you, too," I tell him and he frowns.

"Don't say *too*," he says.

"What? Why?" My doubt is on call, waiting for him to deny me, yet hoping that he won't.

"I don't know . . . it just makes me feel like you are just agreeing with me." He looks down. I remember the promise I made to myself last night that I would do whatever I can to help him conquer his self doubt.

"I love you," I say and he looks up at me. His eyes soften and he gently presses his lips against mine.

"Thank you," he says when he pulls away.

I roll my eyes at how flawless he looks in a plain white T-shirt and black jeans. He never wears anything except plain white or black T-shirts and black jeans every single day, but he looks perfect, every single day. He doesn't need to follow whatever trend is hot; his simple style suits him so well. I put on my clothes from last night and he grabs my purse for me before we head downstairs.

We find Karen and Ken in the living room. "I made some breakfast," Karen says cheerfully.

I feel slightly uncomfortable with Karen and Ken knowing I stayed with Hardin, again. I know they seem to be perfectly fine with it, and we *are* adults, but that doesn't stop my cheeks from blushing.

"Thank you." I smile and she gives me a curious look; I know I will get some questions when we are in the greenhouse. I walk into the kitchen and Hardin follows. We both fill our plates with food and sit at the table.

"Are Landon and Dakota here?" I ask Karen when she comes in. Dakota will probably be confused seeing me with Hardin again after being with Zed last night, but I shake off the negative thoughts.

"No, they went to Seattle for the day to do some sightseeing. Were you still wanting to work on the greenhouse today?"

"Yes, of course. I just have to run to my room and change my clothes," I tell her.

"Excellent! I'll have Ken bring the bags of soil out from the shed while you're gone."

"If you wait until we get back, Hardin can help him?" I half-ask, half-offer, looking to Hardin.

"Oh, you will be around today as well?" she asks, her smile growing. How can he not see that people care about him?

"Uh . . . yeah. I was going to just hang out here today . . . I guess. If that's cool with y-you?" he stutters.

"Of course! Ken! Did you hear that, Hardin is going to be here all day!" Her excitement makes me smile and Hardin roll his eyes.

"Be nice," I whisper in his ear as he plasters the fakest smile I have ever seen across his face. Then I giggle and kick his foot with mine.

chapter seventy

I remove my clothes and take a quick shower, even though I'm going to get dirty gardening with Karen. Hardin waits patiently, fiddling through my underwear drawer to keep himself busy. When I'm done, he tells me to pack enough clothes to spend another night with him, which makes me smile. I would spend every night with him if I could.

As we drive back, I ask him, "Do you want to get your car and take it to your dad's?"

"No, I'm okay. As long as you stop swerving all over the road."

"Excuse me? I am an excellent driver," I say defensively.

He snorts but keeps his mouth shut. "So what made you decide to get a car, anyway?"

"Well, I got the internship, and I didn't want to keep taking the bus or depending on other people to take me places."

He looks out the window. "Oh . . . did you go alone?"

"Yeah . . . why?"

"Just wondering," he lies.

"I was alone; that was a bad day for me," I say and he flinches.

"How many times did you and Zed hang out?" he asks.

Why is he bringing this up now? "Twice: we went to dinner and a movie, then the bonfire. It wasn't anything for you to worry about."

"He only kissed you once?"

Ugh. "Yes, only once. Well, besides the time that . . . you saw.

Now can we move on from this? You don't see me asking about Molly, do you?" I snap.

"Okay . . . okay. Let's not fight. This is the longest we have ever gotten along, so let's not ruin it," he says and reaches for my hand. His thumb rubs small circles on my skin.

"Okay," I say, still slightly annoyed. The image of Molly on his lap makes my vision blur.

"Aww, come on, Tess. Don't pout." He laughs and pokes my side.

I can't help but let out a giggle. "Don't distract me! I'm driving!"

"This is probably the only time you'll ever tell me not to touch you."

"Not likely—don't be so full of yourself."

Our laughter blends together and it's a lovely sound. He brings his hand to my thigh and rubs his long fingers up and down.

"You sure?" his raspy voice whispers and my skin tingles. My body responds to him so quickly, my pulse drumming heavily. I gulp and nod, causing him to sigh and pull his hand away. "I know that's not true . . . but I'd rather not have you driving off the road, so I'll just have to finger you later."

I swat at him, blushing. "Hardin!"

"Sorry, baby." He smiles, raising his hands in mock innocence and looking out the window. I love when he calls me baby; no one has called me that before. Noah and I had always thought that the ridiculous pet names people called each other were too juvenile for us, but when Hardin calls me something, my blood sings in my veins.

When we get back to his father's house, Ken and Karen are in the backyard waiting for us. Ken looks out of his element in jeans and a WCU T-shirt. I've never seen him dressed so casually, and in fact he looks a little like Hardin this way. They greet us with a smile that Hardin tries to return, but he looks uncomfortable as he shifts on his heels and buries his hands in his pockets.

"Ready when you are," Ken says to Hardin. He looks just as uncomfortable as Hardin, though he's more nervous, whereas Hardin seems apprehensive.

Hardin looks at me and I give him an encouraging nod, surprised that I have suddenly become someone he looks at for reassurance. It seems that our dynamic has changed dramatically, making me happy in a way I hadn't expected.

"We will be in the greenhouse, so just bring the soil in there," Karen says and gives Ken a small kiss on the cheek. Hardin looks away from them, and for a second I think he may give me a kiss, too, but he doesn't. I follow Karen to the greenhouse and when we walk inside I gasp. It's huge, bigger than it looks from outside, and she wasn't joking when she said it needs a lot of work. It is practically empty.

Dramatically, she puts her hands on her hips with chipper glee. "It is quite the project, but I think we can do it."

"I think so, too," I say.

Hardin and Ken come in, carrying two bags of soil each. They are both silent as they drop them where Karen directs before walking back out. Twenty bags of soil and hundreds of seeds and dozens of flowers and vegetable plants later, we have a pretty good start.

BEFORE I REALIZE IT, the sunlight has started to fade and I haven't seen Hardin in a few hours. I hope he and Ken are both still alive.

"I think we've done enough for today," Karen says and wipes her face. We are both covered in dirt.

"Yeah, I better check on Hardin," I tell her and she laughs.

"It means a lot to us, Ken especially, that Hardin has been

coming around more, and I know we have you to thank for that. I take it that you two worked out your differences?"

"Sort of . . . I guess we did." I let out a little laugh. "We are still very different." If only she knew.

She gives me a knowing smile. "Well, different is sometimes what we need. It's good to be challenged."

"Well, he is definitely challenging."

We both laugh and she pulls me in for a hug. "You sweet girl, you have done more for us than you know." I feel my eyes tearing up and I nod.

"I hope you don't mind that I've been staying overnight. Hardin has asked me to stay again," I tell her and try not to make eye contact.

"No, of course not. You both are adults, and I trust you're being safe."

Oh God. I know my cheeks are a deeper shade of red than the bulbs we just planted. "We . . . uh . . . we don't," I stammer. Why am I talking about this with Hardin's soon-to-be stepmother? I am mortified.

"Oh," she says, equally embarrassed. "Let's go inside."

I follow her into the house, where we both take our dirty shoes off at the door. I can see into the living room, where Hardin is sitting on the edge of the couch and Ken is in the easy chair. Hardin's eyes immediately find mine and relief flushes through them.

"I'll make some late dinner while you get cleaned up," Karen says.

Hardin stands up and walks over to me. He seems glad to be out of the room with his father.

"We'll be back down soon," I say and follow Hardin up the stairs.

"How was it?" I ask as we enter his room.

Instead of answering me, he wraps his fingers around my

ponytail and brings his lips to mine. We stagger back against the door and he presses his body against me. "I missed you."

My insides liquefy. "You did?"

"Yes, I did. I just spent the last few hours with my father in awkward silence, and then sharing a few even more awkward comments here and there. I need a distraction." He runs his tongue along my bottom lip and my breath catches in my throat. This is different. Welcome, and very hot, but different.

His hands travel down my stomach and stop at the button on my jeans.

"Hardin, I need a shower. I am covered in dirt," I say, laughing.

His tongue runs along my neck. "I like you this way, nice and dirty." He gives me that smile with those dimples.

But I gently push him back and grab my bag before heading to the bathroom. My breathing is ragged and I'm a little disoriented, so when I try to close the bathroom door only to have it stop midway, I'm confused. Until I look down and I see Hardin's boot.

"Can I join you?" He smiles and pushes his way into the bathroom before I can answer.

chapter seventy-one

His fingers grip the bottom of his shirt, pulling it over his head, and he reaches behind me to turn on the shower.

"We can't just take a shower together! We're at your father's house, and Landon and Dakota could be back anytime," I say. The idea of seeing Hardin completely naked under the shower makes me squirm but this is too much.

"Well, then I'm going to take a nice hot shower while you stand there and overanalyze." His pants drop to the floor, along with his boxers, and he steps past me and into the water. The bare skin on his back is tight, pulled against the muscles there. He faces me, his eyes moving up and down my covered body, the way mine are on his naked one. The water covers him, making his tattooed skin glisten. I don't realize I'm staring until he closes the curtain abruptly, hiding his perfect figure.

"Don't you just love a hot shower after a long day?" His voice is muffled somewhat by the sound of the water, but I can still catch its smugness.

"I wouldn't know; some rude naked guy stole my shower," I huff and hear him chuckle.

"A *sexy* rude naked guy?" he teases. "Just come in before the hot water goes away."

"I . . ." I want to, but taking a shower with someone is just so intimate, too intimate.

"Come on, live a little. It's just a shower," he says and opens the curtain. "Please." He reaches his hand out and my eyes scan his long, inked torso, gleaming from the water sliding down his skin.

"Okay," I whisper and undress while he watches every move I make. "Stop staring," I scold him and he pretends to be wounded, placing his hand over his heart.

"Are you questioning my nobility?" He laughs and I nod slowly, trying to fight my smile. "I am in*sulted*."

He reaches his hand out to help, and I can't believe I'm actually doing this, showering with someone. I try my best to cover myself with my arms as I wait for him to move from under the water.

"Is it weird that I love how you're still shy around me?" he says, unfolding my arms, removing my shield. I stay quiet and he gently tugs my arms to bring me more under the water, which he's blocking with his body. His head dips down, soaking my bare shoulder.

"I think it's so appealing to me because you are so shy and innocent, yet you let me do dirty things to you." His breath feels hotter than the water against my ear. I blink as his hands travel down my arms slowly. "And I know for a fact that you like when I say dirty things to you."

I gulp and he smiles against my neck. "See how your pulse quickens . . . I can practically see it under your delicate skin." He taps his index finger over the pulse point in my neck. I have no idea how I am standing; my legs have turned to mush, along with my brain.

His fingers running over my body make me stop worrying about the fact that we aren't alone in the house; they make me want to be reckless and let Hardin do whatever he wants to me. When his long fingers wrap around my hips, I involuntarily lean into him.

"I love you, Tessa. You believe me, don't you?" he asks.

I nod, wondering why he is asking me this right now, after we have said it so many times in the last twenty-four hours. "Yes, I believe you." My voice is hoarse and I clear my throat.

"Good. I have never loved anyone before." He goes from playful to seductive to serious so fast, I can barely keep up.

"Ever?" I think I already knew this, but it feels so different actually having him say the words, especially when we are like this. I thought he would have his head between my legs right now, not be expressing his feelings.

"No, never. Not even close," he admits.

I wonder if he has ever had a girlfriend before—no, I don't want to know if he has. He told me he doesn't date, so I'm going to stick with that.

"Oh," is all I can say.

"Do you love me the way you loved Noah?" he asks.

A sound between a cough and a gasp comes out of my mouth, and I look away from him. I grab the shampoo off the shelf. I haven't even washed anything yet and we have been in here several minutes already.

"Well?" he presses.

I don't know how to answer that. It's totally different with Hardin than it was with Noah. I loved Noah, I think. I know I loved him, just not like this. Loving Noah was comfortable and safe; it was always calm. Loving Hardin is raw and exciting; it sparks my every nerve and I can't get enough of him. I never want to be away from him. Even when he drove me crazy, I missed him and had to fight myself to stay away.

"I take that as a no," he says and turns away from me, letting me have full access to the water. I feel cramped in the tiny space and the air is too thin, too clouded with steam from the hot water.

"It's not the same." How do I explain this to him without sounding insane? His shoulders slack. I know if he was to face me he would be frowning. My hands wrap around his waist and

I press my lips against his back. "It's not the same, but not how you're thinking that means," I say. "I love you in a different way. Noah was so comfortable to me he was almost like family. I felt like I was supposed to love him but I really didn't, not in the way I love you at least. It wasn't until I realized I loved you that I saw how different love was from what I thought it was. I don't know if that even makes sense." A pang of guilt hits me for saying I didn't love Noah, but I think I knew that from the moment I kissed Hardin for the first time.

"It does." When he turns back around, his eyes are much softer. The lust, then apprehension are gone, replaced by . . . love? Or relief . . . I can't tell but he leans down and kisses my forehead. "I just want to be the only person you ever love; that way you are mine."

How could he be such a jerk before and say these loving things to me now? Despite the hint of possessiveness in his tone, his words are sweet and surprisingly humble for him.

"In the ways that count, you are," I promise him. He seems pleased with my answer as his smile returns.

"Now, can you move so I can get this dirt off me before the water goes cold?" I say and gently push him out of my way.

"I'll do that for you." He grabs the cloth and pours soap on it. I hold my breath the entire time he gently scrubs the dirt off my body, and shiver as he passes over the sensitive spots, his touch lingering on them.

"I would have you wash me, but I won't be able to stop what would happen after." He winks at me and I blush. I want to find out what would happen after, and I would love to touch every inch of his body. But Karen has probably already finished cooking and might come looking for us soon.

I know the responsible thing to do would be to agree to leave the shower, but it's hard to concentrate on being responsible when he's naked in front of me. I reach for him, gripping his length in my palm, and he steps back against the shower wall. He stares at me as I pump him slowly in my hand.

"Tess," he groans, resting his head back against the tiled wall.

I keep my hand on him, willing him to groan again. I just love the noises he makes. I glance down, admiring the way the water is spraying us, helping my hand to glide easily over him.

"You make me feel so fucking good."

His gaze on me makes me a little nervous, but the way his teeth are pressed together and the way his eyelids flutter, it's as if he's trying to keep them open to urge me to pleasure him further. My thumb rubs across the head of his penis and he curses under his breath.

"I'm going to come now, already. Fuck." His eyes close and I feel the warmth of his release mix with the hot water, and I can't help but stare until only the water is left on my hand. Hardin leans over, out of breath, and presses a kiss to my mouth.

"Amazing," he whispers, kissing me again.

After I am dirt-free and feeling calm, yet wound up from Hardin's touch, I dry off quickly and put on my yoga pants and a T-shirt from my bag, then brush my hair and pull it into a bun. Hardin wraps a towel around his waist and stands behind me, watching me through the mirror. He looks so heavenly and god-like and perfect and mine.

"Those pants are going to be distracting," he says.

"Have you always been such a pervert?" I tease and he nods.

IT ISN'T UNTIL WE WALK into the kitchen that I realize how we look, both coming down with wet hair. It is obvious that we just showered together. Hardin doesn't seem to mind, but then, he has no manners.

"There are some sandwiches over on the counter," Karen proclaims cheerily, pointing near where Ken sits with a stack of folders in front of him. She doesn't seem to be surprised or mind our appearance; my mother would lose her mind if she knew what I just did. Especially with someone like Hardin.

"Thank you so much," I tell her.

"I had a nice time today, Tessa," Karen says, and we start discussing the greenhouse again while we each gather up a sandwich and sit down to eat.

Hardin eats in silence, glancing at me from time to time.

"Maybe we can do some more work next weekend," I suggest, then catch myself. "Never mind, the weekend after," I say, laughing.

"Yes, of course."

"Uh, is there a theme or something with the wedding?" Hardin interrupts.

Ken looks up from his work.

"Well, there isn't really a theme, but we have chosen white and black for the décor," Karen says nervously. I'm sure this is the only discussion they've had with Hardin about the wedding since he lost it when Ken told him about it.

"Oh. So what should I wear?" he asks casually. I want to reach over and kiss him after seeing his father's reaction.

"You're coming?" Ken asks, clearly surprised but very happy.

"Yeah . . . I guess." Hardin shrugs and takes another bite of his sandwich.

Karen and Ken smile at each other before Ken gets up and walks over to Hardin. "Thank you, son, this means a lot to me." He pats Hardin on the shoulder. Hardin stiffens but rewards his father with a small smile.

"This is great news!" Karen says and claps her hands.

"It's nothing," Hardin grumbles. I move to sit next to him and put my hand over his under the table. I never thought I could get him to agree to the wedding, let alone actually talk about it in front of Ken and Karen.

"I love you," I whisper in his ear when Karen and Ken aren't paying attention.

He smiles and squeezes my hand. "I love you," he whispers back.

"So, Hardin, how are your classes going?" Ken asks.

"Good."

"I noticed you moved your classes around again."

"Yeah, and?"

"You're still majoring in English, right?" Ken goes on, unwittingly pressing his luck; I can see that Hardin is getting annoyed.

"Yep."

"That's great! I remember when you were ten and you would recite passages from *The Great Gatsby* all day, every day. I knew you were a literature whiz then," his father says.

"Do you? Do you remember that?" Hardin's tone is harsh. I squeeze his hand, trying to signal him to calm down.

"Yeah, of course I do," Ken says calmly.

Hardin's nostrils flare and he rolls his eyes. "I find that hard to believe since you were constantly drunk, and, if I remember correctly, which I do, you tore that book to pieces because I bumped your scotch and spilled it. So don't try to take a stroll down memory lane with me unless you know what the fuck you're talking about." He stands up as Karen and I both gasp.

"Hardin!" Ken says as he leaves the room.

I scurry after him and hear Karen yelling at Ken. "You shouldn't have gone that far with him, Ken! He just agreed to come to our wedding. I thought we agreed on baby steps! Then you go and say something like that. You should have left it alone!"

Although she sounds mad, I can tell from the breaks in her voice that Karen is really already crying.

chapter seventy-two

Hardin slams his bedroom door as I reach the top of the stairs. I turn the knob, half-expecting it to be locked, but it opens.

"Hardin, are you okay?" I ask, unsure what else to say.

He answers me by grabbing the lamp off the nightstand and slamming it against the wall. The glass base shatters from the impact. I jump back and a small shriek comes out against my will. He paces over to the desk, grabs the small keyboard, and rips it out of the desktop computer, tossing it behind him.

"Hardin, please stop!" I yell.

He doesn't look at me, but knocks the monitor to the ground and starts yelling, "Why? Why, Tessa? It's not like he can't afford to buy a new fucking computer!"

"You're right," I say and step on top of the keyboard, crushing it further.

"What? What are you doing?" he asks as I pick it up and drop it back on the ground. I'm not really sure what I am doing but the keyboard's already broken, and this seems like the best idea at the moment.

"I'm helping you," I tell him, and confusion flashes in his angry eyes before humor takes over. I pick up the monitor and throw it against the floor. He walks over with a small smile on his lips as I pick it up again, but his hands stop mine and he takes the monitor out of my hands and sits it on the desk.

"You're not mad at me for yelling at my dad like that?" he

asks, and cups my cheeks, his thumbs gently caressing them as his green eyes bore into mine.

"No, you have every right to express yourself. I would never be mad about that." He just had a fight with his dad but he is worried about me being mad at him? "Unless of course you're being mean for no reason, which in this case you weren't."

"Wow . . ." he says.

But the small gap between our lips is too tempting. I lean forward and press mine against his, and he immediately opens his mouth, deepening the kiss. My fingers twist into his hair and he groans as I put more force into it. His anger rolls off him like a tidal wave. I push him back a little and he turns me around so the bottom of my back hits the desk. His hands attach to my hips and he lifts me onto the desk. *I am his distraction.* The thought of me being what Hardin needs makes me feel needed in a way I wasn't aware of. I feel more solid now, more necessary in his life, and my head tilts back as he continues to push his tongue against mine, standing between my legs.

"Closer," he moans into my mouth. His hands grip the back of my knees and he pulls me to the edge. My hands tug at his jeans and he pulls his mouth away from mine.

"What . . . ?" He raises an eyebrow at me. He must think I am insane, coming in here and helping him break things, and now trying to undress him. And maybe I am. I don't care at the moment. All I care about is the way the curve of Hardin's collarbones are shadowed by the moonlight coming through the bay window, the way one of his hands is holding my face like I am fragile, despite him trying to break everything in the room minutes ago.

I answer him wordlessly by wrapping my legs around him and pulling him closer.

"I really thought you were going to storm in here and tell me off." He smiles and presses his forehead against mine.

"You were wrong," I remind him with a smug smile.

"Very. I don't want to go back down there tonight," he says, eyes searching mine.

"That's fine. You don't have to."

He relaxes and moves his head to the crook of my neck. I'm surprised by how easy this is between us. I had expected him to snap at me, maybe even try to make me leave when I came in here, but here he is leaning on me. I can tell he is really trying to navigate this relationship the best he can, despite the fact that he is one giant mood swing.

"I love you," I tell him, and feel his lip ring move against my neck as he smiles.

"I love you," he replies.

"Do you want to talk about it?" I ask, but he shakes his head, still buried in my neck. "Okay, do you want to watch a movie? Something funny, maybe?" I suggest.

After a long pause, he looks back toward the bed. "Did you bring your laptop?" When I nod he continues. "Let's watch *The Vow* again."

I laugh. "You mean the movie that you supposedly despise?"

"Yes . . . well, *despise* is a little harsh. I just think it's a sappy, mediocre love story," he corrects.

"Then why do you want to watch it?"

"Because I want to watch you watch it," he answers thoughtfully.

Remembering the way he watched me the entire time we watched it in my room, that night seems so long ago. I had no clue what was coming up between us. I would have never imagined we would come to this.

My smile is all the answer he needs as he grabs my waist and carries me to the bed.

Within minutes, he is snuggled up next to me studying my face as I watch the movie. Halfway through I feel my eyes getting heavy.

"I'm getting sleepy," I say with a yawn.

"They both die; you're not missing much."

I nudge him with my elbow. "You have issues."

"And you're adorable when you're sleepy." He closes my laptop and pulls me up to the top of the bed with him.

"And you're uncharacteristically nice when I'm sleepy," I say.

"No, I'm nice because I love you," he whispers and I swoon. "Sleep, beautiful."

He gives me a small peck on my forehead, and I am too tired to try for more.

THE NEXT MORNING, the light is bright, too bright. When I roll over to bury my head in Hardin's shoulder, he sighs in his sleep and pulls me closer. When I wake up again, he is awake and staring at the ceiling. His eyes are hooded and his expression unreadable.

"You okay?" I ask, nuzzling farther into him.

"Yeah, I'm fine," he answers, but I can tell he is lying.

"Hardin, if there is something wrong . . ." I begin.

"There isn't, I'm fine." I decide to let it go. We have gotten along all weekend; it's a record for us. I don't want to ruin it. I lift my head up and place a single kiss on his jaw and his arms wrap tighter around me.

"I have a few things to do today, so whenever you're ready, can you drop me off at my house?" he asks. My stomach drops, hearing the distance in his voice.

"Sure," I mumble and move out of his embrace. He tries to grab my wrist but I move too quickly. Grabbing my bag, I head to the bathroom to change and brush my teeth. We have been in our own little bubble all weekend, and I fear that without the protection of these walls, he won't be the same.

I'm relieved when I don't run into Landon or Dakota in the hallway, and even more relieved that Hardin is fully dressed when

I return. I want to get this over with. He has cleaned the glass off the floor and the keyboard is in the trash can, the lamp and monitor neatly piled nearby.

Downstairs, I say goodbye to Ken and Karen, though Hardin walks outside without saying a word to either of them. I assure them that Hardin will still be at the wedding, despite the drama last night. I tell them about the computer and lamp, but they don't seem to pay it much mind.

"Are you mad or something?" Hardin asks after ten minutes of silence.

"No." It's not that I'm mad, I am just . . . nervous, I suppose. I can feel the shift between us and I wasn't expecting anything to change from how we were all weekend.

"It seems like it."

"Well, I'm not."

"You need to tell me if you are."

"You're just being distant and now you're having me drop you off at your house, and I thought everything was fine between us," I say.

"You're upset because I have things to do today?" When he says it like that, I realize how ridiculous and obsessive I sound. *Is that why I am upset? Because he isn't hanging out with me today?*

"Maybe." I laugh at my stupidity. "I just don't want you to be distant from me."

"I'm not . . . not on purpose, at least. I am sorry if I made you feel that way." He reaches over and puts his hand on my thigh. "Nothing is going to change, Tessa."

His words calm me, but there is still a sliver of uncertainty behind my smile.

"Do you want to come with me?" he finally asks.

"No, I'm okay. I have some studying to do anyway."

"Okay. Tess, you have to remember this is new to me. I'm not used to having to consider other people when I make plans."

"I know."

"I can come to your room when I'm finished, or we can go to dinner or something."

I put my hand on his cheek, then run it through his messy hair. "It's fine, really, Hardin. Just let me know when you're finished and we can decide then."

When we pull up to his house, he leans over and gives me a swift kiss before climbing out of the car.

"I'll text you," he says, and bounds up the steps to that damned house.

chapter seventy-three

The emptiness that I feel after dropping Hardin off is strange, and makes me feel a bit pathetic. After the short drive back to my room, it already feels as if I dropped him off hours ago. Steph isn't in the room when I get there, but I'm glad. I really do need to study and prepare for my first day at Vance tomorrow: I have to decide what to wear, what to bring, what I am going to say.

Taking out my planner, I plan my week by the hour, then move on to my clothes. Day one at Vance will be my new black skirt and a red top and black heels, not too high but higher than I would have considered wearing two months ago. The outfit is very professional but still feminine. I wonder idly if Hardin will like it.

To keep my mind off him, I complete all of my assignments that are due this week and then some. By the time I finish, the sun has disappeared from the sky and I'm starving, but the cafeteria is already closed. Hardin still hasn't texted me, so I assume he isn't planning on coming over tonight.

Grabbing my purse, I head out to find something to eat. I remember seeing a Chinese restaurant near the little library, but by the time I find the place it's closed. I look up the closest restaurant to me and find a place called the Ice House. When I drive there, the Ice House is small and looks like it's made out of aluminum, but I'm hungry and the idea of finding another place to eat makes my stomach rumble even more. Going inside, I realize it's more of a bar that serves food, and that it's actually quite packed, although to my surprise I manage to find a small table in the back to sit at.

I ignore the glances of the people inside, who must be wondering why I'm here alone, but I always eat alone. I am not one of those people who need someone to go with them everywhere. I go shopping alone, eat out alone, and I have even been to the movies alone a few times when Noah wasn't able to come. I never really have minded being alone . . . until now, if I'm honest with myself. I miss Hardin more than I should, and it troubles me that he hasn't even bothered to text me.

I order, and while I'm waiting on my food, the waitress brings me over a pink drink with a yellow umbrella sticking out of the top.

"Oh, I didn't order this," I tell her but she sits it down in front of me anyway.

"He did." She smiles and tilts her head toward the bar area. I immediately hope that it's Hardin somehow and crane my neck to look. But it's not. Zed gives me a small wave and a dazzling smile from across the room. Nate walks up and takes the empty bar stool next to him and shoots me a smile as well.

"Oh. Thanks," I tell her. It seems that every place around this campus allows underage drinking, or maybe these guys only go to the places that do. She assures me that my food will be ready any minute and wanders off.

A few moments later, Zed and Nate come over, pull the chairs out from my table, and take a seat. I hope Zed isn't angry with me for what happened on Friday.

"You're the last person that I expected to see in here, especially on a Sunday," Nate says.

"Yeah, it was an accident. I was going for Chinese but it was closed," I tell them.

"Have you seen Hardin?" Zed asks with a smile before looking at Nate, who shares a mysterious look with him before turning back to me.

"No, not for a while. You?" I ask them. My nerves are clear in my voice.

"No, not for a few hours but he should be here soon," Nate answers.

"*Here?*" I squeak. My food arrives, but I'm no longer hungry. What if Molly is with him? I won't be able to take it, not after the weekend we just had together.

"Yeah, we come here a lot. I can call him and see when he'll be here?" Zed suggests but I shake my head.

"No, it's fine. I'm going to go, actually." I look around for my waitress to ask for my check.

"You didn't like the drink?" Zed asks.

"No, well, I didn't try it. Thanks for getting it for me, but I should go."

"Are you guys fighting again?" he asks.

Nate begins to say something but Zed shoots him a glare from across the table. What is going on? He takes a sip of his beer and looks at Nate again.

"He said what?" I ask.

"Nothing, he just said you guys were on better terms now." Zed answers for him. The small bar feels even smaller now, and I am desperate to leave.

"Oh, there they are!" Nate says.

My eyes dart to the door to see Hardin, Logan, Tristan, Steph, and Molly—I knew it. I know they are friends, and I don't want to come off as controlling or crazy, but I can't stand Hardin being around that girl.

When Hardin's eyes meet mine he looks surprised and almost afraid. Not this again. The waitress walks by while they make their way to our table.

"Could I just get my food to go, and get the check, please?" I ask her. She looks surprised, and then looks around at everybody who just showed up and nods, then goes back to the kitchen.

"Why are you going?" Steph asks. The five of them sit at the table next to us. I refuse to allow myself to look over at Hardin. I hate the way he is so different around his friends—why can't he just be the same Hardin that I had all weekend?

"I . . . well, I have to study," I lie.

She smiles hopefully. "You should stay—you study too much!"

Any hope that Hardin would scoop me into his arms and tell me he has missed me is gone. The waitress shows up with my food, and I hand her a twenty, then stand up to leave.

"Well, you guys have a good night," I tell them. I look at Hardin and then back at the floor.

"Wait," Hardin says. I turn around and look at him. Please don't let him make a rude remark or kiss Molly again.

"Aren't you going to give me a good-night kiss?" He smiles.

I look around at his friends and they all look a little surprised but mostly confused. "W-what?" I stammer. I straighten my shoulders and look at him again.

"You're not going to kiss me before you go?" He stands up and walks toward me. I wanted this, but now I am uncomfortable with everyone's eyes on us.

"Um . . ." I don't know what to say.

"Why would she?" Molly laughs. *God, I can't stand her.*

"They are like together, obviously," Steph tells her.

"What?" Molly says.

"Keep your mouth shut, Molly," Zed says and I want to thank him, but there is something behind his voice that makes me wonder about his choice of words. This is beyond uncomfortable.

"Bye, guys," I say again and walk toward the door.

Hardin follows me and grabs my wrist to stop me. "Why are you leaving? And why are you even in this place to begin with?"

"Well, I was hungry and came here to eat. And now I'm leaving because you were ignoring me and I—"

"I wasn't ignoring you, I just didn't know what to say or do. I wasn't expecting to see you here. It caught me off guard," he explains.

"Yeah, I am sure it did. You haven't texted me all day and now you're here with Molly?" My voice comes out much whinier than I wanted.

"And Logan, Tristan, and Steph. Not just Molly," he points out.

"I know . . . but you guys have a history and that bothers me." I surely broke the record for the quickest jealous fit.

"It's just that, babe: *history*. It wasn't like this . . . not like us," he says.

I sigh. "I know, I just can't help it."

"I know. How do you think I felt when I walked in there and saw you sitting with Zed?"

"That's not the same thing. You and Molly have slept together." Just saying it stings.

"Tess . . ."

"I know, it's crazy, but I can't help it." I look away.

"It's not crazy. I understand. I just don't know what to do about it. Molly is in our group and she probably always will be."

I don't know what I expected him to say but the equivalent of "too bad" isn't what I wanted to hear. "Okay." I should be happy that he basically told everyone we are dating now, but the whole thing felt so off.

"I'm going to go," I tell him.

"Then I'm coming with you."

"You sure you want to leave your friends?" I snap.

He rolls his eyes and follows me to my car. I try to hide my smile as we get in the car. At least I know he would rather be with me than Molly.

"So how long were you there before I arrived?" Hardin asks as I pull out of the parking lot.

"About twenty minutes."

"Oh. You didn't meet Zed there, did you?"

"No. It was the last place open to eat I could find. I had no idea he was there—or that you would show up. You know, because you never texted me."

"Oh," he says and pauses for a beat. But then he looks over at me again. "So what did you guys talk about?"

"Nothing; he was only at the table for a few minutes before you got there. Why?"

"I'm just wondering." His fingers drum on his knee. "I missed you today."

"I missed you, too," I say as we pull onto campus. "I got a lot of homework done and I prepared everything for my first day at Vance."

"Do you want me to drive you tomorrow?"

"No, that's why I got my own car, remember?" I laugh.

"Still, I could drive you," he offers as we get to my dorm and head inside.

"No, it's fine. I will drive myself. Thank you, though."

Just as I am about to ask him what he did all day—why he hadn't texted me if he missed me so much—my breath gets locked in my throat and panic takes over.

My mother is standing in front of my door with her arms crossed and a deep scowl on her face.

chapter seventy-four

Hardin's eyes follow mine and widen as he sees her. He reaches for my hand, but I pull away and step out in front of him. "Hi, Moth—"

"What the hell are you thinking!" she yells as we approach.

I want to shrink and disappear.

"I . . . what?" I don't know what she knows yet, so I stay quiet. In her anger, her blond hair looks brighter, more angled toward her perfectly drawn-on face.

"What are you thinking, Theresa! Noah has been avoiding me for the last two weeks, and I finally ran into Mrs. Porter at the grocery—and you know what she told me? That you two have broken up! *Why wouldn't you tell me?* I had to find out in *the most humiliating way!*" she shouts.

"It's not that big a deal, Mother. We broke up," I say and she gasps. Hardin stays behind me, but I feel his hand go to the small of my back.

"Not that big a deal? How dare you—you and Noah have been together for years. He is *good* for you, Tessa. He has a *future,* and comes from a great family!" She pauses to catch her breath a moment, but I don't interrupt, knowing there's more to come. She straightens up and says as calmly as she can, "Luckily, I have just spoken to him and he has agreed to take you back, despite your promiscuous behavior."

Anger flares inside me. "How dare *I*? If I don't want to date him, I don't have to. What does it matter what type of family he

comes from? If I wasn't happy with him, that is what should matter. How dare *you* talk to him about this—I am an adult!"

I push past her to open the door. Hardin follows close behind
me and my mother storms in after.

"You have no idea how ridiculous you sound! And then you
show up here with . . . this . . . this . . . *punk*! Look at him, Tessa!
Is this your way of rebelling against me? Have I done something
to make you hate me?"

Hardin is standing by my dresser with his jaw clenched and
hands shoved deep in his pockets. If only she knew that Hardin's
father is the chancellor at WCU and has even more money than
Noah's family. But I won't tell her that, because that has nothing
to do with it.

"This isn't about you! Why do you have to make everything
about you!" My tears are fighting to break free, but I refuse to let
her get the best of me. I hate that when I am angry I cry; it makes
me seem weak, but I can't help it.

"You're right, it isn't about me—it's about your future! You
have to think of the future, not just how you're feeling now. I
know he seems fun and dangerous, but there is no future here!"
She gestures to Hardin. "Not with him . . . this freak!"

Before I realize what I am doing, I am in my mother's face
and Hardin has stepped forward, grabbing me by the elbows
to pull me away from her. "Do not talk about him like that!" I
scream.

My mother's eyes are wide and red-rimmed. "Who are you?
My daughter would never speak to me this way! She would never
jeopardize her future or be so disrespectful!"

I begin to feel guilty, but that's exactly what she wants, and I
have to fight through it to defend what *I* want. "I am not jeopar-
dizing my future! My future isn't even in question here, I'll have
a four-point-oh, and I have a great internship starting tomorrow!
You are beyond selfish to come here and try to make me feel bad

for being happy. He makes me happy, Mother, and if you can't accept that, then you should go."

"Excuse me?" She huffs, but in truth I'm as surprised by what I just said as she is. "You will regret this, Theresa! I am disgusted to even look at you!"

The room starts spinning. I was not prepared to go to war with my mother, not today at least. I knew it would be a matter of time before she found out, but she wasn't even on my radar for today.

"I knew something was going on from the first time I saw him in your room. I just didn't think you would be so quick to open your legs for him!"

Hardin steps between us. "You're taking this too far," he warns her with dark eyes. I think Hardin may be the only person who could actually give my mother a run for her money.

"You stay out of this!" she snaps, crossing her arms once again. "If you continue to see him, I will no longer speak to you, and you surely can't pay for college on your own. *This dorm alone costs me thousands!*" she shrieks.

I'm astounded that my mother would go there. "You're threatening my education because you don't approve of who I am in love with?"

"*In love with?*" she scoffs. "Oh Theresa, my naïve Theresa, you have no idea what love is." She laughs, making a sound that is more like a sickening cackle. "And you think he loves you?"

"I do love her," Hardin interrupts.

"Sure you do!" Her head falls back.

"Mother."

"Theresa, I'm warning you: If you don't stop seeing him, there will be consequences. I'm leaving now, but I expect a call after you clear your head." She storms out of my room, and I go into the doorway to watch her as she stomps away, her heels clunking and echoing down the hall.

"I am so sorry." I turn to Hardin.

"You have nothing to apologize for." He takes my face in his hands. "I am proud of the way you stood up for yourself." He kisses my nose. I look around the room and wonder just how everything came to this. I lean into Hardin's chest and he reaches around me, rubbing the tense muscles on my neck.

"I can't believe her, I can't believe she would act like that and threaten not to help pay for my college. She doesn't pay for all of it—I have a partial scholarship and some student loans. She only pays twenty percent; the biggest thing is the dorms. But what if she really stops paying for them? I will have to find a job on top of the internship," I sob. His hand moves to the back of my head and gently guides my head down to cry on his chest.

"Shh . . . Shh . . . It's okay, we will figure it out. You can move in with me," he says. I laugh and wipe my eyes, but he goes on, "Really, you could. Or we could get an apartment off campus. I have enough money."

I look up at him. "You can't be serious."

"I am."

"We can't move in together." I laugh and sniffle.

"Why not?"

"Because we have only known each other for a few months, and most of that time was spent fighting," I remind him.

"So, we have done a pretty good job getting along this weekend." He smiles and we both burst into laughter.

"You're insane. I am not moving in with you," I tell him and he hugs me again.

"Just think about it—I want to move out of the frat house anyway. I don't really fit in there, in case you didn't notice," he says and laughs. It's true, his small group of friends are the only ones who don't wear polo shirts and khakis every day. "I only joined to piss my father off, but it didn't work as well as I had hoped."

"You could just get an apartment on your own if you dislike the house," I say. There is no way I am moving in with him this soon.

"Yeah, but that wouldn't be as fun." He grins and wiggles his brows at me.

"We could still have fun," I tease.

His wicked smile grows and he brings both hands down to my bottom and squeezes.

"Hardin!" I scold him playfully.

The door opens and my breathing stops. Flashbacks of my mother's anger fill my vision, and I'm afraid she's come back for round two.

So I'm relieved when it's Steph and Tristan who walk into the room.

"Guess I missed something grand. Your mom just flipped me off in the parking lot," Steph says, and I can't help but laugh.

chapter seventy-five

Hardin ends up staying the night in my room after Steph goes to Tristan's apartment with him. The rest of the night we spend talking and kissing before Hardin finally falls asleep with his head on my lap. I dream of a time and place where we could actually live together. I would love to wake up every morning to find Hardin next to me, but it's not realistic. I'm too young, and that's moving too fast.

Monday morning, my alarm goes off ten minutes late, throwing my whole morning off. After I shower and do my makeup quickly, I wake Hardin before plugging in my blow dryer.

"What time is it?" he groans.

"It's six thirty. I have to blow-dry my hair."

"Six thirty? You don't have to be there until nine; come back to bed."

"No, I still have to do my hair and get coffee. I have to leave here by seven thirty; the drive is forty-five minutes."

"You'd be there forty-five minutes early; you should leave at eight." He closes his eyes and rolls back over.

I ignore him and turn on my blow dryer; he takes a pillow and covers his head with it. After curling my hair, I go over my planner again to make sure I didn't miss anything.

"Are you going to just go to class from here?" I ask Hardin as I get dressed.

"Yeah, probably." He smiles and crawls out of bed. "Can I use your toothbrush?"

"Uh, I guess . . . I'll just buy a new one on my way back." No one has ever asked to use my toothbrush before. I mentally picture myself putting it in my mouth after he uses it, but nothing good comes of that.

"I still say you shouldn't leave until eight; think of the things we could do in thirty minutes," he says, and I look over at him and his tempting dimples, and notice the way his eyes travel up and down my body. My own eyes travel to the bulge in his boxers and my body immediately heats. My fingers stop on the middle button of my shirt as he lazily crosses the small room to stand behind me. I gesture for him to zip my skirt, and he complies, but his hands brush my bare skin delicately as he does so.

"I have to. I still have to get some coffee," I say frantically. "What if there is traffic? An accident? I could blow a tire or need gas. I could get lost, or not be able to find somewhere to park. What if I have to park in the very back and then I have to walk a long way and I will be out of breath, so I will need a few minutes to—"

"You need to calm down, baby. You're a nervous wreck." He sends a little breath across my ear. I look at him in the mirror. He looks so perfect when he wakes up, his sleepiness making him look softer.

"I can't help it; this internship means so much to me. I can't take the chance of messing it up." My mind is racing. I will be fine after today, after I know what to expect and can plan my week accordingly.

"You don't want to show up there nervous like this; they will eat you alive." He places a string of small kisses down my neck.

"I will be fine." *I hope.* Goose bumps cover my skin from his warm breath against my neck.

"Let me relax you first." His voice is low and seductive, laced with sleep.

"I . . ."

He trails his fingers over my collarbone and down to my chest. His eyes meet mine in the mirror and I sigh in defeat. "Five minutes?" I ask and beg at the same time.

"That's all I need."

I move to turn around, but he stops me. "No, I want you to watch," he purrs in my ear. I feel the familiar twinge between my legs from his words. I gulp and he moves my hair over my left shoulder and pushes his body against mine. His hand travels down to the hem of my long skirt.

"At least you aren't wearing tights today. I must say I am a fan of this skirt." He pulls it up to my waist. "Especially when it's like this."

My eyes are glued to his hands in the mirror and my pulse is thrumming. His fingers are slightly cold as they slip into my panties; the contact makes me jump slightly and he chuckles into my neck. His other hand is wrapped around my chest, holding me in place. I feel so exposed, but so turned on at the same time. Watching him touch me takes my mind places that I never knew existed. His fingers move slowly inside me and he kisses my neck softly.

"Look how beautiful you are," he whispers against my skin. I look at myself in the mirror and barely recognize the girl before me. My cheeks are flushed a deep red; my eyes are wide and wild. With my skirt bunched up at my hips and Hardin's fingers moving inside me, I look different . . . sexy, even.

My eyes close as I feel my stomach tightening. Hardin continues his beautifully slow assault and I pull my bottom lip between my teeth to stifle a moan.

"Open your eyes," he instructs. My eyes meet his and it sends me over the edge—Hardin standing behind me, holding me, watching me come undone from his touch is all it takes. My head rolls back on his shoulder and my legs start to shake.

"That's it, baby," he coos and tightens his grip around me, holding me up as my vision blurs and I moan his name.

When my eyes open again, Hardin kisses my temple and tucks a curl behind my ear before tugging my skirt back down my thighs. I turn around to face him and check the clock. It's only seven thirty-five.

He really did only need five minutes, I think to myself and smile.

"See, you're much more relaxed and ready to take on corporate America, right?" He beams, obviously proud of himself. I don't blame him.

"Yes, actually. But you make a terrible American," I tease and grab my bag.

"I don't claim to be otherwise," he says. "Last chance for me to drive you. Well, since my car isn't here, I could drive you in your car?"

"No; thank you, though."

"Good luck; you'll do great."

He kisses me again and I thank him and gather my things, leaving him in my room. This morning has turned out to be great despite my alarm being ten minutes off. The drive is quick and clear, so when I pull into the parking lot it's only eight thirty. I decide to call Hardin to pass the time.

"You okay?" he says on the other end.

"Yeah, I'm already here," I tell him. I can picture his self-satisfied expression.

"Told you. You could have stayed for ten more minutes and given me a blow job."

I giggle. "Always such a pervert, even this early in the morning."

"Yep, I am nothing but consistent."

"I won't argue with that." We banter back and forth about his lack of virtue until it's time for me to go inside. I make my way to the top floor, where Christian Vance's office is located, and give the woman in the front my name.

She gives someone a call and a few moments later gives me a huge smile. "Mr. Vance would like to come out himself; he will see you in a second."

The door to the office I was interviewed in opens, and Mr. Vance himself comes out. "Ms. Young!" he greets me. He is dressed in such a nice suit that I'm a little intimidated, but thankful that I dressed professionally. He is holding a thick folder under his arm.

"Hello, Mr. Vance." I smile and reach out to shake his hand.

"Go ahead and call me Christian. I will show you to your office."

"Office?" I blurt out.

"Yes, you will need your own space. It's not much, but it'll be yours. Let's go over your paperwork there." He smiles and then walks off so quickly that I strain to keep up in my heels. He makes a left turn into a hallway full of small offices.

"Here we are," he announces. There is a black tag with my name in bold white letters next to the door.

I must be dreaming. The office is as big as my dorm room. Mr. Vance and I have different ideas of "not much." Inside, there is a medium-sized cherry desk, two filing cabinets, two chairs, a bookshelf, a computer—and a *window*! He takes a seat in front of the desk, so I go and sit behind it. It's going to take some getting used to the idea that this is actually my office.

"So, Ms. Young, let's go over what your duties will include," he says. "You will be expected to go over at least two manuscripts a week; if they are excellent and fit in with what we publish here, then you will send them to me. If they aren't worth me looking at, toss them."

My mouth falls open. This internship is literally a dream come true. I will be paid and receive college credit to read.

"You will start out at two hundred a week, and if you do well after ninety days, you will receive a raise."

Two hundred a week! That should be enough for me to get my own apartment, albeit a tiny one.

"Thank you so much; this is all so much more than I expected," I tell him. I can't wait to call Hardin and tell him about all of this.

"It's my pleasure. I have it on good authority that you are a very hard worker. Maybe you can even tell Hardin how great it is, so he'll come back and work for me again," he says jokingly.

"What?"

"Hardin, he used to work for us before Bolthouse snatched him up. He started as an intern here last year, did great work, and I quickly hired him. But they offered him more money—and let him work from home. Said he didn't like the office setting, so he left us. Go figure." He smiles and adjusts his watch.

I laugh nervously. "I'll remind him how great this place is." I had no idea he had a job. He has never mentioned it to me.

Mr. Vance slides the folder across the desk to me. "Let's get this paperwork out of the way."

After thirty minutes of "sign here" and "initial here," we are finally finished and Mr. Vance leaves me to "familiarize" myself with the computer and office.

But as soon as he walks out and closes the door behind him, all I can think to do is squeal and spin myself around in my chair, at my desk, in my new office!

chapter seventy-six

When I get back to my car after the best first day possible, I call Hardin, but he doesn't answer. I want to tell him about how great my morning has been and ask him why he didn't tell me that he has a job or worked at Vance.

By the time I get back to campus it's only one, since they dismissed me early, being busy with some high-level meetings or something. I basically have the whole day to do nothing, so I end up going to the mall and walking around. After wandering in and out of almost every store there, I go into Nordstrom, figuring I could use a few more outfits for my internship. The memory of Hardin and me in the mirror this morning flashes in my mind, and I realize I could also use some new panties and bras. My undergarments are so plain and I have had them a while. Hardin doesn't seem to mind, but I would love to see his face if I took my shirt off and had a bra that wasn't plain old black or white. I pick through the racks and find a few promising sets. My favorite one is carnation pink and made almost completely from lace. Pulling it off of the rack alone makes me blush, but I really like it. A saleswoman with curly hair and way too much red lipstick walks over to try to help me.

"Oh yeah, that's nice, but what do you think about this one?" she says and holds up something that resembles a hot pink bundle of strings on a hanger.

"Um . . . not really my style," I tell her and look at the ground.

"I see you prefer the *full* underwear?" she asks. Why must we actually discuss my underwear choices? This could not be more humiliating.

"You should try the boy short style; it's sexy without being too sexy," she says and holds up the same light pink set I am holding, only the panties are made differently. Boy shorts. I never cared too much about my panties because no one has seen them; who knew this would be so humiliating and complicated.

"Okay." I give in and she pulls a few more off the rack: a white, a black, and a red set. The red is a little shocking to me, but I have to admit it's intriguing. Even the black and white ones look more exotic than my usual choices because they are made of lace.

Her smile is a wide and scary chasm. "Just try them; they are all the exact same style." I nod politely and take them from her, hoping that if I walk away she won't follow me. Relieved when she doesn't, I find a few dresses as well and a pair of comfortable dress shoes. I have to ask the cashier to repeat my total three times before I finally pay. Fancy underwear is much more expensive than I thought. Hardin had better like it.

When I get back to my room, Steph isn't there and I haven't heard from Hardin, so I decide to take a nap. My new clothes are put away and I shut off the light.

I wake up to an unfamiliar ringtone. I roll over and open my eyes. Sure enough, Hardin is sitting on the chair with his feet up on Steph's dresser.

"Have a nice nap?" he asks with a smile.

"Yeah, actually. How did you get in here?" I rub my eyes.

"Got my key back from Steph."

"Oh. How long have you been here?"

"About thirty minutes. How was your day at Vance? I didn't think you would be back already; it's only six. But here you are passed out, snoring away, so it must have felt like a long one." He laughs.

I prop myself up on my elbow and look at him. "It was great. I got my own office, with my name on the wall outside it—I can't believe it! It's wonderful. I will be making a lot more money than I thought, and I get to read manuscripts; how perfect is that? I'm just afraid that I will mess it up somehow because it's so perfect. You know?" I ramble.

"Whoa, Vance must like you." He raises a brow. "But you'll do fine, don't worry."

"He said you worked there," I tell him, testing his reaction.

"Of course he did."

"Why didn't you tell me? Or that you have a job now? When do you even have time to work?"

"You always have so many questions." He runs his hands through his hair. "But I will answer them," he adds. "I didn't tell you because, well, I don't know why, actually. And I make time to work. Whenever I am not with you, I find the time."

I sit cross-legged and face him. "Mr. Vance really likes you— he said he wants you to work for him again."

"I am sure he does, but no, thanks. I make more than I did there *and* have less work," he brags and I roll my eyes.

"Tell me about your job. What exactly do you do?"

He shrugs. "Read manuscripts, edit them. Same thing you'll do, but more involved."

"Oh. Do you like it?"

"Yes, Tessa. I do." His tone is a little harsh.

"That's good. Do you want to work for a publishing house when you graduate?"

"I don't know what I want to do." He rolls his eyes.

"Did I say something?" I ask.

"No, you just ask too many questions all the time."

"What?" Is he being sarcastic or serious?

"You don't need to know every detail about my life," he snaps.

"I am just making conversation, having a casual discussion

about your job," I say. "Those are just normal things people do—sorry for taking an interest in your everyday life."

He doesn't say anything. What the hell is his problem? I had an amazing day and the last thing I want to do is fight with him. I direct my attention to the ceiling and stay quiet as well. Eventually I learn there are ninety-five panels up there, and forty screws holding them up.

"I need to take a shower," I finally say.

"So go, then," he huffs.

I roll my eyes and grab my toiletry bag. "You know, I thought we were past this, the whole you-being-an-asshole-for-no-reason thing?" I say and walk out of the room.

I take my time in the shower, shaving and reshaving my legs for the dress that I bought to wear tomorrow for my first real day at Vance. I am beyond nervous, but my excitement tops everything. I really wish Hardin wasn't being so rude. All I did was ask him about a job that he didn't tell me about. I should be able to talk to him about that, but there's just so much about him that I don't know, and it makes me really uncomfortable.

I try to figure out how to explain that to him, but when I get back to my room, Hardin's gone.

chapter seventy-seven

I am beyond annoyed at Hardin's unnecessary attitude, but I try to forget it and brush the tangles out of my wet hair and put on the light pink lingerie I bought today. I slip a T-shirt over my head and look over my stuff for tomorrow. All I can think about is where he went; I know I'm obsessive and a little crazy, but I can't help worrying that he's with Molly.

While deciding whether or not to call Hardin, I receive a text message from Steph saying that she won't be back tonight. She might as well move in with Tristan and Nate; she stays there five nights a week and Tristan absolutely adores her. He probably told her about his job on their second date and he probably wouldn't snap at her and leave for no reason.

"Lucky Steph," I say to myself and grab the remote for her television. My fingers press the buttons absentmindedly and I settle on a rerun of *Friends* that I have seen at least one hundred times. I can't remember the last time I watched television, but it's nice to just lie in bed and watch a simple comedy, to escape from the most recent pointless fight with Hardin.

After a few episodes of various shows, I feel my eyes getting heavy. In my sleepy state my anger momentarily disappears and I text Hardin good night, but he doesn't reply before sleep overtakes me.

"Shit." A loud thud wakes me up. I jolt upright and turn on the lamp to find a stumbling Hardin trying to navigate the dark room.

"What are you doing?" I ask him.

When he looks up at me his eyes are red and glossy. He is drunk. *Great.*

"I came here to see you," he says and plops down in the chair.

"Why?" I whine. I want him here, but not drunk and at two in the morning.

"Because I missed you."

"Then why did you leave?"

"Because you were annoying me."

Ouch. "Okay, I'm going back to sleep; you're drunk and you're obviously going to be mean again.

"I'm not being mean, Tessa. And I'm not drunk . . . okay . . . I *am,* but so what?"

"I don't care that you are drunk, but it's a school night and I need my sleep." I would stay up all night with him if I knew he wouldn't say hurtful things to me the entire time.

"It's a school night," he mocks me. "Could you be more of a square?" He laughs like he's just said the funniest thing ever.

"You should just go," I say and lie back down, turning to face the wall. I don't like this Hardin. I want my semisweet Hardin back. Not this drunk jerk.

"Aww, baby, don't be mad at me," he says, but I ignore him. "Do you really want me to go? You know what happens when I sleep without you," he says, just above a whisper.

My heart sinks. I do know what happens, but it's not fair for him to use that against me when he's drunk and taunting me.

"Fine. You can stay, but I'm going back to sleep."

"Why? You don't want to hang out with me?"

"You are drunk and being mean." I finally turn back around to face him.

"I'm not being mean," he says, his expression neutral. "All I said was you were being annoying."

"That's sort of mean to say to someone. Especially when all I did was ask you about your job."

"Oh God, not this again. Come on, Tessa, just drop it. I don't want to talk about that right now." His voice is whiny and he slurs his words.

"Why did you drink tonight?" I don't mind if he drinks; I am not his mother, and he's an adult. The thing that bothers me is that every time he drinks there is a reason behind it. He doesn't just drink for fun.

He looks away from me and toward the door as if planning an escape. "I . . . I don't know . . . I just felt like having a drink . . . well, *drinks*. Can you please stop being mad at me? I love you," he says and brings his eyes to meet mine.

His simple words dissolve most of my anger and I find myself wanting his arms around me.

"I'm not mad at you, I just don't want to backtrack in our relationship. I don't like when you turn on me for no reason, then just leave. If you're mad about something, I want you to talk to me about it."

"You just don't like to not have control over everything," he says and wobbles a little.

"Excuse me?"

"You're a control freak." He shrugs as if it's a known fact.

"No, I'm not. I just like things a certain way."

"Yeah, your way."

"So I guess we aren't done fighting, then. Anything else you want to throw in there while you're are it?" I snap.

"Nope, just that you're a control freak and I really want you to move in with me."

What? His moods give me whiplash.

"You should move in with me—I found an apartment today. I haven't signed anything yet, but it's a nice place."

"When?" It's hard to keep up with the five personalities of Hardin Scott.

"After I left here."

"Before you got drunk?" I ask.

He rolls his eyes. The light from the lamp hits the metal of his eyebrow ring, and I fight to ignore how attractive that is.

"Yes, before I got drunk. So what do you say? Are you going to move in with me?"

"I know you are new at this dating thing, but people don't usually insult their girlfriend and ask them to move in with them in the same sentence," I inform him, chewing my bottom lip to suppress my smile.

"Well, sometimes the said girlfriend needs to lighten up." He grins. Even drunk, he's charming as hell.

"Well, then said boyfriend needs to stop being a jerk," I say to retaliate.

He laughs and moves from the chair over to my bed. "I am trying not to be a jerk, I really am. Sometimes I can't help it." He sits on the edge of the bed. "I'm really, really good at it!"

"I know," I sigh. Regardless of this episode tonight, I know he really has been trying to be nicer. I don't want to make excuses for him, but he has done much better than I expected.

"So you will move in with me?" He smiles hopefully.

"Jesus, let's take this one step at a time. I will stop being mad at you for now," I tell him and sit up. "Now come to bed with me," I instruct. He raises an eyebrow as if to say, "See, control freak," but stands up to pull his jeans off anyway. When he removes his shirt he puts it on the bed before me, and I love that he wants me to wear his shirts as much as I want to.

I pull my shirt off to slip his over my head when he stops me.

"*Fuck,*" he blurts out and I look up. "What are you wearing?" His eyes are dark and wide.

"I . . . I got some new underwear today." I flush and look away.

"I see that . . . Fuck," he repeats.

"You already said that." I giggle. The light in Hardin's eyes is blazing for me—and it makes my skin tingle.

"You look incredible." He gulps. "You always do, but this is just . . ."

With a dry mouth I look down to where his boxers strain against his growing bulge. The energy between us has changed for the fifth time tonight.

"I was going to show you earlier, but you were too busy being a jerk."

"Mmm," he mumbles, clearly not paying attention to what I'm actually saying. He places his knee on the bed and looks my body up and down again before climbing on top of me.

His lips taste like whiskey and mint, and the combination is heavenly. Our kisses are soft and teasing, coming together and drifting apart, his tongue playfully gliding over mine. His hand wraps into my hair and I can feel his erection press against my stomach as he brings his body closer to me. He lets go of my hair to hold himself up on his elbow and use his other hand to touch me. His long fingers run along the undersides of my lace bra, dipping down inside of it and back out. He licks his lips as he cups me with his large palms, rubbing up and down.

"I can't decide if I want this to stay on . . ." he says. I couldn't care less; I am too mesmerized by his graceful fingers on my skin.

"Off it is," he says and unclasps my bra. I arch my back for him to pull it off and he groans as his crotch presses against mine.

"What do you want to do, Tess?" His voice is shaky and uncontrolled.

"I already told you before," I say as he pushes my panties to the side. I wish he wouldn't have drunk tonight, but maybe his half-drunken state will make me seem less awkward.

I cry out as his fingers enter me and I wrap one of my arms around him, trying to grasp on to something, anything. I reach between us with my other hand to palm him. He groans and I squeeze gently and stroke him lightly.

"You're sure?" he pants. I can see the uncertainty in his clear green eyes.

"Yes, I am sure. Stop overthinking it." Boy, have the tables turned, that I'm the one saying this to him.

"I love you. You know that, don't you?"

"Yes." I press my lips against his. "I love you, Hardin," I say into his mouth.

His fingers continue pumping in and out slowly and his mouth moves to my neck. He sucks at my skin harshly, then slides his tongue over the ache to soothe it. He repeats this over and over, and my entire body is on fire.

"Hardin . . . I am . . ." I try to say and he quickly pulls his hand from me, kissing me as I whimper. He scoots back and hooks his fingers around my panties, pulling them down my legs. He places both of his hands on my thighs and squeezes gently before kissing down my stomach and blowing on my wetness. My body involuntarily lifts off the bed and his tongue moves up and down while he wraps his arms around my thighs, keeping them apart. Within seconds my legs begin to shake and I grip the sheets and he continues lapping his tongue around me.

"Tell me how good it feels," he says against me.

Strangled sounds escape my lips as I try to say something, anything. Hardin continues to say dirty things, licking me between them, forming a delicious pattern as my body shakes and my toes curl. When I regain consciousness he brings his mouth back up to mine, a strange taste on his lips. My chest is heaving and my breath is staggered.

"Are you . . ." he begins.

"Shh . . . Yes, I am sure," I tell him and kiss him, hard. My hands claw at his back, then pull his boxers below his hips. He sighs as the restriction disappears, and we both moan as our skin touches again.

"Tessa, I . . ."

"Shh . . ." I tell him again. I want this more than anything and I don't want him to keep talking.

"But, Tessa, I need to tell you something . . ."

"Shh. Hardin, please stop talking," I beg and kiss him again. I grab his erection and slide my hand up and down its length. His eyes close and he sucks in a sharp breath. Instinct takes over my actions and I brush my thumb over the tip of him, wiping away the dampness there and feeling him pulse in my hand.

"I'm going to come if you do that again," he gasps. Suddenly he pulls up and jumps off the bed. Before I can ask where he is going, he pulls out a small packet from his jeans.

Oh. This is really happening.

I know I should be afraid or nervous, but all I feel is my love for him, and his for me.

The anticipation of what is coming next fills me with wonder, and time seems to slow down while I wait for him to return to the bed. I had always thought my first time would be with Noah, on our wedding night. We would be in a huge bed in some fancy bungalow on a tropical island. But here I am in my small dorm room, on my small bed with Hardin, and I would not change a single thing about it.

chapter seventy-eight

I have only ever seen condoms in sex ed class, where they seemed so intimating. But right here, right now, I just want to yank it out of Hardin's hand and put it on him as fast as I can. I am thankful that Hardin can't hear my indecent thoughts, even if his words are far dirtier than any thought I've ever had.

"Are . . ." His voice is low.

"If you ask if I am sure, I will kill you."

He smiles and laughs, waving the condom between his thumb and forefinger. "I was going to say, are you going to help me put this on, or should I do it?"

I bite my lip. "Oh. I want to . . . but you have to show me how," I say, realizing that learning about condoms in sex ed really didn't prepare me for how this moment feels, and I don't want to mess this up.

"Okay." He sits on the bed and I sit up cross-legged. Stretching out to me, he kisses me swiftly on my forehead. When he tears the packet open, I hold my hand out, but he just chuckles and shakes his head. "I'll show you, this way." Taking my hand, he pulls out the little disk and uses our entwined hands to place the condom above him. It feels slippery to the touch. "Now it goes down," he says, his cheeks flushed. As both of our hands slide the condom over his hard skin, his eyes narrow and he grows a little larger.

"That wasn't so bad for a virgin and a drunk," I joke.

He raises an eyebrow at me and smiles. I am glad we are

being playful and not so intense; it makes me less nervous for what is about to happen.

"I'm not drunk, babe. I had a few drinks, but arguing with you sobered me up, as usual." He flashes his dimples and runs his thumb across my bottom lip.

I'm relieved by his answer. It's not like I want him passing out halfway through or puking on me. I laugh a little at my thoughts and look at him again. His eyes are clear, not glazed like they were an hour ago.

"Now what?" I say before I can stop myself.

He laughs, taking my hand and wrapping it around his length. "Eager?" he teases and I nod. "Me too," he admits, and I love the feel of his hard flesh in my hand. Shifting his body, he hovers over me. With one knee he parts my legs, spreading them wide, and I feel his fingers rub against me.

I wonder if he will be gentle with me . . . I hope so.

"You're soaking wet, so that will make it easier." He inhales. His lips meet mine and he kisses me slowly, his tongue teasing mine. His lips seem to be molded against mine, made just for me. Pulling back slightly, he kisses the corners of my mouth, followed by my nose, and then my lips again. My hands go to his back in a desperate attempt to pull him closer to me.

"Slow, baby, we need to go slow," he whispers against my earlobe. "It's going to hurt at first, so just tell me if you want me to stop. I mean it, okay?" he says gently and looks straight into my eyes, waiting for my answer.

"Okay." I gulp. I have heard that losing your virginity hurts but it can't be that bad. I hope not, at least.

Hardin kisses me again. I feel the silky condom brush against me, causing me to shudder. Seconds later he presses into me . . .

It's such a foreign feeling . . . My eyes screw shut and I hear myself gasp.

"You okay?"

I nod and he moves farther into me. I wince at the pinch-
ing feeling deep inside. It's just as bad as everyone says—if not
worse.

"Fuck," Hardin groans. His body is still, unmoving, but it's
still incredibly uncomfortable.

"Can I move?" His voice is so strained and raspy.

"Yeah," I say. The pain continues, but Hardin kisses me all
over, my lips, my cheeks, my nose, my neck, and the tears forming at the corner of my eyes. I put my focus on squeezing Hardin's
arms and feeling his warm tongue on my neck.

"Oh God," he moans and rolls his head back. "I love you, I
love you so much, Tess." He breathes against my cheek. The comfort of his voice mutes my pain slightly, but it persists as his hips
slowly roll against mine.

I want to tell him how much I love him, but I am afraid if I
talk, I will cry.

"Do you . . . fuck . . . do you want me to stop?" he stutters. I
can hear the pleasure and worry battling in his voice.

I shake my head and watch him in amazement when his eyes
close tightly again. His jaw is clenched in concentration; his hard
muscles contract and pull beneath his inked skin. The pain almost completely disappears as I watch him coming undone. He
brushes my cheekbone with his fingers and kisses me again before burying his head in the crook of my neck. His breath is stag-
gering, hot and wild against my skin. Bringing his face to mine,
he opens his eyes. I would take the pain over and over to be able
to feel this way, this deep-seated connection to Hardin that takes
me somewhere I never knew existed. The emotion in his brilliant green eyes as he looks into mine unleashes the tears from
my eyes; it sends me reeling out into the oblivion and then teth-
ers me back to him. I love him and I know without a doubt he
loves me. Even if we don't last forever, if we end up never speak-

ing again, I will always know that in this moment he was every-thing to me.

I can tell that it's taking everything in him to control himself, to keep this slow pace for me, and I love him all the more for it. Time slows and stops, speeds and stops again as he moves in and out of me. The salty taste of sweat is on his lips as he kisses me, and I want more. I kiss his neck and the spot under his ear that I know drives him crazy.

He shivers and moans my name. "You're doing so good, baby. I love you so much."

It doesn't hurt anymore, but it is still uncomfortable, and there is a slight sting each time he thrusts into me. My lips move to his neck and my hands tug at his hair.

"I love you, Hardin," I manage to say.

He moans and brings his swollen lips to mine. "Oh, baby, I am going to come. Okay?" he says through clenched teeth.

I nod and kiss his neck again, sucking gently on his skin. Har-din's eyes never leave mine as he comes; promises of forever and unconditional love are made as he tenses and gently falls onto me. I can feel the heavy thrumming of his heart against my chest, and I kiss the top of his dampened hair. His chest stops heaving and he lifts up, pulling out of me. I wince at the sudden empti-ness as he pulls the condom off and folds it over and places it on the floor atop the foil wrapper.

"Are you okay? How was it? How do you feel?" His eyes search my face and he looks more vulnerable than I thought pos-sible.

"I'm okay," I assure him. I press my thighs together to dull the ache. I can see the blood on my sheets, but I don't want to move.

He wipes his hair away from his forehead. "Was it . . . was it what you expected?"

"It was better," I answer honestly. Even with the pain, the

whole experience was exquisite. I find myself already fantasizing about the next time.

"Really?" He grins. I nod and he leans closer, pressing his forehead to mine.

"How was it for you? It will be better once I have more . . . experience," I tell him.

His grin fades and he presses his fingers under my chin, tilting my head to make me look at him. "Don't say that; it was great, baby. It was better than great, it was . . . the best," he says and I roll my eyes. I am sure he has been with far better girls who actually know what to do and when to do it.

Answering my thoughts, he says, "I didn't love them. It is a completely different experience when you love the person. Honestly, Tessa. It's incomparable. Please don't doubt yourself or degrade what we just did." His voice is so soft and sincere, I feel my heart swell and I kiss the bridge of his nose.

He smiles and wraps an arm around my waist, pulling me to his chest. He smells so good; even sweaty Hardin is my favorite scent.

"Does it hurt?" He runs his fingers through my hair and twirls a piece over his index finger.

"Sort of." I laugh. "I'm afraid to stand up."

He squeezes me tighter and kisses my shoulder. "I've never been with a virgin before," he says quietly.

I look up at him and his eyes are soft, not mocking in the least. "Oh." My mind produces a hundred questions about his first time. The when, where, who, and why. But I push those thoughts away—he didn't love her. He has never loved anyone but me. I don't care about the women in his past anymore. They are just that: his past. I only care about this beautiful, flawed man who just made love for the first time in his life.

chapter seventy-nine

An hour later, Hardin asks, "Are you ready to get up?"

"I know I should, I just don't want to," I tell him and rub my cheek against his chest.

"I don't want to rush you, but I really have to piss," he tells me and I laugh, climbing off him and the bed.

"Ow . . ." I say before I can stop myself.

"You okay?" he asks for the thousandth time. His hand reaches out to help steady me.

"Yeah, just sore." I cringe when I look at my sheets.

He looks over at them. "Yeah, I'll toss them." He pulls the sheets off the small bed.

"Not in here. Steph will see them."

"Okay? So where?" He bounces up and down on his heels. He must have been holding his bladder for a while.

"I don't know . . . can you put them in a Dumpster or something when you leave?"

"Who said I was leaving? So, what—you sleep with me and then kick me out?" His eyes dance with amusement. He grabs his jeans and boxers off the floor and puts them on. I grab his shirt and hold it out to him.

I smack him on the butt. "Just go pee, and take the sheets out on your way, just in case." I don't know why I care so much, but the last thing I need is Steph drilling me for information about losing my virginity.

"Sure. I won't look like a creep or anything, carrying bloody sheets to my car at night."

I scowl at him and he balls the sheets up and walks to the door. "I love you," he says before walking out.

Now that he has left the room I have a little time to collect myself. I wonder if I look as good as I feel, which is warm and oddly at peace. The memory of Hardin hovering over me while he entered me makes my stomach clench. Now I know why people make such a big deal about sex. I really have been missing out, but I know that if my first time wouldn't have been with Hardin, it wouldn't have been so amazing. When I look in the mirror, my mouth falls open at my reflection. My cheeks are glowing, my lips are swollen. I squish my cheeks and move my hands around; somehow I look different. It's the slightest of changes, and I can't quite put my finger on it, but I like it. I take a second to admire the small red marks dotted across my breasts. I don't even remember him making them. My mind takes me back to him making love to me, his mouth hot and wet against my flesh. I am snapped from my thoughts by the door opening, causing me to jump slightly.

"Admiring yourself?" Hardin smirks and locks the door.

"No . . . I . . ." I don't know what to say, since I'm just standing in front of the mirror completely naked, fantasizing about his lips on my skin.

"It's cool, babe, if I had your body I would stare at myself in the mirror, too," he says and I flush.

"I think I'm going to take a shower," I tell him while trying my best to cover myself with my hands. I don't want to wash his scent off my body, but I need to wash everything else off.

"I'll take one, too," he says. I raise an eyebrow at him and he holds up his hands mockingly. "Not together, I know. However . . . if we lived together we could."

Something has changed in him, too, I can see it. It's the way his smile is a little deeper and his eyes brighter. I don't reckon that anyone else would be able to spot it, but I know him better than anyone, despite the many secrets of his that I plan to uncover.

"What?" He cocks his head to the side.

"Nothing, I just love you," I tell him and his cheeks redden slightly and his face splits into a grin, mirroring mine. We both seem to be giddy and high on each other. I love this. When I move to grab my robe, he steps in front of me.

"Have you at least thought about living with me?" he asks.

"You just asked me yesterday. I can only make one life-altering decision at a time." I laugh.

He rubs his temples. "I just want to sign the paperwork soon. I have got to get out of that damned frat house."

"You could just get it on your own?" I suggest again.

"I want it to be ours."

"Why?"

"Because I want to spend as much time with you as I can. Why are you so hesitant? Is it the money? I would pay everything, of course."

"No you wouldn't," I scoff. "If I was to agree to this, I would contribute—I'm not looking for a free ride." I can't believe we are actually discussing this.

"Then what is it?"

"I don't know . . . we haven't known each other that long. I had always thought I wouldn't live with anyone else until I was married . . ." I explain. That's not the only reason; my mother is a huge reason, along with the fear of having to rely on someone else. Even Hardin. That's what my mother did. She relied on my father's income until he left, and after that she leaned on the slim possibility of his return. She always expected him to come back for us, but he never did.

"Married? That's an ancient idea you have there, Tessa." He chuckles and sits down in the chair.

"What's wrong with marriage?" I ask. "Not between us. Just in general," I add.

He shrugs. "Nothing wrong with it, it's just not for me."

This has taken too serious a turn. I don't want to discuss marriage with Hardin, but it does bother me that he says marriage isn't for him. I haven't ever thought about actually marrying him, it's way too early for that. Years too early. But I would like the option eventually, and want to be married by the time I'm twenty-five and then have at least two children. I have my whole future planned.

Had, my subconscious reminds me. I *had* everything planned until I met Hardin and now my future is constantly changing and shifting.

"That bothers you, doesn't it?" he asks, breaking my thoughts.

Hardin and I making love has tied an invisible string between us, uniting our bodies and minds. The changes in my plans are for the better . . . right?

"No." I try to hide the emotion in my voice, but it comes out heavy. "I just have never heard anyone say flat-out they don't want to get married. I thought that's what everyone wants—that's the central point of life, right?"

"Not exactly. I think people just want to be happy. Think of Catherine; look what marriage brought her and Heathcliff."

I love that we speak the same narrative language. There is no one else who would speak in this way to me, the way that I understand the best.

"They didn't marry *each other*—that was the problem," I say with a laugh. I think back to the time when there had been so many parallels between my relationship with Hardin, and Catherine's with Heathcliff.

"Rochester and Jane?" he suggests. Hardin's mention of *Jane Eyre* pleasantly surprises me.

"You're joking, right? He was cold and withholding. He also

proposed to Jane without telling her that he was already married to that madwoman he had locked in the attic. You aren't making very many valid points here," I say.

"I know. I just love hearing you ramble about literary heroes." He brushes the hair off his forehead, and in a childish moment, I stick my tongue out at him.

"So what you're saying is that you want to marry me? I can promise you that I have no bat-crazy wife hidden in my house." He takes a step toward me. There's no wife, sure, but it's the other things he hides that worries me.

My heart is beating out of my chest as he closes the gap between us. "What? No, of course not. I was just speaking in terms of all marriage. Not us specifically." I am naked and talking to Hardin about marriage. What the hell is happening in my life?

"So you're saying you wouldn't?"

"No, I wouldn't. Well, I don't know—why are we even discussing this?" I hide my face in his chest and feel him shake with amusement.

"I was just wondering. But now that you've presented me with a valid argument, I may have to reconsider my no-marriage stance. You could make an honest man out of me."

He sounds serious, but there is no way he is. Right? Just as I begin to question his sanity, he laughs and kisses my temple.

"Can we talk about something else?" I groan. Losing my virginity and talking about marriage is way too much for my mushy brain.

"Sure. But I am not dropping the apartment thing; you have until tomorrow to give me an answer. I won't wait forever," he says.

"How sweet." I roll my eyes.

"You know me, Mr. Romantic," he says and kisses my forehead. "Now, let's get a shower. You standing here naked makes me want to throw you on the bed and fuck you all over again."

I shake my head and pull out of his embrace before wrapping my robe around my body. "Are you coming or what?" I say and grab my toiletry bag.

"I would love to come, but I guess a shower will have to do for now." He winks and I swat his arm as we walk into the hall.

chapter eighty

B y the time we both take a shower and lie back in bed it's almost four in the morning.

"I have to be up in an hour," I groan against his chest.

"You could sleep until seven thirty and still make it on time," he reminds me. Rushing my morning doesn't sound very appealing, but I do need the sleep. Thankfully, I took that nap, so I hopefully won't be dead on my feet during my first day of actually working at Vance.

"Mmm . . ." I mumble against his skin.

"I'll fix your alarm," he says and I drift off.

MY EYES ARE BURNING from lack of sleep as I try to curl my unruly hair. I line my watery eyes with brown eyeliner and put on my new ruby dress. The neckline is square and just low enough to accentuate my bust without being immodest. The hem ends just above my knees and the small brown belt across my waist gives the illusion that I took longer to get ready than I actually did. I consider putting on a little blush, but thanks to my night with Hardin, my cheeks are still glowing. I slip into my new shoes and check myself out in the mirror. The dress is quite flattering, and I look better than I deserve. I glance over at Hardin wrapped in the blanket on my tiny bed, his feet dangling off the edge, and I smile. I wait until the very last minute to wake him. I consider not waking him at all, but I am selfish and want to kiss him goodbye.

"I have to leave," I say and gently shake his shoulder.

"I love you," he mumbles and puckers his lips without opening his eyes. "Are you going to class?" I ask after I kiss him.

"Nope," he says and rolls back over.

I place another kiss on his shoulder and grab my jacket and purse. I want to crawl back in bed with him so badly. *Maybe living with him wouldn't be so bad; we spend almost every night together anyway.* I shake the thought from my head. It's a bad idea; it's too soon. Too soon.

Still, I spend the entire drive imagining getting an apartment with Hardin, picking out curtains and painting walls. By the time I hit the elevator at Vance, I've already picked out the shower curtain and bathmats, but when the elevator reaches the third floor a young man in a dark navy suit steps on and breaks my concentration.

"Hello," he says and reaches for the elevator buttons. Seeing that the button for the top floor has already been pushed, he leans back against the wall of the elevator.

"Are you new here?" he asks. He smells like soap, and his eyes are a crispy blue, which is a strange contrast to his dark hair.

"I'm just an intern," I tell him.

"Just an intern?" He laughs.

"I mean, I am an intern, not an actual employee," I correct myself nervously.

"I started as an intern a few years ago and was hired on full-time. Do you go to WCU?"

"Yeah, did you?"

"Yep, just graduated last year. Glad that's over with." He chuckles. "You'll like it here."

"Thanks, I already love it," I say as we step off the elevator.

As I go to turn the corner, he says, "I never caught your name."

"Tessa, Tessa Young."

He smiles and with a small goodbye wave says, "I'm Trevor. Nice to meet you, Tessa."

The same woman from yesterday is at the desk and this time introduces herself as Kimberly. She smiles, wishes me good luck, and gestures toward a table full of food and coffee. I smile and thank her, grabbing a sprinkled donut and a cup of coffee before I head back to my office. On my desk I find a thick pile of paper with a note from Mr. Vance telling me to begin my first manuscript and good luck. I love the freedom of this internship—I can't believe my luck. Digging into my donut, I pluck the note off the paper and get to work.

The manuscript is actually really good, and I can't seem to put it down. I'm only a third of the way in when the phone on my desk rings.

"Hello?" I say, then realize I have no clue how to answer my own office phone. Wanting to sound more grown-up, I add, "I mean, Tessa Young's office." I bite my lip and hear a small laugh on the other end.

"Ms. Young, there is someone here to see you. Shall I send him in?" Kimberly asks.

"Tessa. Call me Tessa, please," I tell her. It seems disrespectful to have her call me Ms. Young; she is far more experienced and older than me.

"Tessa," she says, and I can picture her friendly smile. "Should I send him in?" she asks again.

"Oh yeah. Wait . . . who is it?"

"I'm not sure . . . young guy . . . um . . . he has tattoos, lots of tattoos," she whispers and I laugh.

"Yeah, I will come out to get him," I tell her and hang up.

That Hardin is here both thrills me and scares me. I hope everything is okay. When I walk out into the lobby he is standing with his hands in his pockets and Kimberly is on the phone. I get the feeling that she is only pretending to be on the phone, I can't tell for sure. I hope that it doesn't seem like I am taking advantage of the great opportunity Mr. Vance has given me by having visitors on my second day.

"Hey, is everything okay?" I approach him.

"Yeah, I just wanted to see how your first full day was going." He smiles and rolls his eyebrow ring in his fingers.

"Oh. It's great I—" I begin, but stop when Mr. Vance strides toward us.

"Well . . . well . . . well . . . Come to grovel for your job back?" He smiles wide at Hardin and pats him on the shoulder.

"You wish, you old wanker," Hardin says, laughing, and my jaw drops. Mr. Vance chuckles and raises his fist before playfully nudging Hardin in his ribs. They must be closer than I thought.

"So what do I owe the honor? Or are you here to stalk my new intern?" He looks over at me.

"The second. Stalking interns is my favorite pastime." I look back and forth between them, unsure what to say. I love seeing this playful side to Hardin; it doesn't come out much.

"Do you have time to get some lunch, if you haven't already?" Hardin asks me. My eyes dart to the clock on the wall; it's already noon. The day has gone by quickly.

I look at Mr. Vance and he shrugs. "You have an hour each day for lunch. A girl's got to eat!" He smiles and says goodbye to Hardin before disappearing down the hall.

"I texted you a few times to make sure you got here, but you didn't answer," Hardin tells me when we step onto the elevator.

"I haven't looked at my phone, I got sucked into a story," I tell him and I reach for his hand.

"You're okay, right? We are okay?" he asks, his eyes locked into mine.

"Yeah, why wouldn't we be?"

"I . . . I don't know . . . I was just getting worried because you weren't answering me. I had thought . . . maybe you were starting to regret last night." He looks down.

"What? Of course not. I honestly didn't check my phone. I have no regrets from last night, not a single one." I can't hide my smile as the memories invade my thoughts.

"Good. Well, that's a damn relief." He lets out a breath.

"You drove all the way here because you thought I was having regrets?" I ask. It's a little extreme, but flattering all the same.

"Yeah . . . well, not completely. I also wanted to take you to lunch." He smiles and lifts my hand to his lips.

We step off the elevator and walk outside. I should have brought my jacket. I shiver and Hardin looks over to me.

"I have a jacket in my car. We can grab it, then walk around the corner to Brio—it's really good." We walk to his car and he pulls a black leather jacket out of his trunk, which makes me laugh. He must have an entire wardrobe in there. Ever since I met him he's been pulling clothes out of that trunk.

The jacket is surprisingly warm and smells like Hardin. It engulfs me, of course, so I shake my arms to push the sleeves up.

"Thank you." I kiss him on his jaw.

"It looks good on you—perfect fit."

He takes my hand as we walk down the sidewalk; we earn a few strange glances from the businessmen and -women on the streets. Sometimes I forget how different we appear on the outside. We are polar opposites in almost every way, but somehow it works for us.

Brio is a small but quaint Italian place. The floor is covered in beautiful multicolored tiles and the ceiling is a mural of heaven, with chubby smiling cherubs waiting outside white gates, and a pair of angels—one white and one black—locked in an embrace beyond them. The white angel seems to be trying to pull the other through the gates to the other side.

"Tess?" Hardin says and pulls me by the sleeve.

"Coming," I mumble and we walk to the table, which is set in the back of the restaurant. Hardin sits in the chair right next to me instead of across, pulling his chair closer and resting his elbows on the table. He orders for both of us, but I don't mind since he's been here before.

"So you and Mr. Vance are really close, then?" I ask.

"I wouldn't say that. But we know each other well enough." He shrugs.

"You seemed to really get along, I like seeing you that way."

The hint of a smile tugs at his lips and he puts his hand on my thigh. "Do you now?"

"Yes, I like to see you happy." I feel like there is more behind his and Mr. Vance's relationship than he is telling me, but for now I am not going to push it.

"I am happy. Happier than I thought I would be . . . ever," he adds.

"What has gotten into you? You're getting soft on me," I tease and he chuckles.

"I can knock over a few tables, bloody a few noses to remind you," he says and I push my shoulder into his.

"No, thanks." I giggle.

Our food arrives and I thank the waitress. The food looks amazing, and I inhale the great aromas before taking a bite. Hardin ordered us some sort of ravioli, and it's delicious.

"Good, huh?" he brags and fills his mouth with food. I nod and do the same.

After we're finished, Hardin and I bicker about who is going to pay for lunch, but he ends up winning.

"You can pay me back later." He winks behind the waitress's back.

When we walk back to VP, Hardin follows me inside. "You're coming up?" I ask him.

"Yeah, I wanted to see your office, then I will go. Promise."

"Deal," I tell him and we step onto the elevator. When we reach the top floor I give him his jacket back and he shrugs it on. My eyes widen at how hot he looks in the leather.

"Hey, it's you again." The guy in the navy suit says as we walk down the hall.

"And it's you again." I smile.

His eyes dart to Hardin, who introduces himself.

"Nice to meet you. My name is Trevor; I work in finance." He give a little wave, then says, "Well, see you around," and walks away.

When we walk into my office Hardin grabs my wrist and turns me to face him. "What the hell was that?" he spits out.

Is he joking? I look down at my wrist in his hand and take that as a no. His grip isn't tight, but it holds me in place.

"What?"

"That guy?"

"What about him? I just met him this morning in the elevator." I pull my wrist away.

"It didn't seem like you just met; the two of you were just flirting in front of me."

I can't help it, but I let out a laugh that's more like a bark. "*What?* You're insane if you think that was flirting. I was being polite and so was he. Why would I flirt with him?" I try to keep my voice down. Causing a scene will not be good for me.

"Why wouldn't you? He was nice and clean-cut, suit and all," Hardin says.

I realize that he seems more hurt and worried than angry. My instincts tell me to cuss him out and tell him to get the hell out, but I decide to take a different approach. Just like when he was breaking things at his father's house.

"Is that what you think? That I want someone like him, someone unlike you?" I ask in a gentle voice.

Hardin opens his eyes wide, taken aback. I know he expected me to blow up at him, but this change of pace slows him down and he contemplates what to say next. "I don't know . . . maybe." His eyes meet mine.

"Well, you're wrong, as usual." I smile. I need to talk to him about this later, but my need to make sure he knows he has nothing to worry about overpowers my need to correct him.

"I am sorry if you think I was flirting with him, but I wasn't. I wouldn't do that to you," I assure him. His eyes soften and I bring my hand up to his cheek. How can one person be so strong yet so weak?

"I . . . Okay," he says.

I laugh and caress his cheek. I love catching him off guard. "What is he, when I have you?"

His eyes flutter and he finally smiles. I am relieved that I am learning how to disengage the bomb that is Hardin. "I love you," he says and presses his lips to mine. "I am sorry for blowing up like that."

"I accept your apology; now let me show you my office!" I say in a cheery voice.

"I don't deserve you," he says quietly, too quietly. I choose to ignore it and keep my uplifting attitude.

"So what do you think?" I beam.

He chuckles and listens intently as I show him every detail, every book on the shelf and the empty picture frame on my desk.

"I was thinking I want to put a picture of us here," I tell him.

We have never taken any pictures together, and the thought hadn't even crossed my mind until I placed the empty frame there. Hardin doesn't seem like the type who would smile for a camera, even on a cell phone.

"Oh. I don't really do pictures," he says, confirming my thoughts.

But when he sees I'm a little embarrassed by being shut down, he strains to say, "I mean . . . I guess I could take one. Just one, though."

"Let's worry about that later." I smile and he seems relieved.

"Now can we move on to how sexy you look in that dress. It's been driving me crazy since I got here." His voice is a full octave deeper and he takes a step toward me. My body heats immediately; his words never cease to unravel me.

"You're lucky I didn't open my eyes this morning. If I had . . ." He traces his fingertips along the neckline of my dress. "I wouldn't have let you leave."

He brings his other hand to the hem of my dress and caresses my thigh.

"Hardin . . ." I warn. My voice betrays me and comes out as more of a moan.

"What, babe . . . you don't want me to do this?" He lifts me up and sits me on the edge of my desk.

"It's . . ." My thoughts are clouded by his lips against my neck. I dig my fingers into his hair and he nips at my skin. "We can't . . . someone could come in . . . or something." The words are jumbled and don't make much sense. He puts his hands on my thighs and opens them farther.

"There is a lock on the door for a reason . . . I really want to take you right here, on this desk. Or maybe against the window." His mouth travels lower on my chest. The idea of what he is proposing sends electricity through my body. His fingers brush over the lace on my panties and he sucks a breath through his teeth.

"You're killing me," he groans as he looks between my legs to see the white lace set I bought yesterday. I can't believe I am letting this happen, on a desk in my new office on the second day of my internship. The idea thrills me as much as it terrifies me.

"Lock the—" I begin, but we are interrupted by the shrill ring of my phone. I jump straight up and scramble around the desk to grab it. "Hello? Tessa Young speaking!"

"Ms. Young. Tessa," Kimberly corrects herself. "Mr. Vance is leaving for the day and is on his way to your office," she says with a hint of amusement in her voice.

I flush and thank her. Clearly she can sense how irresistible Hardin is to me.

chapter eighty-one

Hardin leaves shortly after he and Mr. Vance finish bickering about a football game. I apologize for having a visitor, but he brushes it off, telling me that Hardin is like family and he is welcome to come by anytime. Visions of Hardin making love to me on the desk take over my imagination and Mr. Vance has to repeat what he said next about payroll three times before I come back to reality.

I go back to reading the manuscript and I am so into it that I don't realize it's after five when I look up again. I am an hour late to leave and have a missed call from Hardin. When I get to my car I call him back, but he doesn't answer. I drive back through moderate traffic, and when I get to my room, I'm surprised to see Steph on her bed. I almost forget she lives here, too, sometimes.

"Long time no see," I joke and drop my purse and pull off my heels.

"Yeah . . ." she says and sniffles.

"Are you okay? What happened?" I sit on her bed with her.

"I think Tristan and I broke up." She sobs. It is a strange sight to see Steph crying—she's usually so strong and sassy.

"Why? What do you mean you *think*?" I ask and put my hand on her back to comfort her.

"Well, we got in a fight and I broke up with him, but I didn't mean it. I don't know why I did it—I was just pissed because he was sitting with *her* and I know how she is."

"Who?" I ask, even though I somehow already know.

"Molly. You should have seen how she was flirting with him and hanging on his every word."

"But she knows you two are together; isn't she your friend?"

"She doesn't care about that. She'll do anything to get male attention." As I watch Steph cry and wipe her eyes, my already strong dislike of Molly grows even more.

"I don't think Tristan would go for her; I see the way he looks at you. He really cares about you. I think you should call him and talk it out," I suggest.

"What if he is with her?"

"He's not," I assure her. I really don't see Tristan running off with the pink-haired snake.

"How do you know? Sometimes you think you know people, but you don't," she says and looks into my eyes. "H—"

"Hey . . ." Hardin says as he bursts into the room and then takes in the sad scene before him. "Um . . . should I come back?" He shifts uncomfortably. Hardin isn't the type to comfort a crying girl, friend or not.

"No, I am going to go find Tristan and try to apologize." She stands. "Thank you, Tessa." She hugs me and looks at Hardin. They exchange awkward glances before she exits the room.

Hardin turns and gives me a kiss. "You hungry?"

"Yeah, actually I am," I tell him. I should do some homework, but I'm actually pretty far ahead. I really have no idea how or when Hardin actually works.

"I was thinking that after we get something to eat, you could call Karen or Landon and see what I should wear to the . . . you know. The wedding." The mention of Landon's name tugs at my heart. I haven't talked to him in a few days and I miss him. I want to tell him about my internship and maybe even about Hardin and me. I haven't decided that yet, but I still want to talk to him.

"Yeah, I'll call Landon. I'm excited for the wedding!" I tell him, then realize I need to get something to wear to the wedding as well.

"Yeah. Me, too. I am so thrilled. Could I be more excited?" He rolls his eyes and I laugh.

"Well, I'm glad you're at least going. It means a lot to your father and Karen."

He shakes his head, but he's come a long way in the short time that I've known him.

"Yeah . . . yeah. Let's go eat," he grumbles and grabs my jacket off the chair.

"Let me change first, geez," I groan. I feel his eyes on me as I undress and grab jeans and a WCU sweatshirt out of my dresser and put them on quickly.

"You look adorable. Sexy office woman by day and cute college girl by night," he teases. My stomach flutters at his words and I lean up on my toes to kiss his cheek.

WE DECIDE TO GO to the mall and eat so that we can go shopping afterward. I call Landon as we sit down and he tells me that he will ask his mother what Hardin should wear and call me right back.

"We can find your outfit first, I guess?" he suggests.

"I don't know what to wear either." I laugh.

"Well, you have the luxury of looking beautiful regardless of what you wear."

"That is not true; you definitely pull off that 'I don't give a crap how I look but I look flawless' look."

He gives me a cocky smirk and leans back in his chair. "I do, don't I?"

I roll my eyes and then notice my phone buzzing. "It's Landon."

"Hey," Landon says, "so she said it would be best if you

wear white. I know it's not the norm, but that's what my mother wants. And at least try to get Hardin in dress pants and a tie. I don't think they are expecting much from him, to be honest." He laughs.

"Okay, well, I will do my best to get him in a tie." I look over at Hardin, who frowns comically.

"Good luck. How's your internship going?"

"It's good. Well, great, actually. It's a dream come true. I can't believe it. I have my own office and I basically get paid to read all day. It's perfect. How are classes? I miss Literature."

Hardin's face turns into a real frown, and I follow his eyes to the middle of the food court. Zed, Logan, and a guy that I have never met before are walking toward us. Zed gives me a friendly wave and I smile before thinking about it. Hardin glares at me and stands up.

"I'll be right back," he says and walks off in their direction. I try to continue my conversation with Landon and watch Hardin at the same time, but I'm not sure what to do.

"Yeah, it isn't the same without you, but I'm so happy for you. At least Hardin hasn't been in class so I don't have to deal with him," Landon says.

"What do you mean he hasn't been in class? Well, besides today. He was there yesterday. Right?"

"No, I figured he dropped again since you left and he obviously can't be more than ten feet away from you at all times," he teases and my heart warms despite my concern over his missing classes.

I look over at Hardin, who has his back to me, but I can tell from how stiff his shoulders are that he's tense. The guy who I don't recognize has a slick smile on his face and Zed is shaking his head. Logan seems uninterested in them and focuses on checking out a group of girls walking by. Hardin takes a step toward the guy and I can't tell if they are messing around or not.

"I'm so sorry, Landon, but I will call you back," I say and hang up. Leaving our trays on the table, I go over to them, hoping in the back of my mind that no one messes with our food.

"Hey, Tessa, how are you?" Zed asks and moves forward to hug me. I feel myself flush and politely hug him back. I know better than to look up at Hardin when our embrace ends. Zed's hair is sticking straight up in the front in a very hot, messy way, and he's wearing all black with this leather jacket that has patches all over the front and back.

"Hardin, aren't you going to introduce your friend?" the stranger says. He smiles and it gives me chills. I can tell he is not a nice guy.

"Um, yeah." Hardin waves his hand between us. "This is my friend Tessa; Tessa, this is Jace."

Friend? I feel like I have just been kicked in the stomach. I try my best to hide my humiliation and smile.

"Do you go to WCU?" I ask. My voice is much more composed than I feel inside.

"Hell, no. I don't do the college thing." He chuckles coolly. "But if all the girls there looked like you, I would be happy to reconsider."

I gulp and wait for Hardin to say something. Oh, right, I am his *friend*. Why would he? I stay silent and wish I had just stayed at the table.

"We are going to the docks tonight; you two should make an appearance," Zed says.

"We can't. Maybe next time," Hardin says. I contemplate interrupting and saying I can, but I am too pissed-off to speak.

"Why not?" Jace asks.

"She has to work tomorrow. I suppose I can drop by later. Alone," he adds.

"That's too bad." Jace smiles at me. His sandy blond hair falls over his eyes and he shakes his head to move it.

Hardin clenches his jaw and looks at him. I feel like I'm missing something. Who is this guy, anyway?

"Yeah, I'll hit you up later when I'm on my way," Hardin says and I stalk away.

I hear Hardin's boots stomping behind me but I keep walking. He doesn't call my name, since I'm sure he doesn't want his friends to think anything, but he keeps following me. I walk faster and dip into Macy's and turn a sharp corner, hoping to lose him. No such luck; he grabs my elbow and turns me to face him.

"What is wrong?" His annoyance is obvious.

"Oh, I don't know, Hardin!" I shout. An elderly woman looks at me and I give her an apologetic smile.

"Me either! You are the one who just hugged Zed!" he yells. We are already attracting an audience, but I am fuming so I don't care at the moment.

"Are you embarrassed of me or something? I mean, I get it, I am not exactly the cool girl, but I thought . . ."

"What? No! Of course I'm not embarrassed of you. Are you crazy?" he huffs. I feel crazy at the moment.

"Why did you introduce me as your friend? You keep talking about living together and then you tell them we are friends? What are you going to do, hide me? I won't be anyone's secret. If I'm not good enough for your friends to know we're together, then I don't want to be." I turn on my heel and walk away to punctuate my little speech.

"Tessa! Damn it . . ." he says and follows me through the store. I reach the dressing rooms and glance at them.

"I will follow you," he says, reading my thoughts.

He will, too. So I turn and head toward the exit of the store. "Take me home. Now," I demand. I stay quiet and at least ten feet ahead of Hardin as we walk out of the mall and to his car. He moves to open the door for me but backs away when I glare at him. If I were him, I would keep my distance.

I stare out the window and think of all the terrible things I could say to him but I stay silent. I'm mostly just embarrassed that he feels like he can't tell people we are together. I know I'm not like his friends and they probably all think I am a loser or not cool enough, but that shouldn't matter to him. I find myself wondering if Zed would hide our relationship from *his* friends, and I can't help but think that he wouldn't. Come to think of it, Hardin has never actually called me his girlfriend. I probably should have waited to sleep with him until he at least confirmed we were dating.

"Are you done throwing a fit?" he asks as we pull onto the highway.

"A fit? You aren't serious!" My voice fills his small car.

"I don't know why it's such a big deal to you that I called you my friend; that's not what I meant. I was just caught off guard," he lies. I can tell he is lying by the way his eyes dart away from mine.

"If you are embarrassed of me, then I don't want to see you anymore," I say. I dig my nails into my leg to keep from crying.

"Don't say that to me." He runs his hand over his hair and takes a deep breath. "Tessa, why do you assume I am embarrassed of you? That is just fucking ridiculous," he growls.

"Have fun at your party tonight."

"Please, I'm not going, I just said that so Jace would lay off."

What I say next I know is a terrible idea, but I want to prove a point: "If you aren't embarrassed of me, then take me to the party."

"Absolutely fucking not," he says through his teeth.

"Exactly," I snap.

"I am not taking you there because Jace is a dick, for one. Two, it's not the kind of place you should be."

"Why not? I can handle myself."

"Jace and his friends are way out of your league, Tessa. Hell, they're even out of my league. They are all stoners and scum."

"Then why are you friends with him?" I roll my eyes.

"There is a big difference between being friendly and being friends."

"Well, why would Zed hang out with him, then?"

"I don't know. Jace isn't one of those guys that you say no to," he explains.

"So you're afraid of him. That's why you didn't say anything when he came on to me," I point out. Jace must be really bad if Hardin is afraid of him.

Hardin surprises me by laughing. "I'm not afraid of him. I just don't want to provoke him. He likes games, and if I provoked him with you he would turn you into a game." His knuckles turn white from his grip on the steering wheel.

"Well, good thing we're just friends, then," I say and look out the window at the beautiful view of the city passing by. I'm not perfect; I know I'm acting childish but I can't help it. Knowing how big a creep Jace is, I get why Hardin did what he did, but that doesn't make it hurt less.

chapter eighty-two

When we get to the room, I plop down on the bed. I am still angry with Hardin but not as angry as I was. I don't want any more attention from Jace than necessary, but meeting him has only raised more questions that I know Hardin doesn't want me to ask.

"I really am sorry. I didn't mean to hurt your feelings," he says. I don't look at him because I know I will turn to mush. He needs to know that I won't put up with him doing things like this. "Do . . . you . . . do you still want me?" he asks, his voice shaky.

When I look over at him, I can see his vulnerability. I sigh, knowing I am not able to hold on to my anger when his eyes are so full of worry.

"Yeah, of course I do. Come here," I tell him and pat the bed next to me. I have no willpower when it comes to this man.

"Do you consider me your girlfriend?" I ask as he sits down.

"Yeah. I mean, it just seems a little silly to call you that," he says.

"Silly?" I pick at my fingernails, a bad habit I have yet to kick.

"You are more to me than some adolescent title." He puts his large hands on both sides of my face. His answer makes my stomach flip in the best way. I can't help the grin that is plastered on my face. His shoulders immediately relax.

"I don't like that you don't want people to know about us— how would we live together if you won't even tell your friends about us?"

"It's not like that. Do you want me to call Zed right now and tell him? If anything, you should be embarrassed to be with me. I see the way people look at us when we are together," he says. So he does notice the way people look at the two of us.

"They only stare at us because we look different, and that's their problem. I would never be embarrassed to be seen with you. Ever, Hardin."

"You had me worried that you were going to give up on me," he says.

"Give up on you?"

"You're the only constant in my life; you know that, don't you? I don't know what I would do if you left me," he says.

"I won't leave you if you don't give me a reason to," I assure him, but I can't think of a single thing he could do to make me leave him. I'm in too deep. Thinking of leaving him sends a pain through my body that I can't bear. It would break me. Even if we fight every single day, I love him.

"I won't," he says. He looks away for a second, then meets my eyes again. "I like who I am with you."

I turn my cheek into his hand farther. "I do, too."

I love him, every part of him. All versions of him. Mostly, I like who I have become with him; we have both been changed for the better by each other. I have somehow gotten him to open up and have brought happiness to him, and he has taught me how to live and not worry about every detail.

"I know I piss you off sometimes . . . well, a lot of the time, and God knows you drive me fucking insane," he says.

"Thanks?"

"I'm just saying, just because we fight doesn't mean we shouldn't be together. Everyone fights." He smiles. "We just fight more than normal people. You and I are very different people, so we'll just have to figure out how to navigate one another. It will get easier," he assures me.

I return his smile and run my fingers through his dark hair.

"We still didn't get anything to wear to the wedding," I point out.

"Oh darn, looks like we can't go." He turns his face into the most insincere frown I have ever seen and kisses my nose.

"You wish. It's only Tuesday. We have all week."

"Or we could skip it and I could take you to Seattle for the weekend?" He lifts an eyebrow.

"What?" I sit up. "I mean, no! We are going to the wedding," I correct myself. "But you could take me to Seattle next weekend."

"Nope, offer's only good for a limited time," he teases and pulls me onto his lap.

"Fine, I guess I'll have to find someone else to take me to Seattle." His jaw tenses and I trace my fingertips over the stubble on his chin and jaw.

"You wouldn't dare." His lips twitch to hold his smile.

"Oh, I most certainly would. Seattle is my favorite place, after all."

"Your favorite place?"

"Yeah, I haven't really been anywhere else."

"Where is the farthest place you've gone?" he asks.

I lay my head on his chest and he lies back against the headboard, wrapping his arms around me. "Seattle. I haven't left Washington."

"Ever?" he exclaims.

"Nope, never."

"Why not?"

"I don't know, we just couldn't afford to after my dad left. My mother worked all the time and I was too focused on school and getting out of that town that I didn't really think of much else, except working."

"Where would you want to go?" he asks, his fingers rubbing up and down my arm.

"Chawton. I want to see Jane Austen's farmhouse. Or Paris. I would love to see where Hemingway stayed while he was there."

"I knew you would say those places. I could take you there." His tone is serious.

"Let's just start with Seattle." I giggle.

"I mean it, Tessa. I could take you anywhere you want to go. Especially England. I did grow up there, after all. You could meet my mum and the rest of my family."

"Um . . ." I actually have nothing to say. He is so strange, he introduces me as his "friend" an hour ago, and now he's taking me to England to meet his mother.

"Let's just start with Seattle?" I laugh.

"Fine, but I know you would love to drive through the English countryside, see the house Austen grew up in . . ."

I can't imagine how my mother would react to me leaving the country with Hardin. She would probably lock me in her attic and never let me out. I still haven't spoken to her since she stormed out of my dorm after threatening me in an attempt to get me to stop seeing Hardin. I want to avoid that inevitable argument for as long as I can.

"What's wrong?" he asks and dips his head down in front of my face.

"Nothing, sorry, I was just thinking of my mother."

"Oh . . . she'll come around, babe." He sounds so sure, but I know her better than that.

"I don't think so, but let's talk about something else."

We start talking about the wedding, but Hardin's phone vibrates in his pocket after a moment. I shift off him so he can get it out, but he makes no move to do so.

"Whoever it is can wait," he says, which makes me happy.

"Will we be staying at your dad's house Saturday after the wedding?" I ask. I need to get my mind off my mother.

"Is that what you want to do?" he asks.

"Yeah, I like it there. This bed is tiny." I crinkle my nose and he laughs.

"We could stay at my place more often. What about tonight?"

"I have my internship in the morning."

"So? You can bring your stuff with you and get ready in an actual bathroom. I haven't been to my room in a while; they are probably already trying to rent it out," he jokes. "Don't you want to take a shower without thirty other people in the same room?"

"Sold." I smile and climb off the bed.

Hardin helps me pack my things for tomorrow and I grow more and more excited to go to the frat house. I hated that house, and still pretty much do, but the thought of a shower in an actual bathroom and Hardin's large bed is too appealing to pass up. He grabs the red set of lingerie out of my dresser and hands it to me with a series of eager nods, and I flush before shoving it in my bag. I pack one of my old black skirts and a white blouse, wanting to space out my new dresses.

"Red bra with white shirt?" Hardin points out. I pull the white shirt out and grab a blue one instead.

"You could bring extra clothes with you so you won't have to bring so much next time," he suggests. He wants me to keep clothes at his place. I love how it's a given that we will stay the night together every night.

"I guess I could," I say and grab my new white dress and a few other random things.

"You know what would make it much easier?" he asks, and pulls my bag over his shoulder as we head outside.

"What?" I already know what he is going to say.

"If we both lived at the same place." He smiles. "We wouldn't have to decide which place to stay at and you wouldn't have to pack a bag. You would have a private shower every day—well, not totally private." He winks playfully. And just when I think he's done, when we get to his car and he opens the door for me, he adds, "You could wake up and make your own coffee in our kitchen and get ready for the day and we could meet up at our place at the end of every day. None of this roommate or frat house shit."

Every time he says "our" my stomach flutters. The more I think about it, the better it sounds. I am just terrified of moving too fast with Hardin. I don't want it to blow up in my face.

As we drive to the house, he puts his hand on my thigh and again says, "Stop overthinking it." I hear his phone vibrating again, but he ignores it. This time I can't help but be a little suspicious of why he isn't picking up the phone, but I push the thought from my head.

"What are you afraid of?" he asks when I don't respond.

"I don't know. What if something happens with my internship and I can't afford it? Or if something happens with us?"

He frowns but recovers quickly. "Babe, I already told you I would pay for the place. It was my idea, and I make more, so let me do this."

"I don't care how much you make. I don't like the idea of you paying for everything."

"You can pay cable, then?" He smirks.

"Cable and groceries?" I offer. I can't decide if I am speaking hypothetically anymore or not.

"Deal. Groceries . . . that sounds nice, doesn't it? You could have my dinner ready every night when I get home."

"Excuse me? It would be the other way around." I laugh.

"We could rotate days?"

"Deal."

"So you're moving in with me then?" I don't think I have ever seen a deeper grin on his perfect face.

"I didn't say that, I was just . . ."

"You know I will take care of you, right? Always," he promises.

I want to tell him that I don't want to be taken care of, that I want to earn things and pay for my own share of things, but I get the feeling he isn't talking just financially.

"I am afraid this is too good to be true," I finally admit to Hardin and myself.

He surprises me by saying, "Me, too."

"Really?" I am relieved that he feels the same way.

"Yeah, the thought crosses my mind all the time. You are too good for me and I am just waiting on you to realize it, and hoping that you don't," he says, his eyes focused on the road.

"That's not going to happen." And I mean it.

He doesn't say anything.

"Okay." I break the silence.

"Okay what?"

"Okay. I will move in with you." I smile.

He lets out a breath that sounds like he has been holding it for hours. "Really?" His dimples pop as he shakes his head and flashes a smile.

"Yeah."

"You have no idea what this means to me, Theresa." He puts his hand over mine and squeezes. Hardin turns onto his street and my mind races. We are really doing this, we are moving in together. Me and Hardin. Alone. All the time. In our own place. Our own bed. Our everything. I am scared as hell, but my excitement is stronger than my nervousness, for the moment at least.

"Don't call me Theresa or I will change my mind," I tease.

"You said only friends and family can call you that. I think I've earned it."

He remembers that? I think I said that right after I met him. I grin. "Point well made. Call me whatever you want."

"Oh, babe, I wouldn't say that if I were you. I have a whole list of perverted things I would love to call you." His smile is wicked, and I find myself wanting to hear his dirty words, but I stop myself from asking and squeeze my legs together. He must notice, because his smile grows.

Just as I'm coming up with a line about how perverted he is, the words are lost in my throat. Pulling up to the house, we see that the yard is littered with people and the street is full of cars.

"Damn it, I didn't know they were having a party tonight. It's fucking Tuesday. See, this is the shit—"

"It's fine. We can just go straight to your room," I interrupt, trying to defuse his irritation.

"Fine," he sighs.

When we walk into the crowded house, Hardin and I head straight for the stairs. Just as I begin to think I made it without running into anyone I know, I spot a mound of greasy, sandy blond hair at the top of the stairs. Jace.

chapter eighty-three

Hardin notices Jace the same time that I do and turns to look at me, then back at Jace, tensing immediately. For a second it seems like Hardin might turn us around, but then Jace definitely spots us, and I know Hardin won't risk antagonizing him by backing away now. All around us, the party rages, but all I can focus on is Jace's mischievous smile, which flat-out gives me the creeps.

As we reach the top of the stairs, Jace gives an exaggerated look of surprise and says, "Didn't think I'd see you two here, you know, since you couldn't make it to the docks and all."

"Yeah, we were just coming here——" Hardin begins.

"Oh, I get why you were coming here." Jace smiles and pats Hardin on his shoulder. I cringe as his brown eyes move to me. "It's definitely a pleasure to see you again, Tessa," he says coolly.

I glance at Hardin, but he is too focused on Jace to notice. "Yeah, you, too," I manage.

"Well, good thing you didn't come to the docks anyway. Cops came and broke up our party, so we moved it here."

Meaning that Jace's slimy friends are here somewhere—more people Hardin doesn't like. I wish we had just stayed at my dorm. By the look in Hardin's eyes I can tell he wishes the same.

"That sucks, man," Hardin says and then tries to continue on down the hall.

Jace grabs Hardin's arm and says, "You two should come down and have a drink with us."

"She doesn't drink," Hardin huffs, annoyance clear in his

voice. Unfortunately, that annoyance seems to encourage Jace even more.

"Oh well. *You* should still come have some fun. I insist," he says.

Hardin looks at me, and my eyes widen as I try to silently say, *No!* But then he nods at Jace. *What the hell?*

"I'll come down in a minute; let me get her . . . settled in," Hardin mumbles, then pulls me by my wrist to his room before Jace can say anything. Unlocking the door to his room, he hurries me inside and quickly closes the door.

"I don't want to go down there," I tell him as he sets my bag down.

"You're not."

"And you *are*?" I ask him.

"Yeah, just for a minute. I won't be long." He rubs the back of his neck with his hand.

"Why didn't you just tell him no?" I ask. For someone who claims he isn't afraid of him, Hardin seems to be very intimidated by Jace.

"I already told you, he is hard to say no to," he says.

"Does he have something over you or something?"

"What?" Hardin's face flushes. "No . . . he's just a dick. And I don't want any trouble. Especially not around you," he says and steps forward to me. "I won't be down there long, but I know him, and if I don't go have a drink with him he will come back up here—and I don't want him anywhere near you," he says and kisses me on the cheek.

"Okay," I sigh.

"I need you to stay in here, though. I know it's not ideal, with the music bumping downstairs, but I can't really think of a way out at this point."

"Okay," I repeat. I don't want to go down there anyway. I hate these parties, and I definitely don't want to see Molly if she is here.

"I mean it. Okay?" he demands in a soft voice.

"I said okay. Just don't leave me up here alone for long," I plead.

"I won't. We should go sign that paperwork tomorrow for the apartment. Right after you get done at Vance. I don't want to worry about this kind of shit again."

I don't want to have to deal with these parties and my small dorm anymore. I want to eat my meals in a kitchen instead of a dining hall, and I want the freedom of being an adult. Spending time on campus and living there only reminds me how young we actually are.

"All right, I will be back soon. Lock the door when I go out and don't open it again—I have a key." He swiftly kisses my lips and turns for the door.

"Geez, you act like someone is going to murder me," I joke, to break the tension, not that he returns the laugh before walking out of the room. I roll my eyes but lock the door anyway; the last thing I want to deal with is drunk people wandering in here looking for a place to fool around.

I turn on his television, hoping to drown out some of the noise from downstairs, but my mind keeps wandering to what's going on down there. Why is Hardin so intimidated by Jace, and why is Jace such a creep? Are they playing their usual immature game of Truth or Dare again? What if Hardin is dared to kiss Molly? What if she is sitting on his lap like before? I hate the jealousy that I feel toward her—it drives me insane. I know Hardin has slept with and fooled around with many different girls, Steph included, but Molly just gets under my skin. Maybe it's because I know she doesn't like me and she tries to shove her fling with Hardin down my throat.

And you caught her straddling him with her tongue down his throat the first time you met her, my subconscious reminds me.

And eventually all these thoughts get to me; I know I should stay put and keep the door locked, but my feet have other plans and before I know it, I am taking the steps two at a time to find Hardin.

When I reach the bottom of the stairs I spot Molly's hideous pink hair and barely there outfit. Much to my relief, Hardin isn't anywhere to be found.

"Well, well, well," a voice from behind me says. I turn to see Jace standing less than a foot away.

"Hardin said you weren't feeling well. He's always lying, that one." He smiles and pulls a lighter out of his pocket. He flicks the top with his thumb, igniting the flame, and brings it to the hem of his jean vest to burn off some of the fringe.

I decide to keep Hardin's lie going. "I wasn't, but I'm feeling a bit better now."

"So quickly?" He laughs, obviously amused.

The room feels much smaller now and the party crowd seems larger. I nod and survey the room, desperate to find Hardin.

"Come, I want you to meet some of my friends," Jace says. His voice never fails to send a shiver down my spine.

"Um . . . I think I sh-should find Hardin," I stutter.

"Aww, come on. Hardin is over there with them anyway," he says and moves to put his arm over my shoulder.

I take a step aside to pretend that I didn't notice his gesture. I consider going back upstairs so Hardin doesn't know I came down in the first place, but I get the feeling Jace will follow me or tell Hardin. Most likely both.

"Okay," I say, giving in. I follow Jace through the crowd, and he leads me outside to the backyard. It's dark but for a few porch lights. I start to feel nervous about following Jace out into the dark yard until my eyes meet Hardin's. His widen with surprise, then anger, and he moves to stand up but then sits back down.

"Look who I found wandering around all by herself," Jace says and gestures to me.

"I see that," Hardin mumbles. He is pissed.

I stand in front of the small circle of unrecognizable faces sitting around what looks like a fire pit made from large rocks, not that there's any fire going. There are some girls there, but mostly it's pretty tough-looking guys.

"Come here," Hardin says and scoots over so there is room for me on the rock that he is sitting on.

I take a seat and Hardin gives me a look that says if all these people weren't around he would be absolutely screaming at me. Jace leans over and says something into the ear of a guy with a ripped-up white shirt and black hair.

"Why aren't you in my room?" Hardin says quietly but forcefully.

"I . . . I don't know. I thought maybe Molly . . ." I begin to say but realize how stupid it sounds.

"You're not serious," he says with a hint of exasperation and runs his hand over his hair. The attention is put back on us when the black-haired guy hands me a bottle of vodka. "She doesn't drink," Hardin says and grabs it out of my hands.

"Damn, Scott, she can speak for herself," another guy says. He has a nice smile and doesn't seem as creepy as Jace or the guy with the black hair.

Hardin laughs lightly, though I can tell it's a fake laugh. "Mind your own business, Ronnie," Hardin says in a light tone.

"So who's up for a game?" Jace asks and I look at Hardin.

"Please tell me you guys don't play Truth or Dare at parties too. Honestly, what is up with playing games, anyway?" I groan.

"Ooh, I like her. Nice and feisty," Ronnie says and I laugh.

"Who says there is anything wrong with playing a few games now and then?" Jace slurs and Hardin tenses next to me.

"No, actually we were thinking of strip poker," another guy says.

"Oh, no way," I tell them.

"What about suck and blow?" Jace says and I cringe and blush. I am not sure what that is, but it doesn't sound like something I want to play with this group.

"Never heard of it. But no, thanks," I say. I see Hardin smile out of the corner of my eye.

"It's a fun game, more fun when you have had a drink or two," a male voice says from somewhere.

I think about grabbing the bottle from Hardin and taking a drink, but I have to get up early and I don't want to have a hangover.

"We don't have enough girls to play suck and blow, anyway," Ronnie says.

"I can get some," Jace says and disappears into the house before anyone can protest.

"Go back upstairs, please," Hardin says quietly so only I can hear.

"If you come with me," I respond.

"Okay, let's go."

But as we stand up, a groan goes up from the circle. "Where you going, Scott?" one of the guys asks.

"Upstairs," he answers.

"Come on, we haven't seen you in months. Hang out for a little while longer."

Hardin looks at me and I shrug. "All right, fine," Hardin says and guides me back to the large stone. "I'll be right back. Stay here this time. I mean it," he tells me and I roll my eyes, finding it pretty ironic that he's leaving me alone with what is supposedly the worst group of people here.

"Where are you going?" I ask him before he walks away.

"To get a drink. You may need one, too." He smiles and goes inside.

I stare at the sky and the fire pit alternately to avoid any awkward conversation. It doesn't work.

"So how long have you and Hardin known each other?" Ronnie asks and takes a swig of liquor.

"A few months," I answer politely. Something about Ronnie is comforting; my senses aren't on high alert with him like they are with Jace.

"Oh, so not long, then?" he says.

"Um, yeah, I guess. Not long. How long have you known him?" I ask, realizing I might as well use this opportunity to get as much information about Hardin as possible.

"Since last year."

"Where did you meet him?" I try to sound casual.

"Party. Well, a lot of parties." He laughs.

"Oh, you're his friend, then?"

"Nosey little thing, aren't you?" the guy with the black hair chimes in.

"Sure am," I reply and he laughs. They aren't so bad, not as bad as Hardin made them out to be. *Where is he, anyway?*

A few moments later Hardin appears with Jace and three girls behind them. What the hell? Jace and Hardin seem to be in conversation and Jace pats Hardin on the back and they both laugh.

Hardin's hands are full with two red cups. I'm just relieved that Molly isn't among the group of girls trailing them. He sits back down on the rock with me and gives me a playful little look. At least he seems to be more relaxed than he was before he walked away.

"Here," he says and hands me one of the cups.

I stare at it for a second before grabbing it from him. One drink won't hurt. I recognize the taste instantly; the night that Zed and I kissed we had been drinking these. Hardin stares at me and I lick my lips to collect the taste of the drink.

"Now we have enough girls," Jace says and gestures to the newcomers.

I look over to them and fight the instinct to judge. They are scantily clad in skirts, and their shirts are identical except the colors. The one in the pink shirt smiles at me, so I decide that I like her the best.

"You aren't playing," Hardin says in my ear. I want to tell him that I will do whatever the hell I please, but he leans into me and puts his arm around my waist. I look up at him, obviously surprised, but he just smiles.

"I love you," he whispers. His lips are cold against my ear and I shiver.

"Okay, so everyone knows how this works," Jace says loudly. "We all need to get in a smaller circle. But first, let's really get the party going." He smirks and pulls something out of his pocket. His lighter appears again and lights the small white object.

"It's pot," Hardin tells me quietly. I figured that it was, even if I haven't actually seen marijuana before.

I nod and watch as Jace brings the joint to his lips and lets out a large puff of smoke before holding it out in front of Hardin. Hardin shakes his head and declines. Ronnie grabs it and inhales deeply, coughing loudly.

"Tessa?" Ronnie says and holds it out.

"No. No, thanks," I say and lean farther into Hardin.

"All right, then, let's play," one of the girls says and pulls something from her purse as everyone moves from their rocks and forms a smaller circle on the grass.

"Come on, Hardin!" Jace groans, but Hardin shakes his head.

"I'm good, man," he says.

"We need one more girl then, unless you want to take the

chance of having Dan's tongue down your throat." Ronnie laughs. Dan must be the guy with the black hair. A quiet redhead with a lot of facial hair takes a hit from the joint and passes it back to Jace. I finish the last sip of my drink and reach for Hardin's. He lifts a brow at me but lets me take it.

"I'll grab Molly. God knows she'll be down," the girl in the pink shirt says.

When I hear her name, my hatred for Molly takes over my common sense and I blurt out, "I'll play."

"Really?" Jace questions.

"Is she allowed?" Dan asks with a smirk and looks at Hardin.

"I can do what I please, thank you," I say and give him an innocent smile despite my bitchy tone.

I know better than to look at Hardin; he already told me not to play, but I just couldn't keep my big mouth shut. I down the rest of his drink, then take a seat next to the girl in the pink shirt.

"You have to sit in between two guys," the girl tells me.

"Oh, okay," I say and get up.

"I'm playing, too," Hardin grumbles and sits down. I sit next to him instinctively, but still avoid eye contact. Jace sits on my other side.

"I think Hardin should sit over here to make things more interesting," Dan says, and the redhead nods in agreement.

Hardin rolls his eyes and moves across from me. I don't get the point of this seating arrangement—why does it matter who sits by whom? When Dan moves to sit next to me, I begin to feel nervous. Sitting between him and Jace is more than uncomfortable.

"Can we start?" the girl in green whines. She is sitting between Hardin and the redhead. Jace grabs what looks like a piece of paper from one of the girls and puts it to his mouth.

What?

"Ready?" he asks me.

"I don't know how to play," I confess and hear one of the girls snicker.

"You put your mouth on the other side of the paper and suck in; the point is to not let the paper fall. If it falls, you kiss," he explains.

Oh no. I look over at Hardin, but he is focused on Jace.

"Start this way so she can see," the girl on the other side of Jace says.

I don't like this game at all. I hope it somehow ends before it's my turn. Or Hardin's. Besides, they seem a little old to be playing these ridiculous games. What is it with college kids wanting to kiss random people every chance they get? I watch as the paper is passed between Jace's and the girl's mouth; it doesn't drop. I hold my breath as Hardin retrieves the paper from the one girl, then passes it to the other. If he kisses one of them . . . I let out my breath when it doesn't fall. The paper falls between the redhead and the girl in the yellow shirt and their lips meet. Her mouth opens and they kiss with tongue, making me look away and cringe. I want to get up and leave the circle, but my body stays still. I am next.

Oh God, I am next. I gulp as Dan turns to me with the paper on his lips. I'm still not entirely sure what I am supposed to do, so I just close my eyes and go to put my mouth on the other side and suck in. I feel hot air through the paper as Dan blows onto it, but I can tell it's too hard and there's no way the paper won't fall. Right as I feel the paper hit my leg, I feel Dan's hot breath as his mouth moves closer to mine. The second his lips brush mine he is pulled away.

I open my eyes, but by the time my mind can catch up to what is happening, Hardin is on top of Dan and has his hands latched around the guy's neck.

chapter eighty-four

I scramble backward with my hands as Hardin lifts Dan's head, his hands still wrapped around his neck, and slams it down into the grass. For a second I wonder if Hardin would have done the same were we on the concrete porch or near the fire pit stones, and I feel like my answer comes in the form of Hardin raising one fist high and slamming it into Dan's jaw.

"*Hardin!*" I scream and climb to my feet. Everyone else just stares, Jace seeming amused and even Ronnie entertained.

"Stop him!" I beg, but Jace shakes his head as Hardin's fist connects again to Dan's already bloody face.

"This has been coming for a while; let them hash it out." He smirks at me. "Want a drink?"

"What? No, I don't want a drink! What the hell is wrong with you!" I yell.

A crowd has now gathered around and people are cheering on the fight. I have yet to see Dan hit Hardin, for which I'm glad, but I definitely want Hardin to stop hurting Dan. I'm too afraid to try to stop him myself, so when Zed appears in the yard, I yell for him. His eyes find me immediately and he jogs over.

"Stop him, please!" I yell. Everyone seems excited about this except me. If Hardin keeps hitting him, he will kill him. I know it.

Zed gives me a quick nod and takes a few steps over to Hardin. He wraps his fist into Hardin's shirt and pulls him backward. Hardin is caught off guard, so he's easily separated from Dan's prone body. Enraged, Hardin takes a swing at Zed, but

Zed dodges his fist and puts both of his hands on Hardin's shoulders. He says something to Hardin that I can't make out and then nods his head toward me. Hardin's eyes are blazing, his knuckles bloody and his shirt ripped from Zed's grip. His chest is pumping up and down rapidly, like he's a wild animal after a kill. I don't make a move to walk toward him; I know how angry he is at me. I can tell. I am not afraid of Hardin the way I probably should be. Even though I just witnessed him completely losing his temper in the worst way possible, I know that he would never physically hurt me.

With the excitement winding down, almost everyone begins to move back inside the house. Dan's crumpled body lies on the ground and Jace leans down to help him up. He stumbles to his feet and lifts his shirt up to wipe his bloody face off, spitting out a mixture of blood and saliva that makes me look away.

Hardin's head turns to look where Dan is and he tries to take a step toward him. Zed holds Hardin tight to stop him.

"Fuck you, Scott!" Dan yells. Jace steps between them. Oh, now he wants to do something. "Just wait until your little—" Dan shouts.

"Shut the fuck up," Jace snaps and Dan's mouth closes.

Dan looks at me and I take a step back. I wonder what Jace meant by "this has been coming for a while." Hardin and Dan seemed fine together a few minutes ago.

"Go inside!" Hardin yells, and I immediately know that he is talking to me.

I decide to listen to him, for once, and turn around and run into the house. I know that everyone is staring at me but I don't care. I push my way through the crowded house and rush up to Hardin's room. I must have forgotten to lock it when I left, and, to add to my horror, there is a big red spot on the carpet. Someone must have stumbled in here and spilled a drink on the tan carpet. Great. I hurry to the bathroom and grab a towel and turn the sink on. I lock Hardin's door once I step inside and furiously wipe the stain, but the water only spreads the spot and makes it much worse. The door clicks and I try to stand before he enters.

"What the hell are you doing?" His eyes move to the towel in my hand then to the spot on the floor.

"Someone . . . I forgot to lock the door when I went downstairs," I say and look at him. His nostrils flare and he takes a deep breath. "I'm sorry," I say.

The anger is radiating off him and I can't even be angry with him because all of this is my fault. If I would have just listened to him and stayed in the room, none of this would have happened.

He runs his hands over his face in frustration and I take a step toward him. His fingers are busted and bloody, reminding me of his fight at the stadium. He surprises me by grabbing the towel from my hands and I reflexively jump back a little. His eyes flash with confusion and he tilts his head slightly as he uses the non-stained portion of the towel to wipe his knuckles off.

I expected him to barge through the door and break things while screaming at me; instead I am granted with his silence, which turns out to be much worse.

"Could you please say something?" I beg.

His words come even slower than usual. "Trust me, Tessa, you don't want me to speak right now."

"Yes, I do," I tell him. I can't stand his angry silence.

"No, you don't," he growls.

"Yes, I do! I need you to talk to me, tell me what the hell happened down there!" I wave my hands toward the window and he clenches his fists by his sides.

"Goddamn it, Tessa! You always have to push and push! I told you to stay in my fucking room—multiple times—and what the fuck did you do? You didn't listen, as usual! Why is it so damn hard for you to listen to what I say?" he yells and slams his fist against the side of his dresser, cracking the wood.

"Because, Hardin, you don't just get to tell me what to do all the time!" I yell back.

"That isn't what I am doing. I was trying to keep you away from shit like what just happened. I already warned you that they aren't a good group of people, yet you prance out there with Jace and then volunteer yourself to play that fucking game! *What the fuck was that?*" The deep veins in his neck are straining against his skin so tightly that I fear they may break through.

"I didn't know what the game was!"

"You knew I didn't want you to play, and the only reason you wanted to play was because Molly's name was mentioned because of this crazy obsession you have with her!"

"Excuse me? *Crazy obsession?* Maybe I don't like the fact that my boyfriend used to sleep with her!" My cheeks flame. My jealousy and dislike toward Molly are a little crazy but Hardin just choked a guy for almost kissing me.

"Well, sorry to break it to you, but if you're going to have a problem with everyone that I slept with, you may want to transfer schools," he exclaims and my mouth falls open. "You didn't have a problem with the girls downstairs," he adds and my heart goes frantic.

"What girls?" My breath catches. "Those three that were playing with us?"

"Yeah, and just about every other girl in this place." His voice holds no emotion as he glares at me.

I try to come up with something to say but I am at a loss for words. The fact that Hardin has slept with all three of those girls and basically the entire female population at WCU makes me nauseous—and the worst part is how he just threw it in my face. I must look like such a fool hanging around Hardin when everyone else figures I'm just one of the many girls he's slept with. I knew he would be pissed-off, but this is too far, even for Hardin. I feel like we have gone back in time to when I first met him and he would purposely make me cry on an almost daily basis.

"What? Surprised? You shouldn't be," he says.

"No." And I'm not surprised, not one bit. I'm hurt. Not about his past, just the way he treated me out of anger. He said it that way just to hurt me. I blink rapidly to stop the tears from coming, but when it doesn't work I turn away and wipe my eyes.

"Just go," he says and walks toward the door.

"What?" I ask and turn to face him.

"Just go, Tessa."

"Go where?"

He doesn't even look at me. "Back to your room . . . I don't know . . . but you can't stay here."

This is not at all what I thought would happen. The pain in my chest grows with every second of silence that passes between us. Part of me wants to beg him to let me stay, and to argue with him until he tells me why he reacted the way he did downstairs, but a bigger part of me is embarrassed and hurt by his cool dismissal. I grab my bag off the bed and sling it over my shoulder. When I reach the door, I look back at Hardin and hope that he will apologize or change his mind, but he turns to the window and completely ignores me. I have no idea how I will get back to the dorms, since Hardin drove me here and I had every intention of staying the night with him. I don't remember the last time I stayed alone in my room, and the thought unnerves me. The drive to this house seems like days ago, instead of hours.

When I reach the bottom of the stairs, someone tugs at the back of my sweatshirt, and I hold my breath as I turn around, silently praying that it isn't Jace or Dan.

It's Hardin. "Come back upstairs," he says, his voice desperate and his eyes red.

"Why? I thought you wanted me to leave." I stare at the wall behind him.

He sighs and grabs the bag from my shoulder and walks back up the stairs. I think about just letting him have the bag and leaving anyway, but my stubborn attitude is what got me in this situation in the first place.

I huff and follow him back to this room. When the door closes he turns around and backs me up against the door.

He looks into my eyes. "I'm sorry." He pushes his hips against mine and puts one of his arms against the door close to my head so I can't move.

"Me, too," I whisper.

"I just . . . I lose my temper sometimes. I didn't really sleep with those girls. Well, not all three of them."

I feel a little relieved but not completely.

"My first instinct when I get angry is to come back even harder, to hurt the other person as much as I can. But I don't want you to leave, and I'm sorry for scaring you by beating the shit out of Dan. I am trying to change, change for you . . . to be what you deserve, but it's hard for me. Especially when you do things to purposely piss me off," he says. He brings his hand to my cheek and wipes the drying tears left there.

"I wasn't scared of you," I say.

"Why not? It seemed like you were when I grabbed the towel."

"No . . . well, I was a little when you grabbed the towel, because of the stain on the floor. But really I was more afraid *for* you when you were fighting Dan."

"Afraid for me?" He puffs his shoulders up a little and brags, "He didn't get a hit on me."

I roll my eyes. "I meant that you would end up killing him or something. You could get in a lot of trouble for assaulting him," I explain.

Hardin chuckles. "Let me get this straight: you were worried about the legal repercussions of our fight?"

"Stop laughing. I'm still mad at you," I tell him and cross my arms. I'm not exactly sure what I am upset about except him telling me to leave.

"I am still pissed at you, too, but you're very amusing." He presses his forehead against mine. "You drive me crazy," he says.

"I know."

"You never listen to me and you always fight me on everything. You are stubborn and borderline intolerable."

"I know," I repeat.

"You provoke me and cause me a shitload of unnecessary stress, not to mention you almost made out with Dan right in front of me." His lips touch my neck and I shiver.

"You say the most annoying things and you act like a child when you're mad." Despite the insults he is throwing at me—complaints about things that, deep down, I think he really enjoys about me—my stomach is fluttering as he kisses my skin and continues his light verbal assault. He pushes his hips against mine again, more forcefully this time.

"But all that being said . . . I also happen to be vigorously in love with you," he says and sucks harshly on sensitive skin below my ear.

I push my hands through his hair, making him groan, and he puts both of his hands on my waist, pulling me to him. I know there are more things to be said, more problems to be solved, but right now all I want is to get lost in Hardin and forget about tonight.

chapter eighty-five

In what feels like a desperate attempt to be closer to me as we kiss, Hardin moves a hand to the back of my neck. I can sense all of his anger and frustration being transferred into lust and affection—his mouth is hungry and his kisses sloppy as he walks backward with our lips still attached. He guides me with one hand on my hip and the other behind my head, but I trip over his feet and stumble just as his legs reach the end of his bed, causing both of us to fall back onto it. In an attempt to wrestle control from him, I straddle his torso and pull my sweatshirt and tank top over my head at the same time, leaving me in my lacy bra. His eyes widen and he tries to pull me down to kiss him, but I have other plans.

Reaching behind my back, my rushed fingers find my bra clasp and I unsnap it before pulling the straps down my shoulders and letting it drop to the bed behind me. Hardin's hands are warm as he reaches up and cups my breasts in his large palms, kneading them roughly. Grabbing his wrists, I remove his hands from my skin and shake my head. His head tilts in confusion before I climb down his body and unbutton his pants. He helps me tug them down to his knees along with his boxers. My fingers immediately grip his length—he gasps, and when I look at his face his eyes are closed. I pump slowly before dipping down and bravely taking him into my mouth. I try to remember his instructions from last time and repeat the things that I know he liked.

"Fuck . . . Tessa," he pants and wraps his hands into my hair.

This is the longest he has been silent during any sexual experience we have shared, and I realize much to my own amusement that I missed his dirty words.

I move my body while continuing to please him and end up between his knees.

He sits up and watches me. "You look so sexy like this, with that smart mouth of yours wrapped around me," he says and grips my hair harder.

I feel the heat gathering between my legs and move my head faster, wanting to hear him moan my name again. My tongue laps around the tip of him and he lifts his hips slightly off the bed, pushing himself down my throat. My eyes begin to water and I can barely breathe, but hearing my name fall from his lips over and over again makes it that much better. Seconds later, he removes his hands from my hair and cups my face, stopping me from moving further. The metallic scent of his bloody knuckles hits my nose, but I ignore the reflex to pull away.

"I'm going to come . . ." he tells me. "So if there is anything else you . . . you know, want to do before then, you should stop blowing me."

I don't want to speak, to give away how desperate I am to have him make love to me, so I simply stand up and slide my jeans down my legs and step out of them. When I begin to remove my panties Hardin's hand reaches out and stops me.

"I want you to leave these on . . . for now," he coos. I nod and gulp, anticipation consuming me. "Come here." He gestures and pulls his shirt over his head. Scooting to the edge of the bed, he pulls me onto him.

Our feverish exchange in the beginning has slowed and the angry tension between us has decreased. Hardin's chest is flushed and his eyes are wild. The feeling of sitting on his lap while he is completely naked and ready—and I am only dressed in panties—is exquisite. He presses the small of my back, the length of his one outstretched hand there holding me in place as his lips meet mine once again.

"I love you," he whispers into my mouth as his fingers move my panties to the side. "I . . . love you . . ."

I gasp at the immediate pleasure of the intrusion. He moves his fingers slowly, too slowly, and I instinctively rock back and forth to create a faster pace.

"That's it, baby . . . fuck . . . You're always so ready for me," he groans and I continue to rock against his hand. My breathing and moans intensify—it still surprises me how quickly my body responds to Hardin. He knows every little thing to do and say.

"You are going to listen to me from now on. Am I right?" he says against my neck, gently biting the skin.

What?

"Tell me you will listen to me or I won't let you come."

He can't be serious. "Hardin . . ." I plea and try to move faster, but he stops me.

"Okay . . . Okay . . . just please," I beg and he smirks. I want to slap him for doing this right now. He is using my most vulnerable time against me but I can't find my anger through my need for him. I am all too aware of his bare skin against mine, only my thin panties between us.

"Please," I repeat and he nods.

"Good girl," he says in my ear and guides my hips to move again as his fingers pump in and out.

I feel myself inching closer and closer to the edge in no time at all. Hardin whispers filthy things in my ear, the foreign words urging me on in a way that I can't describe. They are completely filthy but welcome, and I grip on to his arms to keep myself from falling off the bed as I come undone under his touch.

"Open your eyes. I want to watch what only I can do to you," he instructs and I do my best to keep them open as my orgasm overtakes me.

Afterward, my head falls onto his chest and my arms wrap under his arms, hugging him tight as I try to catch my breath.

"I can't believe you tried to . . ." I begin to scold him, but he silences me by running his tongue along my bottom lip. My breath comes out in spurts as I am still recovering from my high. I reach my hand down in between us and grab hold of him. He winces and pulls my lip between his, sucking lightly. I decide to take a page from the Hardin Scott sex handbook and grip him harder.

"Apologize, and I will give you what you want," I say as seductively as I possibly can into his ear.

"What?" His face is priceless.

"You heard me." I keep my face neutral and pump him in one hand and slide my fingers over my soaking panties with the other.

He whimpers as I rub him against me.

"I'm sorry," he blurts, his cheeks a deep shade of red. "Just let me fuck you . . . please," he begs and I laugh. My laughter is cut short by him reaching over to the nightstand and pulling out a small packet. He wastes no time putting the condom on and kissing me again.

"I don't know if you are ready to do it this way, with you above me. If it's too intense, tell me. Okay, baby?" And like that he's back to the sweet and gentle Hardin.

"Okay," I answer.

He lifts me up slightly and I feel the condom brush against me and then fullness as he lowers me onto him.

"Oh my," I say and close my eyes.

"Is it okay?"

"Yeah . . . just . . . d-different," I stammer.

It hurts, not nearly as much as before, but the feeling is still unpleasant and foreign. I keep my eyes closed and move my hips a little, trying to decrease the pressure.

"Good, different, or bad?" His voice is strained and the vein in his forehead is showing.

"Shh . . . stop talking," I say and move again.

He moans and apologizes, promising to give me a minute to adjust. I have no idea how much time passes before I move my hips again. The discomfort eases dramatically the more I move, and at some point Hardin wraps his arms around my back, hugging me close to him as he moves to meet my hips. This way is much better, him holding me as we move together. One of my hands rests on his chest, holding my weight as my legs start to tire. I ignore the burn of my muscles and continue to ride his body this way. I keep my eyes open to watch Hardin as a bead of sweat rolls down his forehead. Watching him like this, with his lower lip pulled between his teeth, his eyes so focused on my face that I swear I can feel the burn from them on my skin, is overwhelming in the best way.

"You are everything to me. I can't lose you," he says as my lips move over his neck and shoulder. His skin is salty and damp and perfect. "I'm close, baby, so fucking close. You're doing so good, baby." He groans and moves his hands up and down my back as I try to pick up speed. He laces his fingers through mine and the intimacy of the gesture makes me weak. I love his encouragement and I love him.

I feel my stomach tightening as Hardin grips the back of my neck with one hand. He continues to whisper how much I mean to him as his body grows tense. I stare, completely consumed by his words and the way his thumb is brushing over my clit, bringing me to a quick and powerful release. Our moans intertwine along with our bodies as we finish. He practically falls back, lying on the bed, and takes me with him. I barely notice him discarding the condom as I come back to reality.

"I'm glad you followed me down the stairs," I finally say after a long but pleasant silence. With my head lying on his bare chest, I can hear his rapid heartbeat slowing.

"Me, too. I wasn't going to, but I had to. I am sorry for telling you to leave. I can be an asshole sometimes," he says.

I lift my head up and look at him. "Sometimes?" I smile.

He lifts one of his hands off my back and pokes me on the nose with his index finger, making me giggle. "You weren't complaining five minutes ago," he points out.

I shake my head and lay it back down onto his clammy skin. My fingers trace the simple heart-shaped tattoo near his shoulder and I notice the goose bumps raise on his skin. It isn't lost on me that the heart is colored in with solid black ink.

"That's because you're better at that stuff than you are at dating," I tease.

"I won't argue there." He chuckles and moves my hair from my face. One of my favorite things that he does is when he caresses my cheek. His fingertips are rough, but they somehow feel like silk against my skin.

"What happened between you and Dan? I mean before tonight?" I ask. I probably shouldn't, but I have to know.

"What? Who told you there was a problem between Dan and me?" He lifts my chin to look at him.

"Jace. He didn't say what it was, though; he just said it was 'coming for a while.' What did he mean by that?"

"Just some bullshit thing that happened last year. It's nothing for you to worry about. I promise," he says, and smiles a smile that doesn't extend to his eyes but I don't feel like pushing it.

I'm just happy that we worked through our problem for once and that we are getting better at communicating with one another.

"You're going to meet me after you leave Vance tomorrow, right? I don't want anyone to take that apartment before us," he says.

"We don't have any furniture," I remind him.

"It comes furnished. But we can add things or change whatever we want after we move in."

"How much is it?" I ask. I know I don't want to hear the answer to that. I can only imagine how expensive it is if it comes already furnished.

"Don't worry about that; all you need to worry about is how much the cable will be." He smiles and kisses my forehead. "So what do you say? You're still in, right?"

"And groceries," I point out and he frowns. "But yes, I am still in."

"Are you going to tell your mother?"

"I don't know. I will eventually, but I already know what she's going to say. Maybe I should let her get used to the fact that we're together first. We are so young and already moving in together, I don't want to send her into a mental ward." I let out a laugh despite the slight pain in my chest. I wish things could be simple with my mother and she could be happy for me, but I know that isn't plausible.

"I am sorry that this is happening between the two of you. I know it's my fault, but I'm far too selfish to remove myself from the situation."

"It's not your fault. She is just . . . well, she is the way she is," I say and kiss his chest.

"You need to get to sleep, baby; you have to be up in the morning and it's almost midnight," he says.

"Midnight? I thought it was much later," I say and roll off him and lie in front of him.

"Well, if you weren't so tight, I would have lasted longer," he says into my ear.

"Good night!" I groan in embarrassment.

He laughs and kisses the back of my neck before turning the light off.

chapter eighty-six

The next morning, bright and early, I scramble around Hardin's room, gathering my things to take a shower.

"I'm coming with you," he groans, but I laugh.

"No, you're not. You know it's only six a.m., right? What happened to your seven-thirty rule?" I tease and grab my bag.

"I am going to walk you there." I love his raspy morning voice.

"Walk me where? To the bathroom?" I scoff as he rolls out of bed. "I'm a big girl. I can walk myself down the hall."

"You're doing an amazing job at listening to me so far." He rolls his eyes, but I see the amusement in them.

"Fine, Daddy, walk me to the bathroom," I whine playfully. I have no intention of listening to him, but I decide to humor him for the moment.

Hardin raises his eyebrow and smirks. "Don't call me that again, or I'll have to take you back to bed." He winks and I hurry out of the room before I am too tempted to stay.

He follows behind me and sits on the toilet while I shower. "You're going to have to take my car," he says, which utterly surprises me. "I'll get a ride to campus to grab yours so I can go over to the apartment."

I didn't think about any of this last night, which further shocks me, since I usually plan everything out so well. "You're going to let me drive your car?" I gape.

"Yeah. However, if you wreck it don't bother coming back," he says.

Part of me knows he is somewhat serious. But I laugh and say, "I should be worried about you wrecking mine!"

He tries to open the curtain, but I pull it closed again and hear him chuckle. "Just think, babe, after today you will be in your own shower every morning." His voice carries over the water as I rinse the shampoo from my hair.

"I don't think it will really hit me until we are actually there."

"Wait until you see it; you will love it," he says.

"Does anyone know that you are getting an apartment?" I ask. I already know the answer.

"No, why would they need to know?"

"They don't, I was just wondering."

The faucet creaks as I shut the water off. Hardin holds a towel open for me as I step out and wraps it around my soaked body.

"I know you well enough to know that you think I am hiding the fact that we are moving in together from my friends," he says.

He's not wrong. "Well, it does seem a little odd that you're moving out of here but no one knows."

"That isn't because of you—it's because I don't want to hear their shit about dropping out of the fraternity. I will tell them all—even Molly—after we move in." He smiles and wraps his arms around my shoulders.

"*I* want to be the one to tell Molly." I laugh and hug him back. "Deal."

After multiple attempts to keep Hardin's hands off me as I get ready, he hands me the keys to his car and I leave. The moment I get in the car my phone vibrates.

Be careful. I love you, the text reads.

I will. You be careful in my car :) I love you. xo

I can't wait to see you again. Meet me at five. Your crap car will be fine.

You should watch what you say or I may accidently hit a parking median in yours. I smile to myself as I send my reply.

Stop pestering me and go to work before I come down there and peel that dress off you.

As appealing as that sounds, I put my phone back onto the passenger seat and start the car. The engine gently purrs to life, unlike the loud roar of mine. For a classic car it drives much smoother than mine; he really takes care of it. When I turn onto the freeway my phone rings.

"Jesus, you can't go twenty minutes without me?" I laugh into the phone.

"Tessa?" a male voice says. *Noah.*

I pull my phone away from my ear and look at my screen to confirm my horror.

"Um . . . sorry, I thought . . ." I stammer.

"You thought it was him . . . I know," he says. His voice is sad and not at all hateful.

"I'm sorry." I don't deny it.

"S'okay," he says.

"So . . ." I am not sure what to say.

"I saw your mom yesterday."

"Oh." The pain from Noah's sorrow-filled voice and the reminder of my mother's hatred for me causes my chest to ache.

"Yeah . . . she is pretty pissed at you."

"I know . . . she threatened to stop helping me with college."

"She will get over this, I know she will. She's just hurt," he says.

"She is hurt? You're *kidding me,* right?" I scoff. He *cannot* be defending her.

"No, no—I know she is going about it the wrong way, but she's just angry that you are . . . you know with . . . him." The disgust in his voice is evident.

"Well, it isn't her place to tell me who to be with. Is that why you called me? To tell me that I shouldn't be with him?"

"No, no—Tessa, it's not. I just wanted to make sure you are okay. This is the longest we have gone without talking since we were ten years old," he says. I can picture the frown on his face.

"Oh . . . I'm sorry for snapping at you. I just have a lot going on right now and I thought you were calling to—"

"Just because we aren't together anymore doesn't mean I wouldn't be there for you," he says, and my heart aches. I do miss him; not my relationship with him, but he's been such a huge part of my life since I was a child, it's hard to let that go entirely. He was there for me through everything, and I hurt him, without even calling to explain or apologize. I feel terrible about how I left things with him, and tears well up in my eyes.

"I'm sorry for everything, Noah," I say softly and sigh.

"It'll be okay," he says back, equally softly. But then, as if needing to change the topic, he says, "So I heard you got an internship," and our conversation continues until I arrive at Vance.

When we get off the phone he promises to talk to my mother about her behavior toward me, and I feel like a huge weight has been lifted from me. Of anyone, Noah could always manage to get her to calm down when she was at her worst.

The rest of my day goes smoothly. I spend the entire day finishing my first manuscript and making notes for Mr. Vance. Hardin and I text on and off to nail down the details on where to meet, and before I know it the day is over.

When I arrive at the address Hardin sent me, I'm surprised to find that it's about halfway between campus and Vance Publishing. My drive would only be twenty minutes if I lived here, when I live here. It still seems like such an abstract idea, Hardin and I living together.

I don't see my car when I pull into the parking lot, and when

I try to call Hardin's phone I get his voicemail. *What if he changed his mind? He would tell me, wouldn't he?*

Just as I start to panic, Hardin pulls my car into the lot and parks next to me. At least, it looks like my car, but it also looks different. The silver paint is no longer chipped, and overall it looks shiny and new.

"What did you do to my car?" I say when he climbs out.

"It's nice to see you, too." He smiles and kisses my cheek.

"Seriously, what did you do?" I cross my arms.

"I got a paint job. Jesus. You could thank me." He rolls his eyes.

I bite my tongue only because of where we are and what we are about to do. Besides, the paint job does look really good. I just don't like the idea of Hardin spending money on me, and paint jobs are not cheap.

"Thank you." I smile and lace my fingers through his.

"You're welcome. Now let's go inside." He leads me through the parking lot. "You look good driving my car, especially in that dress. I couldn't stop thinking about it all day. I wish you would have obliged my request that you send me naked pictures of yourself," he says, and I elbow him. "Just saying. Would have made class much more interesting."

"Oh, so you *went* to class," I say, laughing.

He shrugs and opens the front door of the building for me. "Here we are."

I smile at his uncharacteristic gesture and walk inside. The lobby of the building isn't what I expected at all. It is all white: white floors, clean white walls, white chairs, white couches, white rugs, white lamps on clear tables. It looks elegant, but very intimidating. A short, balding man in a suit greets us and shakes Hardin's hand. He seems nervous around us, or maybe just around Hardin.

"You must be Theresa." He smiles. His teeth are as white as the bright walls.

"Tessa," I smile and correct him while Hardin bites back a smile of his own.

"It's nice to meet you. Shall we get to signing?"

"No, she wants to see it first. Why would we sign if she hasn't even seen it?" Hardin says in a flat tone.

The poor man gulps and nods. "Of course, let's go up." He gestures down the hallway.

"Be nice," I whisper to Hardin as the three of us walk to the elevator.

"Nope." He smirks at me and squeezes my behind gently.

I glare at him, but his dimpled smile only grows. The man tells me about how great the view is and that this is one of the best and most diverse apartment buildings in the area. I nod along politely, and Hardin stays quiet as we step off the elevator. I am taken aback by the contrast between the lobby and the hallway. It feels like we have stepped into a completely different building . . . even a different time period.

"Here it is," the man says and opens the first door we come to. "There are only five apartments on this floor, so you will have a lot of privacy." He gestures for us to enter, but looks away from Hardin's gaze. He is definitely afraid of Hardin. I can't say I blame him, but it *is* a little entertaining to watch.

I hear my own gasp as I take in the sight before me. The main room's floors are old, stained concrete, except for one large square of hardwood in the space that I assume would be the living room. The walls are brick and beautiful. Damaged but perfect. The windows are large, and the furniture is old-fashioned but clean. If I could design the perfect space, this would be it. It's somehow a throwback to another era, but completely modern.

Hardin watches me intently as I look around, going into the other rooms and letting Hardin and the man trail behind. The kitchen is small and has multicolored tiles above the sink and countertop, adding an indie, fun look. I absolutely love everything about this small apartment. The lobby downstairs had scared me, so I was expecting to hate the place. I thought it would be an overpriced, stuffy apartment, and I'm thrilled that it isn't. The bathroom is small but big enough for us, and the bedroom is just as perfect as the rest of the place. Three walls are old red brick and the fourth is covered with a floor-to-ceiling bookshelf. It has a ladder attached, and I can't help but laugh because I always pictured myself having this exact apartment after I graduated from college. I just didn't think it would come so soon.

"We could fill the shelves. I have a lot of books," Hardin mumbles nervously.

"I . . . just . . ." I begin.

"You don't like it, do you. I thought you would; it seemed perfect for you. Damn it!" He frowns and runs his fingers over his hair.

"No . . . I—"

"Let's go, then, show us another one," Hardin snaps at the man.

"Hardin! If you would let me finish, I was going to say that I love it," I tell him.

The man looks just as relieved as Hardin, whose frown turns into a massive smile. "Really?"

"Yes, I was afraid it was going to be some fancy, cold apartment, but this is just perfect," I tell him and mean it.

"I knew it! Well, I was getting nervous a second ago, but as soon as I checked this place out I thought of you. I pictured you there . . ." He points to the bench in the window. "Just sitting and reading a book. That's when I knew I wanted you to live here with me."

I smile and my stomach flutters at his saying that in front of someone else, even if it's a random leasing agent.

"So we're all ready to sign, then?" The man shifts uncomfortably.

Hardin looks at me and I nod. I can't believe we are really doing this. I ignore the small voice reminding me that this is too soon, that I am too young, and I follow Hardin back into the kitchen.

chapter eighty-seven

Hardin signs his name on the bottom of what seems like an endless page before sliding the whole thing over to me. I grab the pen and sign before I can start overthinking it again. *I am ready for this; we are ready for this.* Yes, we are young and we haven't known each other very long, but I know that I love him more than anything and he loves me. As long as that much is certain, the rest will fall into place.

"All right, here are your keys." Robert, whose name I finally learned from all those pages, hands Hardin and me each a set of keys, bids us farewell, and is on his way.

"Well . . . welcome home?" Hardin says once we're alone.

I laugh and step closer to him so he can wrap his arms around me.

"I can't believe we live here now. It still doesn't seem real." My eyes scan the living room.

"If someone had told me I would be living with you—let alone dating you—two months ago, I would have either laughed in their face or punched them . . . either one." He smiles and takes my face between his hands.

"Well, aren't you sweet?" I tease and put my hands on his sides. "It's a relief, though, to have our own space. No more parties, no more roommates and community showers," I say.

"Our own bed," he adds with a wiggle of his eyes. "We will need to get a few things, dishes and such."

I touch the back of my hand to his forehead. "Are you feeling okay?" I smile. "You're being awfully cooperative today."

He brushes my hand aside, then gives the back of it a little kiss. "I just want to make sure you are pleased with everything here. I want you to feel at home . . . with me."

"And what about you? Do you feel at home here?" I ask him.

"Surprisingly enough, yes," he answers, nodding, and looks around the room.

"We should go get my stuff. I don't have much but a few books and my clothes," I say.

He waves his arms in the air as if he has performed some sort of magic trick. "Already done."

"What?" I ask.

"I brought all of your belongings from your room; they are in your trunk," he explains.

"How did you know I would sign? What if I hated the apartment?" I smile. I do wish I had had the chance to say goodbye to Steph and the room that I called home for three months, but I'll see her again soon.

"Because if you wouldn't have liked this one, I would have found one that you did," he answers confidently.

"Okay . . . Well, what about your stuff?"

"We can get it tomorrow. I have clothes in my trunk."

"What is with that, anyway?" He always has so many clothes in his car.

"I don't know, really. I guess you just never know when you will need clothes." He shrugs. "Let's go to the store and get all the shit we need for the kitchen and some food," Hardin says.

"Okay." My stomach has been full of butterflies since I stepped into the apartment. "Can I drive your car again?" I ask when we get down to the lobby.

"I don't know . . ." He smiles.

"You painted my car without my permission. I think I have

earned the privilege." I hold out my hands and he rolls his eyes before dropping the keys into them.

"So you like my car, then? It drives nicely, doesn't it?"

I give him a coy look. "It's okay."

I lie; I love the way it drives.

Our building could not be located in a better place; we're close to multiple stores, coffee shops, and even a park. We end up going to Target, and soon the cart is full of dishes, pots and pans, cups, and other things I didn't know we would need but seem useful. We save the groceries for another trip since we already have so much stuff. I volunteer to go grocery shopping after my internship tomorrow if Hardin makes me a list of things he likes to eat. The best thing so far about living together is all the small details about Hardin that I would have otherwise never known. He's so stingy with information, it's nice to get some of out him without a fight. Even though we spend almost every night together, by just buying things for our place, I'm finding out things that I would have never known. Like: he likes cereal with no milk; even the idea of mismatching cups drives him insane; he uses two different types of toothpaste, one in the morning and one at night, and he doesn't know why, he just does; and he would rather mop the floor a hundred times before having to load a dishwasher. We agree that I will always do the dishes as long as he mops the floor.

We bicker back and forth in front of the cashier when it comes time to pay. I know he had to put a deposit down for the apartment, so I want to cover our Target haul. But he refuses to let me pay for anything except cable and groceries. At first, he offered to let me pay for the electricity, which he declined to tell me was already included in the rent until I found the proof on the lease. The lease. I have a lease, with a man that I'm moving in with my freshman year of college. That's not crazy, right?

Hardin glares at the woman when she takes my debit card and I give her props because she swipes my card without even acknowledging his attitude. I want to laugh in victory, but he is already irritated and I don't want the night to be ruined.

Hardin sulks until we get back to the apartment, and I stay quiet because I find it amusing. "We might have to make two trips down here to get all the stuff," I tell him.

"That's another thing: I would rather carry one hundred bags than make two trips," he says and finally smiles.

We still end up having to take two trips because the dishes are just too heavy. Hardin's irritation grows, but so does my humor.

We put all the dishes away into the cabinets and Hardin orders a pizza. The polite person in me can't help but offer to pay for it, which earns me a glare and a middle finger. I laugh and put all the trash into the box the dishes came in. They weren't joking when they said the apartment came furnished—it has everything we could need, a trash can, even a shower curtain.

"The pizza will be here in thirty minutes. I am going to go down and get your stuff," he says.

"I'll come, too," I say and follow him out.

He has put my things into two boxes and a trash bag, which makes me cringe but I stay quiet. Grabbing a handful of T-shirts and a pair of jeans out of his trunk, he shoves them into the trash bag with my clothes.

"Good thing we have an iron," I finally say. When I look into his trunk, something catches my eye. "You never got rid of those sheets?" I ask.

"Oh . . . yeah. No, I was going to, but I forgot," he says and looks away.

"Okay . . ." I feel a little uneasy about his reaction.

We haul a load of stuff up the stairs, and right when we reach the top, the pizza guy rings our bell. Hardin goes back down to meet him, and when he comes back up the aroma coming from the box is heavenly. I didn't realize how hungry I'd gotten.

We eat at the table, and it's strange but nice to be eating dinner with Hardin in our place. We're quiet as we devour the delicious pizza, but it's the good kind of silence. The kind that tells me we're home.

"I love you," he says as I put our plates into the dishwasher.

I turn and respond, "I love you," just as my phone vibrates loudly on the wood table. Hardin looks over and taps the screen. "Who is it?" I ask him.

"Noah?" he says as both a declaration and a question at the same time.

"Oh." I know this isn't going to go well.

"He says it was 'nice talking to you today'?" His jaw clenches.

I walk back over and grab the phone, practically wrestling it out of his grip. I could have sworn he was going to crush it in his hand.

"Yeah, he called me today," I tell him with false confidence. I was going to mention it to him. I just haven't found the right time.

"And . . ." He raises his eyebrow.

"He was just telling me that he saw my mother and he was just seeing how I am doing."

"Why?"

"I don't know . . . just to check on me, I guess." I shrug and sit down in the chair next to him at the table.

"He doesn't need to be checking on you," he growls.

"It's not that big a deal, Hardin. I've known him half my life."

His eyes grow colder. "I don't give a shit."

"You're being ridiculous. We *just moved in together* and you're worried about Noah calling me?" I scoff.

"You have no reason to be talking to him; he probably thinks you want him back since you answered the call." He runs his hands through his hair.

"No, he doesn't. He knows that I am with you." I try my best to fight my temper.

He gestures wildly at my phone. "Then call him right now and tell him not to call you again."

"What? No! I'm not doing that. Noah hasn't done anything wrong, I have already hurt him enough—we both have—so, no. I will not say that to him. There is no harm in me being friends with him."

"Yes there is," he says, his voice rising. "He thinks he is better than me, and he will try to take you from me! I'm not stupid, Tessa. Your mom wants you with him too—I won't let him try to take what is mine!"

I step back and look at him with wide eyes. "Would you *listen* to yourself? You sound like a lunatic! I am not going to be hateful to him just because you feel like you have some insane claim on me!" I storm out of the kitchen.

"Don't walk away from me!" he booms, following me into the living room.

Leave it to Hardin to start a fight with me after the amazing day we have had. But I'm holding my ground on this. "Then stop acting like you own me. I will try to compromise and make an effort to listen to you more than I do now, but not when it comes to Noah. I would immediately stop talking to him if he tried to make a move or say anything inappropriate, but he didn't. Besides, you obviously need to just trust me."

Hardin stares at me, and I wonder if his energy is dissipating when at last he simply says, "I don't like him."

"Okay, I get that, but you have to be reasonable. He is not plotting to take me away from you; he isn't like that. This is the first time he has even tried to contact me since I ended things with him."

"And the last!" Hardin snaps. I roll my eyes and head into the small bathroom. "What are you doing?" he asks.

"I'm going to take a shower, and when I get out I hope you're done acting like a child," I say. I'm proud of the way I am standing up to him, but I can't help but feel bad for him. I know he is just afraid to lose me to Noah; he has this deep jealousy because of the way Noah and I "look" together. On paper Noah is better for me, and Hardin knows that, but I don't love Noah, I love Hardin.

Hardin follows me into the bathroom, but when I start to undress he turns and leaves, slamming the bathroom door on his way out. I take a quick shower and when I get out Hardin is lying across the bed in just his boxers. I stay quiet as I open the drawers to find pajamas.

"You're not going to wear my shirt?" His voice is low.

"I . . ." I notice that he folded it and put it on the table next to the bed. "Thanks." I pull it over my head. The familiar minty scent almost makes me forget that I'm supposed to be mad at him. But when I look over at him and his dark mood, I remember all too well. "Well, this was a great night," I huff and take my towel back to the bathroom.

"Come here," he says when I return.

Hesitantly, I walk over to him and he sits up at the end of the bed, pulling me to stand between his legs.

"I'm sorry." He looks up at me.

"For . . . ?"

"Acting like a caveman," he says, and I can't help but laugh. "And for ruining our first night here together," he adds.

"Thank you. We have to discuss these things instead of you blowing up at me." I twirl the hair at the nape of his neck in between my fingers.

"I know." He half-smiles. "Can we discuss you not talking to him anymore?"

"Not tonight," I say with a sigh. I will have to find a middle ground with him, but I am not completely giving up my right to talk to someone I've known half my life.

"Look at us working our problems out." He chuckles ruefully.

"I hope our neighbors won't miss their quiet evenings."

"Oh, they wouldn't have gotten any quiet anyway." His smile shows his dimples to full fire-igniting effect, but I ignore his perverted remark.

"I really didn't mean to ruin the night," he says again.

"I know. It's not ruined. It's only eight." I smile.

"I wanted to be the one to take that dress off you," he states, his eyes darkening.

"I could always put it back on," I say in what is an attempt to be sexy. Without a word he stands up and lifts me over his shoulder. I squeal and try to kick my legs at him. "What are you doing!" I scream.

"Going to get that dress." He laughs and carries me over to the laundry hamper.

chapter eighty-eight

"Too bad we didn't make it to the part about me removing the dress," Hardin whispers into my ear as he pushes me farther onto the bed. As soon as I slid his T-shirt off over my head, he practically tackled me onto our bed and slid the condom on faster than I thought possible.

"Mmm . . ." is the only word I can manage to form as he slides in and out of me. This is the first time we are making love that there is no pain, only pleasure.

"God, baby . . . you feel so good," he groans and rocks his hips against mine. The feeling is indescribable. His lean body fits perfectly between my legs, and his hot skin feels heavenly against mine. I consider responding, to urge him with dirty talk the way that he does me, but I'm lost in him and the pleasure coursing through me as he continues his tender assault.

I grip on to his back, my nails rake down his skin, and his eyes roll to the back of his head. I love to see him this way, so out of control, so primal. He lifts my thigh to wrap around his waist, bringing our bodies even closer. Watching him pushes me to the limit; my toes curl and my leg tightens around his back as I moan his name repeatedly.

"That's it, baby . . . come for me. Show me how good . . . fuck . . . how good I make you f-feel," he stutters, and I feel him twitch inside me. Though he finishes a few seconds before me, his perfect movements continue until I am turned into a pool of boneless mush and am spent. My body is completely relaxed and he collapses on top of me. We lie there in silence just enjoying the feeling of being so close to each other, and within minutes soft snores fall from Hardin's lips.

THE DAYS HERE PASS QUICKLY. Having freedom for the first time in your life will do that. It's still foreign to be in my own place with my own shower, to make my own coffee in my own kitchen. Sharing all of this with Hardin only makes it that much better. I decide upon my navy blue eyelet dress with white heels. I am getting better at walking in them, but I still pack my trusty Toms in my purse just in case. My hair is curled and pinned back and I even put on a little eye shadow and liner. I am really liking this having my own space.

Hardin refuses to wake up, sitting up only long enough to kiss me goodbye. I wonder how he manages to work and do all of his schoolwork when I have yet to see him do either. In a brave move, I grab his car keys and take his car to Vance. If he is skipping classes, he surely won't miss it, right? I forget how much closer we live to Vance now, and I make a mental note to remember to thank Hardin for his foresight, even though he has to drive farther to campus now. That I don't have to drive forty minutes makes my day much better.

When I reach the top floor Kimberly is standing at the conference room table placing donuts in neat rows.

"Whoa, Tessa! Look at you!" She whistles playfully. I flush and she laughs. "Navy is definitely your color." She looks me up and down again. I feel slightly self-conscious, but her smile soothes my thoughts. I have been feeling much more confident and sexy lately, thanks to Hardin.

"Thank you, Kimberly." I smile back and grab a donut and a cup of coffee. The phone rings on her desk and she rushes over to answer it.

When I get to my office, I have an email from Mr. Vance praising my notes on the first manuscript and saying that even though that one was a pass for the house, he looks forward to my evaluation of the next one. I dive right in and get to work.

"Anything good?" Hardin's voice startles me out of my work. I look up, slightly shocked, and he smiles. "Must be, since you didn't seem to notice my arrival."

He looks incredible. His hair is pushed up in the front as always, but the sides are flatter than usual, and he has a plain white V-neck on. The shirt is tighter than usual, making his tattoos even more visible underneath. He is so incredibly hot—and all mine.

"So . . . how was the drive?" he asks with a smirk.

"Really nice." I giggle.

"So you think you can just take my car without my permission?" His voice is low and I can't tell if he is joking.

"I . . . well . . ." I stammer.

He doesn't say anything, just walks over behind my desk and pulls my chair out. His eyes move from my shoes up to my face and he pulls me to stand up. "You look so sexy today," he says against my neck before gently pressing his lips against my skin.

I shiver. "Why . . . why are you here?"

"You aren't happy to see me?" He smiles and lifts me onto the desk.

Oh. "Yeah . . . of course I am," I tell him. I am always happy to see him.

"I may have to consider coming back here after all, just so I can do this every day," he says and puts his hands on my thighs.

"Someone could come in here." I try to be stern, but my tone is shaky.

"Nope—Vance is at a meeting for the rest of the afternoon and Kimberly has agreed to call if she needs you."

The idea of Hardin hinting to Kimberly what we could be

doing in here makes my cheeks heat, but my hormones take over. I glance at the door.

"Locked," he answers cockily.

Without thinking, I pull Hardin closer and immediately put my hand over his crotch, palming him through his jeans. He groans and unbuttons his jeans, yanking them down along with his boxers.

"This is going to be faster than usual, okay, baby?" he says and slides my panties over.

I nod with anticipation and lick my lips. He chuckles and pulls me by my hips to the edge of the desk. My lips attack his neck and I hear the foil packet being ripped open.

"Look at you—three months ago you would blush at the mention of sex, and now here you are letting me fuck you on your desk," he whispers and slams into me.

Hardin clamps his hand over my mouth and takes his bottom lip between his teeth. I can't believe I am actually letting Hardin have sex with me on a desk, at the place of my internship, with Kimberly less than a hundred feet away. As much as I hate to admit it, the idea actually drives me crazy. In the best way.

"Are you going . . . to be . . . quiet . . ." he says in short spurts and moves even faster. I nod and pant, grabbing on to his biceps so I don't fall off the desk from his assault.

"You like it this way, don't you? Fast and hard?" He grits his teeth. I gently bite down on his palm to keep quiet.

"Answer me or I'll stop," he threatens.

I lower my eyes at him and nod, too overwhelmed with sensation to actually speak.

"I knew you would," he says, and flips me over so my stomach is on the desk.

Oh God. He thrusts back into me and moves slowly before

wrapping my hair around his fist and pulling me up so he can kiss my neck. The tension grows in my stomach and his movements grow sloppier—and I know we are both close. With his final thrust he kisses my shoulder before pulling out of me and helping me off the desk.

"That was—" I try to say and he silences me by kissing my lips.

"Yeah . . . it was." He finishes my thoughts before pulling his pants back up. I run my fingers through my hair and wipe under my eyes to make sure my makeup is in place before looking at the clock. It's almost three. The day has escaped me once again.

"You ready?" he asks.

"What? It's only three." I point to the clock.

"Christian said you can leave early. I spoke to him an hour ago."

"Hardin! You can't just ask him if I can leave early; this internship is important to me."

"Babe, relax. He mentioned that he would be out all day and he was the one who brought up you leaving early."

"I don't want anyone to think I am taking advantage of this opportunity."

"No one thinks that. Your GPA and your work speak for themselves."

"Wait . . . so then why didn't you just call me and tell me I could come home?" I raise a brow at him.

"I have wanted to bend you over that desk since your first day here." He gives me a smug smile and grabs my jacket for me.

I want to tell him how crazy he is to come here just to have sex with me on the desk, but I can't deny that I loved it. Looking at him in that T-shirt with those inked muscles, I could never deny him anything.

* * *

AS WE WALK to our cars, he squints at the sun and says, "I was thinking we should go get whatever we are going to wear to that dreadful wedding."

"Good idea," I agree. "But I'm driving your car back home and we can leave my car, then go." I jump into his car before he can protest. He just shakes his head and smiles.

After dropping my car off, we go to the mall. Hardin whines and complains like a child the entire time and I literally have to coerce him with sexual bribes to get him to buy a tie. He ends up getting black dress pants, a black jacket, a white dress shirt, and a black tie. Simple, but perfect for him. He refuses to try everything on, so I hope it all actually fits him. He would take any excuse not to go to the wedding, but I am not going to let that happen. Once we get him settled, it's my turn.

"The white one," he says and gestures to the short white dress in my hand, the other option being a longer black one. Since Karen mentioned that the color scheme was black and white, I figured I would stick to it. Hardin seemed to really like the white dress I wore yesterday, so I decide to listen to him. Much to my annoyance, before I realize what he's doing, Hardin goes from "just carrying" my dress and shoes to paying for them. When I protest, the young girl at the register smiles and shrugs as if to say, "What do you expect me to do?"

"I have to do some work tonight, so I won't be home for dinner," he tells me as we walk out of the mall.

"Oh. I thought you worked from home."

"I do, but I need to go to the library for a little bit," he explains. "I won't be gone too late."

"I'll just go grocery shopping while you are gone," I tell him and he nods.

"Be careful and go before it gets dark," he says.

He makes me a list of things he likes and leaves as soon as we get back to the apartment. I change into jeans and a sweatshirt and walk to the grocery store down the street. When I get back home, I put everything away, catch up on some homework, and make myself something to eat. I text Hardin but don't hear anything back, so I put a plate of food in the microwave for him to heat up when he gets home and lie on the couch to watch television.

chapter eighty-nine

When I wake up, it takes me a few moments to realize I am still on the couch.

"Hardin?" I call out, untangling myself from the blanket. I walk to the bedroom in the hopes he will be in there. But the room is empty. *Where the hell is he?*

I go back to the living room and snatch my phone off the back of the couch. Still no messages from him—and it's seven in the morning. I call, but get his voicemail and hang up. I storm around the kitchen and turn on the coffeepot before heading to the bathroom to take a shower. I'm lucky I woke up on time, because I didn't actually set my alarm. I never forget to set an alarm.

"Where are you?" I say aloud and step into the shower.

As I blow-dry my hair, I go over the possible explanations for his absence. Last night I thought he just got caught up with his work, since he has a lot to make up for or maybe he ran into someone he knew and the time slipped away from him. But at the library? Those things close fairly early, and even bars close eventually. The most likely explanation is that he went to a party. I somehow know this is what happened. A small part of me still worries that maybe he was in an accident; the thought alone hurts too bad to even entertain. But no matter what excuse or story I conjure up in my mind, I know he is doing something he isn't supposed to. Everything was good between us last night and then he goes and stays out all night?

In no mood to wear a dress, I put on one of my old black pencil skirts and a soft pink button-up shirt. Clouds cover the sky my entire drive, and by the time I get to Vance my mood has darkened to match them and I'm infuriated. *Who the hell does he think he is to stay out all night without even telling me?*

Kimberly raises a brow at me when I walk past the donut table without grabbing one, but I give her my best fake smile and walk to my office. My morning passes in a daze. I read and reread the same pages over and over without comprehending any of the words.

There is a knock on my door, and my heart stops. I desperately hope it's Hardin, regardless of how pissed I am at him. Instead it's Kimberly.

"Do you want to go get lunch with me?" she asks sweetly.

I almost decline her offer, but sitting here obsessing over my boyfriend's whereabouts is not helping me one bit.

I smile. "Sure."

We walk around the corner to a small cantina-style Mexican restaurant. By the time we get inside we're both shivering, and she asks to be seated close to a heater. The small table we are given is directly underneath a heater, and we both raise our hands in the air to warm up.

"This weather is unforgiving," she says and prattles on about being cold and already missing summer.

"I almost forgot how cold the winter is," I tell her plainly. The seasons have blended together, and I barely noticed fall slipping away.

"So . . . how are things with Mr. Bad Ass?" she asks with a laugh.

The server brings us chips and salsa, and my stomach growls. I am not skipping my morning donut anymore.

"Well . . ." I debate whether to share my personal life with her. I don't have many friends. None, really, excluding Steph, whom I never see anymore. Kimberly is at least ten years older than me and maybe she has some good insight into the minds of men, something I certainly lack in. I stare at the ceiling covered in strings of beer-bottle-shaped lights and take a deep breath.

"Well, I am actually not sure how things are at the moment. Yesterday things were fine but then he stayed out last night. All night. It was our second night in the apartment and he just never came home," I explain.

"Wait . . . wait . . . back up. Okay, so you two live together?" She gapes.

"Yeah . . . as of Tuesday." I try to smile.

"Okay, so then he just didn't come home last night?"

"Nope. He said he had to do some work and go by the library, but then he didn't come home."

"And you don't think he's hurt or anything, right?"

"No, I really don't." I feel as if I would somehow know if he wasn't okay, like we are tied together in some way that would immediately let me know if he was hurt.

"He hasn't called?"

"Nope. Or texted." I frown.

"I would have his balls if I were you. This is unacceptable," she proclaims.

The server stops by to say, "Your food will be out shortly," and fills up my water. I'm a little thankful for the small interruption, to give me a chance to catch my breath after Kimberly's harsh words.

And then she goes on, and when I realize she's not judging me but sticking up for me, I feel better. "I mean it—you have to make it clear that he can't behave this way; otherwise he will keep doing it. The problem with men is that they are creatures of habit, and if you let this be his habit, you'll never be able to break it. He needs to know from the start that you won't put up with this shit. He is lucky to have you and he needs to get his shit together."

Something about her pep talk gives me more confidence in my anger. I should be pissed. I should "have his balls," as Kimberly so subtly put it.

"How do I do that?" I ask and she laughs.

"Let him have it. Unless he has a damned good excuse, which I am sure he is plotting right now, you let him have it the second he walks through that door. You deserve to be respected, and if he isn't respecting you, then you need to either make him or kick him to the curb."

"You make it sound so easy." I laugh.

"Oh, it's far from easy." She laughs, then grows serious. "But it has to be done."

The rest of our lunch is filled with stories of her college life and how she has had her fair share of terrible relationships. Her blond bob sways back and forth as she shakes her head during almost every story. I find myself laughing so hard I have to dab the corners of my eyes. The food is delicious and I am glad I came out to lunch with her instead of sulking alone in my office.

On the way back to my office, Trevor spots me from near the restrooms and comes over, smiling. "Hello, Tessa."

"Hey, how are you?" I ask politely.

"I'm okay. It's awfully cold out there," he says and I nod. "You look lovely today," he adds and looks away. I get the feeling he didn't mean to say that aloud. I smile and thank him before he heads into the bathroom, obviously embarrassed.

By the time I leave, I have gotten literally no work done so I take the manuscript home with me in hopes of making up for my lack of motivation today.

When I arrive back at the apartment, Hardin's car still isn't in the lot. My anger returns, and I call him and cuss him out on his voicemail, which surprisingly makes me feel a little better. I make myself a quick dinner and get my things ready for tomorrow.

I can't believe it's only two days until the wedding. What if he doesn't come back before then? He will. *Won't he?* I look around the apartment. As charming as it is, it seems to have lost some of its glow in Hardin's absence.

Somehow I manage to get a good amount of work done and am just putting everything away when the door opens. Hardin stumbles through the living room and into the bedroom without saying a word. I hear him toss his boots onto the floor and curse at himself, most likely for falling over. I go over what Kimberly said at lunch today and gather all my thoughts, pushing my anger to its head.

"Where the hell were you?" I yell as I enter the room. Hardin has his shirt off and is removing his pants.

"Good to see you, too," he slurs.

"Are you drunk?" I gape.

"Maybe," he answers, and tosses his pants onto the floor.

I huff and pick them up, throwing them at him. "We have a hamper for a reason." I glare and he laughs.

He is laughing. Laughing at me.

"You have some nerve, Hardin! You stay out all night and most of the day today without even calling me, and then you stumble in here *drunk* and *make fun of me?*" I scream.

"Stop yelling. I have a killer headache," he groans and lies on the bed.

"Do you think this is funny? Is this some sort of game to you? If you aren't going to take our relationship seriously, then why did you ask me to move in with you?"

"I don't want to talk about this right now. You're overreacting; now, come over here and let me make you happy." His eyes are bloodshot from the amount of alcohol he consumed. He holds his arms out for me with a stupid drunken grin on his perfect face.

"No, Hardin," I say sternly. "I'm serious. You can't just stay out all night and not even offer me an explanation."

"Jesus. Would you chill the fuck out? You're not my mother. Stop fighting with me and come here," he repeats.

"Get out," I snap.

"Excuse me?" He sits up. Now I have his attention.

"You heard me, get out. I will not be that girl who sits at home all night waiting on her boyfriend to come home. I expected you to at least come up with a good excuse—but you haven't even tried! I'm not going to give in this time, Hardin. I always forgive you way too easily. Not this time. So either explain yourself or get the hell out." I cross my arms, proud of myself for not giving in to him.

"In case you forgot, I am the one paying the bills here, so if anyone is going to leave, it will be you," he says with a blank stare.

I glance down at his hands on his knees; his knuckles are yet again busted and covered in dried blood.

My mind is still trying to come up with a response when I ask, "Did you get in a fight again?"

"Does it matter?"

"Yes, Hardin! It does matter. Is that what you were doing all night? Fighting people? You didn't even have to work, did you? Or is that your job, beating up people?"

"What? No, that's not my job. You know what my job is. I did work, then I got distracted," he says and swipes his hand over his face.

"By?"

"Nothing. Jesus," he groans. "You are always on my case."

"I'm always on your case? What did you expect to happen when you stumbled in here after being gone all night and day! I need answers, Hardin—I am sick of you not giving me them." He ignores me and pulls a shirt over his head. "I was worried all day; you could have at least called me. I was a mess today while you were out drinking and doing God knows what. You are messing with my internship, and that is not okay."

"Your internship? You mean the one that my father got you?" he says with his foul mouth.

"You're unbelievable."

"Just saying." He shrugs.

How is this the same person who just two nights go was whispering how much he loves me into my ear while he thought I was asleep?

"I'm not even going to respond to that, because I know that's what you want. You want a fight and I won't give you one." I grab one of my T-shirts and stalk out of the room. Before I exit, I turn back to him. "But let me make this clear: if you don't get your shit together—like *now*—I'm gone."

I head to the couch and lie down, grateful for another space to be where he isn't. I allow a few tears to fall before wiping my face and picking up Hardin's old copy of *Wuthering Heights*. No matter how bad I want to go back in there and make him explain everything to me—where he was, who he was with, why he got into a fight, and with whom—I force myself to stay on the couch because that will bother him much more.

Though probably not half as much as the level of control he has over parts of my life is bothering me.

chapter ninety

I put down my book and check the time on my phone. It's a little after midnight, so I should try to force myself to go to sleep. He already tried to get me to come to bed earlier, saying he couldn't sleep without me, but I stuck to my guns and ignored him until he left.

I'm just about to drift into sleep when I hear Hardin scream, "No!!" I jump off the couch without thinking and rush to our bedroom. He is thrashing in the thick blanket and covered in sweat.

"Hardin, wake up," I say gently and shake his shoulder, moving a soaked curl from his forehead with my other hand.

His eyes snap open—they are full of terror.

"It's okay . . . shh . . . it was just a nightmare." I do my best to soothe him. My fingers play in his hair and then brush over his cheek. He is shaking as I climb into bed behind him and wrap my arms around his waist. I feel him relax as I press my face against his clammy skin.

"Please. Stay with me," he begs. I sigh and stay quiet, tightening my grip around him. "Thank you," he whispers, and within minutes he is asleep again.

THE WATER DOESN'T SEEM to get hot enough to relax my tense muscles no matter how high I turn it up. I am exhausted from the lack of sleep last night and the frustration that comes from dealing with Hardin. He was asleep when I got into the shower, and I pray he stays that way until I leave for my internship.

Unfortunately, my prayers go unanswered, and he is standing by the kitchen counter when I get out of the bathroom.

"You look beautiful today," he says calmly.

I roll my eyes and walk past him to grab a cup of coffee before I have to leave.

"So you aren't speaking to me, then?"

"Not right now, no. I have to go to work and I don't have the energy to do this with you," I snap.

"But you . . . you came to bed with me," he pouts.

"Yeah, only because you were screaming and shaking. That doesn't mean you are forgiven. I need an explanation for everything, all the secrets, all the fights—even the nightmares—or I'm done," I surprise him and myself by saying.

He groans and runs his hands through his hair. "Tessa . . . it's not that simple."

"Yeah, it is, actually. I trusted you enough to give up my relationship with my mother and move in with you so soon; you should trust me enough to tell me what is going on."

"You won't understand. I know you won't," he says.

"Try me."

"I . . . I can't," he stutters.

"Then I can't be with you. I'm sorry, but I have given you a lot of chances and you keep—" I begin.

"Don't say that. Don't you dare try and leave me." His tone is angry, but his eyes are hurt.

"Then give me some answers. What is it that you think I wouldn't understand? About your nightmares?" I ask.

"Tell me you aren't going to leave me," he pleads.

Standing my ground with Hardin is proving to be much harder than I imagined, especially when he looks so broken.

"I have to go. I am already running late," I tell him and go to the bedroom to get dressed as quickly as I can. Part of me is happy that he doesn't follow me, but part of me wishes he would.

He is still standing in the kitchen, shirtless, and gripping his coffee mug with white and busted knuckles when I leave.

I mull over everything Hardin said this morning. What could I possibly not understand? I would never judge him for something that causes him to have nightmares. I hope that is what he was talking about, but I can't ignore the feeling that I am missing something very obvious here.

I feel guilty and tense almost all day, but Kimberly emails me the links to one too many funny YouTube videos for my sour mood to last. By lunch, I almost forget the problem at home.

I'm sorry for everything, please come home after work, Hardin texts while Kimberly and I eat from a muffin basket someone sent Mr. Vance.

"Is that him?" she asks.

"Yeah . . ." I tell her. "I stood up to him, but I feel terrible, for some reason. I know I am right, but you should have seen him this morning."

"Good. Hopefully he learns his lesson. Did he tell you where he was?" she asks.

"Nope. That's the problem." I groan and eat another muffin.

Please answer me, Tessa. I love you, he sends minutes later.

"Just answer the poor guy." Kimberly smiles and I nod.

I will be home, I respond.

Why is it so hard for me to hold my ground with him? Mr. Vance lets everyone go a little after three, so I decide to stop by a salon and get my hair trimmed and a manicure for the wedding tomorrow. I hope Hardin and I can work this out before the wedding, because the last thing I want to do is take an already angry Hardin to his father's wedding.

By the time I get home it's almost six o'clock and I have multiple texts from Hardin, which I have ignored. When I get to our door I take a deep breath to mentally prepare for what is to come. Either we will end up screaming at each other, which will lead to one of us leaving, or we will actually talk through it and work it out. Hardin is pacing back and forth across the cement floor when I enter. His eyes shoot up to my figure in the doorway, and he looks relieved.

"I thought you weren't coming," he says and steps toward me.

"Where else would I go?" I say in response and walk past him into the bedroom.

"I . . . well, I made dinner for you," he says.

He is totally unrecognizable right now. His hair is down across his forehead instead of pushed up and back like it normally is. He is wearing a gray hooded sweatshirt and black sweats and he seems nervous, worried, and almost . . . afraid?

"Oh . . . why?" I can't help but ask. I change into sweats of my own, and Hardin's face falls farther when I don't put on the shirt of his that he has clearly laid on the dresser for me.

"Because I am an asshole," he answers.

"Yeah . . . you are," I say and walk back into the kitchen. The meal looks much more appetizing than I thought it would, even though I'm not sure what it is; some sort of chicken pasta, I think.

"It's chicken Florentine." He answers my thoughts.

"Hmm."

"You don't have to . . ." His voice is small. This is such a different scene than usual, and for the first time since I met him I feel like I have the upper hand.

"No, it looks good. I'm just surprised," I tell him and take a bite. It tastes even better than it looks.

"Your hair looks nice," he says. My thoughts travel back to the last time I had a haircut and Hardin was the only one to notice.

"I need answers," I remind him.

He lets out a hard breath. "I know, and I am going to give them to you."

I take another bite to hide my satisfaction with myself for holding my ground with him.

"First, I want you to know that no one—I mean *no one*, except my mother and father—knows this," he says and picks at the scabs on his knuckles.

I nod and take another bite.

"Okay . . . well, here goes," he says nervously before continuing. "One night, when I was around seven, my father was out at the bar across the street from our home. He went there almost every night and everyone knew him there, which is why it was a terrible idea for him to piss anyone off there. This night, he did just that. He started a fight with some soldiers who were just as plastered as him and he ended up smashing a beer bottle over one of their heads."

I have no idea where this is going, but I know it won't be pleasant.

"Keep eating, please . . ." he begs and I nod and try not to stare at him as he continues.

"He left the bar, and they came across the road to our house, to pay him back for smashing the guy's face, I guess. The problem was that he didn't come home—they just thought he did, and my mum was asleep on the couch, waiting up for my dad." His green eyes meet mine. "Sort of how you were last night."

"Hardin . . ." I whisper and grab his hand across the table.

"So when they found my mum first . . ." He trails off and stares at the wall for what feels like forever. "When I heard her screaming, I came downstairs and tried to get them off her. Her nightgown was ripped open and she just kept screaming for me to go . . . she was trying to keep me from seeing what they were doing to her, but I couldn't just leave, you know?"

When he blinks back a tear, my heart breaks for the seven-year-old boy who had to watch those horrendous things happen to his mother. I climb onto his lap on the chair and put my face against his neck.

"Long story short, I tried to fight them off, but it didn't do any good. By the time my father stumbled through the door, I had put an entire box of Band-Aids all over her body to try to . . . I don't know . . . fix her or something. How stupid is that?" he asks into my hair.

I look up at him and he frowns. "Don't cry . . ." he whispers, but I can't help it. I never imagined his nightmares were from something so terrible.

"I'm sorry I made you tell me," I sob.

"No . . . baby, it's okay. It actually felt good to tell someone," he assures me. "As good as it *can* feel."

He pets my hair and winds part of it around his finger, lost in thought. "After that, I would only sleep downstairs on the couch, so if someone came in . . . they would get to me first. Then the nightmares came . . . and they just kind of stuck. I went to a few therapists once my father left, but nothing seemed to help, until you." He gives me a weak smile. "I'm sorry I was out all night. I don't want to be that guy. I don't want to be him," he says and hugs me tighter.

Now that I have a few more pieces of the puzzle that is Hardin, I can understand him more. And just as suddenly as my mood has shifted about him, my opinion of Ken has changed just as drastically. I know people change, and he obviously has improved himself from the kind of man he used to be, but I can't help the anger bubbling inside me. Hardin is the way he is because of his father, because of the drinking, the negligence, and the terrible night that his father provoked an attack against his wife and son, and then wasn't there to protect them. I didn't get all the answers I wanted, but I got much more than I ever expected.

"I won't do it again . . . I swear . . . Just please tell me you won't leave me . . ." he mutters.

Every ounce of anger and entitlement I felt has evaporated. "I won't leave you, Hardin. I won't leave you." And because he looks at me like he needs to hear it, I say it a few more times.

"I love you, Tessa, more than anything," he says and wipes my tears.

chapter ninety-one

We haven't moved from our spot in the chair for at least thirty minutes, when finally Hardin lifts his head from my chest and says, "Can I eat now?"

"Yes." I give him a weak smile and start to climb off his lap, but he pulls me back.

"I didn't say for you to move. Just slide my plate over." He smiles.

I slide his plate over and reach for mine across the small table. I am still reeling from this new information and now I feel a little uneasy about going to the wedding in the morning.

Sensing Hardin doesn't want to discuss his confession further, I take a bite off my plate and say, "You are a much better cook than I expected. Having shown your hand, I expect you'll cook for me more often."

"We will see," he says with his mouth full and we eat the rest of the meal in a comfortable silence.

Later, when I'm loading the dishwasher, he walks up behind me and asks, "Are you still mad?"

"Not exactly," I tell him. "I am still not happy about you being out all night, and I do want to know who you fought, and why." He opens his mouth to speak, but I stop him. "But not tonight." I don't think either of us can handle any more tonight.

"Okay," he says softly. Worry flashes in his eyes but I choose to let it go.

"Oh, and I didn't appreciate you throwing my internship in my face, either. That really hurt my feelings."

"I know. That's why I said it," he answers, a little too honestly.

"I know. That's exactly why I don't like it."

"I'm sorry."

"Don't do it again, okay?" I tell him and he nods. "I'm exhausted," I groan in a small attempt to change the subject.

"Me, too; let's lie down for the rest of the evening. I got the cable turned on."

"I was supposed to be doing that." I scowl at him.

He rolls his eyes and sits next to me on the bed. "You can just give me the money for it . . ."

I stare at the wall. "What time are we leaving here tomorrow for the wedding?"

"Whenever we feel like it."

"It starts at three, so I think we should be there by two," I say.

"An hour early?" he whines and I nod. "I don't know why you insist—" he says but is cut off by my phone ringing.

The look on Hardin's face as he leans over and grabs it tells me immediately who it is. "Why is he calling?" he huffs.

"I don't know, Hardin, but I think I should answer." I grab the phone from his hand.

"Noah?" My voice is soft and shaky as Hardin's glower burns a hole through the apartment.

"Hey, Tessa, I'm sorry to call you on a Friday night but . . . well . . ." He sounds panicked.

"What?" I push, since he always takes longer than necessary to explain stressful situations.

When I look over to Hardin he mouths, "Speaker."

I give him an are-you-kidding look, but end up putting Noah on speaker anyway so Hardin can eavesdrop.

"Your mom got a call from the dorm supervisor about your

final bill being paid for the room, so she knows you moved out. I told her I have no idea where you live now, which is the truth, but she refused to believe me. And so she's coming there."

"Coming here? To campus?"

"Yeah, I guess. I don't know, but she said she's going to find you, and she's being irrational and is really pissed-off. I just wanted to warn you, you know, that she's coming."

"I can't believe her!" I shout into the phone, but then thank Noah before hanging up.

I lie back on the bed. "Great . . . What an excellent way to spend tonight."

Hardin leans on one elbow next to me. "She won't be able to find you. No one knows where we live," he assures me and smooths my bangs off my forehead.

"She may not find me, but she sure will pester Steph and ask every single person she sees in the dorm and make a huge scene." I cover my face with my hands. "I should just go over there."

"Or you could call her and give her our address and let her come here. On your territory, so you have the upper hand," he suggests.

"You're okay with that?" My hands move from my face.

"Of course. She's your mother, Tessa."

I look at him quizzically, given the rift between him and his dad. But when I see he's serious, I'm reminded that he's willing to work on things with his parents, so I should be that brave, too. "I'll call her," I say.

I look at the phone for a while before taking a deep breath and hitting her number. She's terse on the phone, speaking very quickly. I can tell she's saving all her hateful energy for when she sees me in person. I don't give her any details about the apartment or tell her that I live here; I only tell her the address where I am and get off the phone as fast as I can.

Instinctively, I jump out of bed and begin to straighten up our place.

"The apartment is already clean. We have barely touched anything," Hardin says.

"I know," I say. "But it makes me feel better."

After I fold and put away the few items of clothing that were on the floor, I light a candle in the living room and wait at the table with Hardin for my mother to show. I shouldn't be as nervous as I am—I'm an adult and I make my own choices—but I know her and how badly she's going to lose it. I am already overly emotional from the brief glimpse into Hardin's past I was granted an hour ago, and I don't know if I have it in me to go to battle with her tonight. I look over at the clock and see it's already eight. Hopefully she won't stay long, and Hardin and I can get to bed early and just hold each other while we each try to deal with our family legacies.

"Do you want me to stay out here with you or give you two some time to discuss everything?" Hardin asks after a bit.

"I think we should have a little time one-on-one," I say. As much as I want him by my side, I know that his presence will antagonize her.

"Wait . . . I just remembered something Noah said. He said the final bill for my dorm was paid." I look at him questioningly.

"Yeah . . . so?"

"You paid it, *didn't* you!" I half-shout. Despite my energy, it's not really out of anger, just surprise and annoyance.

"So . . ." He shrugs.

"Hardin! You have got to stop spending money on me; it makes me uncomfortable."

"I don't see what the big deal is. It wasn't that much," he argues.

"What are you like secretly rich or something? Are you selling drugs?"

"No, I just saved up a lot of money and don't really spend it. I lived entirely for free last year while I worked, so my paychecks just kept piling up. I never really had anything to spend money on . . . but now I do." He smiles wide. "And I like spending it on you, so don't fight me over it."

"You're lucky my mother is on her way and I only have it in me to go to war with one of you," I tease and he lets out a long chuckle that fades until we're just sitting, holding hands and waiting.

A few minutes later there is a knock . . . well, a *pounding* at the door.

Hardin stands. "I'll be right in the other room. I love you." He gives me a swift kiss before exiting.

I fill my lungs with the deepest breath I can manage and open the door. My mother looks eerily perfect, as always. Not a single smudge mars her heavily made-up eyes, her red lipstick is smooth and silky, her blond hair is neatly piled almost in a halo around her head.

"What the *hell* do you think you're doing moving out of that dorm without telling me!" she shouts without introduction and pushes past me into the apartment.

"You didn't give me much of a choice," I counter, then focus on breathing in and out to stay as calm as I can.

She spins back to glare at me. "*Excuse* me? How did I not give you a choice?"

"You threatened to not help me pay for my dorm," I remind her and cross my arms.

"So, I gave you a choice, but you made the wrong one," she snaps.

"No, you're the one who's wrong here."

"Listen to you! *Look* at you. You aren't the same Tessa that I dropped off at college three months ago." She waves her arms to gesture up and down my body. "You are defying me, even yelling at me! You have some nerve! I have done everything for you, and here you are . . . throwing it all away."

"I am not throwing anything away! I have an excellent internship that pays me very well; I have a car, and a four-point-oh grade point average. What more could you possibly want from me?" I shout back.

Her eyes light up from the challenge, and her voice is full of venom as she says, "Well, for starters, you could have at least changed your clothes before I came. Honestly, Tessa, you look like hell." As I look down at my pajamas, she switches to a new criticism. "And what is this . . . you wear makeup now? Who are you? You're not my Theresa, that is for certain. My Theresa wouldn't be hanging out in some devil worshipper's apartment in her pajamas on a Friday night."

"Do not speak about him that way," I say through my teeth. "I have already warned you."

My mother squints her eyes and cackles. Her head falls back in laughter, and I fight the urge to smack her across her perfectly painted-on face. I immediately cringe at my violent thoughts, but she's pushing me too far.

"And another thing," I say slowly, calmly, to make sure I deliver the pronouncement just so. "This isn't just his apartment. It is *our* apartment."

And just like that, I get her to stop laughing.

chapter ninety-two

This woman I've lived with values her sense of control so much that there are few times I've managed to surprise her, let alone stun her. But here, I have really, truly stunned my mother. Her posture is erect and her face has fallen.

"What did you just say?" she asks slowly.

"You heard me. This is *our* apartment—as in, we both live here." I put my hands on my hips for dramatic effect.

"There is no way that you live here. You can't afford a place like this!" she scoffs.

"Would you like to see our lease? Because I have a copy."

"This whole situation is even worse than I thought . . ." she says, then shifts her eyes to stare behind me, as if I'm not even worth looking at while she calculates her formula for my life. "I knew you were being foolish by messing around with that . . . that boy. But you are just plain stupid for moving in with him! You don't even know him! You haven't met his parents—aren't you embarrassed to be seen in public with him?"

My anger boils over. I glance at the wall, trying to gather some composure, but it's too much and before I can stop myself, I am in her face. "How dare you come into my home and insult him! I know him better than anyone, and he knows me better than you ever could! And I have actually met his family, his father at least. You want to know who his father is? *He's the goddamn chancellor of WCU!*" I scream. "That should satisfy your sad little judgmental streak."

I hate throwing Hardin's father's title around, but this is the type of thing that would jolt her.

Probably because he heard the break in my voice, Hardin comes out of the bedroom with a worried expression. He comes over and stands beside me and tries to pull me back from my mother, just like last time.

"Oh, great! And here's the man of the hour," my mother mocks, and gestures wildly at him. "His father is not the chancellor." She half-laughs.

My face is red and soaked with tears, but I couldn't care less. "Yes, he is. Shocked? If you weren't so busy being a judgmental bitch, you could have *talked to him* and found that out. You know what? You don't even deserve to know him. He has been there for me in ways you never were, and there is nothing—and I mean *nothing*—you can do to keep me away from him!"

"You do not speak to me that way!" she screams and steps closer. "You think just because you got yourself a fancy little apartment and put some cyeliner on that you are suddenly a woman? Honey, I hate to break it to you, but you look like a whore, living with someone at eighteen!"

Hardin's eyes narrow at her in warning, but she ignores him.

"You better end this before you lose your virtue, Tessa. Just take a look in the mirror, then look at him! You two look ridiculous together; you had Noah, who was great for you, and you threw him out for . . . this!" She gestures to Hardin.

"Noah has nothing to do with this," I say.

Hardin's jaw clenches and I silently beg him not to say anything.

"Noah loves you, and I know you love him. Now stop this rebellious charade and come with me. I will get you back into your dorm, and Noah will certainly forgive you." She reaches a hand out authoritatively, as if I'll take it and stroll out of here with her.

I grab the bottom of my shirt with my fists. "You are so insane. Honestly, Mother, listen to yourself! I don't want to come with you. I live here with Hardin and I love him. *Not* Noah. I care for Noah, but it was only your influence that made me think I loved him because I felt like I should. I am sorry, but I love Hardin and he loves me."

"Tessa! He doesn't love you—he is only going to stay around until he gets into your pants. Open your eyes, little girl!"

Something about the way she just called me "little girl" sends me over the edge.

"He has already gotten into my pants, and guess what! He's still around!" I shout. Hardin and my mother share the same shocked expression, but my mother's turns to disgust while Hardin's turns to a sympathetic frown.

"I'll tell you one thing, Theresa. When he breaks your heart and you have nowhere to go . . . you better not come to me."

"Oh, trust me, I wouldn't. This is why you'll always be alone. You have no control over me anymore—I am an adult. Just because you couldn't control my father doesn't give you the right to try to control me!" As soon as the words leave my mouth I regret them. I know bringing my father into this is low, too low. Before I can apologize, I feel her hand connect with my cheek. The shock is more painful than the assault.

Hardin steps between us and puts his hand on her shoulder. My face stings and I bite my lip to keep from crying harder.

"If you don't get the *fuck* out of our apartment, I will call the police," he warns her. The calm tone of his voice sends chills down my spine, and I notice my mother shiver, his tone clearly unnerving her, too.

"You wouldn't."

"You just put your hands on her, right in front of me, and you think I wouldn't call the police on you? If you weren't her mum, I would do much worse than that. Now you have five seconds to get out," he says, and I stare at my mother with wide eyes and bring my hand to my burning skin.

I don't like the way he threatened her, but I want her to leave. After a challenging staring match between the two of them, Hardin growls, "Two seconds."

She huffs and heads toward the door, the loud clamor of her heels echoing off the concrete floor.

"I hope you're happy with your decision, Theresa," she says and slams the door.

Hardin's arms wrap around me in the most comforting and reassuring embrace, and it's exactly what I need right now.

"I'm so sorry, baby," he says into my hair.

"I'm sorry that she said those terrible things about you." My need to defend him is stronger than any concern for myself or my mother.

"Shh. Don't worry about me. People say shit about me all the time," he reminds me.

"That doesn't make it okay."

"Tessa, please don't worry about me right now. What do you need? Can I do anything for you?" he asks.

"Maybe some ice?" I choke.

"Sure, baby." He kisses my forehead and walks over to the fridge.

I knew her coming here wouldn't end well, but I hadn't expected it to be as bad as it was. On one hand I am beyond proud of myself for standing up to her, but at the same time I feel terribly guilty for what I said about my father. I know it wasn't her fault that he left, and it's never been lost on me that she's been terribly lonely for the last eight years. She has never even gone on a date since him; she's dedicated all of her time to me, grooming me into the woman she wanted me to be. She wants me to be just like her, and that just isn't going to work for me. I respect her and how hard she worked, but I need to carve my own path and she has to see that she can't make up for her mistakes through me. I make too many of my own mistakes for that to work, anyway. I wish she could be happy for me and see how much I love Hardin. I know his appearance shocks her, but if she would just take the time to try to get to know him, I'm sure she would love him as much I do.

As long as he could contain his rudeness . . . which isn't likely, but I have noticed the small changes in him. Like the way he holds my hand in public and the way he leans down to kiss me nearly every time I pass him in the hallway of our apartment. Maybe I am the only person he will ever let inside, the only one who he reveals secrets to, and the only one he loves, but that's fine with me. To be honest, the selfish part of me kind of enjoys it.

Hardin pulls the chair out next to me and puts the makeshift ice pack against my cheek. The soft kitchen towel wrapped around it feels great against my sensitive skin.

"I can't believe she smacked me," I say slowly. The towel drops onto the tile floor and he reaches down to pick it up.

"Me either. I thought I was going to lose it," he says and looks into my eyes.

"I thought you were too," I admit and give him a weak smile.

I feel like today has been dragging on for too long; it has been the longest and most draining day of my life. I'm exhausted and I just want to be carried away. Preferably into bed with Hardin, to forget about the downfall of my relationship with my mother.

"I love you too much, or trust me, I would have." He smiles back and kisses both of my closed eyelids.

I choose to believe that he wouldn't actually do anything to her, that he is just speaking metaphorically. Somehow I know that even through all his rage he wouldn't do something terrible, and that makes me love him more. I have come to learn that when it comes to me, Hardin is more bark than bite.

"I really want to go to bed," I tell him and he nods.

"Of course."

I pull the blanket back before lying on my side of the bed. "Do you think she will always be this way?" I ask Hardin.

He shrugs, tossing a spare pillow onto the floor. "I would say no, that people change and mature. But I don't want to get your hopes up."

I lie down on my stomach, burying my face in my pillow.

"Hey," Hardin says softly against my neck, trailing a finger down the curve of my back. I roll over, sighing as I take in the concern in his eyes.

"I'm fine," I lie. I need a distraction. I lift my hand to his face, brushing my thumb over the curve of his full lips. I tilt the metal ring to the side and he smiles.

"Having fun staring at me like I'm some science experiment?" he teases.

I nod, wiggling the metal between my fingers and using my other hand to touch the ring in his brow.

"Good to know." He rolls his eyes and takes my thumb between his teeth before I can pull away. I jerk back, hitting my hand against the headboard.

I move to swat at him, the way I often do, and he grabs my sore hand between both of his and brings it to his mouth. I pout playfully until his tongue swirls around the tip of my index finger in the most provocative way. He continues this across each fingertip until I'm a panting, needy mess—*How does he do this?* Such odd acts of affection from him affect me so intensely.

"Feel good?" he asks, dropping my hand onto my lap. I nod again, at a loss for words. "Want more?" He swipes his tongue across his lips, wetting them. I nod again.

"Words, baby," he insists.

"Yes. More, please." My brain clearly doesn't work. I lean into him, needing his touch, needing him to continue the distraction.

He shifts on the bed, tugging at the strings of my pajama pants with one hand and pushing his hair back from his forehead with the other. My panties are pulled down and left at my ankles as my pants hit the floor. He leans in, settling between my spread thighs.

"Did you know that the clitoris on the female body was made strictly for pleasure? It has no purpose beyond that," he informs me, pressing his thumb against the bud. I groan, pushing my head into the pillow. "It's true; I read it somewhere."

"*Playboy*?" I tease, struggling to form a thought, let alone words.

He seems to find that amusing and he smirks while lowering his head. The moment his tongue finds my sex, I grip at the sheets and he works quickly, combining his fingers with his perfect mouth. I push my hands into his hair, silently thanking whoever it was who discovered this knowledge as Hardin brings me to orgasm, twice.

Hardin holds me tight all night long and whispers how much he loves me. As I start to drift off, I think about the day we just had: my relationship with my mother is damaged, possibly beyond repair, and Hardin shared more information about his childhood with me.

My dreams are clouded by a scared curly haired boy crying out for his mother.

THE NEXT MORNING I am pleased to see that my mother's assault has not left any visible marks. My chest still hurts from the collapse of our already crumbling relationship, but I refuse to dwell on that today.

I take a shower and curl my hair, pinning it up so it isn't in my way as I apply my makeup and pull Hardin's shirt from yesterday over my head. I put little kisses all over Hardin's shoulders and ears to wake him up, and when my stomach grumbles I pad into the kitchen to make us some breakfast. I want to start the day in the best way I can so we can both remain happy and calm before the wedding. By the time I finish my self-imposed kitchen therapy, I am pretty proud of the meal I have prepared. The counter is filled with bacon, eggs, toast, pancakes, and even hash browns. I made way too much food for the two of us, but Hardin usually eats an enormous amount anyway, so there shouldn't be too much left.

I feel strong arms wrap around my waist. "Whoa . . . what is all this?" he asks in a raspy, sleep-filled voice. "This is exactly why I wanted to live together," he says into my neck.

"Why? So I could make you breakfast?" I laugh.

"No . . . well, yes. That and waking up to seeing you half dressed in the kitchen." He nips at my neck. He attempts to lift up the hem of the T-shirt and squeeze the top of my thighs.

I spin and wave a spatula in his face. "Hands to yourself until after breakfast, Scott."

"Yes, ma'am." He chuckles and grabs a plate, piling it with food.

After breakfast, I force Hardin to take a shower despite his efforts to drag me back to the bed. His dark confession and the fight with my mother seem to be forgotten in the morning light. My breath is lost in my chest when Hardin walks out of the bedroom in his outfit for the wedding. The black dress pants are snug but hang off his hips in the most delicious way, and his tie is hanging around his neck while his white button-down shirt is undone, revealing his gorgeous, toned torso.

"I . . . uhh . . . I actually have no idea how to tie a tie." He shrugs.

My mouth is dry and I can't stop staring at him, so I choke out, "I can help you." Thankfully, Hardin doesn't ask where I learned to tie a tie, since his mood would turn sour quickly at the mention of Noah. "You look so handsome," I tell him when I finish. He shrugs and puts the black jacket on, completing the look.

His cheeks flame and I can't help but laugh at the unexpected emotion. I can tell he feels completely out of his element being dressed this way—and it's adorable.

"Why aren't you dressed?" he asks.

"I was waiting until the last minute, since my dress is all white," I tell him and he mocks me playfully.

Finally, after another check of my makeup and grabbing my shoes, I do put the dress on. It's even shorter than I remember, but Hardin seems to approve. His eyes never leave my chest after catching sight of my strapless bra. He always makes me feel so beautiful and wanted.

"As long as all the men there are my father's age, we shouldn't have a problem." He smirks and zips me up. I roll my eyes and he kisses my bare shoulder before I unclip my hair, letting my long curls fall down my shoulders. The pale fabric of the dress is tight against my body, and I smile at the reflection of Hardin and me in the mirror.

"You are absolutely stunning," he tells me, kissing me again.

We scramble around and make sure we have everything we need for the wedding, including the invitation and a congratulations card I bought. As I put my phone into a small clutch bag, Hardin grabs me by the waist.

"Smile," he says and pulls out his phone.

"I thought you didn't take pictures."

"I told you I would take one, so let's take one." His smile is goofy and youthful and it makes my heart swell.

I smile and lean into Hardin as he snaps our picture. "One more," he instructs and I stick my tongue out at the last moment. He captured it at the right moment, my tongue on his cheek and his eyes wide and full of humor.

"That's my favorite," I tell him.

"There are only two."

"Yeah, but still." I kiss him and he snaps another.

"Accident," he lies, and I hear him take another as I give him a look.

NEAR HIS FATHER'S HOUSE, Hardin stops to get gas so we don't have to on the way home. As he is filling up, a familiar car pulls into the parking lot, with Nate in the front seat. Zed parks his car two pumps over from Hardin's and gets out to go inside.

I gasp when I get a good look at him: his lip is swollen, and both his eyes are black and blue. His cheek has a deep purple bruise, and when he notices Hardin's car a furious scowl takes over his handsome, damaged face. What the hell? He doesn't say anything at all, or even acknowledge Hardin and me. Within seconds, Hardin climbs back into the car and takes my hand. I look down at our intertwined fingers and gasp, my eyes trailing over his busted knuckles.

"You!" I say and he raises his brow. "You beat him up, didn't you? That's who you fought and that's why he just ignored us!"

"Would you calm down?" Hardin barks and rolls up my window before pulling out of the lot.

"Hardin . . ." I look over to where Zed has disappeared inside, then back at Hardin.

"Can we please talk about it after the wedding? I'm already on edge. Please?" he begs and I nod.

"Fine. After the wedding," I agree and gently squeeze the hand of his that did so much damage to my friend.

chapter ninety-three

Clearly trying to change the subject, Hardin asks, "So now that we have our own place, I assume you don't want to stay at my father's house tonight still?"

I force Zed's beaten face to the back of my mind. "You'd assume correctly." I smile. "Unless Karen asks us to; you know I won't say no," I tell him.

I am nervous to see Ken after what Hardin told me last night. I am trying to clear it from my mind, but it's harder to accomplish than I thought.

"Oh, I almost forgot," he says and reaches for the radio.

I look over at him and he holds his finger up to tell me to wait. "I decided to give the Fray another try," he informs me.

"Really? And when did you decide this?" I question.

"Well, after our first date at the stream, but I didn't open the CD until last week," he admits.

"That was not a date," I tease and he chuckles.

"You let me finger you. I would say that's a date."

He grabs my hand as I try to swat him and kisses my palm. I giggle and wrap my fingers around his slender ones. Images of me lying on the wet T-shirt while Hardin gave me my first orgasm flood my thoughts and Hardin smirks.

"That was fun, huh?" he boasts and I laugh.

"Anyway, tell me your evolved opinion on the Fray," I request.

"Well, they are not so bad, actually. There is one song that really sticks with me."

Now I am even more curious. "Really?"

"Yeah . . ." he says and his eyes flicker to the road before he presses the button on his radio. Music floods through the small space and I immediately smile.

"It's called 'Never Say Never,'" Hardin says, as if it's new information to me and not already one of my favorites.

We listen to the lyrics silently and I can't fight the silly grin on my face. I know he is slightly embarrassed by playing this song for me, so I don't discuss it. I simply enjoy this tender moment with Hardin.

The rest of the drive is filled with Hardin flipping through songs on the album, telling me what he thinks of each one. This small but meaningful gesture means more to me than he will ever know. I love these moments when he shows me a new side of himself. This side is one of my new favorites.

When we arrive at his father's house, the street is full of cars. Stepping out, I feel the crisp wind blow through me, and I shiver. The thin jacket I wore over my dress doesn't offer me and my small dress much protection, really. Hardin shrugs out of his jacket and lays it over my shoulders. It's surprisingly warm and smells like him, my favorite scent.

"Well . . . look at you being such a gentleman. Who would have thought?" I tease.

"Don't make me take you back to the car and fuck you," he says, and I make a noise between a gasp and squeak, which he finds very amusing. "Do you think you have room in that . . . purse thing . . . to hold my phone?" he asks.

"It's a clutch, and yes." I smile and hold my hand out. He places the phone in my palm, and as I push it into the small purse, I notice his background is no longer plain gray. The small screen holds the picture of me that he snapped while I was talking to him in the room. My lips are slightly parted and my eyes are full of life. My cheeks have a warm glow; it's strange to see myself that way. This is what he does to me—he makes me come alive.

"I love you," I tell him and close the bag without putting him on the spot about his new background.

Inside, Ken and Karen's large house is full of people, and Hardin grips my hand tightly after retrieving his jacket and putting it back on.

"Let's try to find Landon," I suggest.

Hardin gives me a nod and leads the way. We end up finding his stepbrother in the living room next to the china cabinet that replaced the one Hardin broke the first night I came here. Which seems so long ago. Landon is surrounded by a group of men who all look to be at least sixty, and one of them has his hand on Landon's shoulder. A smile appears on his face when he spots us, and he excuses himself from their conversation. He looks very handsome in a suit similar to Hardin's.

"Whoa, I never thought I'd live to see you in a suit and tie." Landon laughs.

"If you keep talking about it, you won't live much longer," Hardin threatens, but there's humor behind his words as he smiles. I can tell he is warming up to Landon, and that makes me happy. Landon is one of my closest friends, and I really care for him.

"My mother will be thrilled. And Tessa, you look beautiful," he says and pulls me in for a hug. Hardin doesn't let go of my hand while I try to hug Landon back, so I do my best with one arm.

"Who are all these people?" I ask. I know Ken and Karen have been here only a little over a year, so it's astounding that there are at least two hundred people here.

"Most of them are Ken's friends from the university, and the rest are friends and family. I only know about half of them." He laughs. "Would you guys like a drink? Everyone will be going outside in about ten minutes."

"Whose bright idea was it to have an outdoor wedding in December?" Hardin complains.

"My mother's," Landon says. "Besides, the tents are heated, obviously." He looks around at the crowd, then back at Hardin. "You should go let your father know that you are here. He's upstairs. My mother is hiding somewhere with my aunt."

"Um . . . I think I'll just stay down here," Hardin replies.

I caress his hand with my thumb; he gives me an appreciative squeeze, and Landon nods. "Well, I have to go for now, but I will see you after," he says and leaves us with a smile.

"Do you want to go outside now?" I ask Hardin and he nods. "I love you," I tell him.

He smiles, full dimples. "I love you, Tess," he says and plants a kiss on my cheek.

Hardin opens the back door and gives me his jacket once again. Stepping out, I see that the backyard has been wonderfully transformed. Two large tents take up most of the yard, and hanging from the trees and the patio are hundreds of small glowing lanterns. Even in the daylight, they are beautiful, and it's all quite a sight to behold.

"I think it's this one," Hardin says and gestures to the smaller of the two tents.

We squeeze through the part in the flaps, and indeed he is right. Rows of wooden chairs face a simple altar, with beautiful white flowers hung on some walls and all the guests in black-and-white attire. About half the seats are full, so we take a seat in the second-to-last row, because I know Hardin doesn't want to be up close.

"I never thought I would be attending my father's wedding," he says to me.

"I know. I am incredibly proud of you for coming. It will mean so much to them. It maybe sounds like you think it will be good for you, too." I lean my head on his shoulder, and he snakes his arm around me.

We begin to talk about the beautiful way this tent has been decorated, in all black and white. Simple and elegant. Its simplicity makes me feel even more like I've been invited to an intimate, personal moment in his family, despite the large number of guests.

"I guess the reception is in the other tent?" he says and twirls a piece of my hair between his thumb and index finger.

"I think so. I bet it's even more beautiful than—"

"Hardin? Is that you?" a woman's voice says. We both turn our heads to the left. An elderly woman in a black-and-white floral dress and flat shoes stares at us with wide eyes. "Oh my heavens, it *is* you!" she gasps. Her gray hair is swept back into a simple bun, and her minimal makeup makes her look healthy, radiant.

For his part, all the color has drained from Hardin's face as he stands up and greets her. "Gammy."

She pulls him in for a tight hug. "I can't believe you're here. I haven't seen you in years. Look at you, you handsome boy. Well, *man*, now. I can't believe how tall you are! And what are these?" She scowls and points at his facial piercings.

He flushes and gives out an uncomfortable laugh. "How have you been?" he asks her and shifts back and forth on the balls of his feet.

"I am good, dear—I've missed you so much," she says and pats the corners of her eyes. After a beat, she dramatically looks around him at me and asks with notable interest, "And who is this lovely young woman?"

"Oh . . . sorry. This is Tess . . . Tessa. My . . . girlfriend," he answers. "Tessa, this is my gammy . . . my grandma."

I smile and stand up. The thought of meeting Hardin's grandparents had never crossed my mind. I had assumed they were dead, like mine. He has never brought them up, but that isn't surprising. I suppose I haven't, either.

"It's so nice to meet you," I say to her and reach to shake her hand, but she has other plans and pulls me in for a hug and kisses my cheek.

"The pleasure is all mine. What a beautiful girl you are!" she says in an accent even thicker than Hardin's. "My name is Adele, but you will call me Gammy."

"Thank you," I say, blushing.

She claps her hands in glee. "I just can't believe you are here. Have you seen your father recently? Does he know you are here?" she asks, looking back at Hardin.

Hardin bashfully puts his hands into his pockets. "Yeah, he knows. I have sort of been coming here lately."

"Well, that is so great to hear. I had no idea," she says and I can tell she is on the brink of tears again.

"Okay, everyone, if you could all take a seat, the ceremony will begin shortly," a man with a microphone says from the raised platform up front.

Gammy pulls Hardin by the arm before he can protest. "Come sit with the family—you two shouldn't be all the way back here." He looks back at me and gives me a look that says "help me," but I just smile and follow them to the front. We take a seat next to someone who looks a lot like Karen and I assume is her sister. Hardin takes my hand in his, and his grandmother looks down and smiles at our affection before putting her hand on his other one. He stiffens a little but doesn't remove it.

Ken walks to his place, and the look on his face when he spots his son sitting in the front row is indescribable: heartwarming and heartbreaking at the same time. Hardin even gives him a small smile, which Ken happily returns. Landon stands next to Ken on the stage, but Hardin doesn't seem to mind; he would never have agreed to be up there anyway.

When Karen enters, a collective sigh sounds through the room. She looks so beautiful as she walks down the aisle. Her face when she spots her groom makes me lean into Hardin's shoulder. Happiness is radiating off of her, and her smile lights up the tent. Her dress is brushing against the floor, and her cheeks are glowing, adding to the ambience.

The ceremony is beautiful and I find myself with wet cheeks when Ken's voice cracks into a small sob as he recites his vows to his bride. Hardin looks over at me and smiles, removing his hand from mine and wiping my cheeks. Karen makes a beautiful bride and their first kiss as husband and wife earns cheers and applause from the crowd.

"Sap," Hardin teases as I lay my head on his shoulder while the crowd files out.

After a bit, we accompany Hardin's grandma to the other tent, and I was right—it's even more beautiful than the first one. Up near the walls of this tent are tables draped with white cloth and topped with black napkins and centerpieces of black and white flowers. The ceiling is covered in lanterns just like the yard, and they cast a subtle glow throughout the room, reflecting nicely off the glassware and glossy white plates. The middle of the tent is cleared for what appears to be a dance floor with black and white tiles, and waiters are standing at the ready, waiting for everyone to get their seats.

"Now, don't you disappear. I want to see you again tonight," Hardin's grandmother says and leaves us.

"This is the fanciest wedding I have been to," he says and looks at the white cloth draped across the ceiling.

"I haven't been to a wedding since I was a child," I tell him and he smiles.

"I like that," he says and kisses my cheek.

I am not used to his public displays of affection, but I could get used to them quickly.

"Like what?" I ask as he sits down at one of the tables.

"That you haven't been to a wedding with Noah," he says and I laugh to avoid frowning.

"Me, too," I assure him and he smiles.

THE FOOD IS DELICIOUS. I go for the chicken, and Hardin chooses the steak. They set things up in a buffet line to keep it casual, but the food is anything but. I drag a piece of chicken through the creamy sauce and bring the fork to my mouth—but Hardin snatches it from me, smiling as he chews the bite. He coughs a little, trying to master chewing and laughing at once.

"That's what you get for stealing my food," I tease him, popping a new piece into my mouth before he can grab it.

He laughs, leaning into my shoulder, and I catch the woman across from us staring. Her expression isn't amused as she watches Hardin press his lips against my shoulder. I stare back at her equally harshly and she looks away.

"Do you want me to get you another plate?" I ask Hardin, loud enough for the rude woman to hear my offer. She looks over at the man next to her and raises a brow. He doesn't seem to be paying attention to her, which annoys her further. I smile and place my hand over Hardin's. He's as oblivious as the man across the table, and I'm glad.

"Uh, yeah, sure. Thank you."

I lean down to kiss his cheek and make my way back to the line for food.

"Tessa?" a familiar voice calls. I look over to see Mr. Vance and Trevor standing a few feet away.

"Hello." I smile.

"You look breathtaking," Trevor says, and I thank him quietly.

"How are you enjoying your weekend?" Mr. Vance asks me.

"It's great. I've been enjoying my weeks of late as well," I assure him.

"Oh, sure." He laughs and grabs himself a plate.

"No red meat!" Kimberly says from behind him. He pretends to shoot himself in the temple, and she blows him a kiss. Kimberly and Mr. Vance? Who would have thought? I will have to press her for details on Monday.

"Women," he teases and fills her plate as I do Hardin's.

"I'll see you in a few." He smiles and walks back to his date. She waves at me and gets the young boy on her lap to do the same. I wave back, wondering suddenly if she has a child.

Trevor leans in and answers my thoughts. "It's his son."

"Oh," I say and look away from Kimberly.

Trevor keeps his eyes on Mr. Vance. "His wife passed away five years ago, right after he was born. He hasn't dated anyone until Kim, and they've only been seeing each other for a few months, but he is head over heels for her." He turns to me and smiles.

"Well, now I know who to hit up for all the office gossip," I joke and we both laugh.

"Babe . . ." Hardin says and wraps his arm around my waist, clearly in an attempt to claim his territory.

"Nice to see you. Hardin, is it?" Trevor asks.

"Yeah," Hardin answers shortly. "We better get back to our seats; Landon is looking for you." He pulls me closer to him, silently dismissing Trevor.

"I'll see you later, Trevor!" I smile politely and hand Hardin his plate of food as we walk back to the table.

chapter ninety-four

W here's Landon?" I ask Hardin when we take our seats.
He takes a bite of a croissant. "I don't know."

"Um, you said he was looking for me?"

"He was, but I don't know where he is now."

"Hardin, you shouldn't talk with your mouth full." His grand-mother appears behind him.

I notice him take a deep breath before he turns to her. "Sorry," he mumbles.

"I wanted to see you before I go—God knows when I will see you again. Can you save a dance for your gammy?" she asks oh so adorably, but he shakes his head. "Why not?" she asks him with a smile.

I realize now that it wasn't just shock that had Hardin rattled before. There's a tension between them that I can't quite put my finger on.

"I am on my way to get Tessa a drink," he lies and leaves the table.

His grandmother laughs uncomfortably. "Well, he's some-thing, isn't he?" I am not sure what to say; my first instinct is to defend him, but it seems she is joking.

She turns to me sharply. "Is he still drinking?"

"What? N-no," I stutter, completely caught off guard. "Well, he only drinks every once in a while," I clarify as I see him walk-ing toward us with two flutes full of pink liquid.

He hands me one and I smile and lift it to my lips. It smells sweet when I tip the glass back to take a drink, and the bubbles spritz lightly, tickling my nose. It tastes just as sweet as it smells.

"Champagne," he informs me and I thank him.

"Tessa!" Karen practically shouts right before she wraps her arms around me. She has changed out of her wedding dress and into a white knee-length wrap dress, not that she looks any less stunning. "I am so thrilled that you two came! How was it?" she asks. Karen is the only person who would ask how her own wedding was; she is too kind.

"It was so lovely; it was beautiful." I smile.

Hardin puts his hand on the small of my back and I lean into him. I can sense how uncomfortable he is between his grandmother and Karen, and now Ken is making his way over to us.

"Thank you for coming," Ken says to Hardin and holds out his hand to shake.

Hardin obliges and quickly shakes his father's hand. I notice Ken start to lift his arm up to hug Hardin, but he lowers it before following through. Still, Ken's face is full of excitement and joy.

"Tessa, you look beautiful, dear." He hugs me and then eagerly asks, "Are you enjoying yourselves?"

I can't help but feel a little awkward around him now that I have a deeper insight into who he was all those years ago. "Yeah. It's a nice setup you've got out here." Hardin does his best to praise his father. I put my hand on his back and rub small circles to ease him.

Hardin's grandmother coughs and looks at his father. "I didn't know that you two were speaking."

Ken rubs the back of his neck, a habit that I suspect Hardin got from him.

"Yeah. Let's talk about this another time, Mother," Ken says and she nods in agreement.

I take another drink out of my glass and try not to dwell on the fact that I am drinking underage in front of adults. In front of the chancellor of my school.

A waiter in a black vest walks by with a tray of champagne, and when Ken grabs a flute I cringe. But he hands the glass to his new bride and I relax, extremely glad to see that he isn't drinking.

"Want another?" Hardin asks me and I look at Karen.

"Go ahead, it's a wedding," she tells me and I smile.

"Sure," I say and Hardin leaves to get me another glass.

We talk about the wedding and the flowers for a minute, and when Hardin comes back with only one flute, Karen gets concerned and asks him, "You don't like the champagne?"

"Oh yeah, it's good, but I already had a glass and I'm driving," he replies, and Karen looks at him with adoration clear in her brown eyes.

She turns to me. "Do you have time to come by this week? I ordered some seeds for the greenhouse."

"Yes, of course. I am free anytime after four all week," I say.

The pleased yet astonished look on Gammy's face is obvious as she looks back and forth between Karen and me. "So how long have you two been seeing one another?" she asks Hardin and me.

"A few months," Hardin tells her quietly.

Sometimes I forget that no one outside of our—well, *Hardin's*—group of friends knows that we despised each other up until two months ago.

"Oh, so no great-grandchildren for me anytime soon?" She laughs and Hardin's face flushes.

"No, no. We've only just moved in together," Hardin says, and Karen and I both spit champagne back into our glasses at the same time.

"You two moved in together?" Ken asks.

I had not expected Hardin to tell them today. Heck, I hadn't even been sure he would tell them at all, given how he is. I am shocked and a little embarrassed at my reaction, but mostly pleased that he has no problem admitting it.

"Yeah, we moved into Artisan a few days ago," he explains.

"Wow, that's a nice place, and closer to Tessa's internship," Ken remarks.

"Yeah," Hardin says, clearly trying to measure how everyone feels about our bombshell.

"Well, I am very happy for you, son." He places his hand on his son's shoulder and I watch with a neutral expression. "I never imagined you would be this happy and so . . . at peace."

"Thank you," Hardin says and actually smiles.

"Maybe we could come by sometime and see it?" Ken asks, and Karen's eyes lower.

"Ken . . ." she warns, clearly remembering the time Ken pushed Hardin too far, as am I.

"Uh, yeah, I guess you could," Hardin says, surprising us all.

"Really?" Ken asks and Hardin nods. "Okay, just let us know when is good for the two of you." His eyes are slightly glossy.

Music begins to play through the tent and Karen grabs Ken's arm. "That's our cue—thank you both so much for coming," she says and leans in to kiss my cheek.

"You have done so much for this family, you have no idea," she whispers in my ear before pulling away, tears shining in her eyes.

"Time for the bride and groom's first dance!" a voice announces through the speakers. Hardin's grandmother walks away as well, following the crowd to watch.

"You just made their day," I tell Hardin and kiss his cheek.

"Let's go upstairs," he says.

"What?" My head is a little fuzzy from the two glasses of champagne I just finished.

"Upstairs," he repeats, sending that familiar electricity through me.

"Now?" I laugh.

"Now."

"But all these people . . ."

He doesn't respond; instead he takes my hand and leads me through the crowd and out of the tent. When we get inside the house, he grabs me another glass of champagne, and I try not to let it spill as I rush up the stairs to keep up with him.

"Is something wrong?" I ask him as he shuts the bedroom door and locks it.

"I need you," he says darkly and pulls his jacket off.

"Are you okay, though?" I ask, my heart already beating out of my chest.

"Yes, I just need a distraction," he groans and steps toward me, grabbing the glass and setting it on the dresser. He takes another step, encircling my wrists in his hands and then lifting them over my head.

I will gladly be his distraction from the overload of everything downstairs—seeing his grandmother for the first time in years, watching his father get remarried, agreeing to let them come to our apartment. That is a lot for Hardin in such a short period of time.

Instead of asking him any questions or pushing him further, I grab him by the collar of his shirt and push my hips out to meet his. He's already hard. Groaning, he lets go of my wrists, allowing me to comb my fingers through his hair. When his mouth moves over mine, his tongue is hot and sweet with the lingering taste of champagne. Within seconds he is reaching into his pocket and pulling out a foil packet.

"We've got to get you on birth control so I can stop using these. I want to really be able to feel you." His voice is husky and he pulls my lower lip between his, sucking lightly and seductively, making my body crave him even more.

I hear him unzip and he hisses as my hands reach down and

push his pants and boxers down to his knees. Hardin's hands go up the front of my dress and he hooks his long fingers around my panties and pulls them down. I clumsily step out of them, using his arms to steady myself. He chuckles lightly before connecting his lips with my neck. His hands squeeze my hips before he lifts me up and I whimper a little, wrapping my legs around his waist.

My hands grip the top of my dress in an attempt to pull it down, but he pleads into my neck, "No, leave it on. This dress is so incredibly sexy . . . it's so sexy, yet white and virginal looking . . . and fuck . . . it's so hot. You're so beautiful." He lifts me up farther, then lowers me onto him. My back is against the smooth door and Hardin begins guiding me up and down. There is a fever and a desperation in him that I have not seen at this level before, and I feel as though I am ice and he is fire. We are so completely different, yet the same.

"Is . . . this . . . okay?" he stutters, his arms wrapped around my back to keep me steady.

"Yes," I moan. The feeling of him taking me this way, against the door, my legs around his waist, is very intense but heavenly all the same.

"Kiss me," he begs.

I slide my tongue across his lips before his mouth parts, allowing me access. Tugging at his hair, I do my best to kiss him as he moves in and out of me faster and faster. Our bodies are moving vigorously, but our kiss remains slow and intimate.

"I can't get enough of you, Tess, I . . . fuck. I love you," he says into my mouth and I gasp and moan, that feeling growing in the pit of my stomach.

A few grunts escape his lips and I cry out, both of us reaching our climaxes. "Let go, baby," he instructs, and I do just that. He leaves his lips pressed against mine, swallowing my moans as he tenses and spills into the condom.

With a few heavy breaths his head falls onto my chest and

he continues to hold me in place for a few seconds before lifting me and then lowering me to stand on my own feet.

I tilt my head back against the door and catch my breath as he neatly puts the condom back into the wrapper and puts it into his pocket before pulling his pants back up.

"Remind me to throw that away as soon as we get downstairs." He laughs and I giggle. "Thank you," he says and kisses my cheek. "Not for what we just did, but for everything."

"You never need to thank me, Hardin. You do as much for me as I do for you." I look into his bright green eyes. "Actually, more."

"No way." He shakes his head gently and takes my hand. "Let's go back down before someone comes looking for us."

"How do I look?" I ask, running my fingers through my hair and wiping under my eyes.

"Freshly fucked," he teases and I roll my eyes. "You look beautiful."

"So do you," I tell him.

ALMOST EVERYONE IN THE TENT is dancing by the time we return, and it seems that our absence has gone unnoticed. As we take our seats another song begins. I recognize it: "Never Let Me Go," by Florence and the Machine.

"Do you want to dance?" I ask Hardin, even though I am sure I already know his answer.

"No, I don't dance," he says and looks over at me. "Unless . . . you want to?" he adds.

I am surprised by his offer and thrilled that he would dance with me. He holds his hand out for mine, but really I'm the one who leads us onto the checkered dance floor, moving quickly in case he changes his mind. We stay in the back, a good distance from the crowd.

"I don't have a clue what to do." He laughs.

"I'll show you," I assure him and place his hands on my hips. He steps on my feet a few times, but he catches on quickly. Never in a million years would I have even entertained the thought that Hardin would be dancing at his father's wedding.

"Sort of a demented song to play at a wedding, isn't it?" He laughs into my ear.

"Not really; it's sort of perfect," I say and lean my head on his chest.

I am aware that we aren't actually dancing as much as we are just swaying back and forth holding each other, but that's fine with me. We stay that way for the next two songs, which end up being two of my favorites. "You Found Me" by the Fray makes Hardin laugh as he holds me close to him. The next, a pop song by a boy band, plays, making me smile and him roll his eyes. During both, Hardin gives me some background on his grand-mother. She still lives in England, but he hasn't seen or spoken to her since she phoned him on his twelfth birthday. She took his father's side during the divorce and defended his drinking, essen-tially blaming Hardin's mother for everything, which was enough for Hardin to not want to speak to her again. He seems very com-fortable sharing this information with me, so I stay quiet, only nodding and humming in acknowledgment of his remarks.

Hardin makes a few jokes about how annoying and whiny all the songs being played are, and I laugh at him.

"You want to go back upstairs?" he jokes and lowers his hand on my back.

"Maybe."

"I'll have to give you champagne more often." I move his hands back up to my waist and he pouts, which makes me laugh even more. "I'm actually having a pretty decent time," he admits.

"Me, too. Thank you for coming with me."

"I wouldn't want to be anywhere else."

I know he doesn't mean the wedding but just with me in general. The thought sends warmth through me.

"May I cut in?" Ken asks as the next song begins.

Hardin frowns and looks at me, then back to his father. "Yeah, but only one song," he grumbles.

Ken laughs and repeats his son's words: "One song." Hardin lets go of me, and Ken's hand goes around my back. I swallow down the uneasy feelings I hold for him. He keeps the conversation light as we dance and my ill feelings are further muted as we laugh at an obviously drunk couple swaying back and forth next to us.

"Would you look at that?" Ken then says, his voice full of wonder.

I turn to see what he's referring to and hear my own small gasp as I spot Hardin awkwardly swaying back and forth with Karen. She laughs as he steps on her white shoes, and he smiles an embarrassed smile. Tonight has been better than I could have dreamed.

After the song ends, Hardin quickly finds his way back to me, and Karen follows. We tell the happy bride and groom that we're going to go, and we all exchange hugs once again, Hardin's being *maybe* incrementally less stiff than earlier. Someone calls Ken's name and he nods at them. He and Karen say their final goodbyes and thank us once again for coming to the wedding before disappearing into the crowd.

"Oh, my feet are killing me," I say. This is the longest I have worn heels in my entire life and I am going to need a week to recover.

"Would you like me to carry you?" he says in a mocking, baby-like voice.

"No." I giggle.

As we are leaving the tent, Trevor walks by with Mr. Vance

and Kimberly. Her smile is bright and she winks at me after look-ing Hardin up and down. I try to stifle my laugh and end up coughing.

"Did you save me a dance?" Mr. Vance teases Hardin.

"No, absolutely not." Hardin laughs back at him.

"You're leaving so soon?" Trevor looks at me.

"We have been here for a while, actually," Hardin answers for me and pulls me away from them. "Nice to see you, Vance," he calls over his shoulder as we walk out of the tent.

"That was rude." I scold him when we get to his car.

"He was flirting with you. I am entitled to be as rude as I please."

"Trevor wasn't flirting; he was just being nice."

Hardin rolls his eyes. "He wants you, I can tell. Don't be so naïve."

"Just be nice to him, please. I work with him and I don't want any problems," I say calmly. Tonight has been too good a night to ruin over his jealousy.

Hardin smirks evilly. "I could always just have Vance fire him."

I can't help but laugh at his cocky response. "You're insane," I snort.

"Only when it comes to you," he says and pulls onto the street.

chapter ninety-five

I love coming home!" I proclaim with a squeal as we walk into the apartment, only to then realize it's freezing. "Except when you turn the heat off." I shiver and he chuckles.

"I still haven't figured that thing out yet; it's too high-tech."

As Hardin tries to figure out the thermostat, I grab a blanket off the bed and two from the closet and drop them in a heap on the couch, then go back to the bedroom. "Hardin!" I call.

"Coming!"

"Can you unzip me?" I ask as he comes in, looking frustrated from his handyman moment.

I flinch from the coolness of his fingertips against my bare skin. He apologizes, then hastily unzips the material, and it drops to the floor. I take my shoes off and find that the concrete floor is freezing as well. Hurrying to the dresser, I grab the warmest pajamas I can find.

"Here, let me give you something," he says and walks to the closet, pulling out a gray hooded sweatshirt.

"Thanks." I smile. I don't know what it is about being in Hardin's clothes that I love so much; it's almost as if wearing them brings us closer. I never did this with Noah, except once when I borrowed a sweatshirt while camping with his family.

Hardin seems to like when I wear his clothes, too. He watches me slip the sweatshirt over my head with lustful eyes. I notice him struggling to get the tie off and I pad over to help him. He watches me silently as I pull the thin fabric from around his neck and set it aside before grabbing a pair of thick, fuzzy, purple socks that my mother got me for Christmas last year.

It dawns on me that Christmas is only three weeks away, and I start to wonder if my mother will still want me to come home. I haven't been home since I left for college.

"What are those?" Hardin chuckles and flicks the balls of fur at the top of my ankle.

"Socks. Warm socks, to be exact." I stick my tongue out.

"Nice," he teases, then changes into sweatpants and a sweat-shirt.

By the time we get back to the living room, the apartment has warmed up somewhat. Hardin turns the television on and lies on the couch, pulling me onto his chest and encasing us in the mound of blankets.

"I was wondering what you were doing for Christmas," I say nervously. I don't know why I feel shy asking him about this when we already live together.

"Oh well, I was going to wait until next week to bring it up, with everything being so chaotic over the last week, but since you did . . ." He smiles, his face holding the same nervousness that I feel. "I'm going to go home for the holiday, and I would like it if you would come with me."

"Home?" I squeak.

"To England . . . to my mother's house." He looks a little sheepish as he hedges, "I get it if you don't want to. I know it's a lot to ask, and you've already moved in with me."

"It's not that I don't want to, it's just . . . I don't know . . ." The idea of going to another country with Hardin is thrilling, but terri-fying. I have never even left Washington.

"You don't have to answer me tonight, but let me know soon, okay? I will be leaving on the twentieth," he explains.

"That's the day after my birthday," I tell him.

He moves suddenly and lifts my head up. "Your birthday? Why didn't you tell me it was so soon?"

I shrug a little. "I don't know. I haven't really thought about it, I guess. Birthdays aren't really a big deal to me. My mother used to go all-out on my birthdays, making each one special, but not in the last few years."

"Well, what would you like to do for your birthday?"

"Nothing. Maybe we can go to dinner?" I don't want to make a big deal out of it.

"Dinner . . . I don't know," he teases. "A bit extravagant, isn't it?"

I giggle and he kisses my forehead. I force him to watch the new episode of *Pretty Little Liars* and we end up falling asleep on the couch pretty quickly.

I wake up sweating in the middle of the night. Lifting myself off Hardin, I peel off the sweatshirt and go over to turn the heat down when a small blue light blinking on Hardin's phone piques my curiosity. I pick the phone up off the counter and swipe my finger across. Three new messages.

Put the phone down, Tessa.

I have no reason to go through his phone; that's insane. I set it down and walk back toward the couch, only to be stopped by the vibration of another text message arriving.

Just one. I will only glance at one. That's not so crazy, right? I know it's insane to be looking through Hardin's messages, but I can't seem to stop myself.

Call me back dick, the message reads. Jace's name covers the top of the small screen.

Yup, reading that was a terrible idea. It didn't get me anywhere at all, and now I feel guilty for going through Hardin's phone like a crazy person . . . but why is Jace texting Hardin, anyway?

"Tessa?" Hardin's voice croaks, causing me to jump, and the phone slips out of my grasp. It falls to the floor with a crack.

"What was that? What are you doing?" he asks through the dark room, the only light being cast from the television.

"Your phone went off . . . and I grabbed it," I half-lie and scramble on the floor to pick up the phone. The screen now has a small crack along the side. "And I cracked the screen," I add.

He groans wearily. "Just come back to bed."

I set the phone down and lie back on the couch with him. But I don't fall asleep for a long while.

THE NEXT MORNING, I wake up to Hardin trying to move out from under me. I shift against the back of the couch to let him get up, and he grabs his phone off the counter before going to the bathroom. I hope he isn't too pissed about me breaking his screen. If I wouldn't have been so nosy, this wouldn't have happened in the first place. I pull myself off the couch and make a pot of coffee.

Hardin's proposal of going to England with him keeps running through my mind. We have already progressed so quickly in our relationship by moving in together at such a young age. Still, I would love to meet his mother and see England with Hardin.

"Deep in thought?" Hardin's voice interrupts me as he comes into the kitchen.

"No . . . well, sort of." I laugh.

"About?"

"Christmas."

"What about it? You can't figure out what to get me?"

"I think I'm going to call my mother and see if she would have even invited me for Christmas. I feel bad not at least seeing first, you know. She will be alone."

He doesn't look thrilled, but he stays calm. "I understand."

"I'm sorry about your phone."

"It's fine," he says and sits at the kitchen table.

But then I blurt out, "I read a text message from Jace." I don't want to hide things from him, no matter how embarrassing the confessions are.

"You *what*?"

"It vibrated and I looked at it. Why was he texting so late, anyway?"

"What did you read?" he asks, ignoring my question.

"A text from Jace," I repeat.

His jaw clenches. "What did it say?"

"Just to call him back . . ." Why is he getting so worked up? I knew he wouldn't exactly be happy that I looked at his text message, but this is an overreaction.

"That's it?" he snaps, which starts to get me annoyed.

"Yes, Hardin—what else would it have said?"

"Nothing . . ." He takes a slow sip of coffee, like it's all suddenly no big deal. "I just don't like you going through my stuff."

"Okay, well, I won't do it again."

"Good. I have a few things to do today, so can you keep yourself busy for a while?"

"What do you have to do?" I ask and instantly regret it.

"*Jesus*, Tessa," he says loudly. "Why are you always on my case!"

"I'm not always on your case. I just wanted to know what you were doing. We are in a relationship, Hardin—a pretty serious one, at that—so why wouldn't I ask where you're going?"

He pushes his mug away and stands up. "You just don't know when to let shit go, is your problem. I don't have to tell you everything, whether we are living together or not! If I would have known you were going to start shit with me today, I would have left before you even woke up."

"Wow" is all I can say before I storm off to the bedroom.

But he's hot on my heels. "Wow what?"

"I should have known that yesterday was too good to be true."

"Excuse me?" he scoffs.

"We had such a great time; you weren't an asshole, for once, but you wake up today and *bam!* You're back to being a jerk!" I scramble around the room picking up Hardin's dirty clothes.

"You forgot the part where you went through my phone."

"Okay, and I am sorry for doing that, but it's honestly not that big of a deal. If there is something on there that you don't want me to see, then there is a bigger problem here!" I yell and shove everything into the hamper.

He points an angry finger at me. "No, Tessa, you're the problem. You're always making something out of nothing!"

"Why did you fight Zed?" I counter.

"We aren't doing this right now," he says in a cool tone.

"Then *when*, Hardin? Why won't you tell me? How am I supposed to trust you if you are keeping things from me? Does this have to do with Jace?" I ask and his nostrils flare.

He runs his hands over his face and then up through his hair, leaving it sticking straight up. "I don't know why you can never just mind your own damn business," he grumbles and walks off.

Seconds later I hear the front door slam and I wipe the angry tears from my cheeks. Hardin's reaction to me asking about Jace is gnawing at my stomach the entire time I clean the apartment. He overreacted; there is something he isn't telling me, and I don't understand why. I am fairly certain it has nothing to do with me, but it just doesn't make sense why Hardin got *so* worked up. I have known since the moment I met Jace that he was trouble. If Hardin isn't going to give me answers, I will have to go another route. I look out the window and watch as Hardin's car pulls out of the parking lot before grabbing my phone. My new source answers on the first ring.

"Zed? It's Tessa," I say.

"Yeah . . . I know."

"Okay . . . well, I was wondering if I could ask you something?" My voice comes out smaller than I intended it to.

"Um . . . where is Hardin?" he asks, and, given his tone, I suspect he holds a small grudge against me for blowing him off after he was so kind to me.

"He isn't here."

"I don't think this is a good idea—"

"Why did Hardin fight you?" I ask before he finishes.

"I'm sorry, Tessa, I gotta go," he says and the call ends.

What the hell? I hadn't been one hundred percent sure he would tell me, but that wasn't the reaction I was expecting, either. My curiosity is now piqued more than before and my annoyance is as high as ever.

I try to call Hardin again, but of course he doesn't answer. Why would Zed act that way? Like he was almost . . . afraid to tell me? Maybe I was wrong and this does have to do with me? I don't know what's going on, but none of this makes sense. I take a step back and reevaluate the situation. Am *I* overreacting? Hardin's frantic expression when I asked about Jace replays in my head, and I'm sure I'm not misreading this.

I take a shower to try to calm my nerves and settle my mind, but it doesn't work; this feeling in the pit of my stomach pushes me to come up with another option. When I get out of the shower, I blow-dry my hair and get myself dressed while I decide what to do next.

I feel a little like Miss Havisham in *Great Expectations*, plotting and scheming. I had never cared for her character, but suddenly I find myself relating to her. I can now see how love can make you do things that you normally wouldn't, like become obsessive and even a little crazy. Though, in reality, my plan really isn't all that crazy or nearly as dramatic as it seems in my head. All I'm going to do is find Steph and ask her if she knows why Hardin and Zed got into a fight, then see what she knows about Jace. The only thing that makes this plan crazy is that Hardin will lose it when he finds out that I called Zed and went to Steph.

Now that I think about it, Hardin hasn't taken me around any of his friends since we moved in together—making it likely none of them actually know about our new living arrangement.

BY THE TIME I leave the apartment, my thoughts are jumbled and I end up leaving my phone on the counter. It begins to snow as soon as I pull onto the freeway, so it takes me over thirty minutes to get to the dorms. They look the same as I remember—of course they do. It has been only a week since I left them, even though it seems so much longer.

Marching up the hallway, I ignore the rude stare from the bleach blonde who yelled at Hardin for spilling vodka outside her door. That first night that Hardin stayed in my dorm with me seems so distant; time hasn't made sense since I met him. When I knock on my old door, there's no answer. Of course she isn't here; she's never here. She spends the majority of her time at Tristan and Nate's apartment, and I have no idea where that is. Even if I did, would I go there?

I get into my car and try to formulate a new plan while I drive around. This might have been easier if I hadn't forgotten my phone, but just as I'm about to give up on my radical decision to practically stalk my old roommate, I pass Blind Bob's, the biker bar I went to with Steph. Recognizing Nate's car in the lot, I pull in. I take a deep breath before getting out, and when I finally do, the cold air burns my nostrils. The woman at the front smiles at me when I enter, and I'm relieved when I spot Steph's red hair from across the room.

If only I had known what was to come.

chapter ninety-six

Nervousness overtakes me as I walk through the smoky bar. Why did I think this was a good idea? Hardin is going to be furious with me, and Steph may just think I'm insane.

When she sees me, a big smile fills Steph's face and she practically shouts, "Tessa, what the hell are you doing here?" before pulling me into a hug.

"I . . . well, I was looking for you," I say.

"Is everything okay? Or did you just miss me?" She laughs.

"I just missed you." I decide to go with that for now.

"I haven't seen you in ages, Tessa," Nate teases and then hugs me. "Where has Hardin been hiding you?"

Tristan appears behind Steph and wraps his arms around her waist. By the way she leans back against him, I know they have worked through the fight over Molly.

She smiles. "Come sit with us—it's just us for now."

For now? I wonder if she means that Hardin will be here soon? I follow the three of them to a booth, dreading the answer to that question. A question I choose not to ask, and instead order a burger and fries. I haven't eaten all day and it's past three in the afternoon.

"And I'll make sure there is no ketchup," the waitress says with a knowing smile and walks back to the kitchen. Clearly she remembers the scene Hardin made the last time I was here.

I pick at my manicured fingers as I wait for the waitress to bring me my Coke.

"You missed one hell of a party last night, Tessa," Nate says. He lifts his glass and gulps down the remainder of his beer.

"Yeah?" I smile. The most frustrating part of my relationship with Hardin is that I never know what I'm allowed to tell people. If I were in a normal relationship, I would respond with "Oh yeah, we had a great time last night at his father's wedding." But since my relationship is far from normal, I stay quiet.

"Yeah, it was wild. We went out to the docks instead of the frat house." He laughs. "We get away with more at the docks and we don't have to clean up after."

"Oh. Does Jace live at the docks?" I try to keep my tone neutral.

"What? No, the docks are boat docks. He works there during the day, though. He lives close by them."

"Oh . . ." I chew on my straw.

"It was freezing, and Tristan here was plastered and jumped into the cold-ass water." Steph snorts, and Tristan flips her off playfully.

"It wasn't too bad; my body was numb the second I hit the water," he jokes.

My food arrives along with Tristan's wings and a round of beers for the three of them.

"You sure you don't want a beer? She won't card you," Nate tells me.

"Oh, no, I have to drive. Thanks, though."

"So how's your new dorm?" Steph asks and steals a fry from my plate.

"My what?"

"Your new dorm?" she repeats slowly.

"I don't have a new dorm." Did Hardin tell her I moved into another dorm?

"Uh, yeah, you do, because you don't live in mine anymore. All of your stuff was gone and Hardin said you changed dorms, that your mom flipped out on you or something." She takes a big swig from her beer.

I decide that I don't care how pissed Hardin gets at me—I'm not going to lie. I'm infuriated and embarrassed that he is still hiding our relationship. "Hardin and I moved into an apartment," I tell them.

"*What?*" Steph, Nate, and Tristan say at the same time.

"Yes, last week. We moved in together about twenty minutes from campus," I explain. All three of them are looking at me as if I have grown a second head.

"What?" I ask harshly.

"Nothing. It's just . . . wow . . . I don't know. That's just a really huge surprise," Steph says.

"Why?" I snap. I know it isn't fair to direct my anger toward her when it's meant for Hardin, but I can't help it.

She frowns and looks like she's pondering something. "I don't know; I just can't picture Hardin living with someone, that's all. I didn't know you two were that serious. I wish you would have told me."

As I am about to ask her what she means by that, Nate's and Tristan's eyes dart to the door, then back to me. When I turn around, I see Molly, Hardin, and Jace standing in the doorway. Hardin shakes some snow from his hair and wipes his boots on the straw mat. I turn around quickly, my heart beating out of my chest. There are too many things going on at once: Molly is with Hardin, which pisses me off beyond words. Jace is with Hardin, which confuses the hell out of me. And I just told everyone that we moved in together, which they seem unsettled by.

"Tessa." Hardin's voice is angry from behind me.

I look up at him, and his face is twisted in anger. He is trying to control it, I can tell, but it's about to boil over. "I need to talk to you," he says through clenched teeth.

"Right now?" I say, trying to sound casual but hard-edged.

"Yes. Now," he answers and reaches out to grab my arm. I quickly climb out of the booth and follow him to the corner of the small bar. "What the hell are you doing here?" he says quietly, his face inches from mine.

"I came to hang out with Steph." Not exactly a lie, but not the truth, either.

He calls me out. "Bullshit." He is struggling to keep his voice down, but we've already drawn the attention of more than a few patrons. "You need to go," he tells me.

"Excuse me?" I retort, stealing one of his famous lines.

"You need to go home."

"Home where? Back to my new dorm?" I challenge. The color drains from his face. "Yup, I told them. I told them that we live together—how could you not? Do you know how stupid that makes me look? I thought we were past you trying to keep me a secret."

"I wasn't . . ." he lies.

"I am sick of the secrets and deception, Hardin. Every time I think we are doing so great—"

"I'm sorry. I wasn't trying to keep it a secret. I was just waiting." Hardin's thoughts seem jumbled. I can almost see the internal battle being waged behind his green eyes. His eyes frantically scan the room, and his panic worries me.

"I can't keep doing this—you know that, don't you?" I tell him.

"Yeah, I know." He sighs and pulls his lip ring between his teeth and runs his hand through his damp hair. "Can we go home and talk about this?" he asks and I nod.

I follow him back to the booths where everyone is seated. "We are going to go," Hardin announces.

Jace gives a sinister grin. "So soon?"

Hardin's shoulders tense. "Yeah," he answers.

"Back to your *apartment*?" Steph asks, and I shoot a glare at her. *Not now*, I silently scream at her.

"Your *what?*" Molly cackles. I could have gone the rest of my life without seeing her again, really.

"Their apartment; they live together," Steph says in a singsong voice. I know she is only trying to shove it down Molly's throat, and usually I would applaud her for it, but I'm too angry at Hardin to focus on Molly.

"Well, well, well." Molly taps her long crimson nails on the table. "That's very interesting," she says, staring at Hardin.

"Molly . . ." he warns. I swear I see panic flash across his face.

She raises an eyebrow. "You're really taking this whole thing a little far, aren't you?"

"Molly, I swear to God, if you don't shut the fuck up—"

"What thing? What is he taking too far?" I can't help but ask.

"Tessa, go outside," he commands, but I ignore him.

"No, what is he taking too far? *Tell me!*" I yell.

"Wait. You're in on it, aren't you?" She laughs and continues, "I knew it! I told Jace you knew, but he wouldn't believe me. Hardin, you owe Zed some big bucks for this." She throws her head back and stands up.

Hardin's face is completely pale; all the blood seems to be drained from his entire body. My head is swimming and I'm so confused. I briefly glance at Nate, Tristan, and Steph, but they are all focused on Hardin.

"Knew what?" My voice is shaky. Hardin grabs my arm and tries to pull me away, but I jerk out of his grip and move over to stand in front of Molly.

"Don't play stupid with me, I know you know. What did he do? Split the money with you?" she asks.

Hardin reaches for my hand, and his fingers are ice cold. "Tessa . . ." I jerk away and stare at him, my eyes wide.

"Tell me! What is she talking about!" I yell to him. Tears threaten my eyes, and I struggle to keep down all the emotions storming through me.

Hardin astounds me by opening his mouth and then closing it again.

"Oh my God, you really don't know? Oh, this is amazing. Everyone pull up a seat!" she mocks.

"Molly, don't," Steph says.

"You sure you wanna know, princess?" Molly continues, giving me a triumphant smile.

I can literally hear the blood pounding behind my ears, and for a second I wonder if everyone else can, too. "Tell me," I demand.

She tilts her head slightly . . . but then pauses. "No, I think Hardin should tell her." And she starts giggling, sliding her tongue ring between her teeth, making the most horrendous rattling, worse than nails on a chalkboard.

chapter ninety-seven

Everything is happening too fast for me to comprehend. I'm confused, and when I look around the room, I see that I'm surrounded by people who have taunted me no matter hard I tried to fit in with them, and I know that I can't trust a single one of them.

What's going on? Why is Hardin just standing there? What's happening?

"I second that," Jace chimes in and lifts his beer in salute. "Go on, Hardin, tell her."

"I . . . I will tell you outside," Hardin says, his voice low.

I look into his brilliant eyes, which seem wild with desperation and confusion. I don't know what is going on, but I do know I don't want to go anywhere with him.

"No, you tell me here. In front of them so you can't lie." My heart is already aching and I know that I am not prepared for whatever he is getting ready to tell me.

He pauses, fidgeting with his fingers before he speaks. "I'm sorry." He holds his hands out in front of him. "Tessa, you have to remember that this was way before I even knew you." His eyes are begging for mercy.

I don't trust my voice, and I barely open my mouth when I speak. "Tell me."

"That night . . . that second night . . . the second party you came to, when we played Truth or Dare . . . and Nate asked if you were a virgin . . ." He closes his eyes as if to gather his thoughts.

Oh no. If it was possible for my heart to sink even lower, it would have. This isn't happening. *This can't be happening. Not right now. Not to me.*

"Go on . . ." Jace says and leans forward like this is the best thing he's ever seen. Hardin shoots him daggers, and I know that if Hardin weren't in the middle of single-handedly destroying our relationship, he would kill that vile man on the spot.

"You said you were . . . and that gave someone an idea—"

"Gave *who* the idea?" Molly interrupts.

"Me . . . gave me the idea," he admits. His eyes never leave mine. Which doesn't make this any easier. "That . . . it could be fun to make . . . to make a bet." His head falls, and tears pour from my eyes.

"No," I choke and take a step backward.

Confusion rams into my already-jumbled thoughts, disrupting any attempt to make sense of them, to make sense of what I'm hearing. Confusion is quickly replaced by a burning mixture of pain and anger. All of the memories flooding through me pile and piece together . . .

"Stay away from him." "Be careful." "Sometimes you think you know people, but you don't." "But Tessa, I need to tell you something."

All of the small remarks that were made by Molly, Jace, and even Hardin himself play over and over. There was always something in the back of my mind, a feeling that I was missing something. All of the air seems to be sucked out of the small room, and I find myself almost gasping as the reality of all this sets in. There were so many clues; I just was too blinded by Hardin to see them.

Why would he take it this far? To have me live with him?

"You knew?" I turn to Steph. I can't look at Hardin any longer.

"I . . . I was going to tell you so many times, Tess," she says, her eyes brimming with guilty tears.

"I didn't believe it when he claimed he won, even with the condom," Jace snickers, enjoying the show.

"Right? Me, either! The sheets, though. I mean, how can you deny blood on the sheets!" Molly laughs.

The sheets. That's why they were still in his car . . .

I know I should be saying something, anything, but I can't find my voice. Everything is still moving around me; people in the bar are eating and drinking, not noticing the naïve girl ten feet away from them having her heart shattered. How is it possible that time still moves as I stand here watching Tristan bow his head, watching Steph cry, and, most of all, watching Hardin watch me.

"Tessa, I am so sorry." He takes a step toward me, but I can't even move my feet to run away like I need to.

Molly's harpy voice breaks through the air. "You know, there is a sort of drama here that everyone has to appreciate. I mean, remember last time we were all here and Steph gave Tessa that ridiculous makeover, and Hardin and Zed were trying to battle over who took her back to her room?" She laughs, then continues: "Then Hardin showed up to your room, right? With that vodka! You thought he was drunk! Do you remember when I called him when he was there?" For a moment she looks at me like she actually expects I'll answer her. "But really he was supposed to win the bet that night. He was pretty cocky about it, but Zed kept saying you wouldn't give it up that quick. I guess Zed was right, but you still gave it up quicker than I thought you would, so I suppose it's a good thing I didn't bet any money . . ."

Molly's terrible sounds and Hardin's eyes are the only thing in the bar.

I have never felt this way before. This level of humiliation and loss is worse than I could ever have imagined. Hardin has been playing me this entire time; this was all a game to him. All the hugs, the kisses, the smiles, the laughs, the "I love you's," the sex, the plans—and fuck if this doesn't burn like nothing else in the world. He had every move planned, every night, every single detail, and everyone knew except me. Even Steph, who I thought was becoming a friend. I glance at him, allowing myself a moment of weakness during the shock, and I wish I hadn't. He's just standing there—standing there like my entire world isn't crashing around me and he hasn't completely humiliated me in front of everyone.

"You'd be happy to know that you were worth a pretty penny, though, even though Zed tried to bitch out a few times. But with Jace, Logan, and Zed's money, I hope he at least bought you dinner!" Molly says, laughing.

Jace finishes his beer and howls. "I'm only disappointed that I missed the infamous *I Love You!* announcement in front of everyone. I heard that was a killer."

"Shut the fuck up!" Tristan surprises everyone by yelling. If I wasn't numb, he may have surprised me, too. "Fuck you guys. She has already had enough!"

Hardin takes another step. "Baby, please say something."

And with his little "baby" plea, my brain finally connects with my mouth. "Don't you fucking dare call me that! How could you do this to me? You . . . you . . . I can't . . ." I have so many things in my head to say, but they just won't come out. "And I won't say anything, because that's what you want." I sound much more confident than I feel inside. Inside I am burning, and my heart is on the floor, underneath Hardin's boot.

"I know I messed up—" he begins.

"You messed up? You *messed up?*" I scream. "Why? Just tell me why. Why me?"

"Because you were there," he says. And his honesty only breaks me further. "And a challenge. I didn't know you, Tessa. I didn't know that I would fall in love with you."

His mention of love carries with it the opposite feeling than it has the past few weeks, and I can taste the bile in the back of my throat. "You're sick. You're fucking sick!" I scream and rush to the door.

This is too much for me. Hardin's hand wraps around my arm and I jerk away, turning and slapping him. Hard.

The pain in his expression gives me the most painful satisfaction.

"You ruined everything!" I scream. "You took something from me that wasn't yours, Hardin. That was meant for someone who loved me, loved me truthfully. It was his, whoever he is, and you took that—for *money*? I ruined my relationship with my mother for you. I gave up everything! I had someone who loved me, someone who wouldn't hurt me the way you did. You are disgusting."

"I do love you, Tessa. I love you more than anything. I was going to tell you. I tried to get them not to tell you. I never wanted you to find out. That's why I was out all night, getting them to agree not to say anything. I was going to tell you soon, now that we live together, because then it wouldn't matter."

I have no control over the words tumbling from my lips. "Are you . . . you . . . oh my God, Hardin! What the hell is wrong with you? You think going around convincing people to not tell me is okay? The fact that I wouldn't know would make it all okay? You thought that if we lived together, I would let this go? That's why you were so determined for my name to be on the lease! Oh my God. You are *sick*!"

Every small detail that made me think twice since I met Hardin all points to this. It was so obvious. "That's why you went and got my stuff for me from my room, because you were afraid Steph would tell me!"

Everyone in the bar is staring and I feel so small, so broken and small.

"What did you do with the money, Hardin?"

"I—" he begins, then stops.

"Tell me," I demand.

"Your car . . . the paint . . . and the deposit for the apartment. I thought if I . . . I was going to tell you so many times, once I knew it wasn't just a bet anymore. I love you—I loved you the entire time, I swear it," he says.

"You kept the condom to show them, Hardin! You showed them the sheets, the bloody fucking sheets!" I wrap my hands in my hair and tug at it. "Oh my God! I'm such an idiot. While I was reliving every detail of the best night of my life, you were showing your friends the sheets."

"I know . . . I don't have any excuse . . . but you have to forgive me. We can figure this out," he says.

And I laugh. A real laugh. Despite my tears, I find myself laughing; I'm losing my mind. This scene isn't playing out like in the movies. I'm not holding myself together. I'm not handling the news elegantly with a simple gasp or a single tear trailing down my cheek. I am crying, pulling at my own hair, and am barely able to control my emotions and form a full sentence.

"Forgive you?" I laugh madly. "You have ruined my entire life—you know that, don't you? Oh, of course you do. That was your plan the entire time, remember? You promised you would 'ruin me.' So congratulations, Hardin, you have. What should I give you, money? Or should I find another virgin for you?"

He shifts a little, as if to block out my view of the others at the table. "Tessa, please. You know I love you, I know you do. Let's go home, please, and I will tell you everything."

"Home? That isn't my home. It never has been; we both know that." I try for the door again. I am so close.

"What can I do? I'll do anything," he begs. With his eyes still focused on mine, he bends down. I'm confused for a second before I realize he is getting on his knees in front of me.

"You? Nothing. There is nothing you can do for me anymore, Hardin."

If I knew what to say to hurt him as badly as he has hurt me, I would. And I would repeat it a thousand times, just so he would know how it feels to be so completely blindsided and ripped apart.

I take off for the door, taking advantage of Hardin's position on his knees. As soon as I reach the door, I crash into someone. I look up to find Zed, his battered face still recovering from the injuries that Hardin caused.

"What's wrong?" he asks and grabs my elbows. Then his gaze travels behind me to Hardin and realization fills his eyes.

"I'm sorry . . ." he says, but I ignore him. Hardin is coming, and I have to get the hell away from this bar, from him.

The freezing air whips my hair in front of my face as soon as I get outside. I welcome the feeling, hoping it will cool the burning inside me. Snow has blanketed my car and the streets.

Zed's voice calls from behind me, "You can't drive, Tessa." I keep trudging through the snow, across the parking lot.

"Leave me alone! I know you were in on it! You all were!" I scream and dig for my keys.

"Let me take you home—you are in no condition to drive in this storm," he says. As I open my mouth to scream at him, Hardin walks outside.

I look at the person I once thought was the love of my life, who I thought would make every day after we met special, and wild, and free. And then I look at Zed.

"Okay," I say.

The click of Zed's car being unlocked is my cue to get in as fast as I can. The second Hardin realizes that I'm leaving with Zed, he runs toward the car. His face twists in anger, and I hope for Zed's sake he gets into the car before Hardin reaches us.

Zed jumps in and takes off. I look over and watch Hardin fall to his knees for the second time tonight.

"I am so sorry, Tessa. I had no idea it would get that out of hand—" he starts, but I cut him off.

"Don't talk to me."

I can't stand to hear any more. I can't take it. I'm sick to my stomach, and the pain of Hardin's betrayal is cutting at me, making me weaker and weaker by the moment. I'm convinced that if Zed speaks, there will be nothing left of me. I need to know why Hardin did what he did, but I'm honestly terrified what will happen if I hear it, all of it. I haven't felt pain like this before and I'm not sure how to handle it, or if I can at all. Zed nods, and we drive in silence for a few minutes. I think of Hardin, of Molly, of Jace and the rest, and something in me shifts. Something makes me braver. "You know what?" I turn to him. "Do talk to me. Tell me everything. Every single detail."

With worried eyes he searches my face for a moment, and then, realizing he has no choice, says a quiet "Okay" as we turn onto the freeway.

chapter ninety-eight

THE BET

Everything is spiraling. Every second my paranoia is growing, and I don't know how much longer I can keep it all contained. Preventing this mistake—no, *betrayal*—from spilling, pouring over into my life seems impossible. I think I've convinced Molly and Jace to keep their mouths shut and their egos far away from my relationship. I've just spent the last hour playing their games, lying and strictly not going anywhere near the truth.

"I just don't get the obsession with her. She's not that pretty. I've said it a million times, but not only is she not that cute, she's also pretentious as hell."

Molly won't shut up about Tessa. She hasn't stopped talking about her since she showed up tonight. And now here she sits, her feet dangling off the edge of the dock.

"Look at you using big words." Jace smiles at Molly. "I wouldn't go that far, but she doesn't fit in around here—that's pretty obvious." He looks at me, then away quickly.

He throws something into the water. A bottle. It floats, and I immediately think about what Tessa would say about littering.

Molly's phone keeps vibrating in her hand, and each time she reads whatever's on her screen, I get more and more impatient.

"Enough about her." I look over at Jace, who's wearing the vest of his work uniform. "Are you working today?"

He shakes his head, then looks at Molly. "Nah. I was going to pick up some hours this afternoon, but I'm going to clock out. You guys hungry?"

Molly jumps up from the wooden dock. "Always! Let's go to Blind Bob's. Steph is there."

I consider declining and taking my ass back home to Tessa, where I belong, but something keeps me from using common sense, and before I know it, the three of us are in my car, heading to Blind Bob's. Maybe I'll tell everyone at once, the whole group—killing two birds with one stone and all that—and see what I have to do to keep them from ruining my entire life.

I fucking hate how much power they have over me. Over Tessa. Over our life together. Fuck. I should tell them before we go to London, if Tessa agrees to go with me. I'm sure she will, because she won't be able to say no to visiting the old stomping grounds of her literary heroes.

"Whose car is that?" Molly points to Tessa's parked car, and my stomach drops. I stormed off today, being a complete dick, and now Tessa is here, with my friends. This could go so terribly, so fucking quickly. I won't let it.

Molly says something to Jace that I don't catch, and stupidly, I ignore them, focusing on keeping my feet from running into Bob's.

When I step inside, the two of them are on my heels. I shake the snow from my hair and approach Tessa.

I have to get her out of here—and fast.

"Tessa, I need to talk to you."

"Right now?"

"Yes. Now." I grab ahold of her arm. She pulls away a little.

"What the hell are you doing here?" I ask in a low voice, so only she can hear me. I'm trying to control my anger. I know that this isn't her fault, but being rational isn't exactly my strong suit.

"I came to hang out with Steph."

I can tell she's lying by the nervous way she pulls her bottom lip between her teeth.

"Bullshit." I look over toward the group, and Molly is smiling while staring at Tessa and me. Fuck. "You need to go," I tell Tessa, hoping she'll listen to me.

"Excuse me?" Of course, she won't leave.

"You need to go home."

"Home where? Back to my new dorm?" she says, pressing me. My blood runs cold. They've been talking before I got here, clearly.

This can't happen. Not here, not now.

"Yup, I told them. I told them that we live together—how could you not? Do you know how stupid that makes me look? I thought we were past you trying to keep me a secret."

My chest burns. I swallow my anger down.

I try to lie, to keep this from exploding in this shitty bar. "I wasn't . . ."

"I am sick of the secrets and deception, Hardin. Every time I think we're doing so great—"

I can't find any words. Not a single one that makes sense or sets this right. Nothing. "I'm sorry. I wasn't trying to keep it a secret. I was just waiting."

I don't even comprehend the frantic words coming from my lips. I scan the room, trying to gather my thoughts at the same time. My mind is bouncing, creating the worst possible scenario, and all I know is that I need to get Tessa out of here.

"I can't keep doing this—you know that, don't you?"

"Yeah, I know." God, do I know. I don't want to keep doing this either. I haven't for so long. I just don't know how the hell to fix it. "Can we go home and talk about this?"

Tessa nods, and I gesture to the booth where my supposed

friends are sitting. I walk toward them. "We're going to go," I tell them.

Jace smiles and lights me on fire. I know that look. "So soon?" he says, picking at the tearing scab I've been trying to keep from bleeding out.

"Yeah." I look at Tessa. We need to go, I try to tell her with my eyes.

"Back to your *apartment*?" Steph asks Tessa.

Tessa's eyes go wide, and she looks at me.

"Your *what*?" Molly gapes.

"Their apartment—they live together," Steph says, pounding the words into Molly. Jace's eyebrows pull together, and I watch the two of them take it in.

"Well, well, well." Molly taps her nails on the table, her eyes burning into me. "That's very interesting." Her lip curls up, and I run my hand through my hair, ripping at the roots, panicking.

This is exactly what Molly wants: to have an opening to rip into the little bubble I've tried to keep Tess in.

"Molly . . ."

She lifts a brow. Still looking only at me. "You're really taking this whole thing a little far, aren't you?"

I don't know what I'm saying, but my mouth is moving.

"Molly, I swear to God, if you don't shut the fuck up—"

"What thing? What is he taking too far?" Tessa asks, her voice cracking at the end.

I swear to God—and I know I haven't talked to him in a long time—but I swear if we can just get out of here . . . I will tell her everything. I just need her alone, away from here.

"Tessa, go outside," I try to convince her.

"No. What is he taking too far? *Tell me!*" Tessa shouts. She's not going to leave. I know her too well.

"Wait. You're in on it, aren't you?" Molly laughs, licking her lips. "I knew it! I told Jace you knew, but he wouldn't believe me. Hardin, you owe Zed some big bucks for this." Molly gets up from the booth.

I can feel everyone's eyes on me, but I only care about Tessa and the way her gray eyes are beginning to water.

With a shaky voice, Tessa asks, "Knew what?"

I try once again to remove her from the chaos. This time I reach for her arm, and she jerks away.

Molly seems to get a kick out of Tessa standing so close, challenging her. "Don't play stupid with me. I know you know. What did he do? Split the money with you?"

"Tessa . . ." I touch her fingers, hoping that I can bring her back to me. But she moves my hand away.

"Tell me! What is she talking about!"

Any hope of words coming from my mouth disappears. I try to speak, but I can't.

Molly cackles. "Oh my God, you really don't know? Oh, this is amazing. Everyone, pull up a seat!"

"Molly, don't," Steph pleads. I can't speak. What the fuck is wrong with me?

Molly doesn't stop. I knew she wouldn't. "You sure you wanna know, princess?"

"Tell me," Tessa demands again.

I feel like I'm watching a movie. Watching the scene play out in front of me, and even I want my character to move, to grab Tessa and run away, or at least to fucking speak. Nothing comes.

I try to convince myself that this is better. That the sooner Tessa knows how fucked up I actually am, the better. For her. At least I don't have to say it—I don't have to say anything. Yes, I'm a coward, but we all already know that.

Molly shatters that last plan of mine. "No, I think Hardin should tell her."

"I second that," Jace says, lifting a beer into the air. "Go on, Hardin, tell her."

It wouldn't help anything to use physical violence right now . . . it wouldn't help anything to knock Jace's teeth out. I keep trying to tell myself that as the world spins around me. Black and red, that's all I can see. And gray, Tessa's eyes. Looking at me, begging for answers.

"I . . . I will tell you outside," I say to her. It would be so much worse to tell her in front of everyone. Even though they already know. Fuck—this is so fucked.

I can see the moment she decides she won't be going anywhere with me. "No, you tell me here. In front of them, so you can't lie."

"I'm sorry," I begin, as if that makes any of this better. "Tessa, you have to remember that this was way before I even knew you."

"Tell me."

"That night . . . that second night . . . the second party you came to, when we played Truth or Dare . . . and Nate asked if you were a virgin . . ." I don't know where to start . . . or where to end. I wish she would have just left me before. Out of all the shit I've done, she should have done this so long ago. It would have been so much better. For me, for Tessa. Instead of this public crucifying of her, of me, of what we have.

Had.

"Go on . . ." Jace harasses me.

"You said you were . . . and that gave someone an idea—" My throat catches the words, my mind and body begging me not to do this here.

"Gave *who* the idea?" Molly interrupts.

"Me . . . gave *me* the idea," I choke out while managing to keep my eyes on Tessa's. I need to look away for my own sanity, but I can't. I at least owe her that.

"That . . . it could be fun to make . . . to make a bet." As the words fall between us, Tessa begins to cry. I dig my fingernails into my hand, hoping to draw blood. It would be a distraction from the pain coursing through the rest of me.

Seconds of silent breaths feel like hours of conversation as I wait for someone to speak. Tessa tears her eyes away from me and turns to Steph. "You knew?"

"I . . . I was going to tell you so many times, Tess," Steph says, and I wonder if that's true. It doesn't seem likely, but the tears are pretty convincing.

"I didn't believe it when he claimed he won, even with the condom," Jace chimes in, continuing to pour gasoline all over this fire.

Molly laughs. "Right? Me, either! The sheets, though. I mean, how can you deny blood on the sheets!"

The kind of man—no, boy—who would bring bloody sheets to his friends. I'm exactly like my father. Worse, even.

"Tessa, I am so sorry." I move toward her. I don't know how she can even look at me. I hate myself more than she ever could, and that helps me balance my rage and humiliation until I look at her again.

Molly continues to dice up what's left of both of us. I don't even tell her to shut up this time. I deserve to be reminded of how disgusting I am.

I don't even know if I can actually hear her voice. I can only hear Tessa's sobs coming from next to me as Molly keeps on.

"But really he was supposed to win the bet that night. He was pretty cocky about it, but Zed kept saying you wouldn't give it up that quick. I guess Zed was right, but you still gave it up quicker than *I* thought you would, so I suppose it's a good thing I didn't bet any money . . .

"You'd be happy to know that you were worth a pretty penny,

even though Zed tried to bitch out a few times. But with Jace, Logan, and Zed's money, I hope he at least bought you dinner!" Molly says, laughing.

Jace chugs the rest of the beer. I can see myself in the reflection in his glass, and I swallow down the bile in my throat as he speaks. "I'm only disappointed that I missed the infamous *I Love You!* announcement in front of everyone. I heard that was a killer."

I want it to stop. All of it. I just can't. Tristan is the one who yells, breaking Jace and Molly's taunting. "Shut the fuck up! Fuck you guys! She's already had enough!"

"Baby, please say something," I manage to say. Tessa's expression tells me that my words are knives to her.

"Don't you fucking dare call me that! How could you do this to me? You . . . you . . . I can't . . ." she cries. "And I won't say anything, because that's what you want."

"I know I messed up—" I don't know how to begin. Messed up is the mildest version of what I actually did. Why can't I fucking speak!

"You messed up? You *messed up*?" She's screaming at me now. Her face is red, her eyes wild, and it's not even comforting to me. Usually anger is my friend—my comfort, really. Not now.

"Why? Just tell me why. Why me?" Her pleading voice breaks with a hiccup.

"Because you were there." I try to be honest, no matter how awful it is. "And a challenge. I didn't know you, Tessa. I didn't know that I would fall in love with you."

She reacts like I've smacked her across the face. I wish she would smack me. Punch me. *Anything*.

"You're sick. You're fucking sick!" she yells, looking at me and my friends like we're all the same. Maybe we actually are. I'm more like them than I am like her. I had almost let her convince me otherwise.

When I touch her again, she finally gives me what I want and slaps me across the face. I welcome the pain.

"You ruined everything! You took something from me that wasn't yours, Hardin. That was meant for someone who loved me, loved me truly. It was his, whoever he is, and you took that— for *money*? I ruined my relationship with my mother for you. I gave up everything! I had someone who loved me, someone who wouldn't hurt me the way you did. You are disgusting."

Her words are so much fucking worse than her hand across my cheek. My fingers itch to make a fist, to connect with the hardest metal or wood near me. I try to focus on her again. I'm speaking before I even realize it. A desperate man.

"I do love you, Tessa. I love you more than anything. I was going to tell you. I tried to get them not to tell you. I never wanted you to find out. That's why I was out all night, getting them to agree not to say anything. I was going to tell you soon, now that we live together, because then it wouldn't matter."

"Are you . . . you . . . oh my God, Hardin! What the hell is wrong with you? You think going around convincing people to not tell me is okay? The fact that I wouldn't know would make it all okay? You thought that if we lived together, I would let this go? That's why you were so determined for my name to be on the lease! Oh my God. You are *sick*!"

Her eyes spark, and she looks up, then back at me. "That's why you went and got my stuff for me from my room—because you were afraid Steph would tell me!"

Not exactly, Tessa. I just wanted to keep you hidden. I keep the words to myself.

"What did you do with the money, Hardin?"

"I—" I shouldn't tell her.

"Tell me." She doesn't give me a choice.

"Your car . . . the paint . . . and the deposit for the apartment.

I thought if I . . . I was going to tell you so many times, once I knew it wasn't just a bet anymore. I love you—I loved you the entire time, I swear it!"

"You kept the condom to show them, Hardin! You showed them the sheets, the bloody fucking sheets!" She pulls at her hair. "Oh my God! I'm such an idiot. While I was reliving every detail of the best night of my life, you were showing your friends the sheets."

"I know . . . I don't have any excuse . . . but you have to forgive me. We can figure this out." I try. I know she's beyond that, but I'm still delusional and everything is happening too fast.

"Forgive you?" She laughs. The laugh isn't real, but that makes it worse. "You've ruined my entire life—you know that, don't you? Oh, of course you do. That was your plan the entire time, remember? You promised you would 'ruin me.' So congratulations, Hardin, you have. What should I give you, money? Or should I find another virgin for you?"

Fuck. My eyes burn, my body is determined to fold in on itself. "Tessa, please. You know I love you, I know you do. Let's go home, please, and I'll tell you everything."

"Home? That isn't my home. It never has been; we both know that."

"What can I do? I'll do anything." I move to my knees without a thought. I will beg her, I will plead with her until I'm blue in the face and the bar is closed and the snow is melted. I'll stay here, on my knees, long after winter leaves if I have to.

"You? Nothing. There is nothing you can do for me anymore, Hardin."

Does she mean it? Will she always feel that way? The door opens behind her, and Zed walks in just as she tries to escape the bar. Everything after he touches his hands to her shoulders is a blur. No matter how much sense I try to make out of what's happening, I can't seem to. I try to get up, to stop her.

But she disappears with him, and there's absolutely nothing I can do.

Steph tries to talk to me. "Hardin, I'm sorry that happened—"

"Get up, man," Jace says. I can barely hear any of them.

All I can hear is the wind whipping outside, taking the only good thing in my life far, far away from me.

acknowledgments

The After series wouldn't have been possible without so many people. I could write another book thanking you all (you know that I could, and probably actually would), but I have only a little space here, so I'll make it as short and sweet as possible.

Author's note: First, I want to thank my Hessa shippers/Afternators/Toddlers (least favorite, ha)/original readers (we clearly couldn't decide on just one name, ha). You guys have been here from the start and are literally the best group of people; you are so supportive, and you make my life. Every word was written because of you and your passion for my storytelling. You are amazing and "ilysm."

Wattpad is next, of course. Without you all believing in me and helping me bring After to life, my dreams wouldn't be coming true. Always remember where this started and that you all had a part in creating something so big. Never give up on yourselves, and please remember (I know I tell you too much) that tomorrow is always better than you think it will be. You are important and loved, even when it doesn't feel that way.

Amy Martin, for fighting for my vision and pushing After until they got it.

Candice and Ashleigh, you both have done so much for me, and I could never repay you for any of it.

I want to thank Gallery Books for believing in After and in me, and for giving me Adam Wilson as the best and most lively editor. Adam, you are just straight-up amazing and funny, and your comments always make me laugh. You get me, my sense of humor (cheesy jokes and all), and you get Hardin and Tessa in a way that not many people do. You have been so helpful and made this such a smooth and quick transition and journey.

My parents and my mother-in-law, you loved me and supported me each step of the way.

Kaci, for your lists and encouragement. (Insert our emoji.)

To Jordan, my husband, whom I've loved since I was a kid. You have given me the time to make my dreams come true, and you put up with my endless hours of writing and tweeting. And you only complained a little when I showed you thousands of Hessa edits.

I'm running out of room here, so I have to go. But I love you all so much, and I am so grateful to have all of you in my life.